A DIFFERENT KIND OF COURAGE

Books by Ellen Howard

Circle of Giving
When Daylight Comes
Gillyflower
Edith Herself
Her Own Song
Sister
The Chickenhouse House
The Cellar
The Tower Room
A Different Kind of Courage

A DIFFERENT KIND OF COURAGE

Ellen Howard

A Jean Karl Book
Atheneum Books For Young Readers

Atheneum Books for Young Readers
An imprint of Simon & Schuster Children's Publishing Division
1230 Avenue of the Americas
New York, New York 10020

The text of this book is set in Bodoni.
First Edition
Printed in the United States of America
10 9 8 7 6 5 4 3 2 1

Library of Congress Cataloging-in-Publication Data
Howard, Ellen.
A different kind of courage / Ellen Howard.—1st ed.
p. cm.
"A Jean Karl book."
Summary: While escaping the horrors of war-torn France,
refugee children struggle to overcome the misconception that
their parents are abandoning them.
ISBN 0-689-80774-0
1. World War, 1939–1945—Refugees—Juvenile fiction.
[1. World War, 1939–1945—Refugees—Fiction. 2. Refugees—Fiction.]
I. Title.
PZ7.H83274Chf 1996
[Fic]—dc20 95-49077

For Layla Raine and Zachary

BERTRAND

Paris, France
June 1940

1

BERTRAND TIPPED back his head against the soft plush of the unfamiliar automobile seat. Through the windscreen he could see the gray buildings of Paris move past, and between them, sudden blinding flashes of sky. The automobile raced forward, then stopped with abrupt jerks that threw Bertrand toward the dashboard. Each time, Maman's arm came out to catch him, yet she seemed almost unaware of him. When the car lurched forward again, her arm came away, and she herself leaned to peer out the windscreen, muttering under her breath.

Was it the Germans? Bertrand wondered. He could hear no sound of shelling, no explosions of bombs. Yet the radio had said that the German army was within twelve miles of Paris yesterday. Soon, everyone was saying, they would be in the city with their tanks and trucks and armored cars. Bertrand tried to imagine the enemy in his familiar streets, perhaps even in the rue Lauriston! They would have rifles, of course, and pistols like the one he had seen in a leather holster at the belt of a French soldier the other day. Bertrand had been so close to the soldier that he could not resist reaching out to touch the pistol, but Maman had snatched his hand away.

When Bertrand had left for school this morning, all had seemed as usual. The things that must now be packed in boxes and suitcases in the automobile had been in cupboards and drawers. The mattresses, now tied atop the automobile, had been on the beds, covered with sheets and blankets that later Marie would tidy. Maman had been at work at the hospital, Marie had said. His little sister, Léonie, had been sitting at the kitchen table, making puddles in her farina with her milk and singing a silly nursery school song.

And now Léonie sat in the backseat, whining to be held on Maman's lap, and their things were with them in the automobile, which hurtled them who knew where, and . . . where was Marie? Why had Maman taken him away from his school in the middle of the day? And who was the strange driver who cursed softly beside them? Bertrand's hands clutched at his school satchel in his lap.

Suddenly in his mind was a picture of his toy four-engine airplane, lying in the dirt beside the schoolyard wall where he had dropped it when Maman appeared. "We will miss Bertrand," Mademoiselle had said to Maman. That meant he would not be going back! But he had left his toy airplane in the schoolyard! It was the airplane that Papa had given him before he left for America!

"Maman!" he cried. "Turn around the car. We must go back for my airplane!"

"We cannot go back," Maman said. "I must get you away from Paris while I can."

"But, Maman, my airpl—"

"Close your mouth!" said Maman, the sharpness of her voice shocking Bertrand into silence.

He closed his mouth and swallowed hard, his heart beating fast. In a little while, he could not keep himself from asking, in a small, scared voice, "But, Maman, *where* are we going?"

His mother did not answer.

"*Mon Dieu!*" said Maman. "What now?"

This time the automobile had slowed gently. Before them Betrand could see a long line of automobiles crowding the street, two and three abreast, all traveling in the same direction. There were motorcycles and bicycles too, and people walking, hauling baggage in handcarts and barrows. He saw an ancient wagon, drawn by a still more ancient horse, a man on a magnificent blue-and-gray bicycle with a yellow steering bar, and a woman pushing a baby carriage piled high with bundles.

Maman said they were leaving Paris. But of course, Bertrand realized that he had known they were leaving Paris the moment he saw the loaded automobile. People had been leaving Paris for months. They had begun leaving when Papa left last fall.

"It is not *his* fight," Maman had said bitterly. "These Americans, they do not wish to dirty their hands."

"I imagine the U. S. will come into the war too, sooner or later," Papa had said. "Americans can no more resist a fight than the French can. But all *I* want to do is paint. I'm a painter, not a soldier, Marguerite, and you are a nurse."

"France will need nurses," Maman had said.

But, for a long time after Papa had left, nothing had

changed. "The Phony War," people called it all through the autumn and winter, because the fighting had not begun after all.

Then, in the spring, Bertrand began to hear talk of battles—the French front was broken on the Meuse, the British were driven from Dunkirk. Still, in Paris, life went on pretty much as usual, though the talk was all of the war. As May turned into June, shops began to close, one by one, and several times a week, both day and night, Bertrand heard a noise that Maman said was anti-aircraft guns. Since early June, people had been saying that the German army was advancing on Paris. That was when Bertrand began to feel afraid, and that was when people really began to leave.

Bertrand had watched them go, one or two at a time. M. and Mme Berger from the apartment next door had gone to visit relatives in Dijon. Each morning at school, more and more desks were empty. François had gone and Jean-Paul and Guy. Yesterday, Mme Finkelstein was gone from the bakery shop, which was locked up tight when Bertrand stopped to buy a *baguette*. He had seen the departing automobiles, automobiles like this one with mattresses tied on top—to protect them from the strafing, someone had told him. They were fleeing.

And now we too are fleeing from the Germans, Bertrand thought. But I am not afraid, he told himself, and neither is Maman. He looked up at her face and saw that she bit her lips.

"*Qu'est-ce qui se passe?* What's happening?" said Maman.

"Perhaps it is the police," said the driver. "Are you certain that passes are no longer required?"

Maman reached for her handbag.

"Of course," she said. "We've nothing to worry about."

But Bertrand thought she looked worried.

Bit by bit, they inched forward. The afternoon sun was hot and beat down on the car, making Bertrand feel like one of Mme Finkelstein's *baguettes*, baking in an oven.

Maman lifted Léonie out of the backseat and let Bertrand crawl over into it. She gave them orangeade to drink, and Léonie ceased her whimpering at last and fell asleep on Maman's lap.

Bertrand lay on his stomach on Léonie's crib mattress, which topped the bundles on the backseat. He put his face as near the open window as he could, but with the automobile moving so slowly, there was no breeze. His head felt stuffed with cotton wool, and he could not keep his eyes open, though he needed to know what would happen.

Distantly he heard Maman and their driver talking. The driver was an orderly who worked with Maman at the hospital, Bertrand gathered. Joseph, she called him. Once Bertrand opened his eyes to see a traffic policeman leaning into the window of the stopped car.

"The automobile is not yours?" he said, and it was Maman who answered. "No, Officer, we are delivering it to Dr. de la Chevalérie who awaits us in Chevreuse."

Ah, thought Bertrand.

Later, Bertrand thought he heard Joseph say, "The engine is overheating."

So am I, thought Bertrand drowsily. I am overheating, and I cannot stay awake. . . .

2

"JOSEPH!" BERTRAND woke to Maman's cry. "Joseph, come back!"

Bertrand opened his eyes to see that neither Maman nor the driver was in the front seat. Maman stood alone in the street, outside the automobile.

There was a hissing sound and the smell of something burning. Bertrand saw that a black cloud poured from beneath the hood of the car.

He scrambled to his knees and stuck his head out the open window. Joseph was disappearing down the street, clinging to the back of an open truck filled with French soldiers.

In the front seat, Léonie had begun to cry. Bertrand's mother stopped calling after Joseph. Her arms dropped to her sides, and Bertrand saw how her whole body seemed to sag.

"Maman! Maman!" he called to her. "Let me out of the automobile. Please, let me out!"

Maman's shoulders straightened at the sound of Bertrand's voice. He saw her shake her head, as though annoyed by a fly. When she turned back to the automobile, she had a tight smile on her lips.

"What do you think of that, *mon chéri?*" she said as she opened the car door. "He has run off and left us with a damaged automobile—a woman alone with two children. *Quelle bête!*"

She sat down sideways on the front seat, leaving the door open, and took Léonie in her arms. Bertrand climbed over the seat into the front.

"What are we to do?" he asked.

She seemed to be talking to herself, rather than answering him.

"Someone will give us a ride," she said, "*sûrement.*"

Bertrand looked out the window and saw that their automobile was pulled over to the side of the street and that the other cars and vehicles were streaming slowly past.

Bertrand had no idea where they were. Houses behind walled gardens lined the narrow street. On the next corner was a tobacco shop, its door locked and barred, its windows shuttered.

"Where are we?" he asked Maman.

"Not even out of the suburbs," said Maman, "and the day almost gone."

It was then that Bertrand realized how low in the sky the sun stood. Its slanting rays sent long shadows running beside the passing vehicles.

In his stomach, Bertrand realized suddenly, was an empty rumbling.

"I'm hungry, Maman," he said. "I want my *goûter*, my snack."

The look Maman gave him was distracted, but she reached over the seat for a basket. From it she took a package of *craquelins*. Léonie sat up on her lap and stopped crying. She grabbed a *craquelin* and stuffed it into her mouth. Betrand took a handful. They were dry and difficult to swallow, but they quieted the rumble in his stomach.

All this while, traffic poured ceaselessly through the narrow street, and the shadows grew still longer. Bertrand began to wonder about his dinner and where he would sleep that night. And from her tight, cheerful smile and the shade of shrillness to her voice, he could tell that Maman was worried too.

"*Et maintenant,*" said Maman finally. "Now, Berti, I want you to be a good boy and watch Léonie for a few minutes. I am going just up the street a short distance. I must find another way to continue our journey."

Léonie began to cry again. She held her arms out to their mother.

"*Moi aussi, moi aussi,*" she cried. "Me too, me too."

Bertrand looked hopelessly at Maman. He did not want her to leave him, but, "*Oui,* Maman," he said.

When Maman closed the door of the automobile, Léonie screamed even more loudly.

"*Regarde-toi,* Léonie," he said desperately, wiggling his fingers in front of her. He made a face and clucked his tongue.

She paid him no attention. Her eyes were screwed shut, and her face was growing red.

"Léonie!" he cried, trying to keep sight of Maman as she walked swiftly away from them. "Léonie, look at all the automobiles. Look, look at that one with the chickens on top!"

But Léonie did not look. She howled.

Bertrand searched in the backseat for something to distract her. He spotted her little red case, the one Maman packed with her toys when they went to play in the Bois de Boulogne. He reached for it, opened its lid, and yes, there was Léonie's favorite doll and her ducky pull-toy and three cloth books. He dangled the doll before her.

"Léonie," he coaxed, craning his neck to watch Maman. "Léonie, look here."

Léonie howled, but she opened one eye to peek when she paused for breath.

"See, here is your *poupée*," Bertrand said, dancing the doll on her lap. Maman had disappeared. Where was she?

Léonie closed her mouth and opened both her eyes. Her nose was running, Bertrand noticed with disgust. But she took a long, shuddering breath and reached for the doll with both hands.

"Are you children alone, little boy?"

Bertrand jumped at the sound of a voice.

A woman was leaning out of the window of an automobile drawn up beside theirs. A hat with a great pouf of blue ribbons and veiling rode crookedly on her head. There was a smudge on her nose.

"Little boy, where are your parents?" she demanded.

Bertrand stared at her, silent. What did the woman want? he wondered, his heart racing. He shook his head.

"Are you dumb, child?" the woman said. "Where are your parents, I say!"

Horns were honking behind them. The driver of the woman's car spoke to her, and she made a brushing-away motion with her hand.

"These children seem to have been abandoned," she said.

Bertrand looked up the street in the direction Maman had gone. He could not see her, and his heart seemed to shrink in his chest. Then, among the men gathered before the closed tobacco shop, he caught sight of her brown hat with its jaunty red feather. He pointed.

The woman looked after his pointing finger, and at that moment Maman detached herself from the group of men and came hurrying toward them.

"Madame!" the blue-hatted woman cried, motioning.

In a moment, Maman was between the two automobiles, so close that, if he had reached out the window, Bertrand could have touched her. He felt his heart expand and breathed a sigh.

Maman and the blue-hatted woman and her driver were all talking at once, but Bertrand could not make out the words against the constant traffic noise.

Léonie had settled with her doll into the seat beside him, sucking her thumb. Bertrand could feel the moist heat of her body leaning against his, but he did not shrug her away.

The grown-ups' voices were rising. Bertrand thought there was something frantic in Maman's gestures, and he felt his chest tighten. The blue-hatted woman was shaking her head. The driver had closed his mouth and turned to look over his shoulder at the traffic. He was turning the wheel.

"*Non, non!*" Bertrand heard his mother cry. "Wait! Give me only a moment!"

Ah! Bertrand sighed again.

He reached for his jacket and his school satchel. The movement disturbed Léonie, and she whimpered. Bertrand saw that her eyelids were almost closed. The doll had worked, he thought proudly.

Maman was reaching into the automobile.

"Come along, *mes enfants*," she said.

The driver of the other automobile had jumped out and was rearranging packages to make room for them.

Bertrand found himself squeezed into a tiny space beside a birdcage in the backseat. The wires of the cage poked into his side, but the look on Maman's face made him afraid to protest. She was sliding a suitcase onto the floor at his feet. It forced him to pull his knees up under his chin. Then Maman pushed in beside him with Léonie on her lap, and the automobile door was slammed shut.

The driver eased the car forward and nosed it out into the traffic, through a cacophany of honking horns. Bertrand heard him curse. He saw the small black automobile with Maman's mattress tied to its top slide past out of sight. All of their things, he realized, with the exception of the suitcase at his feet and his school satchel in his lap, were still in it.

"But, Maman," he said, "what of our things? Our toys and clothes and mattresses? Did you bring Léonie's little case?"

Maman was looking straight ahead of her, at the pouf of blue hat in the front seat. She didn't answer, and Bertrand saw with horror that round, wet tears were sliding from her eyes.

3

BERTRAND LEANED his cheek against the wires of the birdcage. Tears crept, hot and silent, from his own eyes and dripped on the birdcage floor.

Big boys should not cry, Bertrand felt, but he could not help himself.

He felt Maman move beside him. She was trying to undo the clasp of her handbag, but Léonie sprawled asleep across her lap obstructed her reach. Bertrand unclasped it for her and, without being asked, drew out her handkerchief.

"*Merci, mon chéri,*" she said, and Bertrand made himself look at her. Her face was wet and blotched, and her red-rimmed eyes smiled at him bleakly as she blew her nose.

Bertrand wiped his own eyes on his sleeve.

"Could we not have waited for an automobile with space for our baggage?" he found the courage to ask.

Wearily, she shook her head.

"*Non,*" she said, and something in her tone made

Bertrand fall silent again. "There was only one way offered us," Maman said after a moment.

In the front seat, the blue-hatted woman swiveled to look back at them.

"It was good fortune we had room for you," she said.

"Indeed it was, madame," Maman murmured. "We are grateful."

"And so you should be," said the woman, turning her face forward again with a shrug of one shoulder.

Bertrand felt his mother sigh deeply. She shifted Léonie and put an arm around him, pulling him against her side and away from the poking wires. In the shelter of her embrace, Bertrand once again felt brave enough to ask, "Maman, where are we going?"

Her voice was weary.

"To your papa," she said.

"To America? All of us?" he asked, but she did not answer further.

Bertrand could feel the heat of her body, moist through her sweaty clothes. Once in a while, the engine rumbled, its rhythm changing as the driver shifted gears. He felt his mother's body grow heavy beside him and heard her breathing deepen. Finally, he closed his eyes.

When he opened them, it was dark. The engine was silent, and through the open windows breathed a cool breeze. Bertrand's legs were cramped, and it was hard to get his breath, Maman's arm lay so heavily across him. He stirred, trying to get more comfortable, and was startled by a snort. He froze, straining into the darkness, and in a moment the snort came again from the front seat, and then again—snoring. It was only the driver snoring, Bertrand told himself. They must have stopped to sleep. Bertrand remembered he had had no dinner and no proper *goûter* either. But, oddly, he did not feel hungry. There was nothing for it but to go back to sleep, he thought. He closed his eyes again.

They relieved themselves in the bushes beside the road in the faint light of dawn. Bertrand thought he had never been up so early. The chill made him shiver in his damp clothes. Maman's suit was wrinkled, and Léonie's curls were tangled and rough. There was nowhere to wash.

"Didn't you think to bring food?" the blue-hatted woman asked when Maman begged a piece of bread for them.

"I had food aplenty, madame," Maman said, drawing herself up. "It was you who insisted I leave what I had behind."

Grudgingly the woman handed over some bread. It was stale, and Bertrand thought it tasted like dust without so much as a swallow of water to wash it down.

Léonie was whining for farina. She wanted to go home, she whined. She wanted her Marie.

"Ssh," Maman told her, rocking her on her lap. "Things will be better soon."

It was growing light when they rejoined the flood of traffic flowing along the highway. Maman let Bertrand sit by the window. Léonie, on her lap, would not be still, but jostled and kicked Bertrand.

"Can't you quiet that child?" asked the woman in the front seat.

"*Non*, madame, I cannot," said Maman.

They were in the country. Fields moved slowly past Bertrand's window. Now and again a farmhouse squatted near the road. They stopped at one, found it deserted, and helped themselves to water from the well. Other cars pulled into the farmyard after them, and people spilled out to take their noisy, jostling turns at the well. Maman washed Bertrand's and Léonie's faces and hands. Bertrand drank until his stomach felt tight. The adults filled bottles and a canteen.

No sooner were they on the highway again than Léonie wet her panties, soaking the front of Maman's skirt as well. Once again, the blue-hatted woman grumbling, they had to stop while Maman found dry clothes for Léonie in the suitcase beneath their feet. There was no clean skirt for Maman. She wiped up as best she could with the drier parts of Léonie's wet dress. Bertrand took advantage of the stop to go into the bushes again. He did not want to be like Léonie.

They found an inn at midmorning. The innyard was crowded with vehicles, and their driver had to park a distance down the highway. They hiked to the inn along the roadside ditch.

Bertrand ran ahead of the others. It was wonderful to stretch his legs. The warm sweet-smelling air rushed past his ears as he galloped. When Maman called after him, he ignored her, and when she found him in the courtyard of the inn some time later, she did not scold. Instead she gave him fresh bread and butter and Camembert cheese.

"There is no meat or milk or fruit to be had at any price," she said.

Bertrand did not care. He had been listening to the grown-ups who milled about in the courtyard. They looked cross or sad or . . . confused? Bertrand thought.

"What does it mean—Paris is fallen?" he asked Maman.

Her face flushed, and her voice spat her answer so angrily that, though he didn't understand, Bertrand decided not to ask again.

"It means," she said, "that our government has abandoned us to the Germans."

Abandoned. That was what the blue-hatted woman had said, but she was talking about *him* and Léonie.

Some time during the afternoon, the lines of vehicles slowed even more. The edges of the highway were littered with stalled cars. Beside some of them people stood or sat, their faces blank. Once a man ran alongside Bertrand's automobile.

"*S'il vous plaît,*" he begged. "Please, my wife is ill. Cannot you find room for her? Only to the next village?"

"We have no room," their driver snarled. "Can't you see?"

Bertrand turned his face up to his mother.

"Maman, perhaps we . . ."

But Maman was staring straight ahead, as though she did not see the desperate man, as though she did not hear him. Her face was stone.

Bertrand fell silent, and in a moment the man's steps flagged, and he fell behind. Bertrand could hear him crying to another automobile. "*S'il vous plaît . . .*"

Finally they were crawling along the highway at a snail's pace, stopping and starting fitfully.

"At this rate, the gasoline will soon be gone," said their driver, and the blue-hatted woman wrung her hands.

Then the automobile came to a stop and did not start up again. Bertrand could see that the road ahead was clogged with vehicles. One car had slid nose first into the ditch, its rear wheels still spinning in the air. Bertrand giggled nervously at the spectacle, but no one else was laughing. The driver switched off the engine and got out, stretching as he did so and groaning. The blue-hatted woman flung open her door too.

"What is it?" she called to the driver's back.

"*Alors, mes enfants,*" said Maman, "we had just as well stretch our legs too."

"Have we run out of gasoline?" Bertrand asked and was surprised when Maman answered him.

"*Non, non,*" she said. "You can see we cannot pass all these vehicles."

Bertrand wandered after the blue-hatted woman.

"Do not go far, Berti," Maman called.

Although there were people all about, talking and shouting, and dogs barking and little children like Léonie crying, Bertrand thought the highway strangely silent. It was the absence of motors, of course, shut off to conserve gas.

Up ahead Bertrand saw a farmer in a blue blouse calming his horse. The horse drew a farm cart piled high with the farmer's belongings.

Bertrand went closer. He was watching the way the muscles rippled on the rich brown shoulder of the horse. *Quelle force!* What power! Bertrand thought. He wished *he* had a strong horse. If he had, he would climb on its back with Maman and Léonie and ride away across the fields. Bertrand watched how the farmer held on to the horse's harness and stroked its neck. He wondered if he might be allowed to stroke the horse. He kept away from its powerful legs as he edged closer to its head.

Suddenly the horse neighed, rearing, its eyes rolling. There was shouting, and Bertrand saw people point to the sky. He realized that the air was filled with the roar of an engine and the sound of explosions. Someone knocked him down. He felt himself rolling down an incline. He scrabbled to get a handhold. But something heavy fell on top of him. His breath was forced from his lungs. There was roaring in his ears and darkness in his eyes and the taste of dirt in his mouth.

"Are you hurt, *mon fils?*" a voice was saying, and the weight lifted from Bertrand's chest.

He did hurt. His head hurt where it had struck the ground, and his chest hurt too. He opened his eyes and saw that the blue-bloused farmer knelt over him.

"Bertrand!" He heard his mother's voice calling. There was panic in its sound.

Bertrand saw that he and the farmer were in the ditch. Around them other people crouched or lay. Above them, on the highway, he could hear screaming. His mother was screaming his name. Other people were screaming, and the horse . . . yes, the horse was screaming too. Bertrand felt the rough way the farmer's hands were hauling him to his feet. Then the farmer had turned away and was up out of the ditch, calling to his horse.

"Be calm, old boy!" he was calling. "Be calm!"

Bertrand's mother scrambled down into the ditch, Léonie in her arms. Bertrand saw how white was his mother's face, how red was Léonie's.

"Are you hurt, Berti?" Maman was asking over Léonie's cries.

"Why did he shove me down?" Bertrand cried, peering past her. He could see that the horse was lying in the road, its head reared up, struggling. The farmer bent over it.

"Old boy," the farmer said, over and over. "Old boy, old boy, old boy . . ."

Bertrand's mother pulled him close, holding his face against her skirt. It smelled of sweat and urine. He struggled to turn his face, to see what had happened to the horse. Why was it lying there helpless on the road? That big, strong horse?

"*Vite, vite!*" Maman said. She had loosed him and grabbed his hand. She was pulling him up the other side of the ditch, away from the screaming horse of the farmer, away from the woman Bertrand glimpsed lying in the road while another woman hung over her, sobbing. A man lay propped against the side of the ditch, his face dazed, clutching his shoulder with one hand. Something red oozed between his fingers.

Blood! Bertrand's eyes widened, and he stared over his shoulder in fascination at the oozing red. Maman was jerking on his arm, trying to pull him out of the ditch. He realized that the engine sound had grown faint. The explosions had ceased.

"*Pourquoi,* Maman?" he panted as he scrambled after his mother. "Why did that man push me?"

She was pulling him across the field, through brambly stubble that scratched his bare legs. Léonie clung to her neck, sobbing.

"He saved your life," Maman said, her voice ragged. She was almost running, and his legs churned and stumbled to keep up. "*Mon Dieu!*" she gasped. "The Germans are strafing the road!"

ZINA

The Kolónia, Villa St.-Sever
Pau, France
June and July 1940

1

THE TREE spread its shade protectively across the steaming lawn. From one branch, thick and parallel to the ground, there hung a rope that Zina was trying to climb, hand over hand. Her arms strained, and her feet groped for purchase on the swaying rope. She had been practicing her climb for a long time, and sweat slicked her bare chest.

"Get off, Zina. Let me take a turn," one of the boys was demanding.

Zina reached her right hand above the left. She grasped the rough rope and pulled herself upward. When she had climbed to the top, *then* she would get off, she thought angrily.

"Zina, Zina," another voice called. "I think it is your father. Your father has come."

She gritted her teeth, and her arms trembled. It was cruel of them to try to fool her, she thought. Everyone at the Kolónia knew how she and Lisa had been watching for Papa's arrival ever since Paris fell to the Germans.

But days had gone by, a week, and more. He had not come.

Her foot slipped. She scrabbled for support, found it, and reached with her left hand.

"*Zdravstvui,* Zinochka, hello," said a voice near her knee.

Startled, Zina looked down into Papa's face.

It *was* Papa, come at last! Gladness filled her throat.

"Look, Papa," she cried. "Look what I can do!"

She reached still higher, the gladness making her strong. She heaved upward, clear to the top, then looked down for his approval.

But Papa was silent, a frown in his eyes.

Zina felt the gladness sinking, felt the hard knot it formed in the pit of her stomach. Her hands loosened, and she slid down the rope, her palms burning. Her feet hit the ground with a thud that jarred her knees and teeth.

Now her papa was looking down on her.

"You should be wearing a blouse, Zinochka," he said. "Ten is too old for a girl to run about half-naked."

She had wanted to hug him. It had been so long since she had seen him that she had a thousand things to tell—how sick she was of living at the Kolónia, how long she had been waiting for him, how much she wanted Papa and Mama and Lisa and her to live together once more. . . .

But the telling sank, as her gladness had sunk, into that heaviness in her stomach.

"*Da,* Papa," she whispered.

His hand came down on her shoulder.

"Where is your mama, Zinochka?" he said. "Where is Lisa?"

And then, before she could find the words to answer,

her big sister Lisa was there, throwing her arms around Papa the way Zina had wanted to do and crying, "Papa, Papa, they said you had come! Thank heaven you got safely away! What is the news from Paris? Did you know that Mama has moved again? Is this your bicycle? Did you ride it all the way?"

Zina slipped from beneath Papa's hand and went to find her blouse.

No one here at the Kolónia, the Russian Children's Colony, minded that she wore only shorts. There were just a few grown-ups to watch over them—Father Konstantin, and Galina Nikolayevna to cook, and Madame Davydova, and Mademoiselle Von Meck. "Your underwear is *gray!*" Mama had cried when she first came from Paris to live near them last December. "Your socks are all holes!" But now, Mama made sure that they were clean and mended and, beyond that, no one noticed or cared what they wore.

Did she want to live with Mama and Papa again? Zina thought rebelliously as she scurried down the echoing hall of the villa. But the tightness in her throat answered. Yes, a thousand times yes, no matter how particular Papa was!

"With his newspaper shut down because of the war," Mama had said, "your father will have no work. I don't know what we'll do for money. . . ."

But they didn't need money to live together, Zina thought as she scrabbled through her suitcase, looking for a blouse. Money or no money, surely now that Papa had come, the family could be together.

Because of the war, Mama had said, was always saying. Everything was always because of the war. Because of the war, Zina and Lisa had been living at the Kolónia for almost a year.

It had started with not going home after camp.

Zina shrugged into the wrinkled blouse she had found and headed back outside, remembering.

Ever since they were little, Zina and Lisa had spent their summers at the Russian children's camp— "So you won't forget that you are *russkaya,* Russian," Papa said. But always before, at the end of the summer, they had gone home to Paris. Until the war, the "Phony War," the grown-ups called it now. Last autumn, instead of going home, the entire camp, or Kolónia, had moved, first to Grenoble and then to Pau in the south of France, the older children to this abandoned villa, the Villa St.-Sever, and the younger ones to a chateau not far away. "Paris is not safe," Mama had written, "because of the war."

For a moment now, as Zina stepped outside, the glare of the sunlight blinded her. Then her gaze fell on what she had not noticed before, the large blue-and-gray bicycle leaning against the wall. She saw that Papa was sitting in the shade of the tree with Father Konstantin. Madame Davydova had brought out cold drinks. Lisa sat at Papa's knee, and Zina noted with a pang that his hand stroked her hair.

"Rumors fly fast on the roads," she heard Papa saying. "I came by way of Vichy, and they say the French government will move there. . . ."

Just war talk, thought Zina. That was all grown-ups ever talked of. Already Papa had ceased to think of *her.*

She turned toward the bicycle, Papa's bicycle. It was far bigger than the bicycle she and Lisa had shared at home. She knelt beside it and rubbed the dust from its fender with the tail of her blouse.

"What a stupendous bike!" said Pyotr, one of the big

boys, coming up beside her. "Where did that come from?"

Zina flushed with shyness and pride.

"It belongs to my papa," she said.

"Was that *your* father who just arrived from Paris? Did he ride it all the way?"

Zina nodded. Pyotr had never bothered to speak to her before.

"I have a bicycle at home," Pyotr said. He bit his lip. "At least, I used to. . . ."

Zina didn't know what to say.

"Those dirty Germans better leave my things alone!" Pyotr said. "Does he let you ride it?"

Zina looked over at Papa. He was deep in conversation with Father Konstantin.

She grabbed the yellow steering bar and pulled the heavy bicycle upright.

"I need help getting on," she said.

Pyotr boosted her onto the seat, holding the bicycle steady. It was a little like climbing into a tree, the feeling of height, of looking down on things. She grasped the steering bar more tightly and shook back her braids.

"Give me a push," she said.

Her toes barely reached the pedals, and then only the one that was up. She gave a pedal a push, then lost it, but found the other one with her foot. The bicycle began to wobble down the path as her feet alternately pushed and groped. She knew that at any moment it would fall over.

Yet, "Hey, look at Zina Sarach," she heard someone call, and from the corner of her eye she saw three boys leave their game and run toward her to watch.

"Where'd she get a bicycle?"

"It's her father's."

"Lucky Zina!" she heard them say.

Moving air touched her cheek. Zina realized that if she slipped off the seat and simply stood on the pedals, the bicycle went more steadily. She felt power surge through her pumping legs.

"A bicycle! A bicycle!" someone was shouting.

She saw Kira and Sofia, two of her roommates, smile and wave.

"Zina's riding a bicycle!"

"Zina! Zina!"

Zina steered the bicycle around a curve. Suddenly, blocking her way, there was her papa!

She swung her leg over the bar and half fell off.

"Papa?" she said when she had wrestled the bicycle to a halt. She did not dare to look at his face.

But Papa was chuckling.

"*Zdorovo*, Zinochka!" he said. "Well done! Perhaps it would be easier for you if I lowered the seat a bit."

Zina looked up into his smiling eyes. She felt the gladness well up again, drowning her anger. She could not speak for the fullness in her throat.

2

"YOU SAID we could go to live with them when Papa came," Zina accused Lisa.

"I said perhaps," Lisa said.

"We have so little space in these two small rooms," Mama had said, "and no money coming in. . . . Father Konstantin is not asking parents to pay right now. Surely, girls, you understand. . . ."

I don't understand, thought Zina.

"At the Kolónia there are other children," Papa had said, his voice hearty. "You would be bored, staying with us old folks, and no one to play with!"

There is no one at the Kolónia for *me* to play with, thought Zina.

Lisa and the other girls who shared their room—Kira, Olga, and Sofia—ignored her.

"You're too young," someone was always saying, and indeed Zina was the youngest child at the Villa St.-Sever. She had been allowed to stay with Lisa—"so I can take care of you," Lisa said, though Zina saw no need.

I'm on my own anyway, Zina thought.

"Go away, pest," the boys were apt to yell when she tried to join them. "This is a man's game."

The boys came over from their adjoining building to share meals in the dining room, to attend the saying of the Liturgy in the chapel on Sundays, to play in the garden. Zina could climb as high as any of them, she thought, run faster than most, kick the soccer ball almost as far. But they would not play with her.

After breakfast each day now that it was summer and there was no school, Father Konstantin taught them religion, just as he had at camp.

"You may sit in, Zinaida Olegievna," he said kindly, "but do not concern yourself if you don't understand. These are advanced lessons."

Zina was certain she understood perfectly well. Still, she was afraid to raise her hand to answer the priest's catechisms. The older ones would laugh at her no matter what she said, she thought.

There is nothing for *me* at the Kolónia, Zina thought. Nothing except the bicycle.

Papa's coming *had* brought the bicycle. There was no space, he said, to store it in his and Mama's rooms.

"You and Lisa must take it in charge," he said. "Take care that it is put indoors at night, out of the dew, and Zinochka, I am relying on *you* to exercise it. A bicycle should be ridden regularly to keep it serviceable."

There was such a lively twinkle in Papa's eyes when he said this that Zina was not at all certain he was not teasing her, but it didn't matter. Riding the bicycle was her joy . . . and pride.

She was bumping along a garden path one sultry July day when she heard her name called.

"Zina. Zinochka!" It was Sofia calling. Her red hair

glowed against the gray of the villa's stone walls, and her freckled arm waved in the air.

Zina braked in a spray of gravel.

Although Sofia was the nicest of her roommates, never before had she used Zina's pet name.

"What?" Zina demanded, suspicious.

"A very great favor, Zinochka," Sofia coaxed, running over to her. "Madame Davydova needs thread. She is mending the sheets, and her spool is almost empty. She says I may ask you to take me to Pau on your bicycle. See, she has given me the money."

Zina looked at the coin in Sofia's outstretched palm. The bigger girls often went by themselves to Pau—to school in season, to the public baths, to the *cinéma*—but she was never allowed without an adult.

"Madame has given her permission?" she said.

Sofia nodded.

"*Pozhaluista*, Zinochka, please. It is so far to walk, and there is no tram this time of day."

It would be an adventure to ride to town on the bicycle, Zina thought. She smiled inside herself to think that Sofia was begging her for a favor that was all to Zina's advantage.

"Hop on back," Zina said.

The drive led steeply downhill from the villa to the street. Zina had only to try to keep her feet on the whirling pedals as the bicycle swept to the bottom. It felt like flying, the wind in her face. But when they reached the street, she found it hard work to pedal and balance the awkward two-girl load. She regretted Sofia's plumpness.

"I'll pedal," Sofia offered, but Zina shook her head. This was her, Zina's, bicycle. Not Sofia's.

She felt the sweat spring out on her upper lip. She could taste its salt in her mouth. Where Sofia's round, freckled arms clutched her waist, her blouse was soaked.

"Whee!" cried Sofia. "It's been ages since I was on a bicycle."

Zina nodded. She had no breath for talking. Up and down, up and down her legs pumped the pedals, and her heart pumped with them.

On the main highway, other traffic joined them—a donkey cart, a group of boys laughing and wet-headed from a swim. The nearer they approached to Pau, the more crowded the road became. Soon they were steering around bedraggled groups of walkers, loaded with bundles—an old woman pulling a child's wagon, a gray-faced woman with three whining children, men in the remnants of uniforms, one limping on an improvised crutch.

Sofia leaned forward to shout in Zina's ear.

"More refugees! I wonder where they all sleep?"

Refugees.

Zina felt tired. Her legs ached.

Is that what *we* are? she wondered. Refugees? It had a forlorn sound to it. But *we* have places to sleep, she thought, at the Kolónia, and Mama and Papa have rooms. Still . . . they no longer lived in their house in Paris.

"Everything," she had heard Mama mourn. "We had to leave everything."

Not everything, Zina thought.

Mama had brought her sewing machine from Paris, and Papa had his typewriter and his camera. Lisa said that Papa had managed to bring some of their silver spoons and forks on the bicycle, and Mama had her jewelry, sewed into the lining of her suitcase, though Zina was not supposed to know that. And we have the bicycle, Zina thought. No one else at the Kolónia had a bicycle, not even Father Konstantin.

"That way!" Sofia shouted, letting go of Zina with one hand to gesture toward a street to their right. "The best shops are on the place de la Mairie."

Gratefully Zina turned the bicycle toward *la mairie*, the town hall. She could see its clock tower rising above the other buildings. They were almost there!

When Sofia jumped off the bicycle, Zina's legs were trembling.

"Want to come in with me?" Sofia asked.

Zina shook her head. She did not want to leave the bicycle unattended on the street. She watched Sofia disappear through the doorway of a small shop and wished that she too had some money. She was remembering how Mama used to let her walk to the *confiserie* with Lisa to buy candy or, in the summer, ices.

Zina leaned the bicycle against the building. Two soldiers were striding toward her on the sidewalk. With a start, Zina recognized the gray German uniform.

Zina stared at the soldiers bearing down upon her. It was a long time since she had seen anyone so clean, so pressed, so . . . gleaming, she thought. They looked over her head—as though I weren't here, Zina thought as she scuttled off the sidewalk into the gutter to let them pass. Then she watched the progress of their square-shouldered backs. No matter who stood in their way, they did not falter, and all the people did as she had done, stepped aside for them. Zina saw the lowered eyes of the drably dressed woman who pressed herself against a shop window. She saw an old man stagger as he hurried off the sidewalk. She saw a little boy burst into tears.

He's scared of them, poor little fellow, Zina thought. The big, goose-stepping bullies!

The Germans were not goose-stepping now, of course, only striding purposefully into the bakery shop, but Zina had seen them marching in the newsreels—shoulders thrown back, arms and legs jerking stiffly forward.

Zina stepped back onto the sidewalk beside the bicycle. The Germans were like toy soldiers, she thought. She put back her own shoulders and pretended she was a toy soldier, mimicking the silly-looking goose step. Up and down in front of the bicycle she marched.

"Heil Hitler!" she mocked in a funny voice.

A hand clamped over her mouth.

"Zina!" Sofia whispered, her voice frantic. "Stop it this minute! Do you want to be arrested? Do you want to be thrown into the dungeons of *la mairie* to be tortured, as they torture *les Maquisards?*"

Zina stared at Sofia.

"*Les Maquisards?*" she repeated. "What are you talking about? I was only playing."

"The resistance," Sofia whispered. "*Les Maquisards* are Frenchmen who are resisting the Germans."

"But the French surrendered," said Zina.

"Not all," said Sofia.

"And they torture them?"

Sofia nodded solemnly, and Zina could see the fear in her eyes.

Zina stole a glance at the yellow brick town hall. Its basement windows were barred, she saw. She felt suddenly hollow.

"You *must* not mock them," Sofia said. "Promise me, Zinochka. Promise."

Zina swallowed hard and nodded. Had anyone but

Sofia seen her? She scanned the faces of the people in the street, but all seemed intent on their own errands. No one met her eyes. Then, suddenly, her heart turned over. The German soldiers were coming out of the bakery, loaves of bread thrust beneath arms loaded with parcels. Had they been watching through the bakery window? she thought in panic.

They were coming her way, striding swiftly.

She could not tear her eyes from them. Her heart pounded, and she felt her throat constrict with fear.

Sofia clutched her arm.

Zina had ceased breathing. The weight of her arms and legs pinned her to the sidewalk.

The Germans bore down on her.

"*Aus dem Weg, du!*" one of them barked, elbowing past.

Zina could feel the place on her shoulder where the German had shoved her. She was shaking, though already the soldiers were several yards away. In the air was the smell of the bread they carried—beautiful crusty white bread, such as Zina had not tasted in a long time. Her stomach squeezed tight with the memory of it, and suddenly Zina was shaking, not with fear, but anger.

"Bullies!" she cried under her breath.

"*Zi*-na!" Sofia's whispered cry brought Zina back to herself. She saw that Sofia crouched in the gutter, her face stark with terror.

They could arrest me, Zina thought. They could torture me in their dungeons as Sofia said, or send me to a camp. That was the fate of many foreigners in France these days.

"We must never allow the children to be sent to a refugee camp," she had heard Mama telling Papa. "Children *die* in those places!"

Zina felt her heart lurch painfully. Her knees gave way, and suddenly she was sitting on the curb.

Sofia patted her arm.

"It's all right, Zinochka," she said. "They didn't see. Next time, you'll know better."

Zina nodded, but she felt tears flooding to her eyes.

"Don't cry, Zinochka," Sofia was saying. "The Germans won't hurt you."

But it was not the Germans Zina was crying about. It was the bread.

3

THE BREAD they were served at breakfast was gray and coarse. Lisa said they ground up dry peas in the flour to make it go further, but Sofia said she thought it was sawdust! Zina noticed that Sofia ate the bread, as they all did. It was not that there wasn't enough food, only that it didn't seem to satisfy and was always the same—bread and tea for breakfast, soup of lentils for lunch, rice and sometimes a little meat for supper with vegetables from their garden. There was never cheese or butter or milk, except for the rare demi-quart Mama managed to give to Zina and Lisa sometimes when they visited in town.

Zina was chewing her bread and swallowing her tea slowly, trying to make it last. All around her was the chatter of the bigger girls and boys, although their numbers were dwindling as more and more parents found ways to send for them.

At the end of the girls' table, Mademoiselle Von Meck was folding her napkin. No one else had a napkin, but Mademoiselle brought her own to table.

"Certain standards must be maintained," she said. "At least I can set an example."

Zina wondered what good an example was that was impossible to follow.

"Young ladies," said Mademoiselle Von Meck now. "I will take a dozen of you to the baths in town today. Who didn't go last time?" She looked down her long nose, through her pince-nez, at the eagerly raised hands and began naming them off until she had counted twelve on her fingers. "Oh, and Zinaida Sarach also," she said, though Zina had not raised her hand.

Zina sucked in her breath with vexation. It was no use protesting that Mademoiselle had said a dozen, and now there would be thirteen.

"We will meet in the hall in ten minutes," Mademoiselle Von Meck said, "with our towels."

Zina stood, with Mademoiselle Von Meck and the other Kolónia girls, in the line of people that snaked across the marble steps of the Public Bath House of Pau. In front and behind them were men, women, children and old people, clutching towels and, if they were fortunate, small gray lumps of soap.

The war seemed to have made everything gray, Zina thought as she moved slowly forward beside Mademoiselle. Soap was gray, bread was gray, even the faces of people were gray, it seemed to Zina.

She thought of the baths she used to take at home, of the big, deep, gleaming tub filled with hot water and scented with Mama's bath oil and the sharp fragrance of a big white bar of soap.

They were near the door now, and Zina read the sign on the wall beside it. TARIFS, it said, and listed the fees for tub baths and showers. There was a new sign beneath it, she saw, printed in shiny black letters: *établissement interdit aux juifs*, NO JEWS ALLOWED. Zina shivered, though the sun was beating hot on her head. She wondered if one day soon there would be a sign that said, *établissement interdit aux russes*.

"*Bystro, bystro,*" Mademoiselle Von Meck was saying. "Quickly, move quickly, young ladies."

She pushed Zina along ahead of her through the heavy doors that were kept open by the moving stream of people shoving against them.

The line parted, men and boys swept in one direction, women and girls in another. Zina felt herself carried along, squashed struggling among the other girls, toward the changing rooms.

"Ouch, infant," Olga said, giving her arm a pinch. "Watch where you're stepping with those big feet!"

Zina shot her a poisonous glance, but Olga did not even see it. She was jockeying for a place on the narrow bench along the wall of the room.

"Young ladies, young ladies!" Zina heard Mademoiselle Von Meck crying in a voice tinged with hysteria. Somehow, Mademoiselle had been separated from them and was waving from a bench on the opposite side of the room. "Fold your things neatly," Mademoiselle was crying. "Stack them together, here with mine. I'll put them in a locker."

Zina did not even try for a place on the bench. She knelt where she was and pulled off her sandals.

An attendant stood beside the door to the bath cubicles, motioning the bathers toward tubs or shower stalls as they were vacated. Zina hoped she would get a shower. It was easier to be quick in a shower. She hoped the water would be hot . . . at least warm . . . at least not absolutely cold.

When she had stripped to her underwear, she grabbed up her towel and went to stand in the line to the cubicles.

"Zi-*na*!" It was Lisa's irritated voice. "Mademoiselle said to fold your clothes and put them with hers!"

Zina glanced around, startled. She saw that Lisa was gathering her things from the floor, an aggrieved look on her face.

"I'm saving you a place in line!" Zina shouted, suddenly inspired.

"Move along!" Kira, behind her, gave her a shove, and Zina was unable to see whether Lisa was appeased.

Yet a moment later, Lisa pushed in next to her.

The attendant pointed to an empty tub cubicle and jerked her head toward Zina.

"You take it, Lizochka," Zina said, hoping that a shower would come up next.

Lisa gave Zina's shoulder a squeeze.

"*Spasibo*, thanks, Zinochka," she said.

But it was another tub that emptied next.

Dragging her feet, Zina entered the tiny, damp, mildew-smelling space. There was a grimy ring around the emptying tub that its last occupant had not cleaned away. The wet floor was gritty beneath Zina's feet. But there was also a tiny sliver of soap in the soap dish! Zina put in the plug and turned on the hot water tap. The water spurted out, and while the tub filled, Zina climbed out of her underwear and stepped over the porcelain rim into the lukewarm water. She lay down in it, her skin puckering into goose bumps, and rested her head against the back of the tub. At least in here she was not shoved and hurried.

Over the gushing of the water, she could hear the voices of the other girls echoing from the high ceiling.

"Ooh!" someone was crying. "This water's ice cold!"

"Someday," she heard Kira's dreaming voice. "Someday I'm going to have a bathroom all my own."

"In America," Zina heard Lisa saying from the next cubicle over. "In America, everyone has a bathroom in their house with the hot water piped right into it. When we go to America, I'm going to take two or three baths every day."

"Who says you're going to America?" came Olga's mocking voice.

"My father says, that's who!"

Zina sat up and listened harder.

"Don't you wish!" Olga's voice was laughing.

But Lisa's answer was smug.

"You'll see," she said. "Papa says there's no future in France for Russians. He says we won't stay here to starve or rot in refugee camps."

"A lot he can do about it." Olga's voice was bitter.

"You don't know." Lisa sounded angry now. "You don't know *what* my father can do. He escaped from Russia after the revolution. He can find a way to get us to America!"

Zina realized the water was threatening to overflow the tub. Hurriedly she twisted the tap to off.

America. That was where all the people were rich and could do whatever they wanted.

She shivered, whether with resentment that Papa hadn't told *her* about America, or with excitement, or the damp, she didn't know. She sank into the water, putting back her head, and felt her hair fan out, floating around her head. That was how her hair would float in the wind, she imagined, as she rode a great white horse across the vast plains of America. The horse would be white, like the ones the Three Musketeers rode in the *cinéma* films, and powerful. Yes, the horse would be white, not gray. Nothing gray in America, she thought.

Zina lifted her head from the water when the cubicle door opened suddenly, and Mademoiselle Von Meck poked in her head.

"*Bystro*, Zinaida, quickly!" Mademoiselle was urging.

BERTRAND

L'École St.-Étienne, near Paris
June, July, and August 1940

1

IT WAS a school, Maman said. But to Bertrand, it looked like a farm, or a nursery perhaps, with that long row of hothouses glinting in the sun. Bertrand sat on a wooden bench in the courtyard, where Maman had told him to wait, and watched people come and go between the buildings. He could hear the voices of children, playing somewhere near. Someone was chanting a hopscotch rhyme, and someone else was laughing.

It seemed to Bertrand a long time since *he* had played, though in fact it was only two days ago that Maman had taken him out of school.

Bertrand looked around him—at the nuns busy at the well, at the workman in a gray smock who was carrying a ladder toward the orchard, at the field of wheat, like a green lawn, in the distance. "You would like it here," Maman had said. "It is safe."

It certainly *seemed* safe, this school-farm. Here it was difficult to remember how afraid he had been running across the fields yesterday away from the German-strafed road, or the terrible fright of waking this morning in a strange room to the sound of strangers' voices.

"*Quelle chance*, Berti!" Maman had said. What luck to find kind people who would take them in for the night and then direct them to this place, so far from the main highway where the danger lay. "Just think, Berti," she had said. "A school. I would wish it were farther from Paris, but at least it is well out of the city. The Germans will not trouble with a school run by nuns."

The sun was making Bertrand sleepy, and he closed his eyes and leaned his head against the warm wall behind his bench. Yes, he would not mind it if they stayed here awhile before they went to America, he thought. It would be fun to have children to play with, fun to stay on a farm. Perhaps the school needed a nurse to care for the children when they were ill. Maman was a good nurse. Everyone said so.

Bertrand started at the sound of Maman's voice.

"*Merci beaucoup, ma mère*," she was saying, and Bertrand opened his eyes to see her coming out into the courtyard with an old nun so small that her starched white coif rode, billowing like a sailing ship, on a head not much higher than his own.

"This is he," Maman was saying to the nun. "This is my son, Bertrand."

The nun held out a tiny hand.

"Shake hands with Mère Marie Jeanne de la Croix, Berti," Maman said.

Bertrand took the nun's hand. It felt like old paper, he thought, brittle and dry. But her smile was young.

"*Bienvenu*, Bertrand. Welcome to St.-Étienne," she said, and her voice was young too.

Then she was talking once again to Maman while Bertrand stood listening.

"But, Mme Cole," she said, "what will *you* do? Will you be quite safe?"

"O, oui, ma mère," Maman said, and Bertrand could hear the relief in her voice. "Without the children I can travel much more easily. I am certain I can make arrangements for their *émigration* once I reach Marseilles. The American ambassador has assured me they can be gotten out of France. I have papers. . . ."

What was she saying? Bertrand felt the warm, safe feeling flee away. Marseilles? Without the children? Without him and Léonie?

"Maman," he cried, panic shrilling in his voice. He pulled at her sleeve. "Maman!"

"Shh, Maman is talking to *la bonne mère.*"

Maman did not look at him, and Bertrand let go her sleeve, suddenly cold. She was leaving him, he thought. She was going away without him.

At St.-Étienne, Bertrand slept in a dormitory with twenty other boys. The room was large, high-ceilinged, with high blackout curtained windows that darkened it all day. Ranged in rows on the bare wooden floor were the beds, white iron and ghostly in the gloom. They creaked in the night when the boys shifted in their sleep.

Léonie was in another part of the house, where the babies and little children were. Sometimes Bertrand thought he heard her crying in the night, but, "Léonie is well cared for," Soeur Marie Micheline told him. "The good sisters will see that she is not frightened. Go back to bed, Bertrand."

Mornings and afternoons, there was school. Mathematics, reading, geography, and finally, at the end of the afternoon, *écriture,* handwriting. Bertrand's hand would cramp, his fingers feel stiff and leaden, as he struggled to practice his letters. The room would grow warmer, the air heavier. His moist arm would stick to his paper. Then, "*Ça suffit,*" the teacher would say, and instantly all the boys were on their feet, dashing for the door.

When Bertrand first came to St.-Étienne, it was haying time. Though the other boys headed for the playground to swing on the monkey bars perhaps, or to shoot marbles, Bertrand was drawn to the fields to watch the workers cut hay. Their scythes would arc through the thick air, catching the sunlight, and Bertrand could see how sharp were the blades. Their sharpness made an ache in his throat, an ache of wanting. If I had something sharp, Bertrand would think, I would not feel so afraid. If I had a knife or a sword . . .

After the hay came the strawberries. The children were expected to help with the picking.

"You are lower to the ground, *n'est-ce-pas?*" said Soeur Marie Irène gaily. "It is not such hard work for you children as it is for us old ones."

Bertrand thought it was very hard work. His back ached as he crawled along the rows, and he felt his neck sting with sweat. When the sister was not looking, he popped berries into his own mouth and felt the sweet juice run down his throat. It is my pay, he thought. Maman didn't leave me here to be a slave! But the thought of Maman made another ache, and the berries seemed to sour. Maman *had* left him here.

"It's just for a little while," she had said, "until I can make arrangements. You will see."

Just a little while. Yet after the strawberries came the gooseberries and the currants. Soeur Irène found straw hats for those children who had none of their own, but still the sweat trickled stinging down Bertrand's neck.

Then it was July, and the workers were putting ladders into the plum trees, and the sisters were busy from dawn to dark with bottling and jam making. The gnats and mosquitoes were a plague. Bertrand scratched until his bites were bleeding sores, and the nuns made him wear white gloves.

There was no schoolroom now, and the days seemed long to Bertrand. But he had made a friend, Henri, a big, sullen boy the others feared. Henri had a wooden sword, and Bertrand found a fence paling with which to fight. They battled the other boys most afternoons, and though Henri mocked Bertrand for his weakness at first, as the days passed, more and more often he prevailed.

"*Sale Boche!*" he cried one day, pretending that Pierre was the enemy. "Dirty German, take that!"

Pierre's stick went flying, and he covered his head with his arms and cried for mercy.

"*Je ne suis pas Boche,*" he cried, but Bertrand kept on whacking. The hard, satisfying thuds thrilled him. He felt strong and unafraid.

"*Arrêtez-vous!* Stop it at once!" Soeur Marie Micheline came flying across the playground. "What shall I do with you, you naughty boy?" she cried, shaking Bertrand until he dropped his fence paling. "It is isolation for you, Bertrand," she said, dragging him away as Soeur Héloïse helped a blubbering Pierre to the infirmary.

"Meditate on your sins, Bertrand," Soeur Marie Micheline said. "You'll have only bread and water for supper tonight."

Sitting alone in the punishment room, Bertrand thought about the battle. I beat him, he thought. I am not afraid now. I can take care of myself.

2

A FLY buzzed near Bertrand's ear.

"You boys have not enough to do," Soeur Marie Micheline was saying.

Bertrand could just see her starched white coif over the heads of the boys in front of him. On this hot August day, she had chosen a bench beneath the courtyard apple tree, with the boys at her feet on the paving stones. Her favorites knelt close to her spreading black skirts. Bertrand had found a place beside Henri at the back.

Bertrand waved away the fly.

"That is why you are naughty," the sister was saying. "A new skill will keep those idle hands away from devil's work."

Bzzz. The fly was back, circling Bertrand's other ear. But before he could move, Henri's hand shot out, imprisoning the fly.

"*Voilà,*" whispered Henri, smirking.

The fly buzzed inside Henri's fist—furiously, Bertrand thought.

Bertrand held his breath as Henri opened his hand

slightly and, before the fly could escape, caught hold of a vibrating wing. He plucked it off, and Bertrand gasped. He hunched over Henri's hands to shield them from the sister's searching eyes.

"*Regarde,*" whispered Henri.

Bertrand, fascinated, watched him drop the fly to the pavement. It spun helplessly, its buzzing frantic. Its remaining wing beat, fragile and powerless to lift its iridescent body. Bertrand wondered if it was afraid.

Henri snickered. He pulled off the other wing.

Now the fly was silent, crawling.

"Bertrand Cole!"

Bertrand shot upright.

"*Oui, ma soeur.*"

"What are you doing, Bertrand?"

"*Rien, ma soeur.* Nothing."

Soeur Marie Micheline pointed to a place in the front row of boys.

"You may come do nothing here, Bertrand," she said.

"But . . ." said Bertrand.

"*Here,*" said Soeur Marie Micheline.

Bertrand shuffled to his feet and made his way forward to the place the nun indicated. He didn't look back, but he could feel Henri's mocking eyes follow him.

The other boys looked obediently at Soeur Marie Micheline. Bertrand wondered if now Henri would also pay attention.

Soeur Marie Micheline handed a basket to Pierre, who had sprung to her side the instant she called him.

Teacher's pet! Bertrand thought.

"You will each take a piece of cloth from the basket Pierre is handing around," said the sister, "and a threaded needle from the pin cushion. Today we will begin to learn *la broderie*, embroidery."

Embroidery! Bertrand stared, aghast, at the smooth face of Soeur Marie Micheline. He heard a snort from behind him.

"Embroidery is for girls!" Henri said from the back row.

Soeur Marie Micheline lifted her eyebrows. Her voice was as smooth as her face.

"Embroidery is a skill that anyone may learn," she said. "Even clumsy-fingered boys."

The boys beside Bertrand looked uncomfortable. He felt them shift and hunch their shoulders.

"The monks of St.-Roch weave tapestries," squeaked Pierre, his voice trembling.

"*Exactement!*" said the sister, nodding. "Needlework is an honorable occupation for men."

"Pah!"

"Henri Beauchamp," said Soeur Marie Micheline, "come forward."

Bertrand waited for Henri to do as the sister ordered, but nothing happened. He shot a quick glance over his shoulder. Henri sat in his place, his eyes narrowed and scornful.

Bertrand looked back at Soeur Marie Micheline. He saw the flush of color that mottled her face. Her eyes glittered.

"Henri Beauchamp!"

"I'm not some *girl,*" said Henri.

"*Non,*" said the sister, her voice brittle. "You are not a girl. You are a wicked boy who will begin this afternoon to learn embroidery."

Henri made a rude noise.

The nun had risen to her feet so swiftly that Bertrand was not even aware of it until he felt her skirts brush past him. In three long strides she was upon Henri, her thin white fingers grasping his ear.

"Méchant!" she cried. *"Diable!"*

Bertrand saw that Henri's ear was scarlet. He was gritting his teeth, but he did not cry out. Soeur Marie Micheline twisted his ear harder. Bertrand saw tears start in Henri's eyes, but still he did not cry out.

Bertrand's heart thundered in his chest. His face felt hot, and his breath came hard and painful. If only he were as brave as Henri . . .

"Moi non plus!" he cried, leaping to his feet before he thought. "I also will not learn sewing."

His words seemed to hang in the breathless silence, and he could hear how small and girlish his voice had sounded. Not brave at all, he thought, but hysterical . . .

"Qu'est-ce qui se passe?" said another voice, the thin, young voice of Mère Marie Jeanne.

"I have on my hands a *petite rébellion, ma mère,*" said Soeur Marie Micheline. "This naughty boy refuses to learn embroidery with his *camarades.*"

Mère Marie Jeanne swept toward them across the courtyard.

"Ça suffit, ma soeur," she said quietly.

Soeur Marie Micheline let go the ear.

Henri did not deign to put up his hand to rub it. He stood glowering at the paving stones.

The boys stared.

Bertrand thought that no one had noticed him.

"I was coming just now," said Mère Marie Jeanne, "to find help for Louis. He is mucking out the pigsty."

Bertrand heard giggles from several of the boys. He saw the color begin to rise into Henri's stolid face.

"Could you spare Henri Beauchamp, *ma soeur?*" said Mère Marie Jeanne.

Soeur Marie Micheline nodded, and Bertrand, glancing about, saw the smug looks of the other boys. Even embroidery was preferable to mucking out pigsties, their faces seemed to say.

"*Ma mère . . .*" faltered Bertrand. He also, after all, had refused the needlework lesson.

But, "Don't be an *imbecile,*" whispered the boy beside him. He pulled him down.

Behind the tiny upright figure of Mère Marie Jeanne, Henri slouched toward the barns. Bertrand wondered, had he won or lost?

Bertrand clutched in his clumsy fingers the tiny silver needle and the square of yellowed muslin. He could not seem to focus his eyes on the crooked stitches. His finger burned where he had pricked it. He scratched a bloody sore on his leg.

"Cut your thread close to the knot," Soeur Marie Micheline was saying.

The boy next to Bertrand nudged him and handed him a basket.

Bertrand blinked the sweat from his eyes. The sunlight glinted off the contents of the basket. Scissors. Several shining pairs of scissors.

He reached for a pair and passed the basket on. He weighed the scissors in his hand. They were small, perhaps four inches long, and heavy for their size. He opened them and ran a finger along an edge. It was sharp. Closed again, the blades made a glittering point, sharp also. Sharp, like a knife.

"Pass forward the scissors when you have finished with them," said Soeur Marie Micheline.

Once again the basket was coming around. Bertrand could hear the faint clash of metal as the scissors dropped into it. The boy on his left pushed the basket into Bertrand's hand. For a moment, Bertrand looked into it. Then he cut his thread and laid his scissors on top of the others with a clinking sound. But when he withdrew his hand, they were still clasped against his palm, smooth and cool . . . and sharp.

He passed the basket to his right and, as he felt it taken from his hand, he slipped the scissors into the pocket of his trousers.

ZINA

Pau, France
September 1940

1

ZINA TRUDGED behind Lisa up the dark, narrow staircase to Mama and Papa's rooms.

"Is it you, *deti*, children?" Mama called from the top of the stairs.

"*Da*, Mama."

They said it together, and Zina giggled because they chorused so perfectly and because she was glad to be here.

Mama was hugging Lisa, and as Zina put her foot on the top step, she felt Mama's arms go around her too. She leaned her head against Mama and felt something inside herself untighten. She hugged back hard, breathing in Mama's warm salty smell with the pungent cooking smells that filled the hallway where they stood.

"Are you hungry, *deti?*" Mama was saying as though they were not always a little hungry.

"*Da*, Mama, *da*," Zina murmured, happy that Mama had something good for them to eat, but sad that it meant the end of the hug.

Mama loosed herself from Zina's grip and led the way down the hall to the door of the rooms.

There were only two rooms, separated by a curtain. The first, the one they entered through the door in the hall, was the kitchen. Here Mama had her tiny gazogene burner, with a pot steaming on it, and two shelves of pans and crockery above the board counter beside the sink. Here also in the corner, strangely, was the toilet— "A great convenience," Mama had said, making, as she always did, the best of things.

"I made some cabbage soup today," Mama said now, drawing aside the curtain to the front room, which was the sitting room and dining room and bedroom in one. "And" —she paused dramatically and waved her hand in the direction of the rickety table set in a corner— "a fresh tomato!"

Zina ran to the table to see. It was true. On the plate, in round red slices, was a fresh tomato.

"You may share it," Mama said, her voice sounding proud.

"Oh, Mama," said Lisa, "*spasibo*, Mama. Thank you."

"It may be the last we can get," said Mama. "Enjoy it."

Zina plopped onto the hard wooden seat of a chair drawn up to the table. Mama brought the pot of soup from the kitchen and ladled it into their bowls. Then she filled their mugs with tea.

No milk today, Zina thought, but the tomato made up for it.

"Where's Papa?" Lisa was asking.

Zina's hand hovered over the plate of tomato. She looked at Mama.

"*Da, da*, take a slice, Zinochka," Mama said. "Lisa

may have the next one. At the employment office. He goes every day to look for work. A man of his ability . . ." Mama sighed, then brightened. "What do you think, Lizochka? The only job he has found so far is teaching bridge to a rich Englishwoman!"

"Bridge? Cards?" Lisa was talking with her mouth full, Zina noticed as she spooned Mama's good hot soup into her own mouth.

"Bridge!" Mama laughed. "Can you imagine? In these times, right here in Pau, there is a woman with nothing more on her mind than improving her card game!" She wiped her eyes with the back of her hand. "*Nu,* it's money. The good Lord knows we need it."

The cool, tangy tomato lay in Zina's mouth like a blessing. There was only one slice left on the plate. Was it hers, or was it Lisa's? She shot a glance at Lisa and saw that Lisa was looking intently at Mama.

I'd just as well not be here, for all the attention they pay me, she thought.

She reached for the tomato.

"Mama," Lisa was saying, "there's a rumor going about . . . They say the Kolónia is closing. We're all to be sent to our parents, they say. . . ."

Zina's hand had stopped, halfway to the tomato plate.

Why didn't anyone ever tell *her* anything? She hadn't heard such a rumor.

She looked at Mama hopefully.

Mama was nodding, and Zina's heart skipped a beat.

"*Da, da,*" Mama was saying. "I'm afraid it is true. The Kolónia has run out of money too. They can't keep on. Father Konstantin came to see your father and me two evenings ago. He says they can keep you to the end of the week. Then we'll have to take you."

A smile was spreading across Zina's face, though at the same time she had a funny feeling in the pit of her stomach.

"But where will you put us?" Lisa was saying. "How will we manage?"

Her face bleak, Mama was looking around the small room, already crowded by the swaybacked brass bed between the windows, the table and two kitchen chairs, and another small old table with Papa's typewriter on it. Mama's sewing machine, in its case, and her suitcases peeked from beneath the bed.

"I don't know," Mama said. Then she smiled, the smile quivering a little at its corners, Zina thought. "We'll manage," she said.

Zina could feel her own smile fading as the feeling in her stomach grew.

"But, aren't you glad, Mama?" she said.

"Of course I'm glad, darling. It will be wonderful to be together again. It's just that . . . *Nu*, never mind. We'll manage."

Zina searched Mama's face. She was still smiling that quivery smile. Didn't she understand that they wouldn't have to live in these rooms for long? Soon they would be going to America. Lisa said that Papa had said so. "If he can find a way," Lisa had said.

He will, Zina thought, wondering if she dared to remind Mama of America. Perhaps it was another of the things Zina was not supposed to know.

She reached again for the last tomato slice, and Lisa let her take it.

"We're going to be on top of each other here," Lisa was saying. "I hate this stupid war. I hate it!"

Zina cocked her head to one side and studied Lisa's discontented face and Mama's anxious one.

Didn't Mama want them to come live with her and Papa? Was that what she meant when she said she didn't know how they would manage? We'll *have* to take you, Zina remembered she had said.

Suddenly the tomato tasted bitter on her tongue.

2

"HA! GOT one!" Zina whispered triumphantly and flicked the squashed flea off her thumbnail. "That makes six for me," she said.

Lisa flopped over onto her back and stared at the ceiling. The girls lay head to head on two cot mattresses, retrieved from the defunct Kolónia. Though the windows were growing gray with dawn, across the room in the brass double bed, Mama and Papa still slept.

"You only got five so far," Zina reminded Lisa in a whisper.

"Shh!" said Lisa. "I don't care. I'm tired of catching fleas. There are always more. Go back to sleep."

Zina scratched her leg. Lisa was right, of course. No matter how many fleas she caught, her arms and legs were covered with bites that turned into sores when she scratched them.

Still, *I* won, she thought.

A sudden sound of feet on the stairs brought Zina sitting upright. It was M. Thibaud, the butcher who kept the shop downstairs. Zina could tell by the clumping of his huge feet.

"Mme Sarach!" M. Thibaud was calling outside their door. "Mme Sarach, there is a shipment of potatoes today. I have just heard it from M. Vuillemin."

Mama was sitting up in bed, clutching her old pink blanket about her shoulders.

"*Merci,* M. Thibaud," she called to him in French, her voice husky with sleep. "*Merci beaucoup.*"

Zina heard the heavy footsteps retreating.

Mama was yawning. She put back the covers and dangled her legs over the side of the bed.

Papa stirred, lifting his head from the pillow.

"*Nyet,* Oleg," Mama murmured. "No need for you to get up. I'll send one of the girls."

Papa settled back. Mama groped with her foot for her slippers.

Zina crawled off her mattress and scuttled on her hands and knees to retrieve the slippers—Mama's pink satin mules with the feather trim.

"Here, Mama," she said, handing one up to her. She stroked the other with her forefinger. It was still pretty, even if the satin was scuffed and the feathers worn.

"*Spasibo,* Zinochka," Mama said softly, taking the other slipper from her hand. "Lizochka . . ."

"I promised I'd help Kira Volkonskaya with her Latin this morning," Lisa said quickly. "With school starting soon . . ."

"*Da, da,*" Mama said with a sigh. "Zinochka?"

It would please Mama if she said she'd go, thought Zina. It would make her glad that Zina was there to help . . .

"Sure, Mama," said Zina.

✖ ✖ ✖

The warehouse, where the potatoes would be sold, didn't open until eight o'clock, but when Zina arrived, shortly after six-thirty, there was a long line already forming in the street. Zina broke into a run and slipped behind the last person in the line seconds before the puffing arrival of a potbellied man wearing a blue-striped work shirt. The man growled at her and frowned, shaking his head.

But I was here first, Zina thought. She turned her back on him.

The ration coupons were pinned inside the pocket of her cardigan, along with the money for the potatoes, tied in a handkerchief.

"Don't lose it," Mama had warned. "And remember, stay in line. They won't let you back in if you wander away."

Zina knew that. She had stood in line for food several times now. One week, it might be rice that was in short supply. The next it was onions, or macaroni, or oil. Even if one had the ration coupons and the money, there would be none in the shops.

In line, Zina shifted from foot to foot, chewing the bread Mama had sent for her breakfast and hugging herself against the morning chill. The potbellied man behind her smelled. Zina stole a glance at his broken leather shoes.

He moved closer to her and scowled.

Zina turned her attention to the old woman in front of her. She wore soft, floppy slippers on her feet and cotton stockings that bagged around her thick ankles. She moaned and muttered under her breath, her head shaking with palsy.

Zina dangled her string bag from her finger. She

swung it idly to and fro. The line, of course, did not move. It was not yet eight o'clock.

Traffic was beginning to pick up. An empty farm cart clattered past, drawn by a gray horse.

Gray, of course. Zina nodded to herself.

She began to dream of the white horse she might ride in America. Its neck would arch, its eyes would flash, its feet would lift high in a jaunty trot. . . .

The line stretched behind her around the corner and out of sight—mostly women and children, an occasional man. The women greeted one another and gossiped. Zina searched faces for someone she might know.

The roar of a motor announced a German staff car. It barreled down the street, scattering pedestrians and frightening horses. Zina caught sight of the officer who sat in the backseat. His spectacles flashed in the sunlight that was beginning to warm the street. Zina quickly lowered her eyes and did not look again until the sound of the motor had faded in the distance.

Suddenly, from the direction in which the car had disappeared, there was a clamor.

"Runaway!" Zina heard someone shout. She could hear screams and the drumming of hooves. A horse and wagon careened around the corner. It seemed for a moment that the wagon balanced on two wheels. Then, with a crash, it went over. Zina saw the driver fly off the seat. He disappeared from view behind the line of people who were shouting and waving their arms. A small child began to shriek. Zina could hear the racket of the wagon being dragged down the street on its side by the terrified horse.

"*Est-ce qu'il s'est blessé?* Is he hurt?" people were calling.

Then she heard, "*Non, non, pas trop, ça va.*"

Zina jumped to see over the heads of the people. The wagon driver was supported by two other men. Blood ran down the side of his face. He didn't look all right to Zina.

"*Ces sales Boches!*" someone muttered.

Suddenly Zina realized that she had stepped out of line. She looked frantically for the old woman who had been in front of her.

There, there she was in her baggy stockings, and the potbellied man in the blue shirt stood just behind her in Zina's place. Zina ran the few steps to them, but the man had stepped forward, pushing his belly against the old woman's back.

Zina's voice quivered, but she made herself speak loudly in her best French, "*Pardon, monsieur.*"

The potbellied man ignored her.

Zina tried to squeeze in front of him.

"*Fiche-moi la paix!* Beat it!" the man muttered.

His smell clogged Zina's throat, and sickness rose to meet it. Zina choked, anger rising with the sickness. This was her place in line! *Her* place!

Then she realized that the clock of the *mairie* was striking. With a lurch, the line began to move. The potbellied man pressed forward against the old woman's back.

Zina opened her mouth to yell at him. This is *my* place, she meant to yell, but no sound came. The words screamed, powerless, in Zina's mind. She put down her head and charged him, feeling the way the man's soft belly gave way to her butting head. Her fists flailed into the softness, like pummeling a pillow, and she heard beneath the sound of his shouts her own sobbing grunts.

"*Laisse-moi tranquille!* Stop bothering me!" the potbellied man cried.

But Zina could not stop. Whomp! Whomp! went her fists. Whomp, whomp, whomp!

Someone grabbed her arms and pulled her away. Her arms hurt where the hard fingers were gripping them behind her. She kicked out with her feet and caught the potbellied man's shin a cracking blow.

"Ow!" he cried, doubling over.

"*Ça suffit!* That's enough!" commanded a voice above Zina's head.

But it wasn't enough, not nearly enough, thought Zina with a sob. Was she nothing, to be treated this way?

She could hear her own ragged breaths and the thumping of her heart. She had been dragged backward out of range of the potbellied man, so she stopped kicking and, like a punctured balloon, hung suddenly limp from the hard restraining hands.

"What's the trouble here?" she heard the voice above her head say.

"I don't know what got into the brat," the potbellied man was saying, rubbing his shin. "I didn't do a thing to her."

That's not true, Zina wanted to say, but she couldn't seem to catch her breath.

She twisted back her head to see who held her and looked into a face beneath a policeman's cap. Her stomach lurched.

"There's no reason for her to attack me," the potbellied man was saying. "The brat kicked me without cause."

That's not true! Again Zina tried to say it, but even as she struggled to think of the French words that seemed to have fled her brain, she heard them being said in an old and trembling voice.

"*Ce n'est pas vrai!*" the old woman was saying. "He stole her place in line."

Then other people were nodding and murmuring and frowning at the man.

"*C'est juste*," they said. "*L'animal!*"

The policeman's hands loosened on Zina's arms. He gave her a push toward the line, and the potbellied man stepped back, leaving a space for her. His face was deep red, and he did not look at her.

"Behave yourself!" the policeman said, and Zina did not know whether he spoke to her or to the man.

The old woman clucked her tongue and patted Zina's head.

I should thank her, Zina thought, but suddenly she couldn't think of that French word either.

So she was silent, numb and shaken, jostled along as the line moved forward until she had reached the warehouse door.

"How many coupons?" someone barked at her. She fumbled in her pocket. The potatoes were weighed and dumped into her bag.

Then, as she turned, she remembered.

"*Merci*, madame," she cried, but the old woman was already gone.

3

ZINA WAS reading one of the "Adventures of Mischievous Marie" in a girls' magazine she had found in a garbage can. She had not mentioned to Mama that sometimes nowadays she examined garbage cans for salvageable food. Few people had food of any kind to throw away, but once she had found a whole orange with only a spot of mold.

In the story, Marie was out to rescue a kitten who had fallen into a well. Zina guessed that, by the end of the story, Marie would be allowed to keep the kitten as a pet.

"Where is Nanou, Mama?" Zina asked, looking up from the page. Reading about Marie's kitten had made her think of her own.

Mama's sewing machine whirred steadily, and Mama's eyes never left the length of fabric that she fed beneath its needle.

"I have told you that Nanou went to live with some kind people who took him in when I left Paris," she said.

"What kind people?" Zina said, though she knew she had asked this too before.

But Mama did not answer, and Zina did not know whether to believe her or not.

"Mama?" she insisted.

"Hush, Zinochka. Mme Seurat's customer needs this skirt by tomorrow, and the light is failing fast."

Zina sighed and went back to her story. It was true that the light from the window was dimmer every moment. Soon Mama would have to switch on the high, bare lightbulb in the ceiling that was no good at all for reading or, she supposed, for sewing either.

Running footsteps pounded up the stairs. It was Papa, Zina knew. The footsteps were too heavy to be Lisa's, who had been sent out on an errand.

Mama's hand lifted from the sewing machine wheel, and she turned her eyes toward the door. As it burst open, she cried, "Oleg, so soon? I haven't even started supper yet, I have so much to finish."

Papa pushed through the brown curtain that hung across the kitchen doorway.

"Lena, you'll never guess!" he was saying. "I've just run into Irina Okuneva—you remember Mme Okuneva from Paris? It's incredible luck. She may be able to get the girls to America!"

Papa was flushed and smiling. He was striding toward Mama, his face alight, when Mama's sharp voice stopped him in midstep.

"Oleg!" she said. She tipped her head toward Zina with a quick motion. Then her voice softened. "Cannot we talk about it later? Mme Seurat will pay me in money if I can finish this skirt by tomorrow."

Papa's eyes also had gone briefly to Zina. He rubbed his hands together.

"Of course, Lena. I didn't mean to interrupt you. Money, you say, and not carrots or onions?" He shook his head. "I suppose we should be grateful," he said.

From deep in the cave, Zina struggled toward a faint glow of light. The darkness in the cave was so thick that Zina had to push it aside with her hands, as though she were swimming. She could feel it pressing against her eyelids, and she strained to force them open. . . .

From her mattress, Zina saw that Mama and Papa were awake and talking in the dim light of the candle that burned on the table beside their bed. Mama sat on the edge of the bed, her pale legs dangling from beneath her nightgown, and Papa sat in a chair, facing her over the table and the tiny point of light.

". . . may not get a chance like this again," Papa was saying, his tone intense and quiet.

"I know, I know!"

Zina could hear the despair in her mother's voice. It made her feel hollow.

"There's no use arguing at this point," Papa said. "It may not even happen. Irina said that the American woman can take only so many. She's arranged for a group visa, and there's just a small chance there might be room for Lisa and Zina."

At her name, Zina could not help but stir.

"Shh!" hissed Mama, and for a moment neither of them spoke.

Zina shut her eyes quickly and held her breath. Then she thought better of that and tried to match the deep, even breathing of Lisa, asleep on the other mattress. Zina's heart was pounding, and she prayed they could not hear it.

She needed them to keep on talking. She needed to

know about going to America, but Papa had not brought it up again all evening. Lisa had come in from her errand. Mama had continued sewing, even after the electric light was switched on, and Lisa and Zina had heated their supper while Papa sat at the other table going through his papers. Zina had finished Mischievous Marie's adventure—Marie *had* been allowed to keep the kitten—and she and Lisa had done their homework, for school had started just a week ago.

Now, after a few moments of silence, Papa spoke again, so softly that Zina had to strain to hear.

"You must prepare yourself, my dear, in case this should come to pass. We may never find a way out of France for all four of us. How much longer can we keep on as we are?"

Something in the sound of Papa's voice made Zina's throat tighten. She could not resist peeking and saw Mama slip from bed to kneel before Papa's chair.

"Hush," Zina heard Mama murmur, but Papa could not seem to hush.

" . . . no work anywhere," he was saying. "The Unoccupied Zone is filled with jobless people—demobilized soldiers, refugees—*you* see them in the streets. Your slaving over that sewing machine for carrots and onions and the occasional franc will not keep food in our bellies, Lena. The French are not employing foreigners now even as farm workers!"

Mama swayed on her knees.

"Hush, hush," she said.

"Just this morning," Papa said, "some ruffian in the street shouted at me to 'go home' when he heard my Russian accent. Me, who has called France home for more than twenty years!"

Zina felt startled. They taunted Papa!

"They drafted Russians when the war began," he was saying bitterly. "We were good enough to be sent to die, but now we do not deserve even work! Unless something happens soon, it will be the camps for all of us!"

"Hush, Oleg," Mama said. "I will think about it. Hush now, hush."

Zina swallowed hard against the tightness in her throat.

"If we didn't have the children to worry about, you and I would have a chance . . ." Papa was saying.

"*Da*, Oleg," Mama said. "You are right, of course." She rose stiffly from her knees and put her arm about his shoulders. "Come to bed now," she said.

Zina had lain still for so long that she felt she could not move if she wanted to. Her feet were icy, but a fever of heat pounded in her head. Her face felt stiff, her lips pressed hard and hurting against her teeth. Her throat ached.

No way out of France for the four of us, Papa had said. If we didn't have the children, he had said.

So they are planning to send us away, she thought. Away to America.

Zina felt a sob rise in her throat. She put her hands over her mouth to stifle it.

She tried to think about the white American horse, but no vision of it would come. Instead, all she could see on the tight-squeezed backs of her eyelids was grayness—cold and fearful—the grayness that was because of the war.

"Papa?" Zina said. "Where is the bicycle? It isn't in the passageway, and I know that Lisa didn't take it. She was going to walk with her friends."

Papa looked up from his newspaper, then folded it

and laid it aside. He took off his glasses and rubbed the bridge of his nose, his eyes closed.

"Come here, Zinochka," he said. "I need to talk to you."

Zina stepped into the room, letting the kitchen curtain fall back into place behind her.

"What, Papa?" she said, feeling suddenly afraid.

Papa patted his knee, and Zina sat down on it. He put his arm around her.

"I have sold the bicycle, Zinochka," Papa said.

Zina looked at him in disbelief.

"Sold the bicycle?"

Papa nodded.

"It was for a good purpose," he said. "So we can send you and Lisa to America."

Zina's heart sank. She had heard no more about America since the night she woke to Mama's and Papa's whispered conversation. "It may not even happen," Papa had said that night, and as the days passed with no mention of America, Zina had lulled herself into believing Mama and Papa would never send her and Lisa away until they found a way to go too.

"A friend of ours, Mme Okuneva—I don't think you would remember her . . ." Papa paused, and Zina shook her head. "*Nu,* Mme Okuneva is a secretary for the YMCA, and that organization is working with an American church group, the Unitarian Service Committee, to take a group of children out of France to live with American families until this war is over."

Zina thought desperately of what she had heard other grown-ups say.

"They say the war *is* over in France," she said. "The Germans won."

"Perhaps," said Papa. He looked doubtful.

"England has not surrendered, and the Free French forces in England continue to resist. . . ."

Zina remembered Sofia's talk of *les Maquisards*.

"In any case, the war is not over in other parts of Europe. There will continue to be refugee problems and food shortages."

"But what does that have to do with our bicycle?" Zina said. "If we must go to America, why don't we *all* go?"

"Ah, Zinochka," Papa said. "Mama and I wish we *could* all go, but leaving France takes a great deal of money and many different kinds of paperwork—visas, passports, affidavits."

"We *have* passports," Zina said. She had seen their green "Nansen" passports, issued to them because they were not French citizens, among Papa's papers.

"*Da*, I know we do. . . . It is all very complicated, and perhaps impossible if we were to wait for an opportunity to go together. That is why we have decided to send you girls ahead with this Mrs. Sharp of the Unitarians. Mama and I will follow just as quickly as we can. In the meanwhile, you will be having an *avantura*, an adventure—living with a kind family in America and going to a fine new school. . . ."

A kind family, Zina thought, like Mama says took Nanou. . . .

"Will we speak French or Russian at the new school?" asked Zina.

"In America, you will speak English," Papa said.

"But I don't know English," said Zina.

"Oh, yes you do," said Papa. "Some of Mama's family live in England, and Mama herself had an English father though she was born in Russia. You have heard her speak English."

Zina was silent. Mama could speak several languages easily. She did not seem to have to struggle for words as Zina sometimes had to do, even in Russian.

"I am confident you will learn English very quickly," Papa was saying. "Remember how you learned French when you first started school?"

Zina slid from his knee and wandered over to the window to watch for Mama to come home. Papa picked up his newspaper and unfolded it again.

Zina was thinking about the bicycle, Papa's beautiful blue-and-gray bicycle with the yellow steering bar! She thought of the emptiness of the passageway downstairs where M. Thibaud had allowed them to keep it.

"Papa?" she said, turning suddenly. "Was there no other way than to sell—"

But Papa was holding up his hand, stopping her.

"I am reading, Zina," he said.

Zina flushed hot with sudden anger and clamped her mouth shut.

BERTRAND

L'École St.-Étienne and Beaucourt, France
October 1940

1

BERTRAND HAD hidden the scissors inside his pillowcase. In the night, when he lay awake listening to the rustlings and sighs of the sleepers around him, he could slip his hand into the case and touch them. He could feel their point against his thumb and imagine them clenched in his fist like a knife. They were a weapon, he told himself—like the guns of soldiers.

With a weapon he would be brave, no matter what. No matter that Papa had gone to America. No matter that Maman had left him here. No matter that France was conquered.

But in October, the air raids began. The sirens would sound, distantly from the nearby towns and villages—perhaps he heard them even from Paris, he thought. Then the chapel bell would clang, and his invincibility would vanish. The sisters would hustle the children across the courtyard to the *caves*, the wine cellars, and Bertrand could not grab the scissors from his pillowcase. Not with everyone watching. Not with no pocket in his nightshirt to hide them in.

The long nightshirt would flap around his legs as he ran, and he would clutch his gas mask in his arms.

Bertrand could hear the French antiaircraft guns firing at the British planes. The sound reminded him of the rattle of explosions that day on the road, and his teeth would chatter as he ran.

Huddled in the *caves*, the sisters would sing, or sometimes Mère Marie Jeanne would read aloud to them. Bertrand knew it was to comfort them, but he didn't feel comforted. He sat on the cold floor, his arms around his legs, and shivered. The singing sounded mournful, and beyond it, always, were the guns.

Once, as they ran to the *caves*, a bomb flash illuminated the small cemetery beside the nuns' chapel. Bertrand stopped, straining into the darkness where, in the instant of the flash, he had seen the Blessed Mother, haloed with light. She had smiled at him, he thought.

Then Soeur Josephine was beside him, sweeping him toward the *caves*.

"*Dépêche-toi!* Hurry!" she was scolding. "What are you thinking, you stupid boy, to stop in the path like that?"

He didn't tell her he had seen the Blessed Mother. That was for me, he told himself. For me alone.

It was a clear-sky night, crisp and cold, perfect for air raids, Bertrand thought. In the next bed, Jean-Luc had begun to play with his gas mask. He blew into it, making the sides flap with an amusing vulgar sound. Bertrand laughed, his laughter shrill with nerves. He reached for his own gas mask.

Soon most of the boys were blowing into their masks and giggling at the noise.

"*Tais-toi,*" grumped Pierre. "Shut up. I'm trying to sleep."

"Ooo," mocked Henri. "*Le pauvre petit!*"

Henri threw his pillow at Pierre's head.

Bertrand laughed and reached for his own pillow, then thought better of it. It wouldn't do to have his weapon discovered. Pierre was a *rapporteur,* a tattletale.

Pierre was wailing. Henri's pillow had hit him square in the face, and a volley of other pillows was raining on his bed.

"*Silence!*"

Instantly the boys dove beneath their covers. Pierre alone sat up in bed, half-buried beneath the pillows. A gas mask made a final flap-flap-flap.

"*Silence,*" repeated Soeur Marie Micheline from the doorway. "Why do you not sleep? Have you said your prayers?"

"*Oui, ma soeur,*" piped Pierre from the pile of pillows.

"*C'est évident,*" said Soeur Marie Micheline, flashing her pocket lamp around the dormitory, "it's evident that you boys have no need of your pillows. I will care for them."

She began unpiling Pierre's bed and stacked the pillows in a cupboard.

"*Voilà,*" she said. "They will trouble you no further." She turned the key in the cupboard lock and then slipped it into her pocket. "It is time for sleep. Has every boy his gas mask close at hand?"

"*Oui, ma soeur.*" It was a subdued chorus.

Soeur Marie Micheline paced between the beds, her lamp held low. Here she twitched into place a disheveled blanket, there retrieved a pair of spectacles that had fallen to the floor. Finally she stood beside Bertrand's bed.

"*Eh bien,*" she said. "I see that you were not of the pillow fighters. I am proud of you, Bertrand."

Bertrand squirmed, knowing the reason he had not thrown his pillow.

"Good news, *mon enfant.*" There was a gentleness to the sister's voice that Bertrand had not noticed before. "We have had a message from your mother. She will arrive tomorrow to fetch you and your sister."

Bertrand felt for a moment as though his heart would leap from his chest.

"*Ma mère? Demain?* Tomorrow?" he breathed.

"*Oui, demain.* After breakfast you will pack your things and go to the office of Mère Marie Jeanne. *Comprends-tu,* Bertrand? Do you understand?"

Bertrand nodded. He was searching for her face in the shadow above the lamp's glow. He felt her fingers brush across his forehead, cool, as he remembered his mother's fingers were cool. Then she turned away with a swish of her skirts, and the light moved on.

"*Formidable!*" whispered Jean-Luc when she was gone. "I wish I could leave this place."

But Bertrand did not respond. Suddenly his heart was beating hard, and his hands were sweating.

Leave this place? For where? he wondered. Where would Maman take them now? Was it possible to go home, or were they going to Papa in America?

Bertrand's eyes felt sore and scratchy. His head ached.

Soeur Marie Micheline had given him a valise to pack his things in. There was not much, only the change of clothes and the straw hat the nuns had given him and a nightshirt and underwear. He did not trust his weapon to the valise. One could be separated from luggage, he had learned. He slipped the scissors, wrapped in his handkerchief, into his trousers pocket when the sisters were not looking. Then he buckled the valise and was ready to go.

To go . . .

Slowly, his feet somehow reluctant, he headed for the door.

"*Au revoir*, Bertrand," Soeur Marie Micheline called after him. "Good-bye."

At the sound of her voice, Bertrand turned and lifted his hand to wave. Suddenly the young nun seemed dear to him. He felt a pull between them, as though he were tied to her in some way he did not understand. She had not been so *very* unkind to him, he thought. And he *had* been naughty. . . .

His hand fluttered in the air, and he felt tears rising to his eyes. He turned abruptly to hide them.

"*Au revoir, ma soeur,*" he said, and knew the words were a whisper that Soeur Marie Micheline could not possibly hear.

Maman had already arrived. Bertrand could hear her voice through the door of Mère Marie Jeanne's office. He could hear Léonie's voice also, a delighted babble that made Bertrand suddenly angry.

Léonie was such a baby, he thought. She didn't even realize that Maman had abandoned them here. She left us with strangers, he thought, his cheeks flushing hot. She didn't care what might happen to us. She didn't care that they would work us in the fields and punish us with bread and water and . . .

He hesitated before the door, listening to the voices. He would show her that he also did not care. She might leave him wherever she wished. He could take care of himself and Léonie too, he thought, putting his hand to his pocket to feel the reassuring shape of the scissors. *He* would not play the baby as Léonie was doing. . . .

He knocked at the door, his anger in the loud rap and sharp pain of his knuckles against the wood.

"*Entrez,*" came the voice of Mère Marie Jeanne.

Bertrand gave the door a shove.

There was his mother, turning toward him.

"*Mon fils!*" she cried. "My son!" and Bertrand saw the light in her eyes, the quick, warm gladness of her smile.

Bertrand did not feel the valise drop from his numb fingers. He felt only the answering smile that stretched his mouth, felt his legs running the few steps it took him to reach his mother, felt her arms around him, pulling him close.

"Maman," he heard his voice cry. "Maman!" He could hear the joyous sound of it and feel the way he clung to her, the way his anger shrank to a tight, hard knot at the center of his joy.

2

"WHERE ARE we going?" Bertrand said.

Once again they were traveling by automobile. This time the driver was an old man. He did not talk to them, but muttered continuously to himself, his mutterings muffled in his mustache.

"Maman? Where are we going now?"

"*Chez Grandmère,*" said Maman. "To Grandmother's. You will like that, will you not, Berti? You have not seen Grandmère since she visited us last year."

Bertrand nodded. He *would* like that, he thought. Grandmère had given him money from her coin purse to buy *bonbons*, and she had taken over Marie's kitchen to bake a *crème caramel* especially for him. She and Maman chattered night and day, he remembered, and they laughed a great deal. When they went walking, they linked arms like girlfriends, and Maman walked slowly to keep pace with Grandmère's limp. Yes, he liked Grandmère, and so did Maman, Bertrand remembered.

Maman would want to stay with them at the house of Grandmère.

"But I thought we were going to America," he said.

"Soon," Maman murmured. "Soon."

"Are there Germans in the village of Grandmère? Are there air raids?" said Bertrand.

Maman frowned.

"Non," she said.

Bertrand leaned back against the seat. A tightness inside him seemed to ease a little.

Maman will stay with us, he thought, and there are no Germans. *Bien.* But nonetheless, he decided, he would keep for a while his weapon.

A small, round, gray-haired woman stood in the doorway of the house, which was also gray, but tall and narrow. She clutched a sweater about her shoulders and waved them up the walk.

"*Venez, venez,*" she called. "Come in."

Bertrand hurried toward her, shivering. It was cold where Grandmère lived—the Jura Mountains near the Swiss border, as Maman had explained to him.

Then Grandmère's arms were folded about him, and Bertrand remembered her fresh, warm smell, like baking bread.

Bertrand felt himself hustled into the house. Its warmth enfolded him as Grandmère's hug had done. He craned his neck to see the stairs that led up into shadows, the tall doors on either side of the narrow hall, the square dark clock on the wall. It all seemed familiar, though he did not remember being here before.

Grandmère was embracing Maman and Léonie.

"*Enfin,* at last," she was saying.

Bertrand found himself echoing her in his mind. *Enfin.* At last they were safe and together; if not at home, chez Grandmère was very like home.

Then, suddenly, he was listening, listening hard for Maman's answer to the question Grandmère had just asked.

"How long can you stay?" she had said.

Bertrand felt himself go cold and still.

"Only a day or two," said Maman. "I must get back to Marseilles as soon as possible. From day to day they change the regulations. No sooner have I the papers in order than something else is required. But I have at least found an escort for the children, an American woman from a church group. Perhaps I will be able to stay for a few days when I come back to fetch Bertrand and Léonie."

This time when Maman left them, Bertrand did not cry as he had done at St.-Étienne.

"You are *mon brave garçon,*" Maman said, but Bertrand did not feel brave.

If she was only going to leave them again, why had she not left them with the nuns, he thought. But, of course, he was glad to be chez Grandmère.

"How I have missed my great big boy," Grandmère said, hugging him.

If only I knew that we could stay here, Bertrand thought. Even without Maman, chez Grandmère was a good place. But he remembered that Maman had said "when I come back to fetch Bertrand and Léonie."

Bertrand hid his scissors behind some books in the nightstand in his small bedroom. He was afraid Grandmère might find them there when she straightened his room, so he made himself useful, offering to make his own bed each morning.

"What did I do before you came, Berti?" she would say. "How did I get my work done without your expert aid?"

How indeed? It seemed to Bertrand that he ran to fetch something for Grandmère a dozen times a day. It saved her poor leg, she told him.

Grandmère needs me, Bertrand thought, and in spite of himself he began to hope. She will not allow Maman to take me away, he thought.

But at night when Grandmère had tucked him in and closed the bedroom door, the old house seemed lonely to Bertrand. He did not like to close his eyes. He did not like the pictures he saw—of the wounded cart horse on the highway, of blood oozing between fingers, of bomb flashes in the sky. He began to think of the vision he had seen that night in the air raid at St.-Étienne. The Blessed Mother had been filled with light, he remembered. She had been big and strong, rising over him, and beautiful.

It was she who sent me the scissors, Bertrand thought one night. She knew that I needed a weapon, even before I saw her. And so I found them.

Stole them, his conscience reminded him.

But it *wasn't* stealing, he told himself, if the Blessed Mother sent them.

He lifted himself on one elbow and fumbled behind the books in the nightstand to find them. They fitted into his hand as though they were made for it, he thought. He rubbed their cool metal against his cheek before he put them back. Then with a sigh he was able to close his eyes.

The day seemed strangely silent, Bertrand thought

as he came down the stairs one morning when he had been at Grandmère's for many days—though he could hear Grandmère singing in the kitchen, some silly song that made Léonie laugh. The kettle was singing too, and something was bubbling on the stove, and the spicy apple smell of beignet wafted to Bertrand's nose.

"*Regarde la neige*, Berti!" Grandmère cried as he entered the kitchen.

Through the steamy kitchen window, Bertrand saw that the world outside was white. He rubbed a circle in the steam with his finger to make a clear peephole. The snow was what made the silence, he thought. Outside the garden was muffled in whiteness, and the usual sounds of traffic, of neighbors greeting one another in the road, of barking dogs and twittering birds was stilled.

Bertrand felt a bubble of excitement expand in his chest.

"Snow," he breathed.

"These are the mountains, Berti," said Grandmère, smiling. "Here it snows early."

"May I go outside to play, Grandmère?" he said.

Already he envisioned the fort he would build of the snow, as Papa said he had done when he was a boy in America. Already he imagined the pile of snowballs he would fashion in case an enemy happened by.

"First the breakfast," Grandmère said. "See what I have made for you this morning."

Bertrand remembered the *beignets* he had smelled as he came downstairs. He sank his teeth into the crusty sweetness of the warm apple fritter that Grandmère handed him.

"I must go to the shops this morning, snow or no," Grandmère was saying. "My pension check will be at the post office, and I wish to confer with M. Durand, the clockmaker. My wedding clock has stopped, and I do not know the cause. I'll put Léonie onto the little sled your *maman* used to ride when she was small. Will you like that, Léonie, to ride on the sled of your mother?"

Léonie clapped her hands.

"*Mais oui!*" she cried.

"Will you come with us, Berti?" Grandmère asked. "You could help me pull the sled."

Bertrand took another huge bite of beignet while he considered. If Maman were here, she would make him go, to help his grandmother. Grandmère found walking difficult, because of her sore leg. He peeked at her to see if she would insist, but she was busy at the sink, washing the frying pan.

I don't *always* have to help, Bertrand told himself. He swallowed and frowned at his plate. He kicked the table leg.

"Berti?" said Grandmère, sloshing the dishwater.

"I was going to make a snow fort," Bertrand said.

Grandmère turned from the sink to look at him. He did not meet her eyes.

"Very well," she said. "You must not leave the garden while we are gone."

"I won't," said Bertrand. He took another bite, but now the beignet felt heavy in his stomach. Suddenly the snow fort seemed a dumb idea, with no one to play in it with him.

3

"À BIENTÔT!" Bertrand heard his grandmother call from the front hallway. He was struggling into the warm clothes his uncles had once worn to play in the snow.

He did not answer her.

He could hear Léonie's babbling and Grandmère's answering laugh and then the sound of the door closing. He stumbled to the window and watched them as Léonie climbed aboard the small green sled Grandmère had had him fetch from the attic. Grandmère leaned forward, staggering a little until she found her balance. Then she trudged away, pulling the sled by its rope. She looked small and frail to Bertrand, and he would have run after them were it not for the heavy clothes, half on, half off.

Descending the stairs once again, Bertrand thought the day even more silent than it had been before breakfast. Now there was no sound of voices from the kitchen, no singing kettle, no bubbling pots.

He paused for a moment, one foot on the bottom step, and listened. There was no sound at all, no footsteps or closing doors, no . . . No ticking of the clock!

Bertrand looked up at the large, square wall clock hanging in the stairwell. It said twenty minutes past three o'clock, but this was morning, Bertrand thought. Nine o'clock perhaps, or ten. Not twenty after three. He remembered what Grandmère had said—the clock had stopped.

Bertrand stood, looking at the wall clock, his woolen hat in his hand. The scarf around his neck itched. His bundled arms stuck out from his sides, stiffened by layers of clothes.

Grandmère loved her clock, he thought. She was always consulting it. Once she had told Bertrand, "Your *grandpère* made that clock for me. It was his wedding present. You come from a long line of skilled watch- and clockmakers, Berti. Perhaps one day you will follow in their footsteps."

Now, suddenly, Bertrand wanted to fix his *grandmère*'s clock. How surprised she would be to come home and find it running again! He pictured telling her that it was he who had repaired it. She would be so proud of him. She would never let him leave her. "*Mon expert!*" she would say.

The snow fort forgotten, Bertrand set about taking the clock from the wall. It was just out of his reach, but by ascending a few steps and standing on tiptoe, he was able to nudge it off its nail. He caught it in his arms as it fell and was surprised and thrown off balance by its weight. He tottered for a moment, hampered by his heavy clothes and by the clock he clutched to his chest. Then he fell, rolling bump, bump, bump down the half dozen steps to the bottom.

He lay there a moment, hugging the clock, then let go of it, and sat up to rub his knees and elbows. He was not a bit hurt, he decided. The layers of clothing had protected him. And *I* protected the clock, he told himself proudly.

But where to work on it?

Bertrand was sweating beneath his clothes. He *could* take them off again. But if he worked indoors, he was apt to get Grandmère's spotless table dirty. Why not take the clock outside? I can fix it *and* play in the snow, Bertrand thought.

There was a bench in the front garden. Bertrand brushed the snow from it with his mittened hand and set down the heavy clock. He would need some tools, he thought. There was a toolbox in the covered entryway to the back door of the house.

Bertrand slogged around the house, lifting his feet high in the billowed, knee-deep snow. It was harder to walk in than he had imagined. Hard for an old lady pulling a sled! He pushed the thought away. He *was* helping Grandmère by fixing her clock.

Soon he was crouched over the clock on the bench, the toolbox open beside him. He tried the screwdrivers one by one until he found the one that fitted the screws holding the clock case together. He had to take off his mittens, and his fingers turned red and numb as he worked, but he scarcely noticed. The inside of the clock was full of springs and gears and other fascinating parts. Bertrand tried to work out their functions. He unfastened and removed piece after piece. Finally, the parts lay scattered over the bench. A spring had fallen into the snow and, though Bertrand looked for it, it had disappeared. The clock case was empty.

Now all I need to do is put it back together, Bertrand thought. He wondered what should go back first.

Bertrand sat back on his heels to think. Something bright caught his eye. Someone was coming, walking up the snowy road, carrying a suitcase. Bertrand squinted his eyes against the glare of the snow. There was something familiar about the way the someone walked, a quick, decisive way of stepping that he recognized. He knew the something bright as well. It was the pink headscarf of Maman!

The clock was not yet repaired.

Bertrand gazed at the parts that littered the garden bench. Maman would say he had broken the clock. She would not believe that he could fix it. She would want to know why he had not gone to the shops with Grandmère.

I should have gone, Bertrand thought with despair. I should have gone to help pull the sled.

But Maman was still some distance away. Perhaps she had not seen.

Bertrand swept the clock parts into the toolbox and closed it with a snap. Perhaps she would not notice the box, he thought. There were a hundred reasons why a toolbox might be in the garden.

Then his eyes fell on the clock case. He knew there was not one reason why a clock should be in the garden.

He looked around, desperate for a hiding place.

Maman drew closer.

His blood was pounding behind his eyes. His breath came fast. He fell to his knees and began to dig in the snow, his fingers numb to the cold. He pulled the clock case from the bench and pushed it into the hole. He covered it with snow.

Maman was almost to the gate. He saw her arm lift. He saw her greeting smile.

Bertrand jumped up. The clock could still be seen. He stepped onto it, trying to cover it with his boots. He tried to pretend he had just seen her. He tried to make his face surprised. He tried to make his mouth smile.

But suddenly his hands were hurting. They stung and ached with cold. His ragged breath tore at his throat. His knees trembled. He tried not to look down at the clock.

"Berti, *mon fils,*" Maman was calling. The gate banged behind her. She set down her suitcase and came toward him, her warm breath visible in the air.

Then, when she was near enough to touch him, her smile faded.

"*Qu'est-ce que c'est?*" she said. "What's this?"

Bertrand blushed. He could not look at the clock beneath his feet. He could not look at Maman's face. He stared at a large brown button on her coat.

"Bertrand?" Maman said.

He could feel her looking at him. His shoulders slumped.

What did it matter? he thought. What did it matter whether Maman punished him. He had not been a help to Grandmère. He had straightened his room only so she would not find his weapon. He had not gone to help her pull the sled. He had not repaired the clock.

"What would I do without *mon expert?*" Grandmère was always saying.

But she would have to do without him. Maman had come to take him away.

BERTRAND AND ZINA

THE JOURNEY

Marseilles, France to Lisbon, Portugal
November and December 1940

1

"BERTI," MAMAN was saying. "Berti, do you hear me?"

Bertrand tried to open his eyes, but the lids felt so heavy. . . . He could feel himself swaying on his feet. He wanted to lie down, but he felt the hand of Maman grasp his chin.

"Wake yourself, Bertrand. *C'est important!*"

Bertrand forced his eyes open. Maman's face was inches from his, and something in her eyes, something in her voice, brought him suddenly alert. He was no longer riding in the taxi, he saw, the taxi in which they had left their hotel before dawn. Now he was standing in a cavernous space, dark except for a few lights shaded against the blackout and the pocket lamps of people hurrying past. The people's footsteps echoed in the heights of a shadowy ceiling where Bertrand, tipping back his head, could see only darkness. Voices echoed too, and the chuffing sounds of trains. . . . Trains! He was in the railroad station, and Maman stood before him speaking urgently. It was time, he realized. She was sending them away, and this was the time when they must go. Bertrand looked past her and saw a strange woman in a vivid red hat holding the sleeping Léonie in her arms. He looked back at Maman.

"This is Mrs. Sharp," Maman was saying slowly and carefully in English. She had been speaking English to him and Léonie ever since she came for them at Grandmère's. "You will have to speak English in America," she had said.

"Mrs. Sharp is the kind lady who will take you to Papa," Maman was saying now.

"'ow do you do," Bertrand said, his tongue still thick with sleep and unhappiness.

Suddenly Maman pulled Bertrand close. His face was against her shoulder, and he felt her arms around him, squeezing hard. He struggled away from her.

"It is time to say good-bye, my son," Maman said in French. "Parents are not allowed on the platform."

"Come with us, Maman," Bertrand said.

Maman's face was in shadow, but he heard the reproach in her voice, the same sort of reproach he had heard in Grandmère's voice when she learned of her ruined clock. But Grandmère had not wanted him to be punished. "It is only a clock," she had said.

"I have explained that I cannot come with you," Maman was saying now. "There is work for me here, work I must do for France. Be a good boy. Take care of your sister." She pushed a satchel into his hands. "Your lunches are in this, and the medicine for Léonie's impetigo," she said. "We will be together again soon."

Swiftly Maman kissed Bertrand on both his cheeks, but he did not kiss her back. Then she rose and turned toward the red-hatted woman. She bent to kiss Léonie.

"*Merci,* Mme Sharp," she said. "God bless you."

Bertrand thought her voice sounded funny, breathless and choked.

"Maman?" he said hopelessly, but he knew that she had gone—to punish him, he thought.

"Come along," Mme Sharp was saying. Bertrand heard the kindness in her voice, but also its hurry. "The other children are gathering on the platform," she said.

Zina turned her head, trying to see over her shoulder to where Papa and Mama stood beside a blackout-shaded light, but Lisa was pulling her through the gate and onto the train platform. Zina wanted to call out to them one last time, but she heard the words she wanted to say only in her head. *Proshchai*, Mama. *Proshchai*, Papa, good-bye!

She could no longer see them in the dim shadows of the railway station— "la Gare St.-Charles," she repeated to herself, feeling it was somehow important to remember the name of the place from which they were embarking on what Papa called their *avantura*.

People hurried behind them, more children, boys and girls, and a few adults. They were following M. Okunieff, the husband of Papa's friend, Mme Okuneva. M. Okunieff would be going on this journey. Zina wondered why he and Mme Okuneva and even Mme Okuneva's old mother were allowed to travel to America with *their* little boy when Mama and Papa were not, but she had not asked. Papa looked angry whenever she brought up the subject of their separation, and Mama looked distressed.

On the platform, the children were being sorted into what M. Okunieff called "squads." Older boys and girls were appointed squad leaders, though there would be grown-ups traveling with them too. The squads seemed to be organized somewhat according to age, Zina saw, for Lisa was directed to an older group in the charge of a competent-looking girl.

A tall, good-looking boy was the leader of Zina's squad. M. Okunieff introduced them, speaking in French.

"Yves Dubouchet, this is Zinaida Sarach."

M. Okunieff hurried away, murmuring something about the baggage, and Zina stood, feeling quite alone, in the middle of the group of strange children.

She could see Mrs. Sharp, in a striking red hat. She was the American lady who had arranged this journey. Zina and Lisa had been taken to meet her some days ago when they first arrived in Marseilles. Now Mrs. Sharp had a notebook in her hands. She was speaking to each child, then noting something in it.

Two other ladies and Mme Okuneva, whom Zina had also met, were handing out mugs of coffee. Zina's hands closed gratefully around hers when it was passed to her. Although Marseilles was warmer this time of year than Pau, nonetheless there was a damp, cold wind blowing on the train platform at this before-dawn hour.

"*Votre nom de famille?* Your last name?" Mrs. Sharp was saying to her.

Doesn't she remember me? Zina wondered, and before she could answer, "Sarach," said Yves.

"Elizaveta or Zinaida?" asked Mrs. Sharp.

"Zinaida," said Yves.

Mrs. Sharp marked in her notebook.

Zina shot Yves an angry glance. She could answer for herself, she thought. She wasn't a piece of baggage, checked into his keeping. But she remained silent. No one listened anyway.

Yves was dividing his squad into partners.

"Whenever we change trains, you must hold hands with your partner," he told them in an officious tone.

Two of the little girls—as alike as two peas, Zina thought—grabbed for each other. They must be sisters, Zina thought. Maybe even twins.

"Very well, Léontine, Émilie," Yves said, "you may be partners. Stella, can you keep track of the little one?"

The girl named Stella nodded. She was sitting on the bench around which the others clustered, and a sleeping toddler slumped beside her. The toddler's face was wrapped in bandages, and on the other side of her was a boy with round, scared eyes.

"Wilhelm and Isaak Reeser," Yves said to the two older, sullen-faced boys, "you be partners. That leaves, let's see, Bertrand Cole . . ."

The boy on the bench started at his name and glanced wildly about.

". . . and you, Zinaida Sarach."

Zina frowned. Why was she the only girl who had to partner a boy?

She opened her mouth to protest, but caught sight of the boy. He was frowning darkly at her, his hand clutching something in his pocket.

Oh, so you don't want *me* for a partner? Zina thought. Well, I don't want you either, but there's little enough we can do about it.

She closed her mouth and shrugged.

The train conductor approached, striding down the platform.

"*En voiture, en voiture!*" he was calling. "All aboard."

"*Allons-y!*" cried Yves, his voice making a sudden funny squawk. "Let's go, everyone."

2

THAT BIG boy had given him *a girl* for a partner! Bertrand pressed into his corner of the train compartment, his face against the cool window glass, as he watched the dawn streak the sky. *The girl* had gone to sleep almost immediately upon boarding. He tried to pull away from her, but he could feel the heat and heaviness of her shoulder against his.

Léonie was asleep on the lap of the doctor woman. Perhaps it was the medicine Maman had given her for her impetigo that made her sleep so soundly. The impetigo made sores on Léonie's face, sores that must be bandaged. It made her cross too.

Mme Sharp said that the big boy, Yves, was their "squad leader." The doctor woman was the big boy's mother. Bertrand had never before met a doctor who was a woman, unless one counted Soeur Héloïse, the infirmarian at St.-Étienne.

It was a relief to Bertrand that there was someone to help him take care of Léonie, though it should have been Maman or Grandmère, even one of the sisters of St.-Étienne or . . . Marie? It seemed such a long time ago that Marie took care of them in Paris! I can't remember what she looked like! Bertrand thought, his heart beating hard. Then he thought of something even more frightening. Did he remember what Papa looked like? It had been even longer since Bertrand had seen Papa. How will I find him in America if I cannot remember what he looks like? Bertrand thought.

Someone was coming into the compartment, and Bertrand, startled, clutched the scissors in his pocket and turned from the window to see who it was.

"*Bonjour,* Bertrand!" said Mme Sharp. "Are you the only one in this compartment who has stayed awake?"

Bertrand was glad to see Mme Sharp. It was to her that Maman had entrusted them. His hand relaxed, and he took it from his pocket. The grown-ups were awake, he saw, looking around at the others, but it was true that the other children were all asleep.

"In that case," said Mme Sharp, "you shall be the first in this compartment to receive your *béret officiel,* and you may explain to the others when they awake that these *bérets* are to be worn at all times. They are the sign that you are in our group. Do you understand?"

She was handing him a beautiful beige *béret.* Bertrand took it into his hands and smoothed the soft, thick wool.

"Is there one for Léonie also?" he asked.

"What a good brother you are!" Mme Sharp was smiling approval. "Indeed yes," she said, "there is a *béret* for Léonie. Do you think she will keep it on her head? It is very important that she wear it, so we don't lose her."

Bertrand drew himself up, though the train lurched at that moment, throwing him against *the girl.* He recovered himself and placed his *béret* squarely on his head, pulling it over his forehead as he had seen French soldiers do.

"I will see that she wears it, madame," he said.

Someone was whimpering. Zina turned her head on the cushioned seat-back, trying to rid herself of the annoying sound.

There was something on her head, she realized. It fell over her ear when she moved. She put up her hand and reluctantly opened her eyes.

It was a hat, a *béret* of soft beige wool! Zina held it in her hands, examining it. Where had it come from? she wondered.

"It's your *béret officiel*," said a voice beside her. It was the boy, Bertrand, her partner. She looked at him questioningly.

"Mme Sharp has given each of us an official *béret* to show that we belong," he said, his face and voice serious. "You're supposed to wear it all the time. That way you won't get lost."

He was a funny old thing, sounding so important, as though he were in charge of *béret* information. Zina couldn't help but smile a bit. It *was* a lovely *béret!*

She put it back on her head, adjusting it by feel. It was now daylight outside, she saw. She looked around the compartment.

Dr. Dubouchet, Yves's mother, was holding the toddler with the bandaged face. That was not an easy task, Zina saw, because the little girl wriggled and pulled on her bandages. It was she who had been whimpering. The man beside Dr. Dubouchet didn't seem to notice. Yves had said that the man was his father, M. Dubouchet, but he didn't act like a father, Zina thought. He had let himself be led to his seat on the train like a little child, and he sat now staring, seemingly unaware of the people around him. Mrs. Sharp sat dozing across from the Dubouchets, her red hat tipped crooked on her head. The twins were giggling, playing some sort of game with each other. The girl called Stella was reading a book. Yves and the sullen-faced brothers had been put in another compartment, she remembered, but Bertrand squirmed beside her. He was still looking at Zina, and his face looked worried.

Suddenly he leaned toward her and whispered.

Zina didn't understand, so she bent her head toward him. He whispered again, urgently.

"*Oú sont les toilettes?*"

He had to go to the bathroom, and he was too shy to ask the grown-ups!

Zina gave him a reassuring smile. Then she stood up and held out her hand to him.

"Are you going somewhere?" said Dr. Dubouchet. "Ah, to the rest room? It's at the end of the car, that way." She gestured, and the toddler, released for a second, almost wriggled from her lap.

Zina nodded her thanks and led Bertrand from the compartment. It was difficult to walk on the moving train. As soon as she matched her steps to the motion of the floor, there would be a lurch, and the motion would change. She showed Bertrand the rest room door and waited for him outside.

He didn't take long. Boys never did, Zina had observed.

"I'll wait for you," he told her when he came out, and so she went in also and used the strange, swaying, drafty toilet. She rinsed her hands in the tiny corner sink and admired her new *béret* in the miniature mirror above it.

True to his word, Bertrand was waiting in the corridor when she came out. He held out his hand to her again in a trusting way.

He wasn't such a bad fellow, Zina thought.

"Why don't you talk?" he said, looking up at her quizzically.

Zina was startled.

I do talk, she started to say, and suddenly realized she hadn't said a word since she bade good-bye to Mama and Papa.

Why hadn't she? she wondered. She shook her head, frowning. I don't feel like talking is all, she thought.

"It's all right," Bertrand said. He took her hand, and this time it was he who led their lurching way down the corridor to their compartment. "I don't mind," Bertrand said.

Bertrand had never before eaten in the restaurant car of a train. They sat at tables for four. He and the quiet girl sat with the twins. The car was filled with beige *bérets*, Bertrand saw, and a smattering of grown-ups' hats. He searched out the red one of Mme Sharp.

A waiter in a white coat brought large cups of *café au lait*, coffee with milk, and a plate of cold toast and jam. The toast was leathery. Bertrand chewed and chewed before he could swallow it. But he noticed that the quiet girl was eating as though she had never tasted anything so delicious. She was very thin, Bertrand noticed, and there were dark smudges under her eyes and an unhealed sore on her lip. She must be *very* hungry, Bertrand thought, surprised.

He had not liked her at first. She was a girl, after all. But she *had* helped him when he didn't know where the rest room was. She was older and taller than he was, but

Bertrand sensed that, like Léonie, she needed taking care of. Except . . . the grown-ups didn't seem to be taking special care of *her. I* shall have to do it, Bertrand thought, and the thought made him feel strong, as he had not felt since the days when he was the expert helper of Grandmère.

"You may have the rest of my toast," he told her, shoving his plate across to her.

She flashed him a little smile, like the one she had given him when he explained about the *bérets*. Then she stuffed the toast into her mouth. A smear of jam purpled her chin. When she drank her *café*, he watched with fascination the way her throat moved with a softly gulping sound.

A group of big boys and girls was leaving the car with a noisy clatter. One of them, a girl with tight, looped-up braids like the quiet girl's, stopped beside Bertrand's table. She thrust a lunch packet at the quiet girl and said something to her in a language Bertrand did not understand. Perhaps that was why the quiet girl didn't talk. Perhaps she didn't speak French. Except . . . she understood him when he spoke to her. She had understood about the rest room.

"Who's that?" he heard someone ask.

The big girl with the looped-up braids replied in French as she hurried to catch up to the others.

"Oh, that's my sister, Zina."

Zina. Bertrand repeated the name to himself. That was her name. Zina. It made him feel that she was his somehow, knowing her name.

"Are you finished, children?" the doctor woman was saying.

Bertrand looked at his quiet girl, who was draining the last drops of her *café* from her cup.

"Let's go, Zina," he said.

3

"I KNOW a game," the girl named Stella said. "Want to play?"

Zina looked at her. She seemed a nice enough girl, with straight short hair and a pleasant smile.

"Her name's Zina," piped Bertrand, talking for her, as everyone seemed to do.

"What about it, Zina?" said Stella. "Want to play?"

Zina thought about it. Although she had a book, she had read it before, and reading on the swaying train made her stomach uneasy. She didn't feel like sleeping anymore.

She shrugged.

"See," said Stella, "the thing is we have to look out windows on different sides of the train. You could stay in here, and I could go out to the corridor window. We get points for things we see. If it's an animal with four legs, like a horse or a cow, you get four points. A flock of sheep is a hundred points, because it's too many legs to count. But if you pass a cemetery, then all your points are taken away, and you have to start over. The one with the most points when we get to the next station is the winner. Want to play?"

Why not? Zina thought as she nodded yes.

"I'll help her," Bertrand was saying to Stella. "She doesn't talk, you know."

Don't I talk? wondered Zina.

Stella was looking at her curiously.

"Why not?" she said.

"Because she doesn't want to," said Bertrand, his voice belligerent. "She doesn't have to talk if she doesn't want to."

No, thought Zina. I don't, do I?

Stella looked puzzled.

"Okay," she said. "You can tell me how many points she gets."

"I'll help her," Bertrand repeated.

Who appointed *you* my helper? Zina thought, but Stella was at the door of the compartment.

"Don't start until I yell ready," she said.

Zina nodded and moved to station herself at the compartment window, Bertrand at her elbow.

Breakfast had made Bertrand's little sister, the toddler with the bandaged face, more cheerful. She was playing with a doll on the floor at Dr. Dubouchet's feet. M. Dubouchet seemed to be dozing, and Mrs. Sharp and Dr. Dubouchet were deep in conversation in English. The twins were playing their endless game.

"Ready!" came the cry from the corridor, and Zina looked out the window. Mrs. Sharp had opened it to let in air. Though it was only midmorning, it was as hot as a summer afternoon. That was because this was the Côte d'Azur, the sunny coast of the Mediterranean Sea, Papa had told her. Paris, even Pau, in November was wintry, but winter came late and briefly to the Côte d'Azur, he said.

"*Une vache!*" shouted Bertrand. "Cow!"

Zina had seen it. She already held up four fingers. Bertrand laughed, and Zina smiled at the delight in his laugh.

They were coming to a meadow with horses, three horses. Zina flashed ten fingers, then two.

"*Douze!*" cried Bertrand. "Twelve and four makes . . ."

He counted it on her fingers.

"*Treize, quatorze, quinze, seize*. Sixteen!"

Again Zina had to smile.

"And four more," cried Bertrand. "There's another horse!"

But Zina was shaking her head, staring at the horse as it moved past the window, growing swiftly smaller, then out of sight behind a curve.

It was a white horse! A beautiful white horse like the one she envisioned in America. She could feel the way her throat was squeezing shut. She was breathing fast, and her head shook harder, no, no, no!

Bertrand was looking at her strangely, his eyes scared as they had been when she first saw him on the platform. He doesn't understand, she thought.

But her throat was closed, tight against words, against cries. I *can't* talk! she realized.

She put her hand on his arm and, with an effort, made her head stop shaking. Then she held up all ten fingers.

"Ten?" said Bertrand, his voice quivering a bit.

She was pleased he caught on so fast. She nodded and pointed in the direction in which the white horse had disappeared.

"Ten points?" said Bertrand.

Again she nodded.

"Ten points for *that* horse?"

She pointed to the white lace doily on the back of their seat, to her collar, also white, to his shirt.

Suddenly his face was lit with a smile. He didn't look scared anymore.

"Because it was white?" he said, and when she nodded, "Because white horses are special?"

She nodded harder.

"So white horses should get more points!"

He understood! Even without words, he understood her.

Zina grabbed him in a hug. She could feel the smallness of his bones and the soft plumpness of his cheek against hers. She held on to him as though her life depended on it.

Bertrand shifted his weight from one foot to the other. They had been standing in line for ages, it seemed to him, in the large covered train station on the French side of the Spanish border.

He had been happy to get off the train for a while. They had been riding all day in one train or another. Once they had even ridden in an autobus. Mme Sharp explained that the train tracks had been washed away by a recent flood. Bertrand saw bits of lumber, a battered tin bucket, even a dog kennel, stranded in the branches of the trees.

He had pointed out all these interesting sights to Zina. Each time they changed trains he had held her hand, as the partners were supposed to do, and he had made sure that she wore her *béret* so she wouldn't get lost in the crowds in the stations. He had tried to look after Léonie too, though the doctor woman seemed to have her well in hand. Léonie had taken a fancy to the doctor woman and to the girl, Stella, and no longer insisted on holding his hand, as she had done at first. It seemed, Bertrand thought, as if she often forgot all about her big brother. But Zina had no one but him.

Hours ago they had shared the lunches their parents had packed for them. Zina's was scanty, and Bertrand had given her a tomato and half his hard-boiled egg. Now he was hungry again, and he imagined that Zina was too, though, of course, she couldn't say so. He hoped they wouldn't have to wait in line much longer.

The grown-ups were herding them together, closer to the passport checkpoint.

"*Mes enfants!*" Mme Sharp was calling. "*Faites attention!*"

Bertrand shot a resentful look at the two naughtiest boys, the brothers from his squad. They were shoving each other, not paying attention as Mme Sharp was asking, but no one punished them. He fingered the handkerchief-wrapped scissors in his pocket. I could make them behave, he thought.

"As your name is called, please come forward so the passport officer can identify you," Mme Sharp cried over the noise of the trains and the voices of people waiting in line behind them.

They will not hear their names, Bertrand thought of the naughty boys.

"Cole, Bertrand!" The officer called his name first. "Cole, Léonie!"

The doctor woman, who had been carrying Léonie, put her down and motioned to Bertrand to take her hand.

Bertrand reached out, but Léonie jerked her plump little hand from his grasp.

"*Mon docteur,*" she cried. "*Ma* Stella!"

"Go along with your brother," the doctor woman was saying. "Stella and I will come soon."

But, "*Non, non, non!*" Léonie wailed. "*Ma* Stella, *mon docteur!*"

"Come on, Léonie," Bertrand said. He was her big brother. She should want to come with him.

"*Non!*" Léonie cried. She put her hands behind her and backed away.

The passport officer was getting red in the face.

"Exactly what is the problem, madame?" he was saying to Mme Sharp.

"She doesn't want to go without her friends, Dr. Dubouchet and Stella Thibert."

"They will be passed with the Ds and the Ts," said the official.

"Léonie," Bertrand said, adopting a tone he had heard Maman use. "Come with me this instant!"

He grabbed her arm.

"*Non, non, non!*" Léonie wailed.

Bertrand felt his ears getting hot. The passport officer was glaring. Mme Sharp and the doctor woman knelt before Léonie, entreating her to go with Bertrand.

"Cannot Dr. Dubouchet carry her through?" Mme Sharp said over her shoulder.

But the official was adamant.

"C comes before D," he said. "There are three more Cs after these before we can begin on the Ds."

Bertrand clung to the arm he had grabbed. He shook it with all his might.

"Stop your *bêtise*, your silliness!" he cried in his fiercest voice. "Léonie, come with me!"

Behind him he heard a snicker. Whirling, he saw it was the younger of the naughty boys.

"Pah!" the boy said to his brother. "Dey are both silly!"

"*Tais-toi!* Shut up!" Bertrand yelled, advancing toward the boy with his arm upraised.

"*Bêtise, bêtise!*" the naughty boy taunted.

Bertrand slapped him hard.

The boy fell back, his eyes blank and stunned, and instantly Mme Sharp captured Bertrand's arm before he could hit out again.

"Bertrand!" she cried, and Bertrand could hear the dismay in her voice.

"Madame!" the passport officer was shouting. "Very well, madame. Let the doctor carry the child through. I will make an exception this time."

Mme Sharp sighed and rose to her feet.

"*Merci beaucoup,*" she said to the officer.

She looked down at Bertrand, and her look made him feel not much older than Léonie.

"No more hitting, Bertrand. It helps nothing," she said.

Bertrand dropped his eyes, unable to meet her look. He wished he could close his ears as well to her disappointed voice. She had thought he was a good boy, but now she would think it no longer.

4

POOR BERTRAND! Zina could see the tears brimming in his eyes as he slouched past her toward the passport checkpoint. She saw how red his face was and the way his shoulders slumped.

But at least the officer was passing him, Zina thought. Bertrand was a French citizen, not an *apatride*, a stateless person as she and Lisa were. "There may be trouble at the borders over the *apatrides*," she had heard Mrs. Sharp say.

"Corbier, Danielle. Corbier, Lilianne. Corbier, Zoë!" the passport officer was calling.

Those were the triplets, Zina realized. She had heard the grown-ups say that there were triplets in the party. She watched as three pretty girls, perhaps a little older than Lisa, went forward to the checkpoint. They were holding hands, and she wondered if they were nervous too.

The Dubouchets were passing through, Yves and a younger sister and the strange, silent father. Dr.

Dubouchet had been allowed to go ahead, carrying Bertrand's little sister.

"Eck, Felix! Eckhardt, Victor! Ehrle, Fritz! Eichler, Dagmar!"

One by one the children went forward. There were twenty-seven in all, Zina knew, and ten grown-ups.

"Graham, Robert! Henri, Olivier! Hirschman, Henriette!"

This last was one of the grown-ups. She was elegantly beautiful, Zina thought, and young. Zina wondered if she, like Papa, had been unable to find work now that much of France was occupied by the Germans? Perhaps she was a Jewess.

"Joy, Charles!"

That was an American man, a friend of Mrs. Sharp.

"Okunieff, Alexis. Okuneva, Irina. Okunieff, Mikhail!"

Those were Papa's friends. Were they *apatrides*? The passport officer passed them through.

"Reeser, Isaak! Reeser, Wilhelm!"

The brothers from Zina's squad shoved forward from the dwindling group still waiting. A grown-up had made them stand still after Bertrand hit one of them. She saw that he had a red mark on his cheek and that his face looked white, beaded with perspiration. Did Bertrand really hurt him? she wondered, and a moment later, he suddenly bent over and vomited at the feet of the passport officer.

"Madame!" cried the officer in an outraged voice. He had jumped back, clutching the bundle of passports.

That can't be because of Bertrand, Zina thought. He must be sick with nerves.

Mrs. Sharp hurried to the sick boy, pulling a handkerchief from her coat pocket.

"Never mind, Isaak," Zina heard her soothe. "Just go on through to Dr. Dubouchet. She'll take care of you."

That was one way to distract the official from his passport, Zina thought.

Then she heard her own name, and her heart leaped to her throat.

"Sarach, Elizaveta! Sarach, Zinaida!"

As she stepped forward, Zina felt Lisa's shoulder brush hers. Beneath the passport officer's frowning scrutiny, she trembled. Would he let them pass with the others? What would happen if he refused?

Then she felt Lisa's hand slip over hers, warm and firm. Lisa was marching at her side, her back straight and her face serious and somehow grown up. Lisa did not deign to give the officer a glance as she stepped carefully around the smelly mess the Reeser boy had made. Zina saw that the passport officer had already snapped shut their passports and opened the next one.

It felt, Bertrand thought, as though they had been traveling forever. Yet he knew that it was only this morning before light that Maman had left them. They had waited hours in line inside the border stations, once on the French side, where Léonie had made such a fuss, and once on the Spanish side, where the twins from his squad had started a craze among the children for showing the customs inspectors the smelly insides of their empty lunch parcels. That had made their own grown-ups smile.

There had been a good meal finally on the Spanish train—chicken, ham and omelette, fruit and black bread and, best of all, chocolate. Bertrand remembered how Zina had gobbled everything until she came to the chocolate. Then she had licked hers slowly, making it last until long after Bertrand's was gone.

By then they were traveling in darkness, with only the dim lights of the train compartment reflected in the black mirrors of the windows. It was like flying through space, Bertrand thought, or swimming through the depths of the ocean. Outside the windows was only blackness. Even the rumble of the train, the murmur of voices, the whistle of the wind were muffled, as though by the vastness outside.

Now Bertrand was holding tightly to Zina's hand. They were climbing the steep steps into another autobus. The bus was brightly lit. Didn't they worry about the blackout? Bertrand wondered, and then he remembered that this was Barcelona, Spain, and the German war did not reach this far. The thought made Bertrand feel lighter somehow, despite his heavy tiredness.

They had changed trains seven times, but this would be their last ride today, Mme Sharp had assured them. The bus was taking them to a hotel where they could go to sleep in beds.

The naughty brothers were jostling against Bertrand's back. Was it on purpose? he wondered with a twinge of fear. Would they try to get even with him for that slap? He tried to ignore them as he edged down the aisle of the autobus, but their jostling made him step on the heel of the girl Stella, and he felt his face redden and his heart pound. Stella said nothing, only stumbled along ahead of him, following the doctor woman who had a sound-asleep Léonie on her shoulder.

"Here," said Bertrand with relief, spotting empty seats. He pulled Zina out of the aisle and away from the brothers. They sank down on the hard wooden seat. Only then did he let go her hand.

Safe, he thought, and then he looked at Zina and again felt uneasy. The smudges beneath Zina's eyes were darker than before, and in the artificial light of the autobus, her white face looked stretched across her cheekbones. Was she sick? he wondered. Was he not taking good enough care of her?

The bus driver was making the motor roar. The lights inside the autobus dimmed as with a lurch they began to move through the lighted streets. Bertrand, leaning his head against the hard back of the seat, closed his eyes and felt himself slipping into a dream, a dream in which a clock ticked loudly high on the wall of the bus, while cold white snow sifted onto his upturned face. The snow wet Bertrand's cheeks and made the face of the clock wet and slippery, so slippery, Bertrand saw, that the hands of the clock were sliding slowly off. But the Blessed Mother bent to pick them up and put them into Bertrand's hands. Bertrand reached to put them back on the clock, certain he could fix it, but they would not fit. They would not fit because they were not clock hands at all, but scissors! "It helps nothing," the Blessed Mother said, her voice deep with sorrow. . . .

With a scream of brakes, the autobus rocked to a stop. Bertrand opened his eyes and saw that the grown-ups were standing up.

"Only a little longer, *mes enfants*, and you can go to bed," Mme Sharp was calling from the front of the autobus. "Come along smartly now and follow me."

5

WHEN ZINA woke the next morning, at first she did not know where she was. She was clinging to the edge of a thick mattress, which sank away from her toward the other side of the bed so she dared not let go. The grayness of the strange room told her that it was early. Dimly she saw that Lisa sat on a cot across the room, rubbing her eyes.

The bedsprings groaned, and Zina felt the mattress shift with the weight of her bedmate.

Then she remembered. She and Lisa had been put in the hotel room of Mme Stepanova, because the old Russian lady needed to be with someone who spoke her own language. Zina rolled over and saw that Mme Stepanova was sitting up, coiling the long braid of her gray hair atop her head. Mme Stepanova was Mme Okuneva's mother, Zina remembered. She, like Zina's parents, had lived in France since the Russian Revolution more than twenty years before, but Mme Stepanova had never learned to speak French.

I wonder, Zina thought sleepily, if she will learn English in America.

"*Vstavai,* Zina," Lisa said, her voice grumpy. "Get up."

The old lady was groaning to her feet, and the mattress beneath Zina flattened. Zina didn't want to get up. She closed her eyes, but Mme Stepanova turned on the red-shaded lamp over the head of the bed. It shone through Zina's closed eyelids.

She heard the padding of Lisa's bare feet across the floorboards and felt Lisa's hand roughly shaking her shoulder.

"You must have your bath this morning," Lisa was saying. "We let you sleep last night."

Zina's stomach stirred. What she wanted was breakfast, not a bath, she thought.

"I'll start your bathwater," Lisa said as she went into the bathroom and closed the door.

The hotel room had a private bath, a real luxury! Zina pushed herself up and swung her legs over the side of the bed. She would hurry. She didn't want to miss breakfast.

"Did you sleep well, child?" asked Mme Stepanova.

Zina nodded.

Mme Stepanova was dressing beneath the tent of her nightgown, her back turned toward Zina.

"Child?" she repeated. "Did you sleep well?"

Again, Zina nodded.

The old woman turned, frowning.

"Why do you not answer me?" she said. "You have not uttered one word."

Zina stared at her. She knew that if she opened her mouth, no sound would come out. She shrugged apologetically.

The old woman turned back to pull up a thick woolen stocking.

"Such rudeness," she muttered. "I would have

thought that Oleg Sarach's daughters would be *baryshni,* well-brought-up girls. Twelve years old, and she doesn't know how to answer a courteous question, *and* still sucks her thumb like a baby!" She shook her head and glared over her shoulder at Zina. "What's wrong with you, child?"

I'm not twelve, Zina thought. I only just turned eleven! But she could feel the shame creeping redly from her neck to her face. She hadn't sucked her thumb since first grade. Why did the old lady say she did?

She looked at her hands, lying limply in her lap as though they belonged to someone else. She should have washed them before she went to bed, she saw. They were grimy, except for her right thumb, which was shining clean.

I must have sucked it in my sleep, she realized, the hollow feeling in her stomach expanding suddenly to fill her chest. I'm sucking my thumb! I can't talk! What *is* wrong with me?

"Your turn, Zinochka," Lisa said, coming out of the bathroom.

But Zina did not move. She sat on the edge of the bed, staring at her clean thumb while her heart beat in her throat.

Bertrand glanced anxiously at Zina. She was staring out of the train window, the passing lights of the outskirts of Barcelona flashing on her white face. Once again she was looking as she had looked this morning in the hotel dining room—drawn and pale, the smudges dark beneath her eyes.

She had seemed better as the day went on. By the time they were walking along the waterfront that afternoon in the Spanish sunshine, her cheeks had been quite rosy. She had run and played with him in the public gardens. He was sure he had seen her smile. But now, once more aboard a train when it should have been time for bed, Bertrand was worried. Her silence seemed deeper to him, her eyes more blank and sunken.

"Settle yourselves for sleep as best you can, children," Mme Sharp was saying.

Bertrand saw that she was pulling a baby blanket from their satchel to make a bed for Léonie on the seat. He wished that he too had a blanket. If he had, he would make a bed for himself and Zina. Except that the old Russian lady took up so much room. He did not understand why she had been put in with them and the twins sent to another compartment. With that fat old woman and the Stella girl and Zina and him all on one seat, it looked as though they would have to sleep sitting up, as across from them, Mme Sharp and the doctor woman and her strange silent husband were preparing to do.

Bertrand felt lonely. He looked across at Léonie, nestled between the two women. Mme Sharp's hand rested on her curls. The grown-ups were closing their eyes, he saw. On his own seat, the old Russian lady snored softly, her chins jiggling against her bosom with the vibration of the train. Stella was reading by the dim compartment lamp. Zina, her face to the window, seemed very far away.

They would ride the train all night, Mme Sharp had told them, and tomorrow they would arrive in Madrid. Bertrand was certain he would not be able to sleep sitting up, uncomfortable, the rush and rattle of the train loud in his ears. Click-clack, click-clack, click . . .

. . . tock, tick-tock, tick-tock. It was the clock, and Bertrand could not reach it however hard he stretched, standing on his tiptoes and reaching his arms toward it.

He needed to put the clock hands back on. If he did not, something terrible would happen. Something terrible would happen to Grandmère, who was not strong enough to pull the clock to the village. Besides, Soeur Marie Micheline was not in the village. She was in the dormitory, embroidering their pillowcases. "I am proud of you, Bertrand," she had said. That was because she thought he could fix the clock, only he could not reach it. Someone was shouting for him to hurry.

"Quickly, *mon ami,*" a man was shouting. "Quickly, the guns . . . the guns!"

Bertrand stumbled to his feet, his heart thundering. In the dim light of the train compartment, he could see a struggle on the seat opposite. He shook the sleep from his head, his hand digging in his pocket for his weapon.

A man was shouting, "*Mon Dieu,* the guns!"

"Hush, *mon chéri.* There are no guns here." That was the doctor woman's voice.

Bertrand realized it was the doctor woman who was struggling with her silent husband, who was silent no longer. It was he who was shouting, and the doctor woman was holding him against the seat. Her voice was soothing him, and as Bertrand watched, clutching his handkerchief-wrapped scissors tightly in his fist, the man subsided. There was a harsh, choking sound. The doctor woman sank back into her own place on the seat, and Bertrand saw the man's hands go to his face. He slumped forward, his shoulders heaving. He was crying, Bertrand saw with horror. That big, grown man was crying like a little boy!

Bertrand fell back onto his own seat, still staring at the man. He slipped his scissors back into his pocket.

Léonie was crying too, though she sat on Mme Sharp's lap and was being rocked to and fro. Bertrand saw that Zina on one side of him and Stella on the other were staring at the man. The old lady had not wakened. Her snoring went on and on, louder than it had been earlier, and her head noddled with the motion of the train.

"My apologies, Martha," said the doctor woman to Mme Sharp. "I am afraid this sometimes happens in the night. I have no help for it."

"Please don't concern yourself," said Mme Sharp. "I understand. He is a sick man. The sooner we get him away from the war, the better."

The doctor woman was nodding sadly. She had taken her husband's hand into hers and was stroking it.

"Sleep now, *mon chéri*," she said to him. "It was only a dream."

Léonie was quieting.

"Hush," crooned Mme Sharp. "Hush, hush."

Bertrand looked at Zina. She was looking at him, and Bertrand thought she still looked afraid.

His own heart was slowing. It was all upside down and backward, he thought—grown-up men having bad dreams and crying while women acted strong. He himself had been having a bad dream, he remembered, blushing.

"Go back to sleep, *mes enfants*," Mme Sharp said.

Maybe, Bertrand thought, listening to the quiet sobs of the man, maybe we were having a bad dream together, he and I. Except there were guns in *his* dream. Bertrand did not remember any guns in his own dream, though sometimes he did dream of guns, small ones like the soldier had been carrying that long-ago day in Paris and big ones like those that boomed in the night while they huddled in the *caves* of St.-Étienne. I do not dream so much of guns anymore, Bertrand realized. Not since I have my weapon.

He reached into his pocket again for the comforting shape of his scissors. They were solid and reassuring inside his handkerchief.

Zina would not be afraid if she knew that I have a weapon to protect her, Bertrand thought. He wished he could put his arm around her, as she had, that once, hugged him, but he had no idea how to do such a thing. Besides, the Stella girl was watching.

He leaned slightly toward Zina until his arm touched hers.

M. Dubouchet was sick. That was what Mrs. Sharp had said. That was why they were taking him to America.

Zina had paid him little attention before, but now, in the darkened train compartment, she remembered that *he* also did not usually speak.

Am *I* sick? wondered Zina. Is that why I cannot talk? Is that why I suck my thumb in my sleep?

Her hands and feet were cold, though her cheeks seemed to burn. Only her arm was comfortably warm where Bertrand leaned against it.

I must be sick, Zina thought. They should be taking care of me, as Dr. Dubouchet takes care of him. But Papa and Mama had sent her away, and no one else seemed to notice.

She could feel tears aching in her throat. The ache spread to her eyes and down to her stomach as the train hurtled through the darkness, carrying her every minute farther from her parents. The pain of the distance throbbed all through her. She wanted to cry, but she knew the crying would be lost in the racketing noise of the train.

6

"HOW MUCH longer till we get there?" Bertrand asked Mme Sharp. He needed to hear her voice and see her eyes turn to him. "Madame? How much longer?"

Mme Sharp was tucking her hair beneath the red hat.

"Not much longer, Bertrand. We should be in Madrid by lunchtime."

But they had not yet had their breakfast! Lunchtime was a long time away, Bertrand thought.

The others still slept, their heads bent at awkward angles, their mouths gaping. It was because they all slept that Bertrand felt so alone. He wanted Mme Sharp to keep on talking, but her voice was weary.

"Go back to sleep, Bertrand," she said.

Bertrand could not sleep. He could not think of more questions either. He looked past Zina, who slept leaning into the corner of the window, her thumb in her mouth, and watched the brick red soil of the Spanish mountains streak past.

Dear Mama and Papa . . .

Zina sat in the window of yet another strange hotel room, writing to her parents. She felt ready to burst with what she needed to say.

It's really too bad that you can't write to me.

It's really too bad that you sent me away, she wanted to say, but knew that she couldn't.

We're in Madrid in the even fancier Hotel Nacional. The dinner was marvelous. Here is the menu:

Hors d'oeuvres—a prawn, a sardine, olives, and salad

Vegetable omelette

Partridge steak with Brussels sprouts

As much fruit as we wanted

That will show them, Zina thought. That will make them wish they had come too!

It was very, VERY GOOD!!! she wrote.

We went for a walk in a park in Madrid. This evening we leave on the 10 o'clock train and will arrive in Lisbon around 4 in the afternoon tomorrow and at 6 we get on the ship.

See how quickly I am going away from you, Zina thought. You will have to hurry to stop me. You will have to come quickly before I get on the ship. . . .

Her pencil wavered.

They couldn't come that quickly if they wanted to, she thought. It was too late, too late. . . .

She leaned over the sill of the open window and looked down into the street. A thin rain drizzled down, making the gray street gleam and streaking with black the gray stone buildings opposite. On the sidewalk people streamed past. Women wore black dresses and shoes, black stockings and head scarves. Their heads were bent, looking down at their feet. The scene seemed to hum, a gentle liquid sound that mingled with the swish of tires on the wet street. When a horse-drawn wagon rolled by, the noise of the horse's hooves was lost in the steady murmur.

Zina leaned her face into the drizzle, feeling it cool the anger from her cheeks. She shut her eyes and let herself drift in the softly flowing sounds.

This is what the ship will be like, she comforted herself. It will carry me to America. . . . She tried to imagine the white horse, but another, even better thought came to her. Perhaps the kind family will give me a bicycle, she thought, a bicycle of my own! It was easier to picture herself riding a bicycle, the warm breeze in her face, her stomach full, no fear of—

A cry pierced the daydream. It was raucous, ugly, a staccato burst of shrieks from the street below.

Zina opened her eyes and looked down. An old woman had stepped from the crowd. She was shouting at another woman in an open window above. Zina saw the mouth of the woman moving, like a gash in her wrinkled face. The woman above jabbed her fist out of the window. Their voices rose, cracked and furious. Their arms jerked. Their black heads shook with rage.

Quickly, Zina drew back her head into the hotel room and jumped from her chair.

"What is the matter, child?" said Mme Stepanova from the bed where she was resting.

Zina shook her head. She stumbled to the bathroom and closed the door behind her. Inside, away from the street, away from the raging old women, she could draw breath.

Always someone spoils things, she thought—that potbellied man in the potato line, the German soldier who shoved me, cranky old Mme Stepanova, the war, especially the war! People are just mean. Mean, mean, mean!

She sat down on the toilet seat and put her hot head in her hands. She rocked back and forth, chanting the word in her mind until it made a calming, senseless sound, meanmeanmean. . . .

Later, Zina found the postcard on the floor beside the window. Her pencil point had broken, but she peeled the wood away from the lead with her fingernails and managed to finish.

Lisa is well, and I am too. I have written what I could. . . . Kisses, Zina.

Their second night on the train, in first-class compartments, they were able to lie down. Bertrand had taken a nap—though he was too old for naps—that afternoon at the Madrid hotel, so he wasn't sleepy. But he lay down obediently, when Mme Sharp told him to, on a mattress pulled from an upper berth and placed on the floor. The doctor woman put Léonie down beside him.

"I want Zina," Bertrand said. "Why can't Zina be with me?"

"Hush, Bertrand," said the doctor woman. "Go to sleep."

"I am counting on you to take care of your little sister," said Mme Sharp.

The train floor rumbled beneath Bertrand. It made his stomach feel jiggly. Léonie smelled of her impetigo medicine and, a little, of pee. She flung out her arms and legs, leaving Bertrand no room. She snuffled through her nose.

It was no fair, thought Bertrand. Léonie didn't want him to take care of her, and Zina did. He had helped Zina that afternoon to find a mailbox so that she could post her card. He had shared with her the best parts of his supper. But still she looked sick. She needed him!

Léonie whimpered in her sleep. She was a hot damp lump beside him, crowding him to the edge of the narrow mattress. He put out his hands and shoved her.

"Ahh!" Léonie wailed, waking. "Ma-man!" she cried. "Berti is pushing me!"

"Did not!" Bertrand cried. "*Tais-toi*, crybaby! Shut up!"

"Que faites vous?" said Mme Sharp in the darkness. She had tied coats over the compartment windows to keep out the corridor light. "What's the matter?"

Bertrand felt her gathering Léonie into her arms.

"Hush, hush, *ma petite*," she was crooning, but Léonie sobbed loudly.

"I did not push her!" Bertrand protested.

"I did not say you did," came Mme Sharp's voice quietly. "Go back to sleep, Bertrand."

Bertrand realized that she was lifting Léonie into the berth with her.

His cheeks were hot with the lie he had told and with his unkindness to his sister. He lay in the dark, feeling the cold seep through the mattress with the vibration of the train. The train whistle wailed, but Léonie had quieted. She was with Mme Sharp in her berth, and Bertrand could hear her deep, shaky breathing. He heard the snoring of the old Russian lady, and one by one he picked out the sounds of the breathing of the others—the doctor woman and her silent husband and, on another mattress, the Stella girl and Zina.

Still, lying on his back with his hand in his pocket, stroking the hard metal of the scissors through the cloth of his handkerchief, Bertrand felt utterly alone . . . and afraid.

7

ZINA LEANED out of the open train window, stretching her arm in the morning sunlight. The warmth soaked through her skin and into her sore muscles. They had been sitting here at the Portuguese frontier for a long time, waiting while their baggage was searched, though not so long as on the Spanish side, where they had been stopped before breakfast and made to get off the train while the grown-ups were questioned. It had been cold then, and Zina had been colder still with dread that they would be stopped, but the officials had passed them through at last. Now, later in the morning, Zina leaned farther out the train window into the sunshine, trying to warm away the tenseness of her body.

The train on the adjoining track was beginning to move, slowly, and she reached for it. She stretched the muscles of her arm, her hand, her fingers, long, longer, longer still. The train was gathering speed. Just a bit farther, she thought, feeling the breeze of its passing. Just a bit . . .

"Put your arm inside the window at once!"

Zina started and bumped her head on the window frame.

"That is exceedingly dangerous, young lady," Mrs. Sharp was scolding as she entered the compartment.

"I'm sorry, Martha," Dr. Dubouchet murmured. "I was settling Léonie and didn't notice."

"One needs eyes in the back of one's head to notice all the mischief this lot gets into," Mrs. Sharp said, flinging herself onto the seat.

With a jerk their own train began to move. It made the other train seem to Zina's glance to stand still for a second, but she didn't look long. Her eyes went back to Mrs. Sharp, who sat fanning herself with her handbag, her face flushed and furious.

Mean, Zina thought. Even Mrs. Sharp was acting mean.

"I would think you would know better, Zinaida," she was saying. "That's no example to set for the younger children."

She nodded toward Bertrand, who had sat bolt upright at the sound of her voice. His eyes were wide, perhaps with the same surprise that Zina felt.

"I had a patient once whose arm was amputated by a train moving past his," said Dr. Dubouchet dispassionately.

"You could have gotten your *whole head* cut off!" burst out Bertrand.

"You see? You see the seriousness of keeping inside the train?" said Mrs. Sharp. "Zinaida, do you?"

Zina nodded. Why is Mrs. Sharp so angry? she thought. Even Bertrand is against me.

But then she looked more carefully at his face, drained white, she saw, with fear.

"Your whole head!" he was whispering, and she realized that he wasn't really ganging up with the grown-ups. He was scared for her.

"Zinaida," Mrs. Sharp said again. "Enough of this silly silence. Speak up. *Do* you understand?"

Zina gave her a pleading look and nodded her head again, emphatically.

"Oh, very well," said Mrs. Sharp. "Don't speak! At least I can't fault *you* for being noisy."

"What *is* the matter, Martha?" said Dr. Dubouchet.

What indeed? thought Zina.

"The last cruel blow!" said Mrs. Sharp. "At least I hope it's the last. I've had a wire. The shipping company has sold our tickets out from under us! They claim they thought we wouldn't arrive in time for the sailing. More likely they were able to get better prices on the black market."

"Sold our tickets?" said Dr. Dubouchet. "What will we do?"

Bertrand was looking from one woman to the other, swiveling his head as though he were at a tennis match, Zina thought, suppressing a giggle that bubbled up on waves of hope and terror. Would this mean they could not go to America after all? I would not need to leave Mama and Papa, she thought, and then she was gripped with a panicky remembrance of an empty stomach, of German soldiers in the streets, of the specter of the refugee camps.

"What *will* we do indeed!" said Mrs. Sharp.

Zina saw Mrs. Sharp look over at her and the other children and draw in her breath sharply. She laid a hand on Dr. Dubouchet's arm and switched from French to English.

She doesn't want us to understand, Zina thought. She doesn't want us to be frightened.

Zina looked out the window. The train was speeding

through open, sunny countryside now. Olive trees stood, gray-green against a blue sky, and Zina saw beside the tracks a neat whitewashed house in a garden bright with blossoms. A man in a black stocking cap straightened from a row of tall yellow flowers and waved as the train blew past.

But Zina did not wave back.

Didn't she want to go back to Mama and Papa? I want them to come with us, she thought, and she remembered how frightened she had been all along that they might be stopped. We've come so far, she thought. Surely, surely Mrs. Sharp will find a way to get us to America!

"Ne t'inquiète pas," Bertrand was saying, tugging as he spoke on her sleeve. "Don't worry. I will take care of you. I can, you know." His voice lowered to a whisper. "I have a secret. It's because of my secret that I can protect you. Zina?"

Zina looked at him and nodded, only half listening.

"Don't be afraid," he said.

I'm not afraid, Zina thought, trying to put the thought into her eyes so that Bertrand would see it. But this time he didn't understand. He kept prattling about "protecting" her with his "secret."

I'm not afraid, Zina told herself, but she wasn't sure. If it wasn't fear she felt, then what was it?

Another school!

Bertrand craned his neck, looking for nuns, as he climbed down the autobus steps. He sniffed the air for the smell of cooking. He hoped the nuns had supper ready, for he was hungry, and if he was hungry, he knew that Zina was too.

But Bertrand didn't see any nuns. The doctor woman had said that this was an agricultural school near

Lisbon, where they were to stay until passage on another boat could be found. Perhaps nuns did not run agricultural schools, Bertrand thought, though this school, like St.-Étienne, was out in the country.

He wished that Mme Sharp had not left them. She had a way of explaining things so that Bertrand always knew what was going to happen next. She had said that she must stay in Lisbon to arrange for another ship. She had said it would be only for a little while. But that was what Maman had said when she left them at St.-Étienne. Bertrand had seen Mme Sharp climb into a taxicab at the Lisbon railway station soon after the children boarded this autobus. He had looked after the departing taxi a long time, his face pressed against the autobus window.

The doctor woman had also left them, along with her silent husband, though her son Yves and his sister were still with them. Bertrand didn't mind *her* going so much, though Léonie had cried. Now Mme Okuneva and two other mothers were in charge. Bertrand had not realized so many mothers were traveling with them. It gave him a pang.

The children were milling around the autobus now, in the graveled courtyard of the agricultural school. They were waiting for instructions. Even Yves, Bertrand's squad leader, seemed bewildered. Bertrand looked for and found Zina, who stood drooping near the autobus door.

"This way, *mes enfants*," a woman's voice called. Perhaps it was Mme Okuneva, but Bertrand could not see over the heads of the other children. It was someone whose French was oddly accented.

Bertrand took Zina's hand and led her toward the arched door of the square brick building that was another school.

8

TWO OF the big girls were playing checkers.

Zina sat in a corner of the large sunny room that had been fitted out for them as a day room. The Paia-Odivelar Agricultural School reminded her of the Villa St.-Sever, only cleaner, and the food was better, she thought. They had been here almost a week. Would that week stretch into months, she wondered, before they could leave for America? Or would they be sent back to France after all?

She was watching the checker players, though she tried to appear as though she were not. She held her head still and let only her eyes move. That way her head did not throb so strongly, and so long as she did not lower her chin, her nose didn't run.

Everyone had colds, it seemed, and the grown-ups would not let them play out-of-doors until they were better, but Zina did not much care. She felt too miserable to play—unless she could play checkers, she thought. But no one had asked her.

"My father's the bravest, best man in the world," one of the checker players was bragging—Zina thought she was an older sister of the twins. "My mother too," the girl added. "I wish I was old enough to help the Resistance as they do."

"My *maman* is fighting the Germans," piped a small hoarse voice. It was Bertrand, Zina saw. "My *maman* is a nurse. She is fighting for France."

Bertrand had come close to the checkerboard, and the girl who had spoken smiled at him.

"You must be very proud," the girl said.

"Ha! I just captured your man, and you didn't even notice," declared her opponent, tossing back her dark curls.

"*Zut alors!*" said the twins' sister, turning her attention once more to the checkerboard.

Bertrand looked thoughtful, Zina saw.

"So I am," he was saying slowly. "I *am* proud." His voice rose with enthusiasm. "She is killing Germans, I bet. I bet she is shooting Germans. Pow! Pow! Pow!"

The curly-haired player laughed.

"*Petit sot!*" she said. "A nurse does not kill. A nurse helps the wounded."

Zina had forgotten her runny nose. She leaned forward, watching Bertrand, and wiped her nose on her sleeve without thinking. Bertrand's face had crumpled, she saw, and she wished she could say something to put that rude girl in her place.

But I can't, she remembered with a jerk of her head that sent pain coursing behind her eyes.

"My parents help the poor Jews escape from the Germans," said the first girl. "My parents don't believe in killing, but they do believe that one must be willing to die for the right. God put us on earth to help one another, my father says, not to blow one another's brains out!"

Bertrand pouted.

"Then he is not brave at all," Bertrand said. "Not like my *maman*. Not if he won't fight."

The girl's voice was so strong and sure that Zina could not help paying attention.

"There are better ways to fight evil than killing," she said. "It takes a different kind of courage to face the enemy without weapons."

"And it's a good way to get *yourself* killed!" spoke up her opponent. "Ha! I've jumped you again."

But now the girl was paying no attention to the checker game. Zina saw that her cheeks were flaming, and her eyes flashed.

"My parents and our village are braver than all the rest of France together," she said. "They won't be harmed while they do God's work!"

"If it's God's work, why are you and your sisters running away from it?" said the curly-haired girl.

Zina realized that the other children in the room had fallen silent. They were watching and listening to the checker players, who faced each other across the board with blazing faces. The twins' sister had half risen, and Zina thought that, regardless of her pacifist words, she was likely to haul off and hit the other girl at any moment.

"Because they cannot do their work so well when they must worry about us," she said quietly, her voice trembling.

The curly-haired girl smirked.

"In other words, they want you out of the way," she said, and Zina's heart was bruised by the words.

Want you out of the way.

The twins' sister could not deny it. I'm not the only one, Zina thought. Lisa and I aren't the only ones whose parents sent them away. The thought was somehow comforting.

The twins' sister sat down. Zina thought it cost her effort, but she was looking at her opponent with clear eyes, and her voice, though low, was as strong and sure as it had been in the beginning.

"*Mais oui,*" she said. "We are only children. We cannot help, except by getting out of the way."

She lowered her eyes to the checkerboard, and as Zina watched, her hand moved toward one of the checkers. She began to smile.

Bertrand still stood beside them, forgotten, his eyes going from one girl to the other, his face bewildered. Zina saw his lips moving, but could not hear what he said. His nose was running, and a tear hung on his blinking eyelash, then fell and rolled down his cheek.

"Oh, ho!" the twins' sister was saying as her checker skipped across the board with a clicking sound. "You are not so smart as you think!"

Bertrand slipped out the side door. He knew they were not supposed to go outside until their colds were better, but he was tired of the overheated day room, tired of girls who talked nonsense.

The day was bright and windy. Bertrand wished, just a little, that he had stopped to get his coat and *béret*, but he dared not risk going back after them. He turned up his collar and hunched his ears into it. He put his hands into his pockets, feeling the reassuring shape of his scissors. Then he headed toward the back of the school building, kicking his shoes in the gravel as he went.

His *maman* was too fighting the Germans! What was

the use of sending him and Léonie away if she only continued to work at the hospital? If that was her plan, he and Léonie could have stayed in the apartment with Marie as they had always done. No, he remembered how she had sat them on the edge of the bed in the hotel room in Marseilles to tell them about going to America. Léonie would not remember, she had said, but Bertrand must tell her when she was older that Maman had not wanted to send them away. It was for their own good that they must go to Papa in America, she said. But she herself must stay in France to fight the Germans.

Bertrand squinted his tearing eyes against the wind and sent the gravel flying with a kick.

Fight the Germans. He was certain that was what she said. "I am a Frenchwoman," she had said. "My duty is clear."

Bertrand gave his head a small shake.

He was *not* a *petit sot*, a little dummy! He knew that for sure. He was older now than he had been when he was so frightened on the road from Paris. He was stronger too, and fiercer, thanks to his friend Henri. He knew how to fight, and he had his weapon. He . . .

Bertrand lifted his head and cocked his ear to listen. A clamor had arisen just ahead, in the rear courtyard. Bertrand rounded the corner of the building, half running, and came upon the source of the noise.

A man—Bertrand thought him one of the workers at the school—had grabbed a duck from the flock that wandered the enclosed courtyard. It flapped and quacked as he carried it by its neck to a large stump. As Bertrand watched, frozen midstep, the man laid the head of the duck on the stump, lifted high the ax he held in his other hand, and brought it down, whack! Then he tossed the bird onto the ground, where it staggered among its hysterical comrades as though, without its head, it could not tell which way to go. Bertrand could not pull his gaze from the sight of the headless duck, the stump of its neck weakly pulsing a red stain that spread across its breast. It lurched in ever more faltering circles. At last he saw it slump down onto the packed dirt of the courtyard.

The man was bending to seize another duck. It squawked and eluded his grasp.

Bertrand felt something brush his arm and realized that Zina was running past him. Where had *she* come from? he wondered, still frozen. She scooped the endangered duck from the ground and held it to her chest as the man advanced on her, brandishing his ax.

"Put down that duck!" the man was shouting. "You, give it to me."

But Zina held tightly to the duck, though it struggled and pecked at her. Her chest was heaving, and her head shook from side to side.

"What are you doing?" the man said.

Zina shook her head.

The man swore, reaching toward the duck with his big, hairy hand.

Zina jumped back, then turned and fled from him.

She ran past Bertrand again and, as though she had released him from a spell, Bertrand turned and ran too.

He could hear the man shouting behind them as they tore around the building toward the tangerine orchard in front. They did not stop running until they had reached the trees.

Bertrand bent over, his hands on his knees, gasping with fear and elation. The man had not followed them, he saw. Zina leaned against a tree trunk, the struggling duck still clasped in her arms.

How brave she was! Bertrand thought, and "*Formidable!*" he said.

Zina was panting. Her face was white, with two scarlet patches on her cheeks. But her lips trembled into a smile when he spoke. She bent and released the duck, who waddled away—half senseless with terror, Bertrand thought—then shook itself and began to preen.

9

"MES ENFANTS," said Mme Okuneva. She was standing in her place at the head of one of the tables in the agricultural school dining room. "Children, I have good news!"

Some of the children put down their spoons and turned to look at her, but Zina kept on eating. Rescuing ducks was hungry work, she thought with pride.

She saw that Bertrand, who sat a few seats down the table across from her, was also slurping his soup.

"Mrs. Sharp has arranged passage for us on the ocean liner *Excambion*," said Mme Okuneva. "We will sail in one week, on December thirteenth. We will be in America by Christmas!"

The children were clapping. As Zina realized the import of Mme Okuneva's announcement, she put down her spoon and joined them. But she thought she wouldn't *really* believe it until they were on board the ship. She knew now that she didn't want to go back to France, even though continuing the journey meant going away from her parents. Once again Zina was allowing herself to imagine America, to imagine good food and hot baths, perhaps even a bicycle of her own, and the kind American family. Maybe that big girl was right. Maybe by going she was *helping* Mama and Papa.

As the applause quieted, she lifted her bowl to drain the last drops of soup. She would think more about that when her head didn't feel so stuffy. She looked down the table, searching for the bread.

It was in front of Bertrand, who had timidly raised his hand.

"*S'il vous plaît, madame,*" he was saying.

"Yes, what is it . . . Bertrand? It is Bertrand, is it not?"

"*Oui, madame.*"

"What is it, Bertrand?"

"When will Mme Sharp come back to us?" he said. "Now that she has arranged the ship, cannot she come back to us?"

"Oh," said Mme Okuneva. "I thought you all knew. Mrs. Sharp has gone on ahead to America. There were a few places on the ship that sailed today. Not enough for all of us, but enough so that she and a few others could go. Mrs. Sharp's own children are needing her at home, you see. She has been away from them for a long time, helping us."

Zina had not thought of that—Mrs. Sharp had children of her own, children she had left in order to help them. That was another thing she would have to think about.

But now she was watching Bertrand. His face had gone pale, and his eyes stared disbelievingly at Mme Okuneva. The woman did not seem to notice. She was speaking now to one of the other boys, who had raised his hand. Bertrand looked down at his plate.

Zina pointed to the bread basket and nudged Stella, who sat beside her.

"Bertrand," Stella said, "pass the bread to Zinaida."

Bertrand did not respond. He was not crying, Zina saw, but he looked as though he might. Didn't he understand that Mme Okuneva's news had been good? Didn't he understand that they were going to America after all?

"Pass the bread," Stella said again, and when he didn't, Yves, who sat next to him, picked up the basket and handed it to Zina.

Mme Sharp had left him! She had said it would be only for a little while, but she had lied. She had gone on a ship without him!

Was it because he had pushed Léonie that night on the train? Was it because she had discovered what a cowardly boy he was?

Bertrand shoved his way through the group of children who were moving down the corridor toward the day room. Someone stepped on his foot.

"Ow!" cried Bertrand. "Watch where you step!" And then he saw that it was the younger of the naughty brothers, the one he had slapped. Bertrand caught his breath in sharply. Had the boy done it on purpose?

"I vatch," the boy said. "It is you who does not vatch." The boy's French was thickly accented—a *German* accent, Bertrand realized suddenly, like the soldiers who had invaded France.

They burst through the doorway of the day room together, and Bertrand's heart was pounding.

Wasn't the boy's name Isaak? Isaak Reeser? Wasn't that a *German* name?

"You did that on purpose, you dirty Boche," Bertrand said.

The boy turned, his face flaming.

"Vhat you call me?"

"Boche," Bertrand yelled. "Boche, Boche, Boche!"

"Take zat back!" said the boy, balling his fists at his sides.

Bertrand faced him, breathing hard. His temples were throbbing, and he could feel the panic rising in his stomach. Everyone was watching! He wanted to run, but instead he stepped forward.

"I'd like to see you make me!" he heard himself say.

The other children crowded around.

"Fight!" someone said. "There's going to be a fight!"

The boy took a faltering step backward, but the wall was behind him. Bertrand's hand slipped into his pocket and met the shape of his weapon.

"I not Boche," the boy said.

"Boche!" shouted Bertrand. "I'll show you how a Frenchman treats the Boche!"

He pulled the scissors from his pocket in a smooth, swift motion he had often practiced when no one was looking. He heard the gasps of the children, and for a moment he hesitated. Then he tightened his grip. He was holding the scissors as he had seen fighters in the *cinéma* hold their knives, the threatening point toward his enemy. Anger seemed to have replaced his fear. It pulsed through his trembling arm. It churned in his belly and welled bitterly in his mouth. He spat.

The spittle struck the boy on the cheek. He blinked.

Bertrand lunged, crying out in the breath-held silence, and as he lunged his eyes met Isaak's. Isaak stood his ground. Bertrand felt his own weight driving forward the deadly point of the scissors. He saw the place where it would strike, the white skin of Isaak's throat. An image of the duck's white breast, stained with red, flashed in his mind. He jerked the scissors back. Too late! He felt them strike, and his fingers opened. He heard a clatter as he stumbled, fell against Isaak, carried them both to the floor. He heard the thump of Isaak's head against the wall, heard the whoosh of Isaak's breath. Then he was flailing his arms, trying, not to hit Isaak, but only to get away from him.

A grown-up's voice was shouting. Bertrand could not understand what it said. It was a woman—Mme Okuneva, he saw as he turned his head to look up. Mme Okuneva was rushing toward them—the children parted before her—crying out in some foreign language. In a moment, as she knelt beside them, her words turned to French.

"*Mon Dieu! Que faites-vous?* What are you doing?"

"*Rien!*" Bertrand cried, scrambling off of Isaak. "Nothing!"

But he *had* done something. Even as he was denying it, Bertrand knew that he had done something worse than he had ever done before.

10

"HE HAD a knife!" Stella was telling Mr. Joy. Mr. Joy had come into the dayroom shortly after Bertrand was sent to his dormitory and Mme Okuneva took Isaak away.

"He tried to kill him!" said a boy with glasses.

"That's *ridicule!*" said Mr. Joy heartily. "Just a *petit altercation*, that's all. *Rien* to get *agité* about. Who's for a *chanson?*"

Mr. Joy's French and English were always getting oddly mixed up together, Zina thought, watching from her corner. He was the American man who had been with them, in another compartment, on the train. He wasn't at all Zina's idea of an American man—not tall nor handsome nor strongly silent like the American *cinéma* stars, but shorter than Yves Dubouchet, and comical-looking with his stuck-out ears, and noisily enthusiastic. He was not living with them at the agricultural school, but he turned up now and again and took the children who were well enough on autobus excursions to the local sights—to the Lisbon World Exposition or some castle in the countryside.

"But he did, he *did* have a knife," Stella insisted. "I saw it!"

"Where is this *couteau* then?" said Mr. Joy. "I don't see a *couteau.*"

The children shuffled their feet and looked at the floor and then at one another.

"Perhaps Mme Okuneva took it?" someone suggested, but Mr. Joy shook his head.

"You see?" said Mr. Joy.

"But he stabbed him," said one of the triplets.

"Only a scratch," said Mr. Joy. "Done with a fingernail, most likely."

He was striding to the head of the room, rubbing his hands together.

"*Allons-y,*" he said. "I say it's time for a *chanson!*"

"There *was* a knife," said Stella, coming to sit beside Zina. "I saw it. Didn't you see it, Zinaida?"

But Zina only shrugged.

" 'It's a Long (Long) Way to Tipperary,' " announced Mr. Joy. "Ready?"

He raised his hands as though conducting a choir and began to sing the strange English words that made no sense to Zina. Some of the children began to sing with him. Zina just sat and watched, her eyes roaming the room.

Beside her, Stella sighed. Then Zina heard her voice join with the others, ". . . to the sweetest land I know . . ."

Stealthily Zina slipped her hand into the pocket of her dress and touched the cool metal surface of Bertrand's scissors.

"Bertrand?"

Mme Okuneva stood framed in the light of the doorway. Her voice didn't sound angry, as Bertrand had expected it would, but he didn't answer. He turned over on his bed to face the wall and listened to her footsteps approach. He cringed, feeling her above him, but the edge of the mattress only sank with her weight as she sat down beside him.

"We must have a talk, Bertrand," Mme Okuneva said.

She waited in the darkness, and Bertrand heard his heart pound louder as the silence stretched out. Why did she not yell at him? Punish him? *Beat* him? Then a dreadful thought struck him. Perhaps she had called the *gendarmes*. Perhaps they were on their way to carry him off to prison!

Finally, when he could stand it no longer, he said, his voice coming out like a whimper, "Is he . . . d-dead?"

"Oh, no! Poor Bertrand, did you think you had killed him?"

Bertrand heard the sympathy in her voice and felt a sob rise in his throat.

"*Nyet, nyet,* he is only a little bruised and scratched. But why, Bertrand, why did you attack him?"

Bertrand began to cry with relief. He could not help himself. I tried to pull back my weapon, he wanted to tell her. I didn't mean to hurt him, he wanted to say, but the crying burst from him as though he were a baby. Wordless, as though he were Léonie! At that thought, he cried harder.

He felt Mme Okuneva gather him in her arms, and the sobs shook his whole body. Wails poured from his open mouth. Tears gushed from his eyes. Snot flowed thick from his nose. It was like a storm sweeping him helpless before it, like the flood that had swept the land they had traveled that first day on the train.

When he came to himself again, Bertrand found himself held tightly in Mme Okuneva's arms, as though washed up in the branches of a strong tree. It felt like being held by Maman.

"There, there," Mme Okuneva's accented voice soothed as she wiped his face. "There, there, it is not so bad as all that."

"B-but it is!" cried Bertrand. "I am such a bad boy!"

Mme Okuneva put him away from her a little and looked into his face. Bertrand could see the gleam of her eyes, steady on him, even in the half dark of the dormitory room.

"*Nyet,* Bertrand. You are not a bad boy. It is true that you should not have hit Isaak. That was a bad thing to do. But you are not a bad boy, you are a good boy. I have seen how you take care of your little sister. I have seen what a good friend you are to Zina. A good boy like you can choose to do good things."

Bertrand hung his head. He thought he would feel better if she would punish him.

"I know that Isaak is not easy to get along with," Mme Okuneva said. "My Misha has told me how rude he can be . . ."

It was I who was rude, Bertrand thought.

". . . but you must understand that he and Wilhelm have had a hard time. They were in a refugee camp when Mrs. Sharp found them. *Recebedou!* It is a very bad camp, Bertrand. Inadequate food. Appalling conditions. Really, it is a wonder they survived. Their mother *is* dead. Their father begged Mrs. Sharp to take them to safety, and indeed, she found a way to get them out."

Yes, thought Bertrand. Mme Sharp could do that. Mme Sharp could do anything, I think, but I wish she had not gone to America without me!

"They have not lived a civilized life for a very long

time, and so they are often naughty and unhappy. Do you understand, Bertrand?" Mme Okuneva said.

Bertrand nodded, though he still could not look at her.

Naughty, he thought. Unhappy. Yes, I understand.

"Do you think, Bertrand, knowing this, that you could choose to be kind to Isaak? Do you think you could tell him you are sorry?"

Again Bertrand nodded. He felt tired. His head was heavy.

Mme Okuneva helped him out of his clothes and into his nightshirt. She found a handkerchief and told him to blow. She washed his face with a cool cloth. Then she helped him under the covers and bent over him. She smoothed the hair from his forehead—again he thought of Maman and had to squeeze his eyes shut to keep back the tears.

"Good night, Bertrand," said Mme Okuneva.

Bertrand kept his eyes closed, but he could feel her standing above him.

"*Je regrette*, madame," he whispered, trying to control the trembling of his lips. "I'm sorry."

"I know," said Mme Okuneva.

11

THIS WAS the day they would sail for America!

Most of the luggage—there were more than fifty pieces in all, M. Okunieff had said—was once again packed and standing in a great pile in the front courtyard of the agricultural school. The children seemed to run in all directions, their voices shrill with excitement.

"I can't find my red notebook," Lisa was saying. "Have you seen it, Zinochka?"

Zina shook her head, and Lisa sighed.

"When are you going to start talking again, Zina? This is getting stale!"

Zina looked at her reproachfully, but the look was wasted. One of the triplets had hauled the notebook from under a bed, and Lisa was paying no attention.

Zina picked up her small bag and walked out of the room. Behind her she could hear Lisa chattering with the triplet. It was an intimate, exclusive sound, a sound that Zina could not be part of. She walked toward the front door, dragging her feet a little as she went. How many places had they stayed in and left? she wondered.

How many good-byes had been said, autobuses and trains boarded, destinations reached? Soon, soon it will be America! she thought, and a shiver ran through her. The excitement of the others was catching, she thought. She felt . . . was it hopeful? Was it happy? Perhaps . . .

Some of the children were already gathered in the courtyard, waiting for the autobus that would carry them to the ship in Lisbon Harbor. Bertrand was among them, she saw. He stood near the younger Reeser boy. They seemed to have called a truce.

Bertrand was different since the fight—had it really been a whole week ago? Zina thought. He no longer followed her about, acting as though he were in charge of her. In fact, she had not yet found an opportunity to get him alone in order to return his scissors. Scissors! She laughed a little to herself. That had been his big secret, his secret weapon! What a funny fellow he was!

Still, she missed him in a way, missed his hand slipping into hers, his face turned to her so trustingly. Since the fight, he no longer put on airs. He no longer sat beside her jabbering. He was . . . subdued. No bragging, she thought. No laughing either.

The autobus was coming. Someone shouted that they had seen it turn into the drive, and children and grown-ups were pouring out of the door of the agricultural school to throw the last suitcases onto the pile of luggage. Mme Okuneva was calling to them to line up for a photograph while the bags were loaded into the bus.

"Are you wearing your *bérets?*" she called. "Let's have a picture of everyone wearing their *bérets.*"

One of the little girls was crying that she could not find her *béret*, and the Reeser brothers, as usual, had run off, but soon they were all being herded together to stand before the arched windows of the school.

"Little ones in front," one of the grown-ups directed. Zina saw Stella push Bertrand's little sister out to stand in front of her, and Bertrand too was put in front, though he instantly knelt as though he thought he was so big he might block the children behind him. He was not, perhaps, *completely* changed, Zina thought.

She squinted into the sun.

"Smile everyone," the gentleman taking the photograph said, and Zina was surprised at how easy it was to smile.

Then they were crowding onto the autobus. Zina made her way down the aisle, jostling the others as she went. They had grouped themselves in squads once more—out of habit, Zina supposed—and she was surrounded by Yves and Stella with Bertrand's little sister, the Reeser brothers and the twins and Bertrand. Bertrand was in front of her, she saw, and suddenly, spotting an empty seat, she grabbed his hand and pulled him in beside her.

"Are we supposed to do partners?" he asked, and Zina nodded, though no one had told her so.

Bertrand flopped onto the seat and craned his neck to look past Zina out the open window of the autobus.

Soon they were going to get on a boat—a big boat, Mme Okuneva had said—and sail to America. Bertrand had heard talk of submarines and torpedoes among the bigger boys. He wanted to ask if their boat would be in danger, but all the grown-ups seemed too busy, and if he asked a big boy or girl, they were apt to think him a coward. Some of them probably already did—for attacking unarmed Isaak with a knife. Bertrand had not yet corrected the notion that he had had a knife.

It *was* cowardly, Bertrand thought now, admitting to himself what he still couldn't say out loud. The girl playing checkers that day had been right about that. But what bothered Bertrand even more was whether it had been more cowardly to change his mind, once begun. Why *did* I pull back? he wondered as he had wondered dozens of times since the fight. What *made* me change my mind?

It had something to do with the way Isaak had stood there unflinching, and something to do with the awfulness of the headless duck, with Zina's daring rescue of its comrade. You can't put a head back on, once it's off, Bertrand thought, or the wings back on a fly. You can't fix it, once you've hurt someone.

He and Isaak were friends now, but still the fight was between them. He knows I tried to hurt him, Bertrand thought, and he'll always know it. He remembered beating Pierre at St.-Étienne, and the memory shamed him now. What if I had really *hurt* Isaak? he thought. What if the scissors had jabbed into his throat as I meant them to? What if I had *killed* him?

There are some things no one can fix, thought Bertrand, and he wondered that the grown-ups who were fighting the war did not seem to know it.

The autobus was bumping, with a familiar swaying motion, over the rutted drive toward the main highway. Bertrand settled back into his seat.

Beside him Zina was rummaging in her bag. Had she brought along something to eat? They had eaten lunch just a short while ago, but then, Zina was always hungry. He looked over to see what would come out of the bag and was startled to see the shine of metal before her hand closed around it. She nudged him with her shoulder and lowered her hand to the seat between them. Bertrand looked down, saw the hand open, saw that she was passing to him . . . the scissors!

He caught his breath. He had thought one of the grown-ups had taken them. They had disappeared, and no one had mentioned them.

He shook his head and looked away quickly.

He could feel her looking at him, feel the question in her eyes. He swallowed hard and licked his lips. I *must* be a coward, he thought.

He could feel himself trembling, feel the sweat in his armpits. He squeezed his eyes shut and tried to imagine what the Blessed Mother would want him to do.

"You are a good boy," he thought he heard her say in Mme Okuneva's voice.

Bertrand opened his eyes and glanced once again at the scissors lying on Zina's open palm.

I don't want to hurt anyone anymore, he thought.

But I am still afraid, a small voice inside him said.

Perhaps . . . perhaps the others were also afraid? Zina was afraid all the time, and yet she had rescued the duck. Isaak—certainly Isaak had been afraid. Bertrand had seen it in his eyes, yet he had not flinched. Even Henri? It was not brave to torture flies, or younger, smaller children. Perhaps even Henri was afraid.

Grown-ups? Maman was afraid. Bertrand had always known it, though he hadn't wanted to know it. She was afraid when Papa left them, afraid on the road from Paris, afraid for herself and for them. That was why she had sent them away, Léonie and him, because she was afraid—not because he couldn't fix Grandmère's clock! The doctor woman's husband was afraid in the night. Could it be that even Mme Sharp was afraid?

So . . . one could be afraid and still act bravely, Bertrand suddenly saw—as Zina had done, as Isaak had done. And one could be good, yet still do bad things sometimes. But one could choose.

Bertrand reached for the scissors. He knew what to do now. The Blessed Mother had not sent them to him, as he had tried to believe. He had stolen them, but there was no way now to return them.

He snatched them from Zina's palm and leaned across her to fling them out the open window of the autobus.

For an instant, they turned in the air, the sunlight glinting from them, and then they were gone.

12

ZINA WATCHED in surprise as the scissors flew out the window.

But Bertrand was grinning.

She smiled back at him a little uncertainly. She didn't know why he had attacked the Reeser boy that night, but she knew that Bertrand wasn't mean. He was a nice boy, and she was glad he didn't think he needed a "weapon" anymore. After all, she thought, there are lots of people taking care of us.

Taking care of us . . . Lots of people . . .

"How about a *chanson*, youngsters?" Mr. Joy was calling from the back of the bus in his funny mixture of French and English. "Turn around your seats, those of you facing forward, and let's show the *mesdames* and Mr. Okunieff what *bons chanteurs* you are!"

Lots of people, Zina thought as she scrambled up to help Bertrand turn their seat toward the back of the autobus. People like Mr. Joy and Mrs. Sharp and the others who had cared for them on this journey. Even Mama and Papa, she thought suddenly, who sent us away so we'd be safe!

She saw that the grown-ups on the bus were smiling. Mme Okuneva, who was scolding the Reeser brothers for playing in the aisle, was scolding gently.

Not all people are mean, she thought. What about the grown-ups at the Kolónia, or the old woman in the potato line, or Mrs. Sharp who had left her own children in order to help them? What about Bertrand, who had tried so hard to be her friend?

Mr. Joy was lifting his arms in his conducting pose. His face beamed out at them, rosy and comical. His ears stuck out.

"Ready?" he cried.

I don't know how to sing it, Zina thought.

"'Row, Row, Row Your Boat,'" Mr. Joy was announcing.

Boat. Zina thought that was another word for ship in English. This must be a song about the ship that would take them to America.

"Row, row, row your boat," Mr. Joy began to sing. "Come on, louder! Gently down the stream. Merrily, merrily, merrily, merrily. Life is but a dream."

Over and over he was singing it, and the children were joining in. The song lilted up and down the autobus aisle, and Zina felt its happiness seeping into her, felt the enthusiasm of Mr. Joy, who was waving his arms and praising them, felt the way the voices blended to make a sound bigger and stronger than any of their voices alone.

Now he was dividing the children into two groups, one on either side of the aisle, and they were singing the song as a round. One group started, and on the second line the other group came in. The voices mingled, their words different, but their melody the same, and Zina felt the song lift her and carry her somewhere deep inside herself where the anger against her parents seethed.

They sent me away, the bitter thought came and, as

quickly, not because they are mean, but because they love me.

She had not allowed herself to think of that for a long time, perhaps because the thought was like a pain. She felt the pain thicken in her throat, and with it was the fear of the big new country over the sea where she would not know how to talk.

"Gently down the stream," the children were singing.

"*Bon, bon*! Good, good!" Mr. Joy cried, waving his arms.

"Only for a little while," Zina remembered her mother had said. "It will be only for a little while, Zinochka, and then, God willing, we will come. I promise."

I had forgotten that, Zina thought. They *want* to come.

"Merrily, merrily, merrily, merrily," the children sang.

As they had the day she watched the murder of the duck, anger and fear and sadness were rising in her throat, and with them a sudden hope. I saved one of the ducks, Zina thought, and she found herself opening her mouth.

"Row, row, row your boat," her lips shaped the silent words.

"Gently down the stream . . ."

She felt a hand slip into hers, and she saw that Bertrand, singing heartily, was holding her hand. It came to her then that it didn't matter whether she sang well or poorly so long as she sang with the others.

"Merrily, merrily . . ."

Zina heard her own voice, only a whisper at first, but gaining strength and volume as the words—the English words she had thought she could not learn—flowed out.

". . . merrily, merrily. Life is but a dream."

ACKNOWLEDGMENTS

The seeds of this story were sown on April 7, 1991, when I heard Mary-Ella Holst of the Unitarian Universalist Service Committee deliver a sermon entitled "A Reckless Kindness," which dealt with the contributions of Martha Sharp Cogan and her first husband, the Reverend Waitstill Sharp, to the founding of the original Unitarian Service Committee in 1940. So my first thanks must go to Mary-Ella for both the idea and subsequent encouragement.

Where Mary-Ella left off, Anne Forsyth, also of the Unitarian Universalist Service Committee, Alan Seaburg, Curator of Manuscripts at the Andover-Harvard Library of the Harvard Divinity School, and most especially Ghanda DiFiglia, who knows more about Martha Sharp Cogan's work than anyone else outside her family, took up to aid my research. My special thanks to Ghanda, not only for her expertise, but also for her friendship.

I appreciate Martha Sharp Joukowsky's permission to pursue information about her mother's life.

But the lion's share of gratitude must go to Clément Brown and Anna Vakar for their openhearted sharing of memories, their careful review of the manuscript, and their warm encouragement. Without them, this book could not have been written.

One person has seen me through the creation of all of my books, put up with my abstraction, supported my vocation, and demonstrated his pride in my accomplishments. Thank you to my husband, Charles Howard, Jr.

This is the tenth novel that Jean Karl, my wonderful editor, has midwifed. Thank you, Jean, for being there at each birth.

Finally, thanks to my Kalamazoo writers' group, who have laughed and cried with me through every word.

NOTE TO THE READER

By the summer of 1940, war had reached France. Hitler's invading army had been victorious, and the country was divided into two zones, the "Occupied Zone," in which the German army governed, and the "Unoccupied Zone," in which a cooperative French government was allowed limited authority. The Unoccupied Zone in the south was overcrowded with refugees, both French and from other countries, who were fleeing Hitler's army and desperate to get out of France. Starvation was spreading; foreigners, including those who had lived in France for many years, were being forced into refugee camps; the deportation to concentration camps of Jews and others the Germans considered "undesirables" had begun.

In this atmosphere, an heroic American woman, Martha Sharp, helped to conceive and carry out a daring plan to rescue from France as many children as possible and take them to the safety of the United States, in much the same way as British children were being evacuated to Canada for the duration of the war. Working under the auspices of the Unitarian Service Committee and the United States Committee for the Care of European Children, Mrs. Sharp and her co-workers hoped that their "Child Emigration Project" would be the first of many groups of children to be taken to safety. It turned out, however, to be the only such group to successfully escape from France.

The group consisted of twenty-seven children and ten adults. The children were American, French, Russian, Austrian, German, and Czechoslovakian. They were Protestants, Catholics, Russian Orthodox, and Jews. They ranged in age from three to sixteen, both boys and girls.

In this fictionalized account of their journey, I have used only the real names of the adults in the party. Bertrand Cole and Zina Sarach are imaginary characters. They were not among the children Mrs. Sharp took to safety. But they might have been.

The PURSUIT of LOVE

BOOKS BY IRVING SINGER

The Pursuit of Love

Meaning in Life: The Creation of Value

The Nature of Love
1. Plato to Luther
2. Courtly and Romantic
3. The Modern World

Mozart and Beethoven: The Concept of Love in Their Operas

The Goals of Human Sexuality

Santayana's Aesthetics

Essays in Literary Criticism by George Santayana (Editor)

The PURSUIT of LOVE

Irving Singer

THE JOHNS HOPKINS UNIVERSITY PRESS
BALTIMORE AND LONDON

Printed in the United States of America on acid-free paper

The Johns Hopkins University Press
2715 North Charles Street
Baltimore, Maryland 21218-4319
The Johns Hopkins Press Ltd., London

Library of Congress Cataloging-in-Publication Data will be found
at the end of this book.

A catalog record for this book is available from the British Library.

To My Father,
Who Knew the Meaning of Love

Contents

Preface

Wittgenstein was mistaken when he said that philosophy leaves everything as it is. He meant to identify philosophy with analytical maneuvers that enable us to solve cognitive puzzles rather than problems about how to live. He was probably reacting against Marx's insistence that philosophy should lead us to change the world instead of merely telling us what it is. At the same time Wittgenstein and Marx were both greatly interested in basic questions about human values and the search for life's meaning. Wittgenstein felt a kinship to religious writers such as Kierkegaard and Tolstoy, and his philosophic work always presupposed a mystical outlook he considered fundamental even though it defied articulation in language. What could not be said could be shown in expressive gestures, in art, and in moral acts. For his part, Marx remained faithful to his Hegelian origins insofar as he believed that the changes philosophy induces must be predicated upon truths about the nature of man's existence as a nonrational as well as rational being.

What Wittgenstein and Marx both neglected is the way in which philosophy is itself a changing of the world. Each new venture in philosophy is not only a refraction or redirection of what previous thinkers have asserted but also a contribution to the intellectual and emotional equipment human beings need in order to create meaningful lives for themselves. Ideas evolve just as morphological structure or behavior does. Concepts that are not useful will not survive, except in the memory of antiquarians. A philosophy that lives on is one that affects, however indirectly, the imaginative efforts of people at some moment of history who are groping to make sense of the realities to which they are subject.

Needless to say, the consequences of philosophy may be very different from anything the philosopher himself could have foreseen. That is in the nature of creativity, as the God of the Old Testament learns when he realizes how corrupt his progeny have become and then decides to destroy almost all of them in the flood. If it is viable, a new way of doing philosophy originates a vital impetus that can alter what human beings recognize as their world. But it cannot control the ends to which it will be put, just as it cannot know in advance whether others will cherish or discard it. Even at its best, it merely offers future men and women an enlarged capacity to create their own meaning in life. They are free to treat it as they wish.

For this reason, no philosophy can provide a final solution to problems about meaning and value. Philosophy may nevertheless serve as conceptual art, as an artifact of the imagination that can elicit and fructify creative responses in other people. However incomplete, each effort encourages the human spirit to confront the mysteries that permeate existence. Writers such as Camus have likened man's search for meaning to Sisyphus' punishment in having to push boulders endlessly up a mountain, only to watch them roll back down again. A more accurate account of our condition occurs in the experience of Penelope, the heroine of Homer's *Odyssey*. She reveals how the imagination operates both in constructing human problems and in coping with them.

In Homer's tale, Penelope must find a means of temporizing while Odysseus is abroad. He has been at the Trojan wars for ten years. The nobles in Ithaca want her, as the queen, to choose another consort from among themselves. In order to fend them off in a tranquillizing manner while also being true to the husband who is ever-present in her thoughts and whom she awaits with unrelenting hope, Penelope promises to marry one of the suitors whenever she finishes a tapestry she is weaving. She works at it during the day, but secretly at night she unravels its intricate design and thereby gives Odysseus more time to make his appearance.

What is Odysseus to Penelope after ten years of absence? Not just a husband, but also an imagined object of her love in relation to whom she defines her worth, her respectability, her ideal state as a woman. Remaining his devoted wife as she does, she gives meaning to her existence. The ongoing tapestry symbolizes the continuance of her marriage and the fact that its integrity depends not only on Odysseus's return but also on her constant anticipation of it.

In the process of making and unmaking, of weaving and reweaving, we may see the normal workings of imagination. Human beings regularly fabricate artful and sometimes fanciful behavior as part of a quest, which is native to our species, for meaningful life. By undoing what it has fashioned with such elaborate care, the imagination employs creative tropes that revise and sometimes reject responses that were previously valued but are now considered outdated or uninteresting. Once Odysseus does come back, he and Penelope must still spend that first long night together sorting out the pieces of their less than perfect marriage. Having done so, they can then build a new relation that takes them beyond their old one.

In some respects everyone's life experience resembles the climbing of a tree. Whether or not our species can be said to have progressed as time passes, we possess the ability in each moment to explore different branches at our present elevation. Having preferred one or another branch, however, we are forced to choose among alternatives that are then within our grasp. It is always difficult to go backward, and possibilities that we neglected usually become unreachable. This fact of life involves freedom, not merely constraint in the choices we can make. It can even be beneficial. Anxieties we might have had as younger persons with seemingly endless prospects for personal development disappear once we need not make the hard decisions that formerly imposed themselves. Many branches that could have beguiled us will no longer necessitate burdensome deliberation if we know that some earlier choice has taken us to a point of no return.

In life—and above all, in the pursuit of love—there may always be new vistas at hand, and therefore new opportunities for the imagination. But they become fewer as we move closer to the top of the tree. Each further branch demands an increasingly uncertain adjustment, and eventually we reach the limit to how far we can go as just the creatures that we are. The search for love as the framework of a meaningful life may nevertheless continue unabated. For most of us, it is a preoccupation that we never outgrow.

In *Meaning in Life: The Creation of Value* I recommended a naturalist perspective on meaning and value, but I did little to clarify various relevant concepts—among them, the concept of love. I had previously published several works on love and sexuality, and I had no desire to summarize their contents. Nor does this book make that attempt. Instead it approaches love from the point of view of meaning and seeks to develop ideas about love as well as meaning in ways that were not apparent to me before. Though I try to profit from material in my trilogy *The Nature of Love*, the present book is written for readers who may have no acquaintance with it.

The Nature of Love was mainly a historical and critical investigation, including analyses of my own but subordinating them to the study of major developments in philosophy and literature from the Greeks to the twentieth century. The current book takes a different approach. It is an extended essay that uses historical references mainly to locate the different issues I discuss and either to remind learned readers about pertinent details or else to provide people who do not know these details with information that will enable them to follow my line of thought. Some of my insights may interest specialists in the history of ideas, but a thorough examination of texts would have been a distraction and is deliberately avoided.

In this book I attempt to provide the reader with a systematic "mapping" of the concept of love. Each chapter lays down a blueprint for charting one or more regions within its domain. The chapter entitled "Love in Society," for instance, deals with different types of love relationships starting with self-love and continuing through parental love, filial love, peer and friendship love, love of one's clan or group or nation, and then ending with love of humanity. In other chapters I discuss the nature of sexual love, married love, and religious love. I analyze each type into components that can help us to understand it. Sexual love I divide into distinct though often overlapping elements that I call the libidinal, the erotic, and the romantic; religious love I study in relation to theological concepts as well as to my ideas about "the love of life." In earlier chapters I distinguish among the love of things, the love of persons, and the love of ideals; between wanting to love and wanting to be loved; and between love as merging and love as acceptance of another's indefeasible uniqueness. In the last two chapters I consider a variety of other issues: the attempt by several thinkers to differentiate between passion and reason, love and civilization, animal and human love. Finally, I suggest a unified theory that draws together the multiple strands within the book as a whole.

In mapping out this diversity of conceptual elements, I write as a humanistic philosopher. I employ literary examples, insights about human nature, and speculative intuitions that may induce further research. As an essay in the theory of love, the present book does not offer counseling or even definitive conclusions. Instead it seeks to provoke thought in the reader, to open new areas for investigation, and to sketch a panoramic view that others may use in their own search for affective as well as cognitive significance.

As in all my writing, *The Pursuit of Love* argues for a pluralist and "self-realizationist" approach. In the reflections that follow, I will try to carry the discussion into areas that modern philosophy has often ignored. There is no telling what we may find. But then, as Stendhal said about *l'imprévu* (the unforeseen), that is what makes life worth living—assuming that we are able to respond creatively.

I am indebted to many people who helped and encouraged me in the writing of this book: Adam Bellow; Herbert Engelhardt; David Goicoechea, and the other participants in a symposium on my love trilogy that was held at Brock University; Jean H. Hagstrum; Eric Halpern; Marvin Kohl; Richard A. Macksey; Timothy J. Madigan; my friends and students at MIT; Arnold H. Modell; participants at a symposium on love at the National Humanities Center, where I read some pages of an early draft; Cándido Pérez Gállego, and his colleagues at the University of Madrid; David Seinfeld; Stephanie D. Smith; Alan Soble; Robert C. Solomon; Richard Wilbur; and the loving members of my family.

I. S.

The PURSUIT of LOVE

Introduction

LOVE & MEANING

In the 1940s and 50s the Kinsey Reports revealed a great deal about American attitudes toward sexuality. Let us imagine that there existed today an Alfred Kinsey of the soul, an investigator who would send out questionnaires about attitudes toward the meaning in or of life. Let us imagine further that he has access to all people now on earth. If such an enterprising scientist were to ask what makes life worth living, a large percentage of his respondents would say it is the experience of love. In the West, that has been a standard belief for well over two thousand years. For better or for worse, it is a belief that has engendered great religions and infused every branch of civilization and of art.

The ideology of love has colonized all parts of the globe. Eastern as well as Western societies have felt its influence. For many people, love embodies the highest ideal that humanity can aspire toward, while also signifying the deepest reality that pervades our being. With this as an article of faith, it is not surprising that the word is used so loosely in everyday language. Sometimes it refers to powerful sexual desire, sometimes to religious or cosmic exhilaration, sometimes to faithful oneness within human relations—just to mention three of the more common uses that belong to the semantic ambiguity of the term.

In the book that preceded this one, I mentioned love as a prime contributor to meaning in life. For a person in love, I remarked, life is never without meaning. The beloved matters supremely to him or her, even if nothing else does. In saying this much, however, I was limiting the argument unnecessarily; I was not extending it as far as it can go. I now see how my reflections about meaningfulness enable me to approach the nature of love in a more radical fashion. For love is not merely a contributor—one among others—to meaningful life. In its own way it may underlie all other forms of meaning. In this book I explore the possibility that by its very nature love is the principal means by which creatures like us seek affective relations to persons, things, or ideals that have value and importance for us. Seen from this perspective, meaning in life is the pursuit of love, circuitous and even thwarted as that can often be.

If we approach love in this fashion, we may possibly resolve some of the thorny controversies that have bedeviled thinkers in the past. For instance, consider the question of whether love is or is not reducible to a need to be loved. Freud, Proust, Sartre, and many others before them have assumed that all love is really a device for getting someone else to give us a love that we desire. From this it would follow that love is just a search for goods one values because of their potential utility to oneself. This is what I have called a merely appraisive attitude. Through appraisal others matter to us and affect our emotions because of benefits we hope to derive from association with them. Philosophers who are unwilling to reduce love to appraisiveness criticize theories that do so by pointing to the human ability, whether innate or learned, to care about the welfare of other people regardless of the effect upon oneself. The concept of bestowal that I introduced in *The Nature of Love* trilogy is my attempt to understand this further capacity. Insofar as love is bestowal, it creates a kind of value in the beloved that goes beyond appraisal. In loving another, in attending to and delighting in that person, we *make* him or her valuable in a way that would not otherwise exist. To that extent, love is more than just a desire to be loved.

Defining human love as both appraisal and bestowal, I sought to effect a synthesis of earlier philosophies. With the tools I was employing, however, I did not (could not) explain why men and women take love as seriously as they do, why they prize it so highly and even devote their lives to it, as many have thought they should. I thereby ignored various difficult questions that are quite fundamental: Why does anyone bother about love? Is it worth cultivating? Is it really essential for the living of a good life? If so, toward whom or what must it be directed? How does it give meaning to one's life, and why should meaning be considered central to its definition? All of these questions are relevant to the problem about whether love is or is not merely a desire to be loved.

When psychologists first suggested, earlier in this century, that all people have a need to be loved, their hypothesis had an enormous impact upon the study of human motivation. Previously the experts had believed that men and women were born with needs for food, drink, warmth, possibly sex—in general, bodily goods for which there was some physiological explanation. To say that human beings have a need either to love or be loved had always seemed too "philosophical," too greatly dependent on nonverifiable and possibly mystical assumptions that scientists in the modern world were determined to avoid. But shortly after the Second World War, evidence about orphaned and institutionalized infants tended to indicate that Freud was probably right when he intimated that people need to receive love as they also need to be fed and protected from freezing temperatures. Some investigators preferred to explain this particular need in terms of other variables, such as a need to be touched or cuddled; and many refused to identify it as an instinct. Within the psychiatric tradition, however, post-Freudians developed sophisticated and convincing ideas about a structural process through which individuals attain not only a talent for getting love but also the ability to give it.

One group of theorists, led by Melanie Klein, claimed that the need to love and the need to be loved are mutually interactive: these needs arise and evolve through a development between themselves. Even if this is true, however, we still must ask why either need occurs. It is not enough to say that organisms such as ours could not survive without a great deal of careful nurturing during the early months of life. Though humans, compared to other animals, are dependent on caretakers for a disproportionately long period of their lifespan, this alone would not explain why they search for love as often and pervasively as they do from the beginning to the end of their existence.

Perhaps we are dealing with an ultimate fact about our species: human nature simply is that way; people are so constituted that they generally experience a need to love and be loved throughout their lives. One might also say that the extraordinary degree of early dependency conduces to so great a need to be loved that it can be satisfied only imperfectly during childhood, and that this relative failure or incompletion causes the need to persist throughout maturity. In our first years we get into the habit of wanting to be loved, which then perpetuates itself. Eventually it becomes enmeshed with social interests, the sex drive, intimations about our mortality, and so forth.

Though this reasoning may plausibly account for the need to be loved, it does not clarify either the need to love or the process through which the two needs are able to achieve their great importance. Our entire existence is characterized by the creation of meaning. Implicit in the need to be loved is the need to have a meaningful relationship with persons that matter to us. For an infant this would naturally be the parent who protects and nurtures it. We may even imagine the neonate feeling not only that it is loved by the breast that places food in its mouth but also that it is then at home in its proper and meaningful environment. The infant is incapable of realizing that such objects cannot love, but it bestows great value upon the breast and (to some extent) upon the person who offers this source of nourishment. In making its primitive bestowal, the infant may already manifest a need to love. Whether or not all later efforts to find meaning through one or another form of love can be traced back to this initial bond, it reveals a fundamental pattern that continues throughout human development as a whole.

The need to be loved could not be satisfied unless there was someone else who had the ability to give whatever love is needed. The infant is unlikely to establish a meaningful relationship or ever learn to love unless its caretakers are willing to offer the love it requires. They must provide love on some occasions at least, and usually many. In doing so, they create a meaningful response to the child's needs while also enabling the child to find and create meaning in its own way. The possibility of interpersonal love, which occurs at both ends of the relationship, depends on the strength and endurance of the meanings that issue from this process. The meaningful tie between mother and child is determined by the fact that each participant offers love while also wanting to be loved, usually by the recipient of its own love. The giving of love occurs with such frequency and regularity as to manifest a need to love, over and above the need to be loved. Under optimal conditions, there results in both persons a reciprocating love, either as an expression of delight and primal gratitude or else as a more effective means of securing the other's love.

The human quest for meaning is therefore interwoven with both the need to love and the need to be loved. It shows itself as a *need-to-love-and-be-loved.* Consider the behavior of Shakespeare's Romeo and Juliet when they establish, jointly and individually, their love for one another. They create the love between them as a means of resolving adolescent difficulties they previously faced; it then requires, and also justifies, their persistent struggle against an environment that is no longer meaningful to them; it leads them into purposive activities directed toward gratifications they could not have had otherwise. So powerful is the fabric of meaning which constitutes the love between Romeo and Juliet that it minimizes the importance of everything else they care about. That is the basis of their tragedy. While presenting its poignant drama, even Shakespeare is not certain that the value in this pursuit of love justifies the calamities to which it leads. But he is willing to further its mythology because he intuits that the network of meaning that it fosters reveals what he elsewhere calls "the nobleness of life."

These words are used by Antony to characterize his love for Cleopatra. For those two, as for Romeo and Juliet, love means more than all the rest of life.

❄

In studying the need to be loved in relation to the need to love, both involving a typically human mode of making life meaningful, we should avoid the tendency to think that either need is more fundamental than the other. Traditional religions and moralities have often insisted that in matters of love it is better to give than to receive. Above all in Christian dogma, God's essence is portrayed as an endless giving of love designated by the term *agapē*. That refers to a purified love that bestows goodness indiscriminately. It is the outpouring of an infinite power to love regardless of merit in the recipient. It resembles the gentle rain that drops, as Portia says in *The Merchant of Venice*, "from heaven / Upon the place beneath." Though different thinkers within the Christian tradition disagreed about man's ability to emulate agapastic love, it was generally accepted as that which defines what love is in itself and at its best.

A similar dogma pervades the philosophy of nonreligious writers who believe that the giving of love manifests a dimension of moral aptitude that is preferable to our innate need to be loved. A recent psychiatrist states: "To many, receiving love effortlessly, as a child does—undeserved love, unearned love—is the glorious ideal. It is my contention that it is a less nourishing and less profound experience than the often painful and arduous experience of supplying the love."[1]

What can justify giving precedence, in this fashion, to loving rather than being loved? Why should any naturalistic or empirically-minded theorists defend this doctrine? They have no reason to preserve the views of orthodox religion, and the nature of "profound experience" is not self-evident. I think this conception, which is not uncommon, results from the belief that *growth* is an underlying ultimate in human nature. And certainly we may say that the ability to love is something we grow into. Even if people are born with that capacity, and with that need, it does not clearly show itself until much has happened in individual development. As opposed to the desire to be loved, the giving of love requires a discernible period of psychological growth. The need to be loved is evident at birth. The need to love, like locomotion or the effort to explore, appears only after we have done some growing.

Human experience is filled with various patterns of growth. We grow into sexual maturity; we grow into being adults; we grow into persons who can take on parental responsibilities; we grow into professionals who are able to exploit our various talents; we may even grow into elderly men and women who feel we have learned something from our many years of living. It is understandable, therefore, that the capacity to love, which flourishes through a development beyond the mere need to be loved, should be treated as an example of growth displaying a more essential need.

This mode of thinking is nevertheless unsatisfying. Its emphasis upon a teleological end or destination prevents it from appreciating the immediacy of life. Though our experience is not limited to any moment in time, none of which is meaningful to us apart from its relation to the past and the future, what exists in the present retains a kind of reality that the past has already lost and that the future has not yet reached. If we are concerned with what is "nourishing and . . . profound" in an experience, we must consider not only growth but also what is important to the individual who is having that experience *in the present.* Some eventual capacity to love is irrelevant to the infant who is aware of little more than the need to be loved by a caretaker on whom it depends for its mere survival. For an infant the goodness in life means getting the love it needs in order to live. If a child develops no further, as happens with those who die soon after birth, we might sense a tragedy in this thwarting of a natural potentiality for growth. But in itself the infant's experience is just as real and important as the adulthood it may some day achieve. The same applies to all the other stages through which we pass.

In each phase of life, we feel the plenitude in being what we are at that particular time. The intellect can direct us toward deferred possibilities of fulfillment, as a student may submit to the necessity of attending school in the hope of acquiring skills he can use at some later date in the world outside. But in making such projections about eventual growth, the intellect operates as part of an experiential totality that occurs in the present. We speak of "changing" our present condition, and in a sense we do so whenever we sacrifice or alter current interests and desires. But in the process we only substitute a *new* present. Saying that growth indicates what is primary in our being can therefore deflect us from the fact that each moment retains its own inclusive identity. Growth belongs to human nature only as one among other components.

Instead of treating either the need to love or the need to be loved as a preferential entry into the nature of love, we require pluralistic analyses that will clarify love's vast diversity. In being a device by which we make our lives meaningful, love expresses our innate creativity. But we are creative in many different ways. Reductivist methodologies ignore the variegated character of our experience. They impose cognitive constraints considered essential for scientific or quasi-scientific understanding. I am convinced this tactic cannot work. It is not true to what we are.

In saying this, I also have in mind psychoanalytic thinkers who cling to Freud's dictum that "the finding of an object is in fact a refinding of it." A recent follower of Freud calls this his "most profound contribution to love."[2] To claim, however, that all finding is merely refinding ignores the newness of each moment as it is lived. Not only is it undeducible in relation to prior occurrences, as Hume recognized, but also it is stained with an iridescence of its own. Throughout his life a man may have sought the company of buxom and motherly women with whom he could be intimate. Having studied the teachings of the Freudians, he may be willing to believe that this particular interest pertains to his having had a mother who suckled him for many months. Yet the details of his former association are largely unknowable and overtly, at least, they do not enter into the phenomenology of his present experience. Even if therapeutic sessions revivified some of the relevant past, they could never signify that what he now feels as an adult is just a refinding of what occurred before.

Of course Freud need not be interpreted as meaning that all finding is *nothing but* refinding. He may only have thought that, in addition to whatever else it is, each finding includes a refinding. But even this moderate interpretation, which many of his adherents have rejected as insufficiently penetrating, is too extreme. In order to link a man's interest in motherly women to his earliest mode of getting nourishment, one would need exhaustive information about his infancy as well as thorough knowledge about the way in which succeeding stages exert a causal influence on his present sensibility. Such information and such knowledge have never been provided by any scientific study. Even the most extensive psychoanalytic investigations no longer claim to have the requisite completeness.[3]

The most we can say, therefore, is that past events have some effect upon the future and that the present reflects, in one fashion or another, much of what happened in the previous experience of every human being. This may encourage us to delve into an individual's past as psychiatrists are able to do, often with considerable expertise. The enterprise can be extremely useful. But what psychiatrists or their patients unearth (to use a word that is reminiscent of Freud's archaeological metaphor) is a creative disposition to link past and present synthetically. Far from being a literal refinding, what appears is usually a reconstruction. It is an artifact of one's current imagination. Not only is it largely new to consciousness, but also it results from an ongoing effort to make both past and present meaningful in terms of each other. Some of the "findings," if that is the right word for these novel explorations, may be reducible to refindings, but there is no way of knowing how much.

We misrepresent the character of an experience, including the experience of psychotherapy, if we think of the past as a reservoir of objects or events that are capable of enduring in the present like bricks mortared into a wall. The past does endure, but what it was in its own present cannot persist intact. Its universe has disappeared even though elements survive through infinite refractions and modulations that now comprise the present moment. There is metaphoric truth in the belief, held by some religious thinkers, that God creates the world continuously. Human experience, like life in general, is always re-creating itself. That is what enables it to survive the incessant dying of actualities that slip into the non-existence we call the past. What remains in time is only a trace or partial residue—that much of the past that has transformed itself into the present. The refound object Freud was seeking will always turn out to be something that is still active in us but it will have been totally reconstituted, like the molecules of a meal we have eaten. To that extent, however, its meaning must always be found in the life we are now living.

The conception I am proposing can help to explain relationships of love that Freud's mechanistic approach misrepresented. His ideas about transference love, for instance, assume that the patient's fixation on the therapist echoes or even duplicates the child's dependence on a parent whose love it desperately needed. Correctly understood, this is surely true. But Freud also discovered, or surmised, that reports about childhood experiences are often unreliable, even fictional. Patients dramatize and sometimes invent stories about their past. To that extent, however, the relationship with a therapist does not reinstate previous events. What unites the two clusters of experience, and enables the later one to be efficacious, is the attempt to establish a meaningful pattern in one's life. Parent and therapist are alike in being authorities. The patient treats them as persons whose love matters greatly to him. He will therefore do and believe whatever is needed to get that love. The refound content represents this endeavor to make oneself lovable in the present as well as the past. In part at least, its meaning must always manifest that creative effort. The patient's search for love may therefore be more important in the therapeutic situation than anything that is either found or refound.

Transference love is rightly called love because it involves so great a bestowal of value upon another person. But it cannot transfer upon that person exactly the same love that was bestowed upon a parent. Since the fabulous accounts, the distorted memories, the outright lies that patients tell—together with their accurate reminiscences—are all part of a meaning in life they are now bringing into being, the therapist can only resemble the parent as one who may possibly abet this creation of meaning. Parent and therapist provide an interpersonal setting in which it can happen. Painful though it may sometimes be, the therapeutic session is like an artistic performance. In the presence of someone he cares about, the patient uses his imagination to make a meaningful presentation of the world as he knows it. If he succeeds, which usually means confronting truths about himself, his achievement may have meaning throughout his life.

However much or little he interacts with the patient, helping him to probe the actual source and nature of his distress, the therapist is also an audience. Even when the patient loves the therapist, as some actors love the audiences for which they perform, this love cannot be fully interpersonal. The patient, like the artist on stage, is seeking approval from someone he cannot know intimately. Such love can be very strong, and therefore comparable to the love for parents. In infancy the audience consists of only the one or two caretakers, which gives the relationship its special intensity. This focusing of attention is repeated when the patient's performance is experienced only by the therapist. On both occasions love creates its multiple meanings through the bestowing and appraising of value, a process that is imaginative, emotional, and felt to have immediate urgency in one's present life.[4]

The distinction between bestowal and appraisal will concern us in a later chapter. Here I need only emphasize that studying love as an attempt to create meaningful lives for ourselves adds a further dimension to those concepts. I realized this several years ago when a friend gave me a puzzling eighteenth-century placard constructed like a very primitive hologram. If you look directly at it, you read the word *Liebe*. If you look at it from the left side, the word you see is *Freiheit*. If you look at it from the right side, *Wahrheit* is the word that appears.

My first reaction was that these three—love, freedom, truth—

are not only different but also incompatible. For if we love someone or something, do we not give up the freedom to range through other opportunities? Our bond creates a gamut of obligations that would not have existed if we had remained aloof and possibly carefree or unattached—in the state of *apétie* (indifference) that the Marquis de Sade admired so much. And if we do become involved, bestowing and appraising reciprocally in the reverberating spiral that mutual love creates, we run a risk of deluding ourselves about the relationship. Love is capable of falsifying perceptions and masking what we truly feel, thereby occluding an actual situation in ways that prevent us from obtaining dispassionate truth. We think of wisdom as a kind of seeing, in other words, elucidation at a distance. But love is plausibly represented as a constraining embrace, often with the eyes closed. Liebe would seem to be quite distinct from Wahrheit as well as Freiheit.

I do not wish to repudiate this first reaction of mine. But I also believe that approaching love as an expression of our search for a meaningful life can indicate how love, freedom, and truth are indeed compatible. The oneness that love entails cannot be imposed. Though people describe their experience of falling in love as if it were a bolt from the blue, even this tempestuous event is the outcome of a destiny they have chosen for themselves—as I argue in the next chapter. Those who fall in love may not have *decided* to feel the great excitement aroused in them by their beloved, but they are free to reject it in one manner or another. If they fall in love with someone they know to be unworthy or generally undesirable, it is they who give this person such vast importance. Their love may be a fatality, but they are nevertheless responsible for its existence.

What looks like a seizure from without—the innocent and hapless individual suddenly struck by an arrow from Cupid's bow—may therefore be taken as a manifestation of meaning being created in accordance with whatever needs or desires the lover accepts as paramount at the moment. This bestowal must have had causal antecedents, but it is a response that is freely accepted and gratuitous.

Though it is always accompanied by relevant appraisals, it also goes beyond them.

In the history of philosophy the realist tradition, much to be admired for its ruthless honesty, details the many ways in which love eventuates in a forfeiture of freedom. A perfect love might not do so, but a perfect love does not exist on earth. In establishing the pair-bonding that often belongs to love, one sacrifices many of the freedoms that human beings have always cherished—above all, the freedom to live one's life in blissful unconcern about what matters to someone else. Love can sometimes exact a considerable sacrifice of alternate pleasures. This may be the price we have to pay for attaining meaning through any interpersonal attachment. What we gain in meaningfulness we may lose in the happiness and even joy of doing everything we wish, particularly if we wish to do it with persons other than the one we love.

I recognize this challenge and will attend to it in later pages of this book. The word *freedom* is ambiguous in a manner that warrants examination. The same applies to *truth*. In one sense we are disqualified from understanding what is really happening when we ourselves are involved in an ardent relationship. We cannot stand back from our love experience and study it with detachment. On the other hand, the truths that a detached spectator may be able to discern are also partial. They reflect a lack of intimate involvement. Some truths can only be attained by participation of the sort that love entails. Though we may agree with the disinterested observer once we have fallen out of love, we will have undergone much that he or she did not. If only in the sense of knowledge by acquaintance, a great deal will be known to us that no one else can fully appreciate. This segment of the truth involves the meaning that we have given to our lives in the act of bestowing and appraising value.

These reflections about love as search for meaning may have particular relevance for our times. We are living during a period in which large numbers of people have renounced their faith in love.

Most of the twentieth century has been an awakening from idealistic attitudes induced by nineteenth-century romanticism and predicated upon the belief that human beings can find infinite sexual harmony through romantic love alone. That idea incorporates much that preceded it in the philosophy of love. Like religious dogma in the West, it treats love as an expression of divinity that appears in ordinary existence when life is fully realized and most consummatory. Like courtly love in the Middle Ages, it locates this all-resolving affect in the passionate oneness that a man and woman can achieve through intimacy with one another. In the modern world, romantic love was often thought to be the basis of married love as well as the love for whatever children issued forth. Under these circumstances sexual love would be compatible with the love of one's friends, one's nation, humanity at large, and even the cosmos as a whole. Throughout its many permutations romanticism treated love between the sexes as a primary source of value and of meaning.

This ideal has been discredited in the view of many in the contemporary world who might well have accepted it 150 years ago. Realist thinkers in science and philosophy have attacked romantic love throughout the twentieth century. Affluence in the industrial countries has led millions to believe that the good things in life can be attained through pleasures and activities that do not require the risk or personal involvement that love demands. By the middle of the nineteenth century, romanticism had itself split into optimistic and pessimistic interpretations. The latter, typified by the philosophy of Schopenhauer, maintained that even the most benign romantic love was not conducive to a happy or truly meaningful life.

In this view, which was elaborated by subsequent theorists, love is the great destroyer of freedom as well as truth. It is considered an enslavement to natural processes, notably those required for the preservation of the species, that snares individuals by deluding them with hopes about everlasting happiness and ever-increasing meaning. By now that sophisticated, but possibly cynical, conception has been widely disseminated. It has convinced large numbers of people that romantic love is undesirable, and possibly other types of love

as well. Whether or not they think it is a pervasive fallacy, many assume that love must generally be deceptive. The elderly had often said this in the past. Nowadays the young seem to agree without much experience of their own. Previous generations may have dreamt of a life of love and interpersonal harmony; ours frequently thinks that enlightened men and women must want to escape this needless pathology. Despite romance novels and sentimental movies that are still very popular, the search for love is in danger of being replaced by the avoidance of it.

As a pluralist, I have no interest in telling anyone how to live. But philosophical exploration can help to reveal values and realities that might otherwise remain hidden or misconstrued. By analyzing love as a fundamental source of meaning, we may attain insights that can be used to defend and even strengthen it. At the very least, we should be able to map out its intricate domain.

I

TWO MYTHS ABOUT LOVE

Ideas in the history of philosophy filter into the emotional responses of ordinary men and women. Having developed in a region of the imagination, they then become concepts that humanity *lives* by. They may nevertheless be misleading and harmful—myths in the pejorative sense. In this chapter I focus on two myths that have dominated much of our thinking about love and have sometimes induced chaotic or confused attitudes in the lives of many people.

The first is a myth about the role of love in the universe. So highly has love been prized that entire religions have been constructed about its ineffable attraction. The idealist tradition in particular has regularly maintained that love "makes the world go round." Love is taken as either the explanation for everything existing as it does, God himself *being* love, or else as a causal power in all the mechanisms that comprise the world. In either event, the pursuit of love would account for each of the affective relationships, including the least successful, that belong to the human condition.

The second myth deals with the inner constitution of love, depicting it as merged identity that unifies separate persons or even objects. The two myths are different, but they often buttress each other. For if the cosmos is a single entity, as we may tautologously believe, everything in it might possibly hunger for the closest and most indelible fusion with all the rest, or at least some part of it. That would happen through the merging ascribed to consummate love.

In different ways the first of these myths underlies almost every religious sect in the Western world and, nowadays, many in the East. Realist and antitheological thinkers have also resorted to it. When Freud offered his own, inevitably metaphysical, suggestions about drives that constitute all vital process, he specified love and death as the two basic factors in life. Under death he subsumed not only the cessation of life but also the following: an innate drive to return to a prior material state, a feeling of destructiveness toward anything that thwarts one's life-force, and an aggressive need to oppose the restraints and countervailing attainments of civilization.

Analyzing love as the opponent of death, Freud drew upon an equally scattered range of meanings. In love, or Eros as he called it, he found not only libidinal drive but also a pervasive impulse that enables human beings to live harmoniously, to construct the amenities of social life, and to further ideals of brotherhood, compassion, and even community with some imagined deity. Freud thought that the drives toward death and toward Eros must always interweave throughout our existence, and he concluded that this, too, was preprogrammed rather than being a merely learned condition. Love and death were the supreme coordinates that define all animate nature.

Without examining this notion at any length, we may recognize it as a principal tenet within a system of beliefs that had been molding for almost two hundred years. Freud's suggestions in this area reflect the theories of philosophy that evolved throughout the nineteenth century as a product of German romanticism. That world view arose from the experience of sensitive individuals in a particular part of Europe who drew upon social traditions that were meaningful to themselves. One might therefore argue that what they call love is mainly an artifact of their culture and neither innate nor universal in our species.

If this is true, we in the modern world are subject to a fundamental error. We tend to think that love is basic to us as human beings, and we may even assign it the metaphysical role that Freud (or, in its own way, Christianity) does. But in actuality, we would only be manifesting the influence of a doctrine that belongs to the history of ideas and has no further import.

This way of thinking deflates and possibly defeats the first of the two myths that I mentioned earlier. But in doing so, it formulates an alternative that may be too extreme. I believe that the critics have overstated their case. Though our experience of love is always related to the concepts that we use in our search for it, and though such concepts exist within a cultural milieu that includes the ideology of some particular society, psychological and biological constants transcend each tradition. It would be foolhardy to claim that throughout the course of human development all men and women have had the same motivation. And yet, one can plausibly hold that the need for love is more or less genetically programmed, and that it can and does appear in persons who belong to virtually any culture. At least to this degree, the first of the two myths would not be a fallacy.

But, it will be said, in various societies that anthropologists have studied there exists no idea of love that is equivalent to the one that Westerners take for granted. Even if this evidence is reliable, however, it cannot prove that people in those societies have none of the yearnings or instinctive needs that we generally recognize as indicating a desire for love. These may exist universally, albeit repressed or redirected by social norms that are hostile to them. Love can contribute to what is meaningful in life despite the fact that different cultures interpret the meaning of love itself in different ways and some may try to thwart it by suppressing all relevant concepts.

For that matter, the occurrence of love is not limited to creatures that have a developed concept of it. There is good reason to believe that animals that lack our intellectual powers may also experience love. Though they behave in ways that are different from our own, language being so important in human nature, members of many other species have a capacity for love that is comparable to ours and sometimes superior.

Animal love is usually less imaginative and less creative than human love—which is not to say that animal love is totally deficient in these respects. It is closer to social and nurturant instincts even among domestic pets whose responses have been tamed by their association with human beings. Our kind of love is more cerebral, and more greatly geared to ideals or distant goals. From this we should not infer that human love is inherently spiritual, or ethereal, in any transcendental sense. It emerges from our biological condition just as animal love issues from the natural forces that propel these other organisms. Human nature is complex. Part of it is typically animalistic and part involves the conceptual and innovative capacities that put our species in a class by itself. Though the spectrum of human love may stretch between limiting poles that are vastly different from one another, love as we experience it generally includes variable components of both thought and emotion, ideology and gut reaction, intellect and quasi-instinct.

Though some people may be shocked at my suggesting it, I believe the conceptual, rather than the instinctive or nonconceptual, is the major determinant in love at first sight. To the person who undergoes that violent upheaval, it may seem that deep organic forces have drawn one into an affiliation that no set of concepts could possibly produce. It is as if the stricken individual has been torn loose from the conformities of reason and society that usually control emotional outburst. The same might be said of the phenomenon known as falling in love, which is a semimystical event that can alter one's entire life.

Certainly the act of falling in love, or love at first sight, deviates from less spontaneous and less emotional patterns of response. Nevertheless, these examples of love—at least as we in the West experience them—are dependent on ideational components that our social life has fostered in us. Under the influence of hormonal pressures, some hypothetical savage may lurch in heated lust toward a likely object of gratification. But we do not consider that a case of love at first sight or falling in love. These include mental strands that poets and novelists, historians and philosophers, have artfully woven and infinitely rewoven throughout the patterns of civilized attitudes. The thoughts of those creative men and women pervade our feelings and our ordinary language. We inherit a world outlook from which we cannot detach ourselves completely. In its totality it manifests an erotic imagination that has blossomed over a period of centuries, attaining greater specificity in each person as he or she develops individually. La Rochefoucauld said that some people would never have fallen in love if they had not heard about it. In a sense this is true of everyone.

Many variations can occur from society to society and from one cultural tradition to another. Within its own parameters, each case of falling in love or love at first sight reveals one or another system of affective concepts. When the passionate experience actually occurs, one may feel an abrupt and cataclysmic upheaval in oneself. It has been carefully nurtured, however: the "bolt from the blue" is an explosive product of conceptual forces that have been working toward this event for many years and through devious channels. Without a basis in instinct, the relevant concepts might never have come into existence. But without the appropriate concepts, divergent as they are in different cultures, the biological impulses would never be experienced as the stirrings of love. Falling in love and love at first sight both result from lengthy and extensive preparations within the regions of intellect and imagination as well as emotionality.

I emphasize this point because I wish to argue that, even in these extraordinary occurrences, all love takes time to develop. It is never something that just *happens*. It is an outcome of much that has already happened. Even Stendhal, that wise and brilliant Romantic, recognized that "passion love" cannot exist without a period of crystallization. In general, love is an achievement, an attainment, a formation of positive and purposeful adjustments that have been evolving in the individual for quite a while and will continue to do so. The phrase *I love you* expresses, whether truthfully or otherwise, both an accomplished desire and an ongoing willingness to enter into whatever behavior will be necessary for love to survive and to flourish. The words signify much more than the fervent but possibly momentary feeling that may be venting itself by means of them.

We have been systematically misled by fables that present love as a kind of sudden magic. Think of *Turandot*, the opera by Puccini based on the play by Carlo Gozzi. In the first act, the wandering prince Calaf observes the beheading of a suitor who failed to answer Turandot's riddles. She is the emperor's daughter and very desirable, but she is also cruel and unrelenting in her hatred of men. Calaf has every reason not to risk his life in pursuit of her hand: her riddles may be unanswerable, and despite her beauty she would seem to be a monster. Calaf is nonetheless carried away by love that smites him after he sees her for the first time. He feels that life without her would be unbearable. He is reconciled to dying if his perilous quest ends in failure. When he strikes the great gong at the end of Act 1, announcing his desire to compete, he can no longer control himself; it is as if he were indeed under a magic spell.

We in the audience accept this as the markings of love, and it makes for exciting opera. It is a fantasy that enlivens our imagination and lends itself to intensely emotional music. But though the fictional representation may have aesthetic validity, its truthfulness resides in a condensation and reconstitution of reality. We would get closer to the psychological facts if Calaf confessed—as it were, to his analyst—that the concept of manliness with which he was reared requires him to undertake desperate adventures such as this, to challenge women who are domineering and appear to be unconquerable, to prove his superiority over lesser males, to supplant the emperor as a father figure whose power and possessions he can acquire by marrying into the ruling family, and so on.

We may possibly trace some of these motivations to biological imperatives in all males. At the same time, they affect Calaf as they do because he belongs to a developmental history of ideas that infuses his feverish adoration in the manner of Western romanticism. Even if we ascribe his love of Turandot to his wanting to confront retroactively the hostile and loveless mother that he may have had, there are other ways in which he could have satisfied that need. Calaf's actual response derives from the culture in which the opera originates—its fashionable concepts, its ideologies, its governing types of imagination. None of that came into existence all at once. It is a human syndrome that took centuries to be constructed, and for those of us in the modern world who have been formed by it, its affective reality renews and enlarges itself through gradual accretions within our own being.

Should we therefore conclude that the first of the two myths is a fallacy? If the characteristic examples of love that we have mentioned are largely products of our cultural inheritance, how can they reveal an ultimate force that explains existence and makes the world go round? Even among human beings, there would seem to be no preordained mode of response that shows forth a universal striving for love. How could one claim that anything of the sort inheres in reality as a whole?

It would indeed be perilous to make that assertion. We human beings have a tendency to project upon the universe whatever our ideals and strongest yearnings urge us toward. At the same time, our emotional demands are also part of reality. Although the need for love has no unitary essence and appears in different array throughout the diversity of varied cultures, it may be present in all human beings. As I have suggested, a family resemblance to it can be detected in other species as well.

The belief that something comparable occurs in the cosmos at large is a nonverifiable extrapolation. That is why such views are scorned by most scientists and find a haven in religious faith. In an obvious sense, the evidence does not support them. But these ideas may nevertheless be highly meaningful as an insight into the nature of human affect. If we experience a need to love, we may possibly feel that the same is true for many other creatures. We may even think that our mutual craving has metaphysical import. Nietzsche remarked that "all desire wishes for eternity . . . deep, deep eternity." To discard these intimations entirely, to assert that they are merely expressions of a beguiling fallacy, is to substitute a different faith. We are free to do so, and perhaps we should. But we are not necessarily mistaken if we do not.

❄

Later in this book I will return to the idea that even in its earlier stages love is something that takes time to develop and does not merely happen. But here I wish to consider the second of the two myths. It appears most vividly in a fable that recurs throughout countless works of philosophy and literature, pervading in fact the mentality of all civilized people. Plato's *Symposium* presents the fable in the famous speech of Aristophanes. Plato there suggests the notion that love consists in a search for union with one's alter ego. Not only does the lover want to be reunited with his "other half," the other part of himself, from which he has been split off but also, Aristophanes says, the desired condition is a state in which the different individuals are merged or fused with one another.

Plato himself transmutes the principle of reunion through merging into a conception of the supreme philosopher imbued and at-one with the ultimate form of goodness—which is to say, the highest ideal and the basic reality within the universe. Christian mystics would later use this idea to support their belief that love of God culminates in the return to him through a total merging with him.

Throughout the centuries the concept of love as merging has been a fundamental theme that lends itself to many variations. It occurs in Descartes' assertion that love between the sexes is inherently the desire to create a homogeneous union with which each participant can identify him- or herself. Belief in the feasibility of merging underlies all romanticism and most idealist philosophies in the nineteenth century. It explains their adoration of "organic unity" in love of every sort.

The scholarly world would be greatly enriched by a detailed and systematic history of the idea of merging. At present I wish to concentrate upon recent claims that love involves at least a *search* for it. This view, which occurs in Sartre's later writings, is fully formulated in two books by Robert C. Solomon. Beginning with the persuasive suggestion that love is a means by which one chooses one's self, that is to say, the self one wants to be, Solomon goes on to define love as the willed creation of what he calls a "shared identity." Solomon argues that love is the creation of a new entity, a new self. He takes this to mean that love craves the "merging of selves." He claims that the merged condition for which love strives is "a *shared self*, a self mutually defined and possessed by two people."[1]

Though Solomon is talking primarily of romantic love, he often sounds as if his definition applies to every other kind of love as well. Presumably, they are all ways of searching for a shared self. At this point it may be useful to consider what William James says about the self in *The Principles of Psychology*. The self, he tells us, is "the sum total of all that [an individual] can call his, not only his body and his psychic powers, but his clothes and his house, his wife and children, his ancestors and friends, his reputation and works, his lands and horses, and yacht and bank-account."[2]

Starting with this as a working (though outmoded) definition of self, I can easily imagine how different persons might establish a loving relationship that includes partial sharing of their selves—that is, a sharing of some of the components in their different selves. I tried to indicate the nature of that oneness in the final chapter of my trilogy, and Solomon also describes the condition in various places in both of his books. But I disagree with his further assertion that lovers always want a literal merging of their selves. Nor do I see any reason to think that their desired union is describable as a *new self*. They may freely give each other access to their own selves, but that is different from trying to create a supervening "shared self."

Lovers normally engage in what I refer to as a "sharing of selves." This happens when they share various manifestations of themselves—lands, horses, yachts, bank accounts, as well as their ideas, feelings, reciprocal desires, and joint aspirations. The personal community that their love fashions for them is indeed a new reality, but it is not a new self in which the old selves completely lose their different identities.

Solomon modulates his conception of love, as Sartre did before him, by insisting that the yearning for total merging is counteracted by the lovers' simultaneous desire to retain their independent identity, the separate and autonomous selfhood that each of them has. According to Sartre and Solomon, love always involves a tension between these two archetypal but contrary inclinations. Both philosophers insist that the very nature of man's affective being requires conflicting opposition of this sort.

That seems to me the point at which their analysis goes astray. There can be the necessary conflict they specify only if love invariably includes a quest for merging. But while some people do wish to fuse with one or another person, and Shelley's love of nature even leads him to implore the West Wind to "be thou me, impetuous one," this is not an ineluctable or universal attitude definitive of love.

I think that Sartre and Solomon, to say nothing of the great romanticist tradition upon which they seem to rely, have been misled by a reification that often occurs when philosophers use terms like *oneness* or *union*. Instead of taking these words to imply an actual merging, our understanding of the relationships that love usually seeks would be furthered, I believe, if we directed our attention to events such as the following: the pursuit of common interests, the harmonious interaction between people who see themselves as separate individuals, the wedding of distinct personalities in mutual experiences that matter to each, the formation of beneficial interdependence. These are all different from the making of a merged self. They signify variable ways in which a sharing between separate selves can occur among human beings. The unity that joins lovers may be designated as a kind of oneness, as when we say that a married couple make one unit in society. The Bible even calls husband and wife "one flesh." Such oneness is not, however, a merging.[3]

Like a joint bank account, love has an identity, but only as something that people experience without losing their own identities. The life that lovers have together creates values that are available to these individuals in the most intimate and important aspects of their existence—the casual spending of time with one another, the enjoying of each other's presence, the desire to give and receive pleasure, the exchange of judgments and impressions, the reaching of decisions that affect them both, the cooperative struggle for goals they care about, the rearing of a family as a combined expression of themselves, the participation in a society to which they each contribute, the feeling on various occasions of reciprocal excitement, joy, or sorrow.

In each situation there will be separate perspectives within the totality that love establishes. The lovers may be united in facing a problem together, but their responses to it can differ vastly. Even unanimity is never tantamount to "shared identity." Far from being a prerequisite, that would make love impossible—which may explain why Sartre's views on the subject (though not Solomon's) are generally so pessimistic.

In choosing their particular type of relationship, lovers may often seek the interdependence to which I referred. Solomon and Sartre find love paradoxical because they think the merging in love involves submissive dependence on another person that inevitably undermines the autonomy each lover also wants. But if we substitute the concept of *inter*dependence, this paradox evaporates. When the participants are interdependent, they each accept the other as a separate and autonomous person whose own self-interests are equally important and worthy of respect. Neither of them sacrifices him- or herself, and each is strengthened by the independence of the other. The result can be a joint and mutually rewarding recognition of their individual autonomy.

Interdependence implies a preservation of self, and therefore it precludes the possibility of merging. Nor is there a shared self that supervenes upon the lovers. Accepting themselves as indefeasibly different persons despite their oneness through love, they constantly reaffirm their autonomous condition even though they give up various freedoms. As interdependent beings, they are compensated for whatever sacrifices they make by the benefits each derives from association with the other. Ambivalence and emotional uncertainty can exist in this state of affairs, but nothing that is necessarily paradoxical. When we discuss the nature of autonomy, in a later chapter, we shall have more to say about interdependence as an element in love.

Merging is basically a metaphor for the making of physical and chemical compounds. Streams merge when they unite and become a river, the water in them being itself a merging of hydrogen and oxygen. The idea that love is merging treats it as analogous. But this analogy is misleading. We attain greater accuracy if we realize that the unity of love is more like the responsiveness between violin and piano in a Mozart sonata or the concerted rhythm of paddlers in a canoe. What each person contributes is systematically distinct, and the outcome is not a merging of their identities so much as a highly coordinated integration of them. The lovers' personalities are not lost but only combined and intermeshed, like links that crisscross within a fence, or like the hazel and the honeysuckle knotted together in medieval love-literature, or like the interfoliate oak and linden trees that Baucis and Philemon become in Ovid's *Metamorphoses*.

In the Ovidian fable Jupiter promises to grant anything the lovers wish. They have been married for many years and are now very old. They do not fear death, but each dreads the grief that one of them must undergo when the other dies. They therefore ask, as their only desire, that they die at the same time. Jupiter honors their request. But with the graciousness of a deity, he does something more: he turns them into trees standing next to each other. The man becomes an oak, his wife a linden; and foreverafter their leaves intertwine as a manifestation of their love. In that image we may see the oneness that is love. There is no suggestion of a merging. The unity of the lovers resides in the pattern of their intermeshing. No absorption or loss of identity has occurred, no supplanting of uniqueness, but rather an intimate sharing of different selves and a beneficial interdependency between them.

Sometimes the selves make a neat matching as if they were parts of a two-figure statue that has been cleanly broken and can now be recemented. That was possibly what Aristophanes meant when he spoke about the "welding" of alter egos. The bond is then a joining at the superfices. It is what I call a "wedding" of two selves. Love often requires something more dynamic and tumultuous than that, as Solomon insists, but this may only be a matter of individual taste.

We should not prejudge the types of union that different lovers may institute. Certainly we should not assume that any one type is essential in order for love to exist.

In an attempt to deal with these problems from a contemporary psychiatric point of view, Willard Gaylin has recently suggested that the concept of fusion be substituted for the concept of merging. Where the latter suggests a swallowing up, Gaylin states, the former implies a melting that is truly indicative of love. We do in fact talk about the melting glances of lovers, and they themselves may say that their "hearts" melt when they think about one another. But the definition of fusion that Gaylin gives hardly serves to distinguish it from merging: "[Fusion] literally means the loss of one's identity in that of another; a confusion of ego boundaries; the sense of unsureness as to where I end and you, the person I love, begin; the identification of your pain with my pain and your success with my success; the inconceivability of a self that does not include you; and the inevitability that your loss will create a painful fracture of my self-image that will necessitate a long and painful rebuilding of my ego during a period of grief and despair."[4]

Love does sometimes take this form, particularly when it is pathological, and much of the ideology in romanticism encourages even healthy individuals to identify love with feelings such as these. They are nevertheless inessential to love, and absent in many instances of oneness that fully satisfies our need for love. The myth of love as merging or fusion becomes a fallacy when interpreted as providing necessary or sufficient conditions.

In the writings of David Hume one finds a more illuminating account of love and sympathy, which he considers innate modes of responsiveness. He describes people as if their minds were "mirrors to one another," whose rays are "often reverberated."[5] He compares human beings to stringed instruments that can vibrate and resonate reciprocally. Affections pass from person to person, he remarks, as "correspondent movements": "[Like] strings equally wound up, the motion of one communicates itself to the rest."[6]

Hume's ideas about community as an affective reverberation recur throughout nineteenth-century romanticism, despite the latter's usual emphasis upon merging. They contribute to the pervasive irony in a novel of Henry James entitled *The Reverberator*. There the sensitive young man reverberates so thoroughly to the presence of the woman he loves (or rather, would *like* to love) that he never succeeds in translating his delicate feelings into suitable action or emotion.

Like most of James' novels, *The Reverberator* portrays the failure of love. Though love is a reverberation between the separate but interwoven selves of different people, nothing in the bond this creates guarantees emotional success. The concept of merging or fusion always carries with it fantasies of magical power. Since we are not chemical elements, like sodium and chlorine becoming salt, there would *have* to be some kind of magic for us to merge with one another through love. But no such magic exists. In the real world, the most we can plausibly hope for is a beneficial interaction between separate persons.

At the same time we must always remember that the bond love initiates is more than just a concern about the welfare of another person, or even a mutuality of interpersonal concern. It is also evidence, sometimes an overt proclamation, that what matters to each matters inherently to both—and often very deeply. What harms or benefits one of the lovers will be experienced as something that harms or benefits the other as well. It is as if each defines his being in terms of what the other is, wants, believes, and represents. The two may eventually think and feel alike; they may communicate in ways that outsiders deem uncanny; when they express themselves jointly or take action together, they may *appear* to be a single entity. That is why I used, and will progressively analyze, terms such as *oneness*, *union*, and *interdependence*. Love is a pervasive interpenetration that not only causes each person to care about the other but also to reject, and frequently to dread, the possibility of life without the other. In accepting the beloved, the lover accepts this as the nature of their relationship. It is part of the peculiar bestowal and appraisal that love involves.

Though love is a gratuitous bestowal (for nothing can force it to exist) and related to many appraisals, not all of which we may realize that we have made, it is something we ourselves create. It depends on prior instincts to some extent; yet we must always learn how to recognize and employ them. The idea of merging is very seductive: to many people it has glowed as a beautiful prospect. That is why its mythological expression has had such great importance in art and literature as well as in philosophy. Nevertheless it is a confection of the mind, a sugary fable, and potentially dangerous. If it truly (even partly) revealed what lovers want, one could possibly agree with those who maintain that love should be avoided.

2
PERSONS, THINGS, IDEALS

In our attempt to understand love, we must approach it from a pluralistic stance. Love is not a single or uniform condition. It encompasses a number of separate attitudes, as evidenced by crucial differences among the love of things, the love of persons, and the love of ideals. These modalities may often overlap, but they need to be distinguished from one another.

I begin by emphasizing that the word *things* is here being used in a somewhat artificial manner. I am not talking about a love that would be limited exclusively to physical entities or even material objects—a sizzling steak or a sports car or a lustrous strand of hair. Such objects are properly called things. They exist as units within the world of matter. We love and often cherish them as such. They are not persons, and they are not ideals. But neither are they identical with a whole gamut of other entities that I also include in the "things" category: acts, sensations, feelings, emotions, and any other aspect of one's experience or behavior that might be loved.

These are not all objects in the sense that shirts or apples are, but they may nevertheless be loved in a similar fashion. Nor is there anything problematic about this fact. A good night's sleep is not the same as a pleasant walk through the woods in autumn; and yet the love of each may be comparable. The different entities loved as things are alike in being the passive recipients of our attention or delight. Unlike persons, they cannot return our love. Unlike ideals, they are specific, often concrete actualities rather than sheer possibilities. Despite their diversity, we treat them all *as if* they were things that can be loved as physical objects ordinarily are.

The love of things has often been maligned in both Western and Eastern cultures. We have been told that a good life requires the subordination, even the elimination, of whatever appetite we may have for materiality, or things in general. Misers are scorned because they love money, sometimes even the metallic currency itself. In Molière's comedy, Harpagon is portrayed as foolishly doting on the gold coins that he hoards in a casket buried in his garden. Throughout the ages traditional moralists have reviled gluttons and lechers because such persons direct their affective impulses toward material pleasures that are loved for themselves alone. Eastern religions have frequently wanted to eradicate all desire, on the assumption that one can thereby escape the unwholesome lure of things sensory or physical, any of which might drag us down by eliciting a love for them. Western religions have generally been more circumspect, but they too proffer the idea that a perfect or definitive love must be wholly spiritual.

The love that Christians, Jews, and Moslems are usually encouraged to emulate is one that issues from the nonmaterial essence of the deity in which they believe. Though God is said to love the world and all that it includes, he is thought to love everything as an emanation of his own creative ideality. Human beings he loves as persons somehow kindred to himself. A love of things, a love of matter that appears in its own brute facticity within a world governed ultimately by physical laws, is not the kind of love that Western religions have advocated any more than the Eastern ones.

In the West, and implicitly in the East, there has nevertheless lingered a pagan and naturalistic respect for the love of things. The various churches have had to tolerate it, and they have often tried to co-opt it for their contrasting purposes. In our culture it is exemplified by the belief, among ordinary people as well as philosophers, that artists of every sort rightly love the materials they use in their aesthetic productions. We admire a painter's love for the colors he places on his canvas and organizes into formal patterns that are meaningful to him. Without the love of things, there would be no love of art and no love of food or clothes or furniture or gorgeous sunsets.

In its devious manner, nature has contrived for men to love the delicate face or supple figure of a woman, and for women to love the strength or muscularity of a man. These traits may have some fundamental importance for the reproduction of our species, but in themselves they are not uniquely or inherently sexual. Most societies have accepted the love directed toward such attributes as a legitimate love of things, basically material perhaps but not necessarily libidinal.

Life would be severely diminished, as it has been in the few puritanical societies that have survived for any length of time, if people were not allowed to enjoy the love of things without being made to feel guilty. In a sense even puritanical societies allow this kind of love, though they usually limit it to a special class of preferred objects. Rectitude will not consist in loving the pleasures of vanity or sexual indulgence or gourmet dining, but it may be identified with loving a tidy house or a starched collar, or any other adherence to decorum. While leisure and exuberance are condemned, the puritan devotes himself to the physical agencies that create frugality and efficiency. Though his religion reviles what it calls "heathen" attitudes, he has a similar love for a bountiful crop or a well-cooked meal. The love of things undoubtedly occurs among people everywhere and at all times.

At the opposite extreme from the materiality manifested by a love of things, there is the spirituality inherent in a love of ideals. Through idealization, the making of ideals, people create a meaningful and even significant life for themselves. The pursuit of ideals is typically human. It embodies a characteristic search for perfection that is distinctive to our species. Different cultures, and different individuals within each culture, strive for different kinds of ideals; and such divergency can lead to conflicts that cause dissension and sometimes war. But without the plethora of ideals that appear in all civilized existence, there would be neither civilization nor the good life as we recognize it.[1]

Unlike the love of things, which can be commonplace and relatively innocuous, the love of ideals is potentially harmful as well as frequently magnificent. We stand in awe of the heroic soldier who risks his life in battle even though he knows that the odds are against his coming out alive. We see him as one who has given himself to an ideal of service and self-sacrifice for the good of his people. It is because he too believes in the goodness of loving such ideals that he can find within himself the courage and the fortitude required under the circumstances.

Our hearts leap up at the prospect of this, or almost any other, dedication to an ideal. We feel that we are in the presence of something that makes our humanity more valuable. I think this feeling is justified. But we must also remember that without the militant enthusiasm that readily accompanies a love for ideals, there would not be as much hatred in the world as there is and always has been. Certainly people would be less destructive and less prone to ridiculous self-righteousness if they were not goaded by a love of ideals that blinds them to the lovability of whatever someone else desires.

This blindness is not inevitable in love, but it is usually hard to resist in view of our eagerness to feel enthusiastic about anything we believe in. Even when they are moderate rather than abusive or extreme, ideals often contribute to xenophobia and revulsion toward the love that others feel with equal strength. We think of the canine virtues as hostility toward strangers and devotion to the pack. Among human beings these traits become idealized despite the factional hostility to which they lead. They attain their power in being ideals that have been instilled from early childhood.

For many people, love is itself an ideal, and possibly the greatest of them all. As such, it can easily coalesce with an ideal attachment to persons. In the love of persons, others are experienced as autonomous beings and not merely as commodities to be used. But persons may also, and simultaneously, be commodities to one another. To love someone *as* a person in no way detracts from the realization that he or she is nevertheless an object in the material world, a conglomeration of varied properties we treat as things. While loving these attributes in themselves, as things, we can surely feel love for the person whose attributes they are.

If in loving men or women we loved only their attributes, our love would be nothing but a love of things. Even that need not exist. Though we are valued commodities for one another, we may not always make the kind of bestowal that is required for love of any sort to occur. To love another as a thing is to reduce that individual to whatever attributes we love in him. To love him as a person, to have a love of persons directed toward this particular human being, we must respond to him as something more than just his properties. We love him as a complete entity, a totality, a whole that may not be greater than the sum of its parts but that nevertheless retains a distinctive and irreducible quality to which they all contribute.

To love another person as a person is, in large degree, to focus upon the uniqueness of this man or woman. One might say that everyone is unique, whether or not he is loved. As a matter of trivial fact, each of us has a being that occurs at a specific time, occupies a delimited space, and consists of properties that cannot be wholly duplicated. This may even be true of everything, not just persons. The love of persons is a way of attending to such uniqueness and giving it importance in our mutual relations. It enables us to surmount our interest in benefits we get from other people. We love them as just the persons that they are, though also profiting from their utility to us.

The love of persons is an advanced capacity that may not be realized in everyone. It occurs less often than the love of things or the love of ideals. Even the most primitive human being will attach himself to something in his environment that fascinates and delights him. This happens in every culture. In highly developed societies individuals may become so demoralized or depressed that they no longer love the many things that most people care about—food, possessions, fellow creatures who can yield pleasure directly or indirectly. All the same, a love of things is pervasive and would seem to exist at every stage of human evolution.

For its part, the love of ideals occurs, in varied ways, throughout civilized existence. It contributes to the very structure of group psychology. Human beings are socialized through patterns of communal behavior that impose their constraints by subsuming them under one or another set of ideals. The individual accepts the demands of his society because he has acquired an incipient love of the same or similar ideals. In loving them, he satisfies the programmed need to feel that he retains at least a measure of oneness with the particular group to which he belongs. That is why there is honor among thieves and distorted idealism among murderers.

In loving another person, however, men and women create an affective bond that is required by neither their material nor their social existence. Even if it is a universal potentiality, as I believe, the love of persons is more haphazard than either the love of things or the love of ideals. It is frequently absent from life in the family. In the world at large, wholesome and satisfying relationships may often amount to little more than partnerships or companionable federations among people who merely keep their usefulness for one another in some harmonious balance. The love of persons may only be a relatively recent, and far from predominant, development of the human spirit.

For most of us in Westernized culture, the ideal of love is more closely associated with the love of persons than with the love of things or the love of ideals. In the West, the concepts of courtly love, married love, and most of what we think of as romantic love have usually been oriented toward the love of persons. Both realist and idealist traditions have extolled it as an achievement that brings out the best in human nature. It is because the love of persons means so much to human beings that they often experience the ravages of jealousy. A casual attitude toward sexual or marital relations would not issue into the sorrows of an Othello or Scarlett O'Hara. Men and women of their sort are fundamentally very idealistic, and the ideal that fuels their suffering is interpersonal love as an all-resolving necessity. It throbs within their fevered imagination as a transcendent goal they cannot live without. It was, in fact, invented to make life meaningful for people such as they.

If this goal were given less importance, if it required less than absolute allegiance, there would be no jealousy. A lover would calmly recognize that the qualities he admires in his beloved are also valued by others, and he might well accept her inclination to experience love with them as well as him. Why has that benign and possibly commendable attitude always been uncommon among lovers? It is not enough to say that men and women become overly possessive in their emotional life because they are afraid of being *dis*possessed. Though this must be a major consideration, since no human being has an infinite amount of love to parcel out, jealousy also arises from other causes.

First, there is the lover's feeling that he or she has not been adequate *as* a lover, which is to say, as one who is truly dedicated to the grand but elusive ideal of love. Jealousy presents itself as the fear that someone else is getting the love we want for ourselves and also deserve to have. But the jealous lover secretly feels he is unworthy of so great a good. Deep down he fears that the beloved is attracted to some real or imagined rival because this other person provides a superior love he cannot emulate.

It is not merely a question of relative talents or desirable attributes. That would reduce jealousy to envy. We envy people who are better than us in matters that we care about. But this need not involve a fear that we have failed in relation to an ideal basic to our humanity. That kind of failure undermines our self-esteem and makes us feel we are somehow degenerate. A tennis player may envy the champ's astounding backhand without feeling that he himself is worthless as a human being. The lover who is jealous does have this feeling. The ideal of interpersonal love is so powerful in him he assumes that only his massive shortcomings can explain the beloved's ability to take an amorous interest in anyone else. Whether or not the rival is good at lovemaking, or especially receptive to it, the jealous man suspects that his own capacity for love is deficient and that he alone is to blame. This frequently becomes a self-fulfilling belief, since jealousy prevents us from loving as we should.

The second cause of jealousy that I wish to note derives from self-love, which—as I will argue in a later chapter—is basic to all love in general. To love ourselves successfully we need to know that others also love us. This validation is threatened when the individual we love turns to another. Most people can tolerate such anxiety, but the jealous person cannot. His unsatisfiable appetite for self-love demands unlimited acceptance by the beloved. She must recognize his unique and endless need while also enacting absolute fidelity regardless of his merits.

Metaphysical hunger of this sort may generate in some people the assurance that God provides the love we seek, but among human beings no such perfection can exist. Those of us who think otherwise are living in delusion that can register as the agonizing pain of jealousy. For then all signs of freedom or independent judgment on the part of the beloved will be taken as proof that our self-love is being thwarted. Feeling we have been denied the total love we desperately desire, we end up hating the beloved and giving her good reason to hate us in return.

❄

In various philosophical traditions the love of persons has been dismissed as either unattainable or undesirable. Fundamental in Plato's thinking about love is his belief that the lover of wisdom, the philosopher, will transcend the love of persons as he also rises above any love of things. This conviction dominates much of Western philosophy, rationalist as well as empiricist. It is illustrated by Spinoza's claim that only a love for being as a whole can free us from our bondage to the ordinary world.

Throughout his argument Spinoza assumes that ardent attachment to another person, particularly when it takes the form of sexual love, is either madness or ontological folly. In order to liberate ourselves, he insists, we must achieve a love for reality itself—a love he interprets as an intellectual appreciation of how everything is as it is. This kind of love, it would seem, is the only type he considers worth having. Certainly it is the love he deems most praiseworthy.

In taking this view, Spinoza not only neglects the variegated character of a love between persons, but also he assumes that the kind of love available to philosophers like himself must be the highest love. We need not sneer at the arrogance or self-preferment in this assertion. We know that lovers are often richly poetic in describing what they love. In as great a man as Spinoza such expressions of adoration may be seen as merely hyperbolic. In any event, it would be hard to take them as veridical. I am suggesting that they are not.

As against Spinoza's way of thinking, we may say that authentic love can exist without being directed toward reality as a whole. Through the love of persons we accept another as the particularity that he is. Whether or not we have an interest in reality as such, we bestow value upon the person before us. If we were merely to subsume him under one or another general law, we would be treating him as a thing. If we saw him as just the embodiment of virtues and vices, he would only represent some ideal that matters to us. Having attributes that can be classified, and possibly quantified, human beings are loved or hated as things are loved or hated. And they can also be approved or condemned, honored or vilified, in their proximity to or distance from an ideal. In being loved as *persons*, however, people are accepted and respected in themselves, as what they are and have become, given the unique configurations of their individual development. Loving another as a person does not mean accepting or respecting all the attributes he has. Some of them may be repellent. But if we love this person, we accept him in his totality, despite his unacceptable and even hideous imperfections. By enacting such acceptance, we make the bestowal of value that is relevant to loving another as a person.

Spinoza thinks that the love of persons cannot be rational, that it must be irrational. Possibly that is his fundamental mistake. Loving a person is inherently neither rational nor irrational. It is a form of life that human beings cultivate, sometimes irrationally but often with no loss of rationality. They frequently consider it an emotional fulfillment worth striving for, and they sometimes feel guilty when they have not attained it.

There is no reason to believe that the Spinozistic saint, loving God or Nature in an intellectual vision that enables him to embrace the universe, is best qualified to understand or evaluate the love of persons. On the contrary, many other men and women are better qualified than he: people who are sensitive to the suffering of others, people who have a natural disposition toward nurturance, people who are cheerfully gregarious and therefore capable of *liking* others, people who enjoy the good things of life (above all, good health) and are capable of sharing their serendipity in acts of spontaneous generosity, people who have acute awareness of the physical and moral beauty in others, or people who acquire the ability to maximize their own pleasures through the fostering of pleasurability in someone else.

This enumeration could continue much further, of course. I mention these loving dispositions only as evidence that the love idealized by a rationalist philosopher like Spinoza cannot explain or suitably approximate the love of persons.

When Plato formulated his own arguments for rejecting the love of persons, on the grounds that it undermines all philosophic love, he emphasized that love always seeks for goodness. We do not love something, he insisted, unless we think that it conduces in some fashion to what is desirable. In the final section of the *Symposium*, Socrates states that "love is the desire for the perpetual possession of the good."

To the extent that this implies that by its nature love reduces to the love of ideals, we may find such essentialism unpalatable—as we may also repudiate Freud's attempt to reduce love to what is, in effect, the love of things. But though the love of persons is not reducible to either of the other modalities, Plato is right in believing that it comes into being only *because* we desire some goodness that exists in another person. Love requires and includes appraisal as well as bestowal. Appraisal is both causal and constituent. Bestowal goes beyond appraisal, but in ways that need not negate its great importance in the experience of love.

Over and above this, Plato's thought has further utility. Without committing ourselves to the metaphysics that underlies his philosophy, we may agree with him that no love can be justified unless it satisfies our perpetual desire for goodness. This is true for the love of persons as well as the love of things and the love of ideals. Each can provide its own definitive value, but none of them is necessarily good or inherently better than the other two. A destructive love of ideals is worse than a harmless love of things or even a self-deluding but inconsequential love of persons.

❄

To determine how we can adjudicate among these competitive forms of love, we may resort to another Platonic principle. Throughout his teaching, Plato speaks of harmony as that which reveals what is most desirable. In a similar vein, we can assert that an experience that harmoniously integrates beneficial possibilities of all three modalities is better than one that does not.

To say this is to acknowledge that the different forms of love need not occur in isolation from one another, and indeed that they should not. Nothing prevents our love of another person from also including love of the particular traits that belong to that person as well as love of the ideals that he or she represents. The three modes then contribute to our mutual attunement. They overlap and pervasively interact. In their harmony, each love strengthening the other two, do they not create a bond that is better than any alternative? Do we not have good reason to think that the cooperation among the three eventuates as an affective unity superior to what is proffered by one of them alone?

We should not assume that everyone will agree about the relative value of these components, even when they are harmonized. But the need for love that combines them in a single experience is both profound and powerful in human beings. It shows itself in the concepts of religious love that have accumulated over a period of centuries and that have mattered greatly to millions of people. In loving God, the devout believer seeks to love him as a supernatural person whose attributes can be loved as things are loved and whose divine essence reveals what is ultimately ideal in the universe.

The love of God thereby seeks to unite all three modalities. When theologians say that God *is* love, they must be taken as speaking metaphorically. For love as we know it is either an attitude, a disposition, a gamut of feeling and behavior, or else it is an ideal for which we strive. Love cannot literally be a person. Only in mythology is it personified, as Aphrodite, or Eros, or the like. Yet God, whose being the theologians define as love, is said to be a person, albeit supernatural.

This conception of God as love will always be beset by massive problems. If we think of God as the final source of goodness, as that which bestows upon reality the very possibility of anything having value, he could be the cosmic order, the laws of nature, the material substratum from which all goodness must originate. He would then be loved only as a thing is loved, and our faith becomes idolatry. The situation is even more anomalous if he is considered the essence of absolute ideality. For that may very well be loved merely as a possibility, whether or not it exists.

On the other hand, we cannot love God exactly as we love a person in the world. He must belong to a special ontological category, and that requires a love for him that is more than any ordinary love of persons. He must be loved as a person beyond time and space who is the highest of all conceivable ideals while also being the final wielder of power in the universe. Can we really understand what is being said? Is it logically coherent? If it is not, or if it impedes our search for meaning, why should anyone cultivate this kind of love?

Theology may or may not be able to justify its attempt to combine the three modalities. The idea of a living God who is love may be radically confused. This is a question I cannot address here. What has most relevance for our present purpose is the fact that so much human thought and imagination have gone into the effort to envisage this harmonization among the different modes of love. Even if there is no transcendental being toward whom all three can be directed, the importance of uniting them in valid as well as valuable experiences provides a challenge that even a humanist can appreciate.

In a later chapter I will return to the nature of religious love. In the meantime, what could serve as a working hypothesis for understanding which love is best for creatures such as us? The following may be of help: Love is most rewarding when it harmoniously integrates the love of persons with a love of ideals that progressively enrich experience and a love of things that fully satisfy our needs. This standard is intentionally vague; it leaves room for great diversity among different instances of love. To my way of thinking, that is an advantage and not at all a defect. In their pluralistic orientation, the subsequent chapters will try to show its many implications.

3
SEXUAL LOVE

The distinction among love of persons, things, ideals is augmented by another that intersects with it. In each of these modalities, there exists a complexity of different dispositions that structure their own types of love. Though it may be arbitrary in some respects, I find the following categorization useful: sexual love; love of self; parental love of a child; filial love of a parent; peer love; group or social love; religious love. Each of these can embody the love of persons, things, and ideals; and each of them interacts with the others in ways that are distinctively human. Moreover, as we shall see, none of them is unitary within itself: they all have subdivisions that are worth studying on their own.

In thinking about the different types of love, we must always realize not only that they are frequently compatible with one another but also that they evolve and readily succeed each other. Apart from the fact that love can blossom or disintegrate, as everyone knows, it may also undergo transmutations that are less easily recognized. Is married love the same when husband or wife has died or been affected by Alzheimer's disease? The surviving spouse may think that his or her love remains unaltered. But this is an illusion, and sometimes a harmful one. Originally there may well have been an interpersonal love, so magnificent perhaps that we want to believe that it can never disappear. But if the beloved is no longer living and mentally intact, our bond has ceased to be interpersonal love. It has changed into something else: nostalgia and hopeless desire for a oneness that has been destroyed, or else moral commitment to the pitiful creature who can still receive our love but cannot return it. Devotion to the dead or devastated spouse is marital love transformed beyond its earlier state. It has become amalgamated with a love of humanity focused upon that very special individual with whom we once had a sharing of selves and for whom we now feel unremitting concern. Whether better or worse than what we previously had, this new relationship illustrates the fact that love, like life itself, is a plastic process. It varies in conformity with temporal vicissitude. It rarely stays the same for very long.

❄

Though I start with sexual love, I do not consider it uniquely indicative of love in general. In the development of each person there are other kinds that will have preceded it—love received from one's parents, as well as filial love and friendship among peers. In the history of ideas, concepts of religious love existed long before humanity began to idealize the possibilities of love between or within the different genders. For us at the end of the twentieth century, however, that is the phenomenon that dominates our thinking about love. In the last two hundred years sexual love has frequently been deemed the only relationship that can truly reveal the nature of love. For many people it serves as the justification for interpersonal intimacy and as the prerequisite for a lasting family, a good society, and an adequate participation in nature. Various philosophers have argued that religious love is a projection or extension or indirect expression of sexual love, and some have claimed that all other love is also reducible to it.

In the nineteenth century, when romanticism was a kind of super-religion that infused and transfigured all of the traditional dogmas in the West, sexual love was treated like a natural deity much as nature itself had been deified in the previous century. More precisely, sexual love was seen as a sacred manifestation of nature parallel to the descent of Christ showing forth the infinite goodness of God the Father. At the beginning of the nineteenth century the joint divinities, nature and its epiphany in sexual love, generally appeared benign. As holy ingredients in animate existence, they could make possible not only happiness but also fully consummate experience. They were taken as the meaning of life, thereby revealing what was needed for ordinary men and women to attain meaningful lives, on earth, here and now, within our mortal dispensation.

The utopia promised by communist, and some other, ideologies—themselves a product of benign romanticism—could thus be achieved at once. The man and woman who were made for each other by nature in its loving concern for sexual goodness would create the requisite paradise. This idea was anticipated in Shakespeare, as I mentioned earlier. Antony clasps Cleopatra and asserts: "The nobleness of life / Is to do thus, when such a mutual pair / And such a twain can do't." By the nineteenth century the mutual pair no longer had to be rulers or even aristocrats. Every man and woman capable of sexual love could experience the nobleness that natural life affords through this supreme self-realization.

In later decades the new religion lost its ebullience. Doubts set in, as they must have for the early Christians when the Second Coming failed to occur after years of expectation. Romanticism survived, but its defeated hopefulness turned into pessimism about life. Only in or through death could the nobleness of love be found. For many devotees the world seemed so wretched and corrupt that nothing but *Liebestod* (love-death, the love that finds fulfillment only after death) could be a viable option for human beings. Between these extremes of benign and pessimistic romanticism, there existed many gradations of belief—as there would in all religious faiths.

In the twentieth century the pendulum has swung back and forth. Skepticism about the dogmas of romanticism has been accentuated by the realist approach that underlies the scientific study of human motivation. No one doubts that some people do experience the ecstasy of sexual oneness and that others, thwarted by social or personal impediments, despair of ever enjoying love in the world as we know it. But realists interpret the *meaning* of all this in ways that repudiate the metaphysical assumptions of idealism in general and romanticism in particular. The realists consider sexual love a device by which organisms arrange for the repeated and harmonious gratification of physical needs related to reproductive drives that are programmed in the species and devoid of any ideality.

This meager sketch may serve as an entry into the ambiguities that have always attended the concept of sexual love. I can best illustrate them by citing a scene in Verdi's opera *Rigoletto*. From the very beginning of that work, the duke of Mantua is presented as a libertine who enjoys the sport of seducing women whose beauty or youthful charm arouses his sexual appetite. In the opening scene we see him scheming lecherously during an orgy at court; in the final act he visits a prostitute and uses amorous language with her in protestations that are blatantly parodistic. For him love would seem to be just playful lust. But in the duke's first recitative and aria in Act 2, he tells us that his feelings for Gilda are different from any that he has previously experienced. He claims that she has elicited in him a true and abiding love that makes him care about her happiness rather than his own selfish pleasures. The music that Verdi gives the duke at this point is thoroughly convincing. He is made to sound like an innocent young man suddenly infused by the purity and quasi-religious enthusiasm of romantic love. When the courtiers who have abducted Gilda carry her into the duke's bedroom, however, he rapes her in his usual libertine manner.

We in the audience can only wonder at the duke's aria in the second act. Why did Verdi present him as one who feels authentic love? Did he think that the grim melodrama would be too outlandish if the duke appeared as a monster who has never experienced even a glimmer of what is truly sexual love? Did he surmise that we could more easily accept the self-sacrificial love that Gilda later manifests if the man for whom she dies is shown to have had at least a modicum of loving sentiment?

Without discounting such explanations of Verdi's intention, I interpret his art as revealing through this aria the ambiguous and uncertain character of sexual love in general. It often harbors illusions about the other person and oneself. It is a state in which one may not always have reliable access to what one really feels. As Stendhal understood, better perhaps than any other writer on the subject, the passionate lover can never be sure that his response is more than just a mask to hide motives of vanity, possessiveness, and sexual hunger.

The duke of Mantua, like Don Juan in Molière's play, is a very young man who has been bombarded by conflicting ideologies of the period in which he lives. He does not know which of his tumultuous feelings are authentically his own. Like Don Juan in all his transformations, the duke is more than just a libertine. By giving him vivid and melodious music, Verdi shows him to be a lover of beauty and to that extent one who pursues an uplifting goal. He fails as a human being because his ability to love other persons is not properly developed. Though she dies, Gilda succeeds because hers is. In his imperfection, however, the duke shows how sexual love fluctuates between our longing for the ideal and our craving for what is merely appetitive. It may possibly satisfy both, but that is an achievement one can never presuppose; and in any event, it may or may not amount to a love of persons.

In view of these ambiguities, we may wonder how sexual love is related to the other kinds of love that I have listed, such as peer love or friendship. In the Western world, at least, sexual love has often been condemned as obsessive desire like the duke of Mantua's. To the extent that this is correct, the attitude does not presuppose oneness with its object or even friendliness toward it. At the same time, we usually recognize that love and sex are not reducible to each other. The concept of sexual love encourages us to think that the two may be harmoniously combined even though they include different types of interest.

All passions that are powerful reveal a bestowal of value inasmuch as the object toward which they are directed has been given vast importance. This nodule of created meaning exerts the requisite force within the affective orbit that passion defines. Nevertheless, such bestowal need not be an acceptance of the other as she is in herself. Appetite is often blind or oblivious to the being of someone it finds attractive. It readily fixates on an attribute that may satisfy its own impulsive need regardless of what the other person is or wants. Sexual love can include desires of this sort, but also it extends beyond them.

In the legend of Tristan and Iseult the lovers often claim that they do not love each other, their passionate attachment having been forced upon them by the poisonous potion they drank unawares. But in their relationship we perceive much more than just sexual obsession. Tristan and Iseult are indeed true lovers, as the narrator tells us. Apart from their having drunk the potion, they are made for each other. Their oneness may even represent the ideal dimensions to which all sexual love aspires. Throughout their tribulations, it is the fellowship or emotional friendship between a heroic man and woman that binds them so securely. Their sexual needs are a part of that love, but insufficient to constitute it by themselves. The tragedy of Tristan and Iseult issues from the fact that the society they inhabit cannot accept their love as what it is, as something very different from mere sexual appetite or indulgence.

Though this love story, like many others, pivots upon the conflict between love and society, it also reveals that sexual love is itself a social phenomenon. Not only is the concept an example of cultural accretion transmitted through the language and customs that are second nature to us, but also the relevant experience creates a new community of two. Through sexual love we attain friendship with someone who is normally outside our immediate family and yet accessible for cherished delights that were easily available in early childhood. The carefree nudity that little children experience in each other's company, the fondling they receive from their parents, the warmth and direct assurance that give them the feeling of being wanted—all this is put in jeopardy once they grow up. Through sexual love they are able to find another person with whom they can reinstate the kindly relationship that was formerly so enjoyable.

By associating with members of their society, particularly peers, children acquire the ability to care about other persons. It is part of their social development. They learn how to feel benevolent toward people who are like themselves in some but not all aspects of their personality. In modern philosophy we may turn to Hume as one of the first to have understood how much of sexual love is well-intentioned rather than purely appetitive. When Hume talks about the constituents of what he calls "the amorous passion," his analysis anticipates much of our contemporary thinking about healthy-minded oneness afforded by love between the sexes. At times Hume does revert to seventeenth-century ideas about falling in love being wholly inimical to the friendship of married love. But in general he recognizes that most sexual desire can be harmonized with the humane interests required by a life in society. This harmonization is effected by the amorous passion.

Unlike Kant, whose problem about sexual love arises from his assumption that sex and love are fundamentally contradictory, Hume sees no inherent conflict between them. Kant thought that since sexual appetite is always selfish and appropriative, it makes authentic love for its object virtually impossible. As against this kind of belief, Hume emphasized the ways in which kindliness, reproductive drive, and the sense of beauty interpenetrate within loving sexuality.

Kant concluded that only through marriage could the inconsistency of sexual love be overcome. He believed that married love contains an ethical element that enables human beings to reconcile their simultaneous desires for sex and love. Hume's approach seems to me much more promising. He implicitly asserts that sexual love creates its own fellowship, whether or not it occurs within the bounds of matrimony, and he sees that it unites moral and aesthetic sensibilities with those that are mainly sexual.

At the same time, Kant's ideas about love alert us to an inner relationship between love and marriage that Hume did not understand. Though falling in love may involve an intensity of feeling that is basically different from the comfort and orderliness of marriage, as Hume insists, all sexual love contains a desire for continued oneness with the beloved. Plato touches on this point when he says that love is a striving for *perpetual* possession. In the relationships between men and women in most societies, this longing for permanence translates into the constancy of commitment that marriage entails. To this extent, sexual love and married love are internally related to one another. The former may never issue into the latter, but it contains within it a yearning for the lasting and possibly undying union that matrimony has often signified in the Western world.

This much of Kant's argument, to which I will return when I discuss the nature of marital love, can prove to be very helpful. It explains details of the Don Juan legend that might otherwise have eluded us. In all the versions of that myth, Don Juan is masterful at getting women to feel sexual love for him, while he only feigns it in relation to them. He generally succeeds by promising marriage, and in Molière's *Dom Juan* he actually marries each of his victims. In that play, too, he describes an occasion on which his sexual passion was aroused by seeing the endearments of a recently married couple. In his amatory experience, marriage is not an extraneous phenomenon. It is part of what he wants but cannot encompass authentically. That contributes to his difficulties with sexual love.

In the nineteenth century, when Don Juan turns into an idealistic searcher for perfection who moves from one woman to another in his quest for the absolute, we are led to believe that he has a real love for each of his women. Nevertheless, it is a limited love since it precludes the possibility of permanence. As in the other versions of the myth, Don Juan's inadequacy as a human being consists in the anomaly of his wanting sexual love while also resisting its aspiration toward intimacies that last instead of being transient. This is his dilemma. He ends in hell because he cannot solve it. Though displaying the grandeur and the glory of instinctual freedom that men have always cherished, he finds no way of transmuting it into the permanent love that men (and women) also desire.

❄

Much has happened in the philosophy of sexual love since Hume and Kant did their work two hundred years ago. In the hope of furthering the traditions that each of them established, I suggest an analysis in terms of three concepts: the libidinal, the erotic, and the romantic. These are terms I draw from ordinary language, but I am not reporting on dictionary definitions and I am willing to concede that my usage may be stipulative at times. I wish to show that sexual love is a condition that unifies all three of these dispositions.

The libidinal is often considered innate. Even the most empirically-minded psychologists can agree that reproductive drive occurs in human experience and behavior as a vital energy that seems to be instinctual. It operates through physiological mechanisms in us as in all animals. In most other species the libidinal is geared to estrus in the female and pheromonal stimulation in either sex. Having lost these constraints, human beings are more pervasively libidinal. But also they have cultivated the other two components in sexual love as a means of both taming and enriching what might otherwise be an uncontrollable drive. This is not to say that the erotic and the romantic are "sublimations" of the libidinal. It only signifies that human nature exists as it does by virtue of its ability to develop all three in a way that prevents the libidinal from being the sole determinant.

Libido is the force of nature that realist philosophers have usually emphasized in analyzing love. Lucretius described libido as a wild and merciless agency in all of life, a ferocious, unrelenting principle that filled him with hatred as well as awe. Realists who belonged to advanced periods of science, Schopenhauer and Freud for instance, identified it (more coolly) as a means by which each species assures its own reproduction. When Freud reduced love to libido, he attested to the primordial character of this need for reproduction. He was certain that it governed, however indirectly, all affective relations within the species.

Since human nature is so complex and so greatly given to nonmaterial refinements that civilization cultivates, Freud's conception was predicated upon two assumptions that he retained throughout his theorizing. First, he thought that observation of species other than the human generally reveals libido operating in an unalloyed and repetitive fashion that must be innately programmed. Second, he was convinced that human nature followed similar laws despite the many differences between us and other organisms. As a biologist and psychologist, he had only to decipher the intricate changes that libido underwent in becoming human.

The first of Freud's assumptions may seem obvious to pet owners. Humanized as my dog may be, he takes a brazenly libidinal interest in a wide array of other dogs. His attitude toward them is assertive and physically explicit. There appears to be no concern for privacy or civility within that canine world. It is as if all members of the species recognize a general duty to make themselves available for reproductive purposes. The females may refuse to be mounted at the wrong time or by a mate they consider unsuitable, but prudishness is not part of their repertoire. The libidinal instinct would seem to function automatically, even autonomously, as an impersonal mechanism that overrides whatever values each dog may otherwise have.

As a matter of fact, we know that this way of characterizing canine relationships—and probably libidinal behavior within most other species—is far too simplified. On closer observation, we notice that the pet we are walking through the park pays scant attention to dogs that are very old or very young, too big, or just too frightening in their response to him. Even so, Freud's generalization about nonhuman species may be accepted as more or less accurate. But the second assumption, about libido being similar for humans and nonhumans, is highly problematic. This belief is not entirely founded on empirical data, and it lends itself to both weaker and stronger versions that are very different from one another.

The idea that libido operates in us much as it does in other organisms is inadequate since there are no objective criteria for deciding what to consider either similar or dissimilar. Different spectators comparing the behavior of a young man entering a singles bar with the behavior of my dog striding through the park might agree about many obvious facts and yet differ in the extent to which they find the two patterns of response truly comparable. No one would say that the situations are identical in all respects. The degree to which they are thought to be alike will vary with each observer's interpretation of the relevant events. With equal validity, different people may see different meanings and entertain vastly different conceptions of what is happening.

As in many disagreements about what is "really" going on, we are being presented with alternate instances of what I call idealization. For reasons of his own, each observer concentrates upon some element in an objective state of affairs and gives it extraordinary importance. He bestows great explanatory value upon it, which causes him to reach generalizations that others might not make. In emphasizing parallels between human and nonhuman libidinal behavior, Freud creates an idealization of this sort. His views were shocking at the time he published them because even the scientific community was accustomed to stressing the differences between libido in us and in other creatures.

The weaker version of Freud's idea contents itself merely with documenting cross-specific similarities. They are certainly worth noting, but in themselves they do not explain much. The stronger version attempts to understand all affective behavior in terms of the drive for reproduction. "Aim-inhibited" effects of sublimation and repression would thus be reducible to the "aim-uninhibited" desire for coitus in the sense that the latter denotes a fundamental element of human nature while the former are only secondary. I have discussed the philosophical implications of Freud's libido theory elsewhere.[1] Here I need only remind the reader that this much of it is speculative and nonverifiable. It is metaphysics rather than science.

In trying to explain why libidinal drive is so often thwarted in human beings, Freud introduced but hardly developed the notion of "organic repression." He thought there was something within the reproductive program, as it evolved in *Homo sapiens*, that is inherently imperfect or self-defeating. Though more or less the same as in other organisms, human libido as Freud conceives of it was impaired when our species renounced the quadrupedal posture of its ancestors. Standing erect, human beings lost the olfactory acuity that serves the libidinal needs of other animals with great effectiveness. At the same time, sexual receptivity in women extended itself beyond a single estrus period. In that regard libido became more uniform in male and female. Neither of them can overcome organic repression, however, and that would account for much of the discomfort and frustration that often attends libidinal impulse.

Freud's tentative ideas about organic repression may have only limited value. They can nevertheless serve as a reminder that, far from being able to explain all affect, libido has a more circumscribed role in human sexuality than Freud himself believed. Though we are dimorphic like other animals and reproduce through behavior that is often similar, the drive for propagation has a highly modulated effect upon us even as sexual creatures. Whether or not we posit that libido in us was impaired at a crucial stage of evolution, it always functions under conditions of restraint that are peculiar to the human race. These appear in the sexual love that belongs to the natural program of our species. Libido has an important place in such love, but the erotic and the romantic are more definitively human.

❄

Using the word *erotic* in this context, I harken back to the Greek god Eros. He is the son of Aphrodite, the goddess of love and beauty. In later iconology he is often portrayed as a little boy, sometimes even a two- or three-year-old, as a way of symbolizing traits that are not directly reproductive. In having none of the wrinkles and blemishes that people dread as they get older, children with their baby fat have often seemed uniquely beautiful to adults. There is little evidence that children think in these terms, but that does not matter. Under the sign of Eros we experience flesh as in itself a beauty to behold. Through the erotic we see it not as an abstract perfection like the beauty of a mathematical proof but rather as a physical charm with sexual overtones.

When Freud first formulated his theories about childhood sexuality, he horrified his contemporaries because they thought that he was besmirching the purity to which human beings have access in the first stages of their individual development. Freud's critics would not have felt this way if they had recognized that sexuality can be beautiful, in children as in adults. All the same, I think they were right to resist Freud's idea that sex drive becomes prominent in human beings shortly after birth. Freud seemed to identify the sexual with the libidinal, whereas childhood sexuality is usually erotic and nonlibidinal. In later life, the erotic may readily cooperate with reproductive impulses, but even then it cannot be reduced to them.

To a large extent, the erotic is an aesthetic phenomenon. On most occasions, it has no effect upon the genitals. To say that it is an offshoot or transformation of the libido serves only to beg the question. Freud's conception of the libido, together with ideas about sublimation and repression that he introduced to make it comprehensive, led him to conclude that virtually any interest that people have in relation to one another must be explicable as the workings of reproductive energy. He failed to appreciate the degree to which pleasures of seeing, touching, tasting, smelling, and even yearning might be sexual in another fashion.

Through the erotic we can enjoy the real or imagined presence of someone for whom we do not have libidinal desire. The most voluptuous nudes in the history of painting can provide great delight to the grasping eye of a sensitive and virile male, but they rarely arouse responses that are explicitly genital. The erotic attachment exists in its own dimension. It is part of the pleasure we take in bodies subsumed within some ideal of beauty, health, or vitality. We create these ideals through acts of the imagination that make life meaningful. Though this aspect of human nature belongs to a dynamic field of forces that also includes the reproductive, neither is derivative from the other. The erotic is an ultimate fact of our being, following patterns of response that retain their own identity even though they are bound by the physical and biological necessities they too must serve. Nothing is gained by trying to reduce the erotic to the element of sexuality that is reproductive in origin.

Different though they may be, the erotic and the libidinal are never wholly independent. They should be seen in their relation to one another. They are, so to speak, competitive but also cooperating comrades within the extensive enterprise of sexuality. At times in a person's life when one of them is weak, the other may be strong as if to compensate. Older people often turn to the erotic *because* their libidinal capacities have largely disappeared. The man who once relished the excitement of fornication may find that he now likes merely talking to young and beautiful women. He begins to see nubile females as if they were delightful daughters whose company he enjoys.

On the other hand, young people frequently cultivate the erotic as a way of taming what might otherwise be unmanageable demands that the libido makes upon them. Girlie magazines and pornographic movies often provide this service to those who need it. Dialectical relations between the erotic and the libidinal are extremely intricate. If scientists, philosophers, and novelists ever learn how to benefit from each other's expertise, we may someday make great discoveries about these interactions within human sexuality. In trying to understand the nature of sexual love, one must start with the recognition that many of the interests and most of the intimacies that belong to it are primarily erotic rather than libidinal.

When, on some enchanted evening, young lovers see each other across a crowded room, they may initially experience little more than the promise of good will that shines in the other's eyes. Their steadfast gaze may sometimes assure them that coital conjunction is a viable possibility, but also there might be nothing of the sort operating in or around their consciousness. As Stendhal says about crystallization that leads to passionate love, it can originate in a glance that mainly conveys "the promise of happiness." This happiness need not involve coitus; it can occur in the absence of genital gratification. It often comes through enjoyment of sight and hearing, and much of it is largely cerebral.

If the lovers meet and begin to dance, like Romeo and Juliet in their first encounter, they are likely to savor their physical contact as the expression of much that is extraphysical. Think of the symbolism in touching and being held, in feeling oneself move in musical rhythm across the floor, in gliding with another person for no extraneous purpose and in the presence of others who consider such behavior entirely innocent. The lovers' gestures are coordinated and yet free. In their interpersonal unity, male and female experience the delightful responsiveness of their movements while also having a general sense of bodily enjoyment. Human beings cherish this facet of their sexuality. They cultivate it for itself, for its own inimitable goodness.

Ordinarily we think of the erotic in terms of tactile relations, particularly when they are gentle and nonassertive. But sight may actually be the most erotic of our sensory acuities. In flourishing at a distance, vision enables us to caress an object that we do not touch and may not be able to reach. Through sight we enjoy other persons without intruding upon them. We expand our sexual love not only through an exchange of glances but also through a visual feasting upon the delectable appearance presented to us. In its own way sight can be as immediate and titillating as touch, while also arousing greater possibilities for the imagination—whole vistas, as we say, which touch would never comprehend. The word *imagination* itself implies (though very misleadingly) the having of images that are either visual themselves or translatable into the visual.

It was by reference to the imagination that I sought to understand bestowal when I first began my writing on the nature of love many years ago. Throughout the trilogy that ensued, I tried to show the panoply of imaginative values in the many idealizations that I studied. I now wish to emphasize that even in sexual love imagination can occur in different forms or types. It does not operate in the erotic element of sexuality as it does in the romantic, as I will presently argue, or in the libidinal. In the erotic responses of most people the imagination has a distinctive affinity to the visual sense. We see a beautiful outline and our mind begins to dally with imagined pleasures that we associate with this material object. Either literally or figuratively, we dream of situations in which the fascinating image gratifies our longings for emotional comfort, security, and the blissful unity with another person.

This indulgence in the erotic occurs during daydreams, of course, as well as those that happen while we are asleep at night. Whether we are conscious or unconscious, the dream is a visual event permeated by affective significance. While it also includes auditory and kinaesthetic sensations, the experience we have during slumber has always intrigued human beings because they can then see with their eyes closed and with their active life shut down temporarily. The imagination keeps working as before but now in a kind of self-indulgence, like a laborer who returns to the shop after hours in order to make what he himself cares about. In dreams the imagination may proffer simulated culminations for which the libido hungers, but usually it concocts fanciful embroidery for the erotic. The beloved teases us by appearing in one or another fantastic guise that leads to nothing else. Imagination operates like an inspired pair of scissors that snips disjointed fragments from our normal visual life. It puts them together in a playful montage that manifests our love of the erotic itself, while also expressing our love of some particular erotic object.

Without the erotic there would be no civilization, and no desecration of it. It is the erotic that explains the heart-shaped graffiti that mar the concrete slabs of our sidewalks, the walls of famous buildings, and even the harmless trees in which young lovers carve their initials. The amorous vandals are playing with the fantasy that others, possibly succeeding generations, will care about these proclamations of love. By thrusting their personal sentiments upon the visual experience of everyone else, they undermine the loveless restraint to which civilization often devotes itself. But what the erotic is here doing does not entirely differ from what happens when the founders of civilization construct palaces or monuments or religious shrines to express the love they likewise feel for someone else. In both kinds of activities the erotic play of imagination is largely celebrational and devoid of reproductive implications.

The erotic imagination also appears in gift-making, which overlaps with aesthetic efforts of every sort. I used to think that in writing books, as in art work generally, one makes a loving gift to the universe. I now believe that one is also making a gift to oneself, since the creative gesture enables us to have a meaningful life. In either event, we extend ourselves through symbolic representations of what we feel and what we appreciate, much as a lover does when he sends presents to his beloved. As in all giving of gifts, the erotic conveys affective meaning and may eventuate in a relevant type of love.

The erotic is universal among human beings, and within many other species. Various philosophers have speculated about an affinity that causes animate beings to gravitate toward one another. Some have even suggested that it obeys a general law that keeps all things in nature within their appointed courses, pulling or repelling other entities in the systematic fashion that we designate as the cosmic order. Since our immediate concern in these pages is sexual love that human beings feel, we need not linger on these speculations about an ultimate force that keeps the stars in their explosive dance throughout the firmament. I merely wish to suggest that when Empedocles says that love and strife govern all existence, or Dante insists that love makes the world go round, or multitudes of mystics tell us that God's bestowal of goodness inheres in everything, we may have difficulty with their words unless we interpret them as depicting a condition that is somehow analogous to the erotic aspect of love in our own experience.

When we are fully alive, we sense an affective tug that almost anything can exert upon us: not just other persons but also material objects, or even our own person, our own ideas, our own aspirations, and whatever goals our fertile imagination can display before us. It would be far-fetched, even outrageous, to think that the miscellaneous bric-a-brac of mere reality can elicit love on all occasions or even many. I make no such claim. I only suggest that the erotic has enormous extensibility, and that it contributes to sexual and possibly extrasexual love as one among other affective motives that become apparent to us in our moments of greatest vitality. It thereby helps to constitute the meaning in life that we create for ourselves.

To read the equation from the other direction, we can also say that love as a bestowal of value draws upon erotic interests that somehow link us to persons, things, and ideals whether or not we wholly recognize the nature of these subterranean ties. The actualization of erotic potentialities may often be a matter of chance.

Turning some "jolly corner" of our lives, as Henry James called it, we may suddenly notice something in the present or the past to which we actively respond without premeditation. Our response may or may not be love, and it may never bring the kind of heightened awareness for which James is always striving. But when this awareness does occur, it reveals inclinations that leaven life in us. We are then alert to whatever affects our consciousness and makes itself amenable to thought or feeling.

The erotic easily coalesces with human curiosity. When a man peers obsessively through the window at a pretty neighbor, his libidinal stirrings are often minimal. His experience is more likely to be a variant of the erotic. And when a scientist looks through a microscope in order to observe an amoeba's behavior, he too employs a quasi-erotic imagination that reaches out toward this otherwise hidden life. Without the erotic we might not be fascinated, as we are, by painted figures on a canvas or moving pictures on a screen. We are drawn to such objects and activities by affective forces that may be instinctual but not as the reproductive process is.

It is only by referring to the erotic that we can understand many of the cultural variations in sexual response. When women's hemlines were an inch above the ground, men were excited by the shape and mere appearance of an ankle. It took on aesthetic and erotic importance for them. Nowadays, in societies such as ours, that is not likely to happen. Instead men are sensitized to knees or thighs or buttocks or breasts (or even faces, in some Moslem countries) that are partly and variably revealed in accordance with fluctuating fashions. This play of the sexual imagination keeps erotic interest alive while preventing it from reaching too rapid a culmination in libidinal behavior.

In arts of every kind the erotic is not only celebrated as a human consummation but also interwoven with the varied types of aesthetic creativity. What I said about lovers dancing with each other applies to the infinite possibilities of dance itself. As everything in nature that is pendent seems sexual to us, so too do forms and lines in painting or sculpture elicit erotic responses that are often expressive as well as being directly enjoyable. Melody, rhythm, and even timbre in music awaken an acceptance of our sexual being that the erotic has always nurtured. Above all is this evident in the act of performing music, whether in a large orchestra or in a small, highly personalized group. We speak of the making of music as we also speak of the making of love. A hundred men and women playing different instruments and following different cues may not appear to be participants in a lovefest that envelops them all, but the erotic bond between soloists and their accompaniment is obvious (and sometimes embarrassing to watch). Whether they are duo violinists or members of a rock band or performers in a concerto grosso, musicians often respond to one another with the same kind of intimate awareness that one observes in lovers smiling and touching as they rollick in the grass. A friend once told me that when she and her husband play two-part piano pieces together their experience is more exciting sexually than when they have intercourse. This excitement is typically erotic and yet completely aesthetic.

There resides a great mystery in everything erotic, as there is in gravity itself, and I do not pretend to have clarified it. How it is that individuals should feel either affinity or repulsion toward each other may ultimately exceed our powers of explanation. People gravitating erotically about one another, with all the infinite equilibrations that this involves, may be so complex a phenomenon that it will always defy scientific analysis. The erotic, as an affective glue that can bind us to almost anything, may constantly elude the probing of our intellect. In our attempts to understand or appreciate it, we may not get much beyond a sense of wonderment. The same, to an augmented degree, may be true of erotic feelings when the sexuality to which they belong turns into love. This need not distress us unduly. Our world is a place of many mysteries. Once we accept that fact, and respond imaginatively, we can enjoy it as an ever-present marvel. Within its cage, the enlightened spirit can sing with open throat. This may even constitute its truest liberation.

❄

In moving to the romantic element of sexual love, we do not exclude the libidinal and erotic. If the erotic is as pervasive as I have been suggesting it may be, it probably cannot be excluded; and if the libidinal is instinctive in our species, as many biologists argue and as we may well agree, it, too, would be present in every form of sexual love. But the degree and quality of such coherence can differ greatly. When the erotic begins to cooperate with the romantic, it appears more obvious than it did before; when the libidinal is subordinated to the erotic or romantic, it tends to lose its imperious animality. Both of these alternatives become prominent in the kind of sexual love known as "romantic love."

Since it is an element of sexuality, the romantic may never be wholly emancipated from the mechanism of reproduction that must operate in all creatures who survive genetically as we do. But that mechanism can often be attenuated, diminished, or even curtailed. Its relative importance fluctuates in conformity with outer demands from society or the environment and inner inclinations arising from one's will or temperament. In its affiliation with romantic love, the libidinal may at times be hardly discernible. This happens in the puppy love of preadolescence, in the courtly or Platonic love that appears in youth and middle age, and in the sexless infatuations that the elderly sometimes cultivate. Romantic love ranges within a spectrum of libidinal appetite. It can be a torrid passion that glories in its genital yearning, but on other occasions (or in other persons) it can also be so great a banking of those instinctual fires as to make one wonder whether in fact they still exist.

For its part, the erotic cannot be diminished by the advent of romantic love. The romantic both concentrates and augments the erotic. What was diffuse and aimless now becomes focused upon a single individual. The person we love romantically attains more power than other objects in our affective universe. Nothing else will receive as much erotic attention. Our love for this person will seem unique, and through it we may well acquire the capacity to experience her in her own uniqueness. We perceive this quality in her, and possibly her alone, because she is the only one toward whom we have directed so much of our imagination. In making her the center of our erotic interests, we magnify her importance to us. We bestow upon her the special value that she acquires as an object of romantic love.

In a book on human sexuality I distinguished between "the sensuous" and "the passionate" as two means by which people respond to one another. I analyzed the former as the light and playful aspect of sex that finds fulfillment in sensory enjoyment. The passionate I related to the intensely emotional need for oneness that sexuality also includes.[2] The romantic often burns with fervor that it borrows from the passionate, but it may or may not avail itself of the sensuous as extensively as the erotic does. The two distinctions are therefore supplemental, not identical. They impose different, though wholly coherent, perspectives upon sexual love.

What most clearly distinguishes the romantic is its relation to the love of persons. To the extent that we love another person *as* a person, we treat him or her as a being that we accept as-is. We may hope for changes in the beloved, but we do so because that is what the beloved also wants. Though bestowal must always interact with appraisal that equally belongs to love, it is a way of attending to the other person and delighting in whatever properties he or she may actually have. I repeat these descriptions of the love of persons in order to emphasize its frequent role within sexual love. The romantic is the agency for its inclusion.

We may easily see why this must be the case. Libidinal impulse must always remain somewhat indiscriminate as far as persons are concerned. It may direct itself toward someone who can give sexual pleasure, and that is doubtless a part of the innate machinery that affects our choice of whom to love, but the differences between this person and others who are attractive in a comparable fashion will not matter very much. The erotic is also faithless to any individual, and even more volatile. It will bind us to one alluring object after another, often with great rapidity and a sense of flirtatious unconcern. Nor does it limit itself to human beings. Once we think romantically, however, we deploy our sexual energy toward oneness with another person in relation to whom we hope to establish a permanent bond that is not transferable to anyone else. It is as if we really were made for each other.

Throughout *The Nature of Love* I doggedly separated the Romantic from the romantic. The capitalization was intended to distinguish between the modern, typically Western, concept and the interpersonal trope that exists atemporally in human nature. I think our present discussion can have utility for understanding both senses of the word. As a fully developed entity, the Romantic ideal is fairly recent. Though arising out of occasionally similar ideas in the Middle Ages and even the ancient world, it reaches fruition only in the last two or three hundred years.

Nineteenth-century romanticism introduced various concepts that were not at all the same as those of courtly love. But though Romantic theory articulates a view that differs from its medieval antecedents, earlier and later conceptions address themselves to the same romantic element of sexual love. In future centuries there may be post-Romantic systems of thought that will supplant the ones we take for granted nowadays. This is a matter for history to determine. Throughout its evolution, however, the philosophy of love has been a continuing effort to decipher and often to recommend romantic desires that are possibly present, to some degree, in virtually all human beings.

Characterizing the romantic and the passionate as I did just now, I spoke of a search for oneness with another person. But what does this entail? Romanticists in the nineteenth century generally thought oneness that defines romantic love would have to be some kind of merging of the lovers. Once we discard or broadly reinterpret this notion, we see that the romantic can accommodate other kinds of oneness equally well. Perhaps so much of Romantic love has had a tragic ending, both in the lives of real people who adhere to this ideology and in the fictional dramatizations that portray it, because the actual experience of love proves that merging cannot happen. Yet our craving for the romantic may often be successful. Not only do human beings desire lasting oneness with another person, but also they sometimes find it.

Nor is there any need to reduce the romantic to other forms of oneness, as both Freud and various theologians do. Freud explains it as a surrogate for the bond between a child and its mother. The "oceanic feeling" that many lovers experience in each other's arms he ascribes to the blessed peace of the infant at the maternal breast. The search for sexual union is thus explained as a longing to return to the lost paradise of infancy. For the theologians, it is oneness with divinity that we really want, God restoring us to our primal unity with his infinite being.

Freudian and theological conceptions both seek to explicate the romantic in terms of something other than itself. We do better, I think, to take it at its face value. We are the creatures that we are partly because the romantic matters to us. It may occur in differential modes from society to society and from individual to individual, but it remains a universal potentiality of what we normally recognize as human nature. It is a fact of our condition that we crave attachments of this sort.

In much of our experience we desire relations that do not endure. Merely to say that we seek oneness with another person is not to say that we seek *permanent* oneness. But without that search a relationship falls short of being romantic, even when it involves its own kind of love. If someone loved another with the intention of unity that would last only a brief or limited period, we would suspect that this is not truly a romantic attitude. The playwright George S. Kaufman complained to Irving Berlin that "I'll be loving you, always," a line in one of his songs, was too unrealistic. Kaufman suggested that he change it to "I'll be loving you, Thursday." We laugh because we know that this would vitiate the romantic quality of the song. The hope for permanent oneness is at the heart of romantic love. Though romantic lovers know that all emotions are inconstant, and that sexual appetite varies from moment to moment, they seek a relationship that will continue endlessly. Don Juan—as portrayed by George Bernard Shaw, for instance—may find such permanence in his ceaseless striving for ideals. But then he becomes a romantic lover of ideals, not a romantic lover of persons.

Some romantics think their oneness will even outlive death, either as a renewal of the love they attain on earth or as its perfection in the next world. The concept of Liebestod includes the idea that love cannot flourish *until* the lovers die. All this presupposes that true love is really indestructible. In that event, the unity that defines romantic love can surmount death and go on forever.

Important though they are in the history of ideas, notions of Liebestod or eternal love are local phenomena, as lacking in universality as the desire for merging or oceanic feeling. But as we also want to believe we have a permanent home in the universe, so too do we yearn for permanent oneness with some other person. The romantic directs this longing to persons who have erotic value for us and libidinal relevance. In the modern world the institutional goal of romantic sexual love has generally been monogamous marriage. From the early seventeenth century until very recently, Western societies designated the bond of matrimony as the circumstance in which romantic aspirations would be legitimized. It was understood that romantics might often lose their ardor for one another once they lived together and reared a family. Society could easily tolerate that consequence, and in their amatory exhilaration the lovers were willing to run the risk.

Lovers were thus allowed to indulge their desire for the romantic, but only as a prelude to a marital state beyond itself. Married love was the consummation that men and women were expected to pursue, a kind of future validation for whatever premarital fantasies they might also have. If we are cynics, we might say that the intoxicating goodness of romantic love served as an inducement for establishing ties that benefited society or the species more than the individuals themselves. One might even see marriage as an indication of bourgeois parsimony to which the democratic modern world naturally tends. For if we marry the person with whom we have had a romantic love experience, we institute an economy of affective resources. In our relation to a person of the opposite sex, we combine the values of love, sexuality, stable parenthood, and a socially authorized family. In its quest for greater organic wholes, which characterized the dominant idealist philosophy, nineteenth-century romanticism saw marriage as a *Gesamtwerk* (work of artistic synthesis) for interpersonal love parallel to the drive for national unification in politics and the search for absolute spirit in religion.

In our generation marriage has increasingly given up its teleological claim. The young distrust the restraints of earlier societies and see no reason why they should experience romantic love only in the context of eventual marriage. In effect, we have returned to the mentality that prevailed prior to the seventeenth century. Before then it was generally, though not invariably, assumed that matrimony or even marital love was a thing apart from romantic love. At least among the literate people whose testimony we can read, permanent oneness with a person who was loved sexually would not have been limited to the conditions imposed by marriage.

In lower orders of society the situation was very different. Though marriages were generally arranged by the families, and women of all classes were often bartered brides, these pressures must have been less complicated than they were for the aristocrats. Among the poor there were greater taboos against ranging beyond one's immediate surroundings, and therefore greater likelihood that the person one knew and loved would be someone who was socially acceptable as a conjugal mate. We can readily imagine romantic attachments arising in the village square and duly issuing into marriage sanctioned by the two families.

A similar link between the romantic and the marital exists in various medieval romances that depict sexual love within the aristocracy. Chrétien de Troyes' *Eric and Enide* is one among many examples. But with their affluence and sophistication, the nobles would also have had considerable access to romantic possibilities outside marriage. The separation between the romantic and the marital develops as one of the prominent themes of courtly love.

In reverting to the idea of romantic love as something apart from marriage, the present attitude nevertheless retains much of the romanticism of the nineteenth century. Though at a later age than their parents or grandparents, most young people eventually get married to someone they have loved, and they generally hope that the person they marry will provide the permanent oneness they sought in previous relationships. The romantic faith is far from being dead. Our bookstores are inundated with romance novels as never before. And though they give voice to different prescriptions, the panaceas of romantic love that are rife throughout contemporary advertising still lure us into this sexual wonderworld.

Within the imagination, which activates every love, the romantic employs devices that distinguish it from the erotic and the libidinal. A moonlit night in the garden is not inherently romantic. It becomes so by signifying a natural and benign beauty that may change but permanently recurs. Compared to the volatility of human feelings, rhythmic patterns in nature—the full moon appearing as it does each month—represent the everlasting fidelity we crave. The gliding of the moon through a sky it dimly illuminates may symbolize our persistent though gently muted sexual longing. The loveliness of the scene might even assure us that reality itself sustains the affective good we seek. The great poets and artists of the Romantic movement perceived the aesthetic potency in such uses of the imagination. They constructed inspired ideologies around them. Our contemporary conception of the romantic is the offspring of their creative insight.

As I have intimated, the thinking of the nineteenth-century Romantics often presupposes the work of earlier philosophers such as Hume. His emphasis upon kindliness and the sense of beauty helps to clarify the romantic search for oneness, but ignores the hope for a perfect and permanent relation with another person. That sentiment arises from a region of the imagination that Hume does not explore.

Had he done so, Hume might not have felt the need to contrast falling in love and the friendship of married love as sharply as he does. He fails to recognize that the romantic imagination unites these two attitudes. The person who falls in love is overwhelmed by the possibility, which may well be a fantasy, that the beloved is a uniquely appointed alter ego with whom true friendship can be established throughout a socially functional and lasting, even endless bond of the sort that married love represents. The search for continued oneness, which leads the romantic lovers into marriage, is usually an integral part of falling in love. To that extent, the two are not at all inimical.

If married love does occur, as sometimes happens, the spouses may no longer feel the same libidinal passion or erotic sensitivity they formerly experienced when falling in love. But they may see in their present condition a fulfillment of much of what they wanted from the start. If they celebrate and renew their love through sentimental remembrances of their original ardor, or through anniversary dinners, or through second and third honeymoons, they do so not because they want to bring back the emotional turmoil of falling in love, but rather because they cherish the romantic element that was present in it. The imagination is cunning in this manner.

❄

It is also through the imagination, in one of its characteristic modes, that ideals are created. Having analyzed sexuality into the libidinal, the erotic, and the romantic, we may now perceive that the ideal of sexual love prescribes the imaginative harmonization among these three. In principle, each can occur without the other two. But many people, and most moralists in recent centuries, have extolled their coherence within a single relation. One might even say that the romantic includes within itself this longing for integration with the libidinal and the erotic. The concept of romantic oneness would seem to imply that under suitable circumstances libidinal satisfactions will be given to, and received from, a beloved who has a reciprocating erotic awareness.

How can this harmonization occur? The libidinal and the erotic are basically promiscuous. They do not define themselves in terms of any exclusive object, and they usually aspire to immediate pleasures rather than permanent affiliations. If the romantic is to be harmonized with them, this can happen only when a further act of imagination invites us to consider the possibility that the deepest demands of all three may somehow be adjusted to one another. The ideal of sexual love proffers this mutual reconciliation among the libidinal, the erotic, and the romantic as an achievement worth striving for. It is a prospect that has motivated many lovers. Pursuing this ideal gives meaning to their lives, even when they realize how greatly they fall short of what they seek.

Success in this venture requires modifications in our social arrangements as well as our emotional responses. Some people are unwilling or unable to make any such compromise. That has been a statistical norm, and there is no reason to think the future will be different. There will always be those who are simply uninterested in fulfilling the ideal of sexual love. They prefer to keep love and sexuality in separate compartments—assuming they have not given up on both. Even if they have strong inclinations toward one of them, they may not wish to combine and possibly dilute it with the other.

Only in recent years have philosophers really begun to study the nature of human sexuality, as distinct from the nature of love. These are different areas of investigation, each worthy of attention. In talking about sexual love, either as an ideal or as an actuality, we have been discussing the relation between sex and love. They interpenetrate to some degree even when they seem to occur in isolation from one another. As Freud noted several times, *Liebe* refers in German to both love and sexuality; and the most reductivist of psychoanalytic theorists may possibly admit that sexual drive is usually accompanied by a concern about one or another kind of love. Certainly our commonplace thinking about healthy or psychologically desirable sex implies that at least a modicum of love will have been realized as well as physical consummation.

The ideal of sexual love envisages a happy confluence between sexuality and love. It treats lasting and beneficial interdependence between two persons as the making of a good society. To this extent, sexual love is inherently a social love, like friendship or love within the family. I have mentioned the connection between marriage and the romantic, and I will extend that line of reasoning when I consider married love in later chapters. Each form of social love has its own configuration, however, and each depends on its own mode of imagination. In their different ways they enable us to create meaningful relations with other persons and with ourselves. As always, our analysis needs to disclose what is unique about the various patterns as well as their dynamic effect upon one another.

4
LOVE IN SOCIETY

In talking about marital love, we have already entered the domain of social love. Marriage is a communal institution that involves the entire society to which each pair of spouses belongs. Some philosophers have treated sexual love as if it were itself the formation of an independent society, as if the lovers could truly be a separate unit, *seuls au monde* (alone in the world) as Sartre says. But strictly speaking, that is not true. Whether their attachment turns out to be short-lived, as it often is in libidinal or erotic relations, or part of an ongoing quest for romantic permanence, their sexual love cannot create a new society by itself. It may express a rebellious attitude toward the society into which the lovers were born, and it may initiate a lasting bond that survives in defiance of that society. But when this occurs, sexual love takes on public importance it did not have before. It becomes, if not an exemplar of marital expectations, at least a variation upon them.

The basic unit of society is the family. In the Garden of Eden there is no human society. It comes into being only later, when the original couple must take responsibility for the genetic consequences of their sexuality. Marriage is a means of legitimizing sex within the larger community to which it contributes. Married love, or its equivalent under current circumstances, will always manifest goals of whatever society it sustains.

In reviewing the different kinds of social love, the distinction among persons, things, and ideals will prove itself as useful as in relation to sexual love. Though all categorization must be somewhat arbitrary, social love can be seen as extending through a spectrum of different affective interests. At one extreme there is the love of self; at the other, religious love. In between there is parental love of a child, filial love of a parent, peer and friendship love, married love, love of one's tribe or nation, and love of humanity. As in the chromatic spectrum, these blend into one another, and each has subdivisions that are worth studying on their own.

Self-love belongs at one of the poles since it is a limiting case within the range of social love. In an obvious sense we do not have a society with ourselves. We simply are what we are, individuals that flourish or falter in the world of our experience, enjoying our personal life as best we can. Though it is perfectly correct in ordinary language to say that we like and even love ourselves, the logical form of such utterances must always seem odd. Who is doing the loving and what is the object that receives it? If we love ourselves, do we unite two parts of our personality, which then undergo a kind of social love between themselves? Certainly not. There is just a single entity, our particular self, which loves itself. But what exactly does that mean?

When Freud dealt with this problem in his writings about what he called "narcissism," he consciously changed the way in which that word had been used throughout psychiatric literature. Formerly it had always referred to a pathological condition in which someone behaved as if his own body were the body of someone else, showing toward it the same kind of love that lovers would ordinarily express in relation to one another. In a Parisian cabaret I once saw this reenacted by a performing artist. In Freud's usage, narcissism or self-love referred to something totally different. Far from being a pathology, it was a primal state and fundamental in human nature. Nor was it limited to a confusion about one's body.

Freud resorted to the Greek myth about Narcissus because he obviously wanted to retain the symbolism of a mirrored relationship with oneself. As Narcissus falls in love with his own image reflected in a pool of water, so too do people who narcissistically love themselves bestow value upon the person they conceive themselves to be. The idea of self-love would thus encompass the fact that each of us can feel delight in merely being what we are.

Throughout the centuries, love of self has often been maligned as a human defect. In much of traditional theology and religious philosophy, it is assumed that all self-love must be sinful or evil and therefore not really love at all. Self-love is thought to be a fall from grace, a manifestation of pride, as in Lucifer, or else an animalistic substratum that humankind must transcend if it can ever attain authentic love.

In the tradition that Luther represents, only God is capable of love. Christianity had always maintained that God's inexhaustible love consists in a pure bestowal of goodness as opposed to any kind of self-preferment. Those who held this faith had generally been encouraged to emulate Christ by making sacrifices, and even to sacrifice themselves, for the sake of others. Luther concluded that though this reveals the nature of love our immersion in the material world prevents us from attaining it. Our self-love, he thought, corrupts and ultimately destroys our efforts to love God and other people, however well-intentioned we may be. Even the most saintly man or woman would be self-sacrificial in a subtle, and possibly unrecognized, attempt to gain salvation. As all love comes from God, its occurrence anywhere must be an indication of his immanent presence as opposed to any capacity on the part of mere humans. We can only be vehicles of God's love, "funnels" as Luther says. Self-love, through which we try to use the world for our own advantage, prevents us from creating love that is worthy of that name.

In making this argument, Luther claimed to be more authentically Christian than the fathers of the church who had established the orthodox faith over a period of 1500 years. St. Augustine and St. Thomas Aquinas had recognized the difference between earthly and divine love, but they believed there was an aspect of self-love that is entirely commendable. Since God was the good for which we must strive in order to fulfill our nature, the desire to do so through self-love would be beneficial and not at all corruptive. Instead of condemning self-love as a whole, the church had only to instill the kind that leads to the love of God and one's neighbor. *Cupiditas* was that much of self-love that deflected one from the Christian ideal, but *caritas* enabled us to emulate Christ while also loving ourselves in accordance with human nature.

Moderate and commonsensical as this traditional position may have been, it seemed unrealistic to Luther and to the early Christians whose faith he sought to reinstate. They were certain that self-love inevitably reduces to a selfish attitude that is foreign to the proper love of either God or fellow creatures. Catholicism held out the hope that we could learn how to love by cultivating and refining elements of self-love that derive from our natural condition while Lutheranism insisted that *only* through an unmerited descent of God's love can humanity ever achieve the state for which it hungers, the perfection that self-love would otherwise render impossible.

Without taking sides in this theological dispute, I need only note that both alternatives assume that, either totally or in large degree, self-love amounts to selfishness. This seems to me an egregious error. Selfishness is pejorative. It arrogates to oneself value that might have gone to others but that is now being denied them. Instead of sharing money acquired in a communal enterprise, the selfish man contrives to keep it all for himself. To the extent that selfishness is dominant, it makes one disregard the rights and welfare of others, and therefore it precludes a love of them.

But this does not apply to self-love, which exists in a dimension all its own. To love oneself is to have a sense of self-affirmation, assurance about the potentialities of one's being, confidence and even delight in existing as one does. That may or may not be accompanied by pretentiousness or pride. For reasons of self-love, a man or woman can thwart the inclinations toward selfishness that everyone may also have. This was fully recognized by Plato. Like most Greek philosophers, he took it for granted that everything one did would reflect the love of self. But since one loves oneself, he maintained, one wants what is truly good for oneself and that means cultivating moral attitudes that eliminate selfishness or willful self-aggrandizement.

The wisdom of Plato's suggestion has not been adequately appreciated. Even in Freud and Sartre, we find subtle residues of the assumption that self-love reduces to nothing but selfishness. Freud and Sartre are pessimistic about the human capacity for love because they believe that all love is really self-love and that this signifies nothing but the desire to *be* loved. Since primal narcissism underlies the diverse configurations of love, Freud concludes that each of them can only be an insidious attempt to satisfy the love that every person has for himself alone. Similarly, Sartre finds love paradoxical and ultimately futile since it purports to accept another's freedom while also wanting the other to subjugate himself totally to us. On both accounts there would seem to be no viable way of escaping selfishness that is inconsistent with love.

When psychiatric revisionists such as Erich Fromm criticize this approach, they generally argue that loving oneself is possible only if one also loves other persons. This implies: first, that self-love is different from selfishness; and second, that it inherently presupposes an ability to bestow authentic love upon objects other than oneself.

I believe that both these generalizations are true, and that they help us to move beyond shortcomings in Freud and Sartre. Nevertheless the revisionists misrepresent the relationship between love of self and love of others. They wish to give priority to love for something beyond oneself—one's family, the human race, God—and therefore they derive the love of self from that. As Fromm puts it: "If it is a virtue to love my neighbor as a human being, it must be a virtue—and not a vice—to love myself, since I am a human being too."[1] The love of self is thus envisaged and even justified as a *consequence* of loving human beings in general, not merely in the sense that we cannot love ourselves unless we are able to love others but also because self-love is just an application to oneself of the love one also has for others.

This conception is suspect in various ways. It leads theorists such as Fromm to treat the human sense of separateness as a problem that can be solved only by developing love for other people or even the universe itself. Fromm thinks that all members of our species have "transcended nature," inasmuch as their reason alienates them from instinctual responses that define the lives of other animals. This results in a sense of separateness that inevitably creates anxiety, according to Fromm. The only remedy he admits is the achievement of love that effectively unites one individual with another and our species with nature as a whole. Self-love that derives from acceptance of one's being as a separate entity must therefore be a variant of selfishness. It does not cure the original distress, and it subverts a desirable love of self.

But Fromm has misread the map of human ontology. Our sense of individuality is based on innate dispositions just as our love for others is. The realization that we are separate does not always cause anxiety. It often registers the indefeasible character of the uniqueness that is native to consciousness in each of its occurrences. In the experience of an organism that is aware of itself *as* a self, the sense of separateness is a radical datum—an ever-present given that defines one's self. One cannot exist, as just the living creature that one is, without a continual assertion of one's reality. No one could be a self-oriented entity otherwise. To that extent, the love of self bespeaks a desire to flourish as just the meaningful life that throbs within the boundaries of one's own particularity.

For this reason, separateness does not pose the kind of problem that Fromm suggests. On the contrary, it is a precondition for us to love ourselves as what we are. Though we cannot have an adequate self-love unless we also love others, neither love is derivative. The ability to love in no way eradicates our awareness both that we are separate from one another and yet that loving someone else makes it possible for us to love ourselves effectively.

Having misconstrued the nature of self-love, Fromm gives a distorted analysis of the biblical story about Adam and Eve. Before they eat fruit from the tree of knowledge of good and evil, he asserts, Adam and Eve are instinctually in harmony with nature much as the other animals are. Afterwards, on Fromm's account, they experience not only the sense of separateness but also shame, guilt, and anxiety that is typically human. Only by learning how to love each other can they overcome their feeling of loneliness and their constant alienation from nature.

This interpretation falsifies crucial details of the myth. Though it is true that Adam and Eve are not wholly human until they eat of the tree of good and evil, their subsequent sorrows do not result from a sense of separateness. They suffer because they have transgressed and must be punished. Knowledge of good and evil includes the recognition that one can be held accountable for what one willfully does. The expectation of punishment readily turns into painful feelings of guilt. Their sinful conduct alienates them not from nature or themselves, but only from God.

Having defied the divine commandment, Adam and Eve can no longer assume that God will proffer the goodness of his protective love. They realize that they are now estranged from him. Knowing about good and evil, they learn—as all human beings must—that their life will henceforth be precarious. They cannot be sure that God will sustain them either individually or as a couple. Only through faith can they believe that a Creator who metes out such punishment does so for reasons of love. Human anxiety is caused not by self-love but rather by the knowledge of good and evil.

If one knows the difference between what is good and what is evil, one recognizes that the goods of nature must be won through struggle. Having been thrust into that reality, and into this realization, Adam and Eve must always fear that their spontaneous love of self might not be gratified on any particular occasion. In this respect, they have lost their innocence. Like orphaned children who suddenly find themselves adrift in a cold or hostile world, their self-assurance has been severely challenged. The solution for their problem is not to overcome a love of self that results from the sense of separateness, but rather to find appropriate ways to satisfy and to strengthen their self-love in view of the conditions that are now undermining it.

In many mythological sources we find portrayals of the irreducible importance, and even sanctity, in our existing as separate entities. In various legends the hero's name must be kept secret lest it give his enemies power over his unique essence. Throughout the Old Testament the ineffability of the divine spirit is symbolized by the fact that God's name is unknowable. In myths of masculinity the protagonist often claims to be a "man without a name." His ultimate nature cannot be fathomed. It has a hidden residence that must not be disclosed. His separate being remains intact as long as no one knows his name or who he really is.

In the aria from *Turandot* that Luciano Pavarotti has adopted as the expression of his own uniqueness, Calaf says: "My mystery is enclosed within me, / No one will ever know my name." In his self-affirmation, Calaf is not prevented from loving at least one other person. On the contrary, his self-love makes him worthy of loving others as well as being loved by them. When he freely reveals his name to the princess, thereby giving her the right to have him executed, he does not renounce self-love. He merely tests her ability to love him in return. In the process, he enables her to experience love for him that will supplement and fortify her love for herself. Until she learns how to love him as the person he is, she does not have a genuine love of self. To love her own self authentically, she must become a woman who can love a man such as he.

I am suggesting, therefore, that just as we cannot love ourselves unless we are capable of loving others, neither can we love others unless we love the separate and distinct persons that we are in ourselves. We thereby bestow value upon our own separateness while also appreciating the importance of accepting the separateness in others. These conditions are correlative to one another. Neither is more ultimate, neither reduces to the other.

There is no paradox in saying both that we love others and that we wish to be loved by them. It would be a mistake, however, to think that our love for other people is nothing but a circuitous device for getting them to love us. Apart from the fact that loving others is enjoyable in itself, we want to love them, while also being loved by them, because we recognize that we then have greater *reason* to love ourselves. Self-love increases our capacity to extend love beyond ourselves, which then augments our love of self. Only if it excludes further possibilities of love can self-love become injurious.

But, it will be said, is there not bad self-love (apart from selfishness) as well as good? That is what we refer to as vanity, arrogance, self-indulgence, or being too greatly wrapped up in oneself—what the Italians call being *pieno di se* (full of oneself). These are moral imperfections within self-love. They need to be exorcised or corrected, but not in a way that jeopardizes our basic ability to experience the love of self.

One might also say that bad self-love, when sufficiently extreme, is no longer an actual love of self. The blindness and incessant craving of bad or wholly selfish love vitiate love in general. But this peril is not limited to self-love. As we shall see, even a love of humanity deteriorates when it becomes detached from other types of love or militates against them.

❄

Self-love is a prerequisite for every other kind of love that human beings can have. I accept this as a primitive fact of nature. We are not gods, and we delude ourselves if we think that we can bestow love in the selfless way that is sometimes ascribed to divinity. As the source of our existence, God is often called a heavenly father in Western religion and a heavenly mother in others. Having created this idea, the mythic imagination then infers that the love experienced by actual parents may possibly resemble God's love. The Bible speaks of God wanting to be loved by his creation, and theologians claim that God loves himself. How that is possible may be a mystery beyond our comprehension, but it bolsters the notion that parental love can have a definite likeness to the love that is divine. And if God's love pervades the universe, irradiating all existence indiscriminately, can we not believe that parental love is also unconditional?

If we said this, however, we would ignore the character of self-love in human beings and misinterpret the desire to be loved that all of us have. These explain the nature of parental love in ways that are not always evident. The doting mother may insist that she cares only about the welfare of her child. She may undergo frequent sacrifices to protect this organism that is now beginning to live a life of its own, and she may honestly delight in its sheer existence. But she has such responses because her child is an extension of herself. Though they are physically separated, the mother is likely to feel that she is in the offspring that was once in her. Even if she has adopted this child, she treats it like one that could have issued from her own body. Their psychological separation will take much time to occur, and in some mothers it never does. Such are the facts of human nature; analogies to divine love seem quite irrelevant.

This is not to say that a mother's love is merely a way she has of loving herself. Though overly self-sacrificial parents are bad as mothers or fathers precisely because they love themselves poorly and therefore cannot truly love anyone else, those who succeed in loving their children accept the fact that they are different and distinct. This awareness is itself a kind of selflessness. It is a spiritual achievement, and possibly that explains why many people have considered mother's love, at its best, to be the purest of all human loves. Freud thought love a woman has for her child may be the only kind that does not reduce to a desire to be loved. Fromm claimed that a mother's love, and hers alone, is unconditional. He believed that maternal love differs from all other human love, including the father's, in specifying no demands that must be fulfilled.

We liberate ourselves from these pseudoscientific dogmas by remembering how greatly even the most loving of mothers depends on benefits she gets from her child. Not only do gestating and postpartem women undergo physiological processes that create a vital symbiosis, but also the generative experience can reorient the entire gamut of a woman's emotions. The loving mother needs the infant just as it needs her, though obviously in different ways. Her love cannot be unconditional, if only because a baby who totally defeated her hopes and expectations would not be perceived as her *child*. Instead she might see it as a lump of flesh that has issued from her body like waste material upon which she has no reason to bestow much value.

Unloving mothers, those who are revolted by the experience and the outcome of parturition, are not the only mothers who impose conditions upon their children. On the contrary, all mothers do. And since their capacity for love is limited by forces deep within themselves, it inevitably reflects the extent to which their own interests are satisfied. Loving mothers are those who happily accept the mutuality of demands that binds them to their children. They are able to find means by which they can enjoy the neonate while also giving sustenance and gratification to it. Maternal love is predicated upon a reciprocal and harmonious satisfaction of needs and desires. It is never wholly unconditional.

The idea that father's love differs from mother's love is correct in one respect. Without being *more* conditional, father's love has generally involved social and political standards that supervene upon the personal or nurturant goods that mothers can provide. Since most societies thus far have been controlled by men, the ruling males arrogated to themselves not only military power but also emotional means of enforcing their commands. To maintain supremacy, the leaders in each tribe extended or withheld their love for the next generation in accordance with its willingness to accept their authority. Since these leaders were usually older men, and often the fathers in each family, paternal love readily conformed to this system of imposed dominance.

A mother's demands are usually less public, and in that sense less obvious, but they too pertain to the formation of character considered suitable for a young boy or girl in a particular society. The father's love may appear to be more conditional, since it shows itself through laws and commandments that are broadcast overtly in the group. But even when the mother allies herself with the child against the father, her love usually presupposes the standards of her community. Only in that context can she make her own bestowal.

As the roles of male and female have changed in the modern world, these differences among the types of parental love have altered greatly. Though a father cannot bear a child within his body, he can approximate the kind of love that mothers have always felt.

In our generation men are beginning to take that possibility more seriously than before. In the past they often perceived their offspring as mainly proof of their sexual potency and ability to possess a fertile female. That is why they were so much concerned that the children of their wives should be engendered by themselves. But as the child gets older, the father may also perceive in it the evidences of his role as a caretaker. When his son or daughter was born, he might only have felt the pleasure that comes from producing a new bit of life. His love develops into something further, however, if he helps to nurture the child and if he prepares it for its later existence. In having these similar attitudes, father's love and mother's love overlap—to whatever extent their society allows.

In most societies, the mother sees the child as her own and as one that she can love not only because she has given birth to it but also because it turns immediately to her for food and comfort. The father must convince it that he too is trustworthy, and therefore some time may have to elapse before he can experience reciprocal affection with this boy or girl. Without being better or worse as a love for another human being, the father's love will have a somewhat different structure from the mother's even in the least sexist society. Both are alike, however, in being parental and therefore predicated upon the sociobiological necessities through which our species has evolved and preserved itself from one generation to the next.

Having this survival value, parental love is not reducible to any other. As often happens with genetic phenomena, it plays a part in forming habits and conventions that affect wider segments of behavior. Until recently, parental love was conducive to the creation of large families and thus helped to offset the high rate of mortality among humans. In the modern world this greatly cherished love has become more hazardous. In all future centuries the inherent goodness of parental love must always be balanced against the dangers of overpopulation that threaten to destroy the human race. This problem is a new one but, like most others that our species has to face, it involves a conflict between alternate systems of value.

In resolving such conflicts, we create new values, and therefore new meaning in our lives.

❄

As a response to parental love, filial love might seem to be just as instinctual and immediate. But even if there is an innate mechanism that causes children to love parents and that operates in human beings as pervasively as the program needed for parents to love children, the two affective patterns are not equally spontaneous in their occurrence.

The mother who is handed an infant she just now brought into the world has had a long history of learning how to love. The traces of her own infancy remain in her, and she may have greatly anticipated this new advent of life as a chance to reexperience and improve upon her own growth into maturity. If she loves her child, as women often do on first sight, her feeling is the fruit of all her experience as a person who was once a child and now is not. If the neonate was and remains unwanted, she may feel little or no love for it. Assuming that she does love it, however, her bestowal is a focused epiphany of dreams and aspirations as well as the realities of her actual life. The baby has no experience of this sort to draw upon. Its love can occur only gradually, as it begins to live. Filial love is therefore a different kind of love.

Adults often have a tendency to see those who are starting out in life as if they were tiny men or women. We smile with sympathetic amusement at the farcical image of the father stocking the playroom with football equipment for the boy his wife has just presented to him. Though this may never actually happen, it symbolizes the parental tendency to identify children with some later stage of development and to ignore their present condition. An infant is alive and obviously human, but it is also a small machine for survival. It needs to be fueled, to be protected against destructive forces in the environment, and it must recharge its energies through long periods of sleep. Its ability to love others or itself is almost entirely unformed.

However much a newborn child may sense the goodness of the food and drink and comfort that it receives, it does not recognize the parental love that bestows these values. The infant turns to mother or father in an attempt to receive whatever is required to activate its life-support systems. If these efforts succeed, the neonate may possibly assume that it has tapped an everlasting source provided for its benefit. It is as if nature has miraculously contrived to keep it in existence. With experience, the child learns that even the most bountiful of caretakers withholds and sometimes withdraws the goods of life as well as giving them freely.

An infant has two ways of responding to its endangered state. It can express anger, which may even approximate hatred, in having to undergo such galling frustration. It then acts like a cub or kitten that scratches and bites as a means of disciplining the hand that occasionally feeds it. But also, and from an early age, children learn that their personal need is more likely to be satisfied if they show appreciation or incipient gratitude for what they do receive. Though not a matter of conscious thought, and often unrecognized by the circumambient adults, this crucial experience is a major advance for a human being. Love as an explicit and more or less sophisticated attitude develops out of the realization that one's needed caretaker can be cajoled through agreeableness as well as through demonstrations of annoyance. Seduction of that sort is an important step in love, though not the first or the last.

Before this momentous event occurs, there often exists a sense of mutual enjoyment between mother and infant, hugging and being hugged, feeding and being fed, each delighting in the other's presence. All human love may issue out of this feeling of oneness. But in itself it is still a primitive reaction that lacks many of the characteristic responses in love. These appear more definitively once the young child learns how to give the caretaker something similar to the goods it hopes to receive.

The smiles and endearing noises that mean so much to parents are adaptive means by which young but rapidly growing humans expand their capacity for love. One might argue that infants are not able to have the kind of awareness that gratitude normally involves.

They do make ingratiating gestures, however, and those are surely related to what we can eventually perceive as a kind of reciprocation. Whatever the innate basis for this maneuver, it is something each child must learn to do. It is part of its equilibration with the surrounding environment constituted by somewhat mysterious parental giants that are not always as kind or cooperative as the child would like.

The process that functions in this manner contributes to filial love that human beings experience. Not only do love and hate have a dialectical relationship to one another, but also they interact differently at various levels of development. Whatever its age or emotional condition, every child learns sooner or later how to integrate—though often badly—the animosity and affection it feels for parental figures that seem to control its entire life.

The need to cope with the fact of generational dominance is accentuated in human beings since we remain dependent on our parents for a greater proportion of our lives than any other species. Prolonged subservience results from our having lost those instincts that make other creatures self-reliant from the very beginning of their existence. This may also help to explain why we develop in later years such extreme capacities for hatred as well as love, and for the frequent interpenetration of these feelings.

As with all human affect, much of filial love is symbolic and imaginative rather than merely biological. The persons toward whom filial love directs itself are not necessarily one's actual parents. Any benefactor can play the role of father, as any nurturant individual or institution can appear to be an alma mater. The relationship that Greek love often dignified, as in some of the speeches in Plato's dialogues, idealized the bond between an older man who offers wisdom or aesthetic refinement and a boy who acknowledges his indebtedness through reciprocal devotion and varied acts of gratitude. On the island of Lesbos, comparable relations may have been cultivated between mature women and the girls they sought to educate.

Leaving aside the physical interests that would commonly have motivated those who believed in this ideal, we may see it as a model for the highly spiritualized interaction between the human and the divine in Western religion. Nowadays we scarcely marvel, as we should, at the suggestion that men and women are the *children* of God. That platitude has become so well established among religious people that few of them realize how enormous is the mythological belief that they swallow with such ease. In both Old and New Testaments man is recurrently portrayed as a helpless being that can and ought to love God the father. In earlier religions devotees saw themselves as the children of Mother Nature or the Great Goddess, much as Catholics may address the Mother of Christ as if she were also their own mother.

Freud attacked Western religion precisely because it projects upon a transcendental plane the love between child and parent that everyone seeks in multifarious ways on earth. He felt that this could only be a neurotic, and therefore lamentable, attempt to solve the problems of filial and parental love. The father one needs and possibly reveres cannot protect us forever. To think there exists in heaven a parental deity who is similar in his relationship to us but endowed with infinitely greater powers can only be a wish fulfillment. If we believe that we may have anything like filial love for this fictional entity, we plunge into a fantasy world that merely weakens us in our struggles with unabating reality.

So Freud argued, and his view is not without merit. At the same time, however, the Freudian critique is simplistic in maintaining that loving God as one might love one's father is only, and always, a means of overcoming the grief experienced when a beloved parent dies. As theologians like Eckhart in the Middle Ages and Paul Tillich in our century have suggested, religious faith can be directed toward a godhead that transcends the usual anthropomorphic conceptions of divinity. In that event, the language of filial and parental love loses its usual connotations and is less likely to project one's anxieties and desperate hopes. Freud's assertion that religious love is just a metaphoric extension of the child's search for parental love might well be true about religion as most people experience it. But the mystical belief in a "God beyond God," assuming such doctrines can be rendered coherent, may indicate that some religious faith can still be justifiable.

Nor should we deny the wisdom in asserting that we are like little children in our relation to the world at large. Even if we glory in the attainments of our species, as humanists in the Renaissance did, we must also realize how insignificant these achievements are within a cosmic setting that we can hardly understand. All things human depend on forces in the universe that bring us into being and support us throughout our existence while also imposing restraints at every moment. To some extent, that is how every child experiences its filial ties.

Even so, the analogy has obvious deficiencies. Despite our poetic mythmaking, not all of nature is alive. Moreover, the portion that is alive rarely has a loving attitude toward us. And though we participate in life, we need not share the lives of our parents. The separateness of human beings serves as a precondition for filial love, as it does for all other types of love. Only the fetus exists within a parental body, and it too is separable. On the other hand, nature is always coursing through us; we can never emancipate ourselves from it. Our relationship to our parents is not the same, regardless of how greatly we may possibly identify with them.

As in a parent's love for its child, filial love occurs within parameters laid down by the human need for autonomy. Even the most clinging of children will normally free itself of the dependence it once required in order to survive. This may not destroy filial love, but it often changes it into responses that enable the child to emulate the parent rather than submitting to it. In growing up, the child adopts valued aspects of the parental character and thereby incorporates the parent as a creator of meaning. But in most cases, children also become parents themselves. Accepting this role, they often extend a protective attitude toward those who showed love in rearing them. Their parents return to second childhood in the sense that they become, in part at least, the children of their children and feel toward them some of the sentiments they originally felt toward their own mother and father.

The ideal of filial love is so important to human beings that we augment opportunities for experiencing it in later life as well as when we are young. An elderly father may not welcome his increased dependence on his son; he will resent being told how to spend the remaining years of his life. But he may be comforted by the idea that the younger man will share some of his burdens and possibly take care of him in his final illness. A mother may feel hurt because her children no longer respect her code of values, but she too will be glad to think that the management of the family now falls on their shoulders rather than hers. In general, we hope to receive from our children a kind of quasi-parental love directed toward us that may be—if only they are willing to forgive our previous inadequacies—commensurate and even superior to whatever love we once gave them.

Peer love has been neglected and sometimes disregarded, even by thinkers who understand the dynamics of affective relations within a family. It tends to be interpreted either as an incipient stage in sexual love or as a period of latency that enables separation from the parents to become a viable reality. But peer love has a structure all its own, and within the trajectory of individual development it has an essential part to play. It is a form of friendship that matters greatly to children, though as adults they often forget that it ever existed. Moreover, friendship love or friendliness in later life evolves out of the bond that peers can have with one another.

The relationship between parent and child is inevitably vertical. Parental and filial loves move up or down as progressions within a hierarchy of dominance and acquiescence, protection and submission, authority and liberation within the family unit. In contrast, peer bonding cuts across the grain. Peers relate to one another more or less on an equal footing, within a horizontal excursion that takes them beyond filial concerns. Whether as fellow children in day camp or as companions marching off to war, they easily identify with one another. It is as if they were indeed the alter egos referred to in the myth of Aristophanes. They are not bifurcated halves of a prior identity, but the sense of equality may cause each to feel that the peer is virtually another self. Regardless of differences among them, they are socially kindred spirits at this moment in their lives.

Peers are drawn to one another because they find themselves in the same boat, a fairly small one that they have been thrown into by their similar experience of life and often for no biologic reason. If there is a genetic tie, as there would be between siblings or cousins, this may well intensify the bond. But in itself the peer relation is based merely on an awareness of resemblance in one's condition rather than identical lineage. In adulthood it reappears when strangers in some remote corner of the globe suddenly realize that they speak the same language or are nationals of the same country or even grew up in the same town. Though the peers have different tastes or interests, and would ordinarily be jockeying for power, the feeling that unites them arises from a joint recognition that their situations are indeed alike. Unrelated as they may be throughout the gamut of their lives, they see each other as an image of themselves. In some respects it may even be a mirror image.

A person is not the same as his mirror image, and no one has ever thought that what he finds in the mirror is really him. He sees an object of his perception, not to be confused with what he himself is. But the mirror image resembles us in ways that allow us to treat it as our own. Projecting aspects of our appearance upon a solid surface, it flatters us even when it makes us look less attractive than we would like to seem. For it deigns to show us forth. Our peers provide a comparable service. They are living representations of our reality—like ontological performers or actors portraying humanity but without a stage. Once we accept the fact that they have lives of their own to lead, we may come to love them. By seeing ourselves in them, we make them honorary participants in our own self-love.

Originating under these circumstances, peer love introduces an element of the greatest importance in all social love. I am referring to the ability of lovers to experience a sheer and sometimes indiscriminate pleasure in just *being with* each other. Throughout the relationships that define parental and filial love, this pleasure is diluted by the hierarchical nature of the bond. Though mother and infant may feel wholly satisfied in simply pressing against one another, parental and filial relations are generally charged with sentiments that exceed the basic goodness of enjoying the presence of the other person. The parent feels a sense of responsibility; the child sees the parent as a looming authority. But when peers spend their time together, doing nothing out of the ordinary, walking together in silence perhaps or waiting side by side for a bus to arrive, they have access to one another's company merely in being themselves. They are mutually immersed in the flow of their platitudinous lives, and the mutuality itself becomes a precious consummation.

Even when little children play at separate games, in isolation though in the same room, their proximity often seems to provide a meaningful sense of fellowship. They ignore each other most of the time and in fearful moments they will scurry back to their mothers, but they know that others like themselves are present and doing similar things. This feeling of reassurance, which can eventually include affection, will also extend to dolls or animals with whom they can identify. In addition to everything else that happens in this situation, they are learning how to be companionable, and that develops into a capacity for friendship.

When one of my children was small, she received a book about friendship (given to her by a friend of mine) that said "A friend is someone who likes you." This may stand as a necessary condition for friendship, but there is another that seems to me equally important. A friend is not only someone who likes you; a friend is also someone who is *like* you. We cannot hope to be friends with aliens from another galaxy whose minds and manners are totally strange to us. The same applies for organisms on earth that have lifestyles incongruent with ours. It may not matter that the other creature has traits or interests that are vastly different from our own. "A dog is a man's best friend" has doubtless been true for many men. What links the two is the ease with which they engage in similar pursuits and tend to share similar values. At the very least, they cherish their joint participation in what they do together. They are like each other in these areas of their lives, though certainly not in others.

To the man the dog he loves may be a subordinate who must be trained and disciplined; to the dog the man may be a leader of his pack whom he must dutifully follow. To that extent, they are not peers and theirs is not a friendship. The two become friends only after their perspectives have been so thoroughly intertwined that each enjoys the other as a companion whose presence or absence matters to them. They acquire a mutual interest in activities they perform with one another and in each other's company—taking a walk or playing ball or wrestling playfully. They need not have the same interests, but they derive a reciprocal pleasure merely in being with each other and acting as if their interests might be identical.

A man and his dog who are friends behave like peers in childhood. But this can happen only after they have surmounted the many differences between them. Among human beings friendship as a developmental capacity normally manifests a previous experience of peer love. As Harry F. Harlow demonstrated in his experiments with primates, those who have had no peer love when they were young find it difficult to make friends when they grow up. At least, friendship will always be rare and frightening for such individuals. Peer love and friendship in general involve the ability to enlarge one's self-love by including another living entity in it, and both presuppose a sense of likeness to that other creature.

These conditions were understood by Plato and Aristotle, who usually take their clear cases of human love from the relationship between friends. In the *Phaedrus* and in several of the speeches of the *Symposium*, Plato would seem to think of love as primarily the bond embodied in friendship, which he portrays as an adventure of like-minded companions striving to attain the Good. Apart from its sexual and metaphysical overtones, his analysis assumes that the participants are satisfying their self-love by means of each other and that this is feasible because they share a similarity of interests.

In the *Nicomachean Ethics* Aristotle uses Plato's conception to exclude persons who are not alike in moral excellence or who seek one another's company merely for reasons of pleasure and utility. He is willing to admit that these relations often go by the name of friendship, but they cannot meet the more stringent demands that he imposes. What he designates as "perfect friendship" is a social but usually nonsexual love between persons who admire one another as virtuous human beings, who see this much of themselves in each other, and who establish a kind of moral partnership that benefits everyone. What Plato interprets as a mutual search for goodness Aristotle depicts as the basis of an ideal community in which likes are not only attracted to likes but also fulfill their social and political potentialities as the fruition of their perfect friendship.

We may well agree with Aristotle when he says that "a friend is another self," meaning another person whose self is similar to one's own. For this signifies only that friendship results from our ability to perceive a likeness between oneself and the other. But Aristotle also believes that friendship precludes any possibility of moral disparity. A good man cannot have real friendship with one who is bad since their differences in virtue, Aristotle thinks, will make them inimical to one another.

In holding this view, Aristotle ignores the capacity of love to treat someone as if he were better than he is. When he makes this kind of bestowal, the good man expresses a belief (naive as it may be) that deep down the bad man he befriends is likewise capable of goodness. If the recipient of such love can accept it as authentic, a lasting friendship may develop. Moreover, even the most virtuous of human beings must realize how easy it would be for him or her to go astray; and this awareness may also provide whatever sense of likeness is needed for friendship to exist. In love there is no condescension. To the extent that we are able to love, we act as if we are all alike—each of us, as in the words of the Negro spiritual, "standing in the need of prayer."

Since he thinks that every love is a form of self-love and that one truly loves oneself by living up to moral ideals, Aristotle finds no way in which perfect friendship could occur among persons who are not equally good as human beings. But this limits friendship to a select community that closes off the potentialities of love. The closed society defines itself in terms of friendship of this sort. In a closed society we make friends only with those who belong to our socioeconomic class, or share our religious faith, or have the kind of educational background we respect, or possibly embody the aesthetic aspirations we admire.

Such friendships can be very powerful. I have no reason to denigrate their emotional value. But even so they do not account for the affiliations that issue from, and partly constitute, the open society. These result from our willingness to admit similarities between ourselves and people who are nevertheless different from us. To be their friends we must experience a kinship in our relative conditions. That can occur even if we are not the same in any of the ways that Aristotle and the closed society claim to be essential.

The kind of friendship that Plato and Aristotle consider perfect is just a particular instance within the genus, though one that moralists have valued very highly. It illustrates only a special kind of relation between peers or equals. The casual colleague or drinking friend whose banter we enjoy need not be engaged with us in any ascent toward duty or goodness. Nor are we likely to strengthen our friendship by comparing respective virtues. It may be wholly sufficient for us that we derive pleasure from one another's presence, from our mutual enjoyment of each other's "conversation" as Milton uses that word when he describes the harmonious attunement within a happy marriage. Having a friend who is ethically (or intellectually) superior to ourselves can be gratifying to our vanity since we assume that he must find in us some rare and desirable quality that we have not yet recognized. Having a friend who is morally in trouble, or even a criminal, can satisfy our inclination to act creatively for the welfare of someone we like.

These and all other kinds of friendship exist as lateral efforts toward oneness. They reveal how another animate being—above all, another member of our species—has a life that is equivalent to our own. Struggling to survive in the world, as we do too, the friend shows us what we both are despite our separateness. Montaigne said that he loved his friend Etienne de la Boétie for no reason other than "because it was he, because it was I." But also it was Montaigne seeing himself in his friend, despite their differences. They could not have been friends otherwise.[2]

When Freud discusses friendship, he tends to think of it as occurring within a group that is structured by subordination to the ego ideal embodied in a father, a general, a religious leader. As children within a family, or soldiers in the same army, or fellow devotees of a supreme deity, we treat one another as peers and potential friends by virtue of our common subservience. In saying this, however, Freud carries into his analysis more of Platonic and Aristotelian idealism than he strictly requires. For though the types of emotional bonding that he specifies frequently occur, they do not exhaust the great variety of friendships available to men and women. Friendly relations, ranging from the trivial to the most intense, can occur without any acceptance of the same ego ideal.

Indeed, one might analyze peer love and friendship as devices by which the individual *separates* himself from the oppressiveness of authorities such as parents or rulers or whatever gods there be. In carving out their own identities, growing children often gravitate toward one another as fellow sufferers in reaction against the standards of rectitude that have thus far been forced upon them. They are "rebels without a cause," as in the film with that title. Friendship then becomes solidified in the mutual process of helping each other assert the autonomy of his or her being.

The chance acquaintance on a train, the baseball fan one sees at every game, the neighbor who lives through a calamity with us—all these can elicit friendliness that approximates the love that peers experience. Even when the unifying situations involve some minimal self-definition in terms of personal ideals, they are grounded in gregariousness and the touch of nature that makes us all akin. Only on occasion, and then often superficially, are they also joint pursuits of virtue. Idealists are sensitive to the beauty that can exist in friendships predicated upon a oneness between noble souls yearning for the same moral and spiritual ends. Nothing I can say will ever diminish the splendor and profundity in that kind of relationship. Without it human love would lack a great deal that people have rightly treasured. But here, as in the rest of our reasoning, we must never forget that our love of ideals has only a limited importance in the totality of human nature.

❄

This caveat is particularly relevant to discussions about types of social love that are intermediate between friendship and the love of humanity. These are often considered reducible to the types of love we have already mentioned. And indeed marriage based on sexual love can strengthen a parent's desire to love indiscriminately all the members of the family that results from it. Even if one thinks of family love as a summation of parental, filial, spousal, and peer love, which are circumscribed relations, they all have fluid boundaries. They readily extend beyond themselves. Our discussion of peer love has already disclosed how it may reappear in a kind of friendship among members of different species.

At this point we may return to the nature of married love. It is not only a culmination of sexual love and a plausible basis for family love but also the embodiment of a unique type of friendship. Through sexual love men and women overcome the many differences in attitude and hormonal disposition that may have separated them before they attained their erotic, romantic, and libidinal harmony. Having married one another, however, they run the risk of dulling the edge of sexual interest and losing the peculiar attentiveness that is essential in love. For sexual love to survive the social circumstance that has been appointed as its preservation, the married pair must create a friendship that pertains to them alone. They will then see themselves as equal pillars, each in his or her own way supporting the edifice which is the family structure they build together. Their marital love, if it exists, will be predicated upon that cooperative enterprise while also manifesting the concern for each other that issues from both friendliness and convenient access to whatever sexual consummation they desire.

There may be viable and even functional families in which love between the spouses does not occur. Peer love among the children and parental adjustment to one another may keep such families afloat, particularly when the surrounding society buoys them up. But children generally learn how to love, as they also learn to speak a native language, by imitation of what they hear and see about them. If their parents love each other, despite and possibly because of all the difficulties that accompany their stewardship of the family, the children are more likely to find in later life the type of sexual love that will encourage them to start a family of their own. What they feel for a person they can think of marrying will reflect their earlier observations of what their parents felt for one another.

In a somewhat different manner, family love can also encompass sentiments related to human beings greatly distant in time or space. Piety toward one's forebears, which sometimes turns into retroactive devotion bordering on love, is a feeling of that sort. Knowledge about remote ancestors cannot elicit the same affection that one might have toward parents, children, or siblings. Nor are we capable of experiencing a love of future descendents that would be comparable to our love for those who now surround us. Yet we sense an identity with people who share our lineage even though they live in different periods of history. This may only be a diminished form of social feeling, but it helps to explain why some people care about their genealogy. For them "the family" includes a vast array of persons they will never meet or learn much about.

Basic in this kind of social interest is acceptance of a common destiny embodied in our genes. When we look at photographs of great-grandparents who died a hundred years ago, we frequently detect inklings of what we have since become. We not only see our kinship; we also *feel* it. A love of parents, children, or siblings then appears as a segment within the larger love of family. Those who have it bestow importance upon the causal factors that contribute to their own existence. But since we cannot know even the names of everyone who belonged to our family in the past, or will do so in the future, and since those faces in the photographs are sure to look bizarre and unrecognizable in most respects, our sense of identity takes us beyond the immediate family and becomes an intimation, often vague and merely poignant, about humankind itself.

This is not to say that people obsessed by genealogy are outstanding lovers of the human race. On the contrary, they often turn into snobs and convince themselves that their family tree reaches higher than anyone else's. Even so, the ability to love humanity as such must develop out of affective bonds within one's immediate family and within the wider social units that surround or intersect it. Those who love indiscriminately are generally people who have experienced so much love in their childhood background that they feel no impediment to loving almost every person they meet, or else, like Beethoven, they have had so little family love that they end up loving an abstract figment of human oneness that represents in their imagination what they have wanted all along.

In his description of social institutions, George Santayana emphasizes the differences between family ties and love that may have preceded them through sexual intimacy between the parents. However useful romantic love can be as a preliminary to matrimony, he says that it "is but a prelude to life." He considers routine relations within the family itself as more fully indicative of our capacity to live with others, to establish harmonious affiliations with them, and possibly to love them as human beings. "Passion settles down into possession, courtship into partnership, pleasure into habit."[3]

In saying this, Santayana neglects the way in which the family gives rise to values that are very different from possession, partnership, or habit. What seems to me more relevant is the fact that family life generates an available feeling of *home*, a feeling of being *at* home. If we can have love even for people that we do not know, it is because we feel that (potentially, at least) we might be at home with them as fellows within the human species. We sense ourselves belonging to it as we also belong to the family into which we were born.

In a rudimentary fashion, this sentiment is anticipated by the relationship that mother and infant establish with one another under suitable conditions. Each of them, feeling *heimlich* as the Germans say, experiences a casual but enduring reliance upon the primal comfort that the other affords. Psychiatrists have often stated that the image best typifying harmonious social love is that of the babe nursing at the mother's breast. Their mutual bestowal occurs in the total and familiar inclusiveness that embodies the sense of home. Some may see an earlier example of being-at-home in the fetal or embryonic state, but we might quibble about that as a social relation since the two organisms are not yet separated. Nevertheless, Mother symbolizes the home everyone has had or would like to have had. Even when maternal love is meager or sporadic, its aura extends to the family that becomes a little cosmos of sustenance for the developing child. If the child is happy in this environment, it will develop a fertile love of family and a sense of belonging to a place or social setting that feels like home.

Later, as we mature, many strangers present themselves to our experience. Without fitting into clearly specifiable boundaries, they constitute the world of our humanity. Through our life in an adequate family we learn how to feel at home within that world. That is part of the subtext in Robert Frost's poem "The Death of the Hired Man." The farmer's wife tells her husband that the worker who became a part of their family but then left has now come home to die. The farmer spurns the idea that their former hired man has any right to return. "Home," he says, "is the place where, when you have to go there, / They have to take you in." But his wife thinks differently. She believes that home is something "you somehow haven't to deserve."[4]

Taken literally, the farmer's assertion is surely false. No one has to take anyone back. Yet if the family truly was a home, we may be readmitted as an expression of whatever love that bound the members of it. Such love envelops even those who were not born in this family but joined it later. One might remark that the wayward relative or footloose workman is often accepted out of pity or a sense of moral concern. Quite so, but would these sentiments operate as they do if we did not also feel that family love should be available to anyone who has merely lived in the family, whether or not he otherwise deserves such love? And if we are all part of the human world, can we not hope that regardless of what we have done it too will take us back in compliance with a similar ideal?

For that to occur, society as a whole must be a homeland similar to the family. Some theorists have denied that this can ever happen, the family being "natural" while society is not. But though they are founded on genetic and reproductive relationships, families are not uniquely natural. Since man is a social creature who would not be recognizably himself without the language, the concepts, and the modes of awareness he acquires through civilization, other groups are just as natural as the family. Feelings of love or quasi-love directed toward larger social units may therefore flourish with a considerable degree of innate legitimacy. At one and the same time, these feelings are extensions of family love and yet not wholly reducible to it. Having made its most permanent impression during the highly formative years of childhood, family love prepares us for different but related sentiments we may have in relation to our "people"—which is to say, our tribe, or clan, or country, or nation. It imbues such broader groups with its own indelible values.

This becomes apparent if we think of how the word "nation" is used by Shakespeare in various places. In Shylock's great speech about anti-Semitism, he mentions that Antonio "scorned my nation." Similarly, Captain Macmorris, the Irish officer in *Henry V*, feels enraged when Fluellen teases him about his "nation." Neither Shylock nor Macmorris has in mind a political entity such as present-day Israel or Ireland. They identify themselves with interwoven families that constitute a clan or people. A nation, even in the current sense, is ideally a manifestation of some cultural and genetic subdivision within humanity—a "folk," to use what is now a barbarism in English, or *Volk*, as the German language puts it more colloquially. In actuality, our current nations are clusters of these ethnic groupings imperfectly thrown together for one historical reason or another.

The love of one's country has been a sentiment that millions of ordinary human beings have regularly professed in modern times. It is entirely compatible with distrust and even hatred of one's neighbor. For no individual, above all the person who lives next door, need represent the land we claim to love. We generally choose our leaders from men and women who seem to embody what we would like our country to be, whether or not they are capable of ruling effectively. In the age of television, no American president can be elected unless he has the glamor of a media star.

The country is itself a somewhat fictive entity, unified in the imagination mainly at moments of crisis. When it is attacked, many are willing to risk their lives for it although, at other times, they may be inclined to cheat on their income tax. Love of country is often just an excuse for attacking someone out of sheer combativeness—as when soccer fans forget their love of soccer and fight among themselves merely because they support different national teams. Having left their native turf to do business or take a vacation abroad, countrymen band together like brothers, even if they would never dream of speaking to one another back home.

The pride, the patriotism, the chauvinistic prejudice that fuels such moments of social feeling may add up to something less than love. But under these conditions emotions can sometimes express themselves with a fervor that not only rivals romantic passion but also draws much of its strength from a metaphoric deployment of it. Wars would be less common if human beings were not eager to experience the cathartic ebullience that often occurs when enormous populations are carried away by some real or simulated love of country.

The peril in this type of love is readily ignored by people who crave a feeling of oneness with the other members of the group to which they happen to belong. Are they reverting to the infant's dependence on the mother who provides an all-embracing society? But infants do not kill for that. Militant enthusiasm is a problem for the many adults who do. It brings out the best and worst in people who have developed mature capabilities that are distinctive to human beings. That is why it is so dangerous, while also being inspirational and rousing to the spirit.

❄

The move from love of family to love of nation or country is fairly gradual, and most people make this transition with relative ease. But the love of humanity, which is the next progression beyond these other kinds of social love, involves a very big leap. How many people actually cross this chasm? Relatively few, perhaps. In the ancient world such love would seem to have made little or no sense. Aristotle thought that the ideal polis must be a city state that one could traverse by foot without much difficulty. In that event, how could one possibly care about the multitudes of foreigners who lived outside the small world of social feeling that truly mattered? Aristotle did not deny that all featherless bipeds with intellects comparable to those of a typical Athenian might qualify as human beings. But neither he nor virtually any other Greek philosopher would have seen in this definitional circumstance a good reason for loving them, either as individual persons or in their totality.

The idea of love for humanity, and consequently each man or woman within it, takes on importance only among the Stoics and the Jews or Christians of the first century A.D. If one thinks that a single God created everything, and that each human being is fashioned in his spiritual likeness, one may very well conclude that people are all essentially the same. As children of God and members of the same biological species, they constitute a large family of resemblance. At least in principle, one could therefore feel toward them the type of love that ideal siblings might experience.

In the West the fathers of the church defined their religion in terms of the Bible's two great commandments, the first enjoining a love of God and the second a love of "one's neighbor"—that is, any other human being. But these sages also recognized that the love of humanity could create problems. St. Augustine, himself a child of the old dispensation as well as the new, was particularly concerned about the dubious consequences that might result from distributing one's love without discretion. He saw how easily this could undermine the love we owe to our immediate family, and in general to those with whom we live moment by moment. He felt that a hierarchy had to be imposed among the recipients of our love, and he concluded that obligations to our own people should come first. Freud said the same many years later.

Without denying the holiness in loving humans indiscriminately, regardless of propinquity or family ties, as Christ had done,

Augustine argued that we exist in a moral universe that must extend outward from our intimate and daily relations with one another. No one could have contact with all other people, or even a significant number of them, and therefore our love for persons in the actual groups to which we belong requires our special attention. Though love for the human race is inherently commendable, it would have to be secondary or modulated in its effect. "All . . . men are to be loved equally; but since you cannot be of assistance to everyone, those especially are to be cared for who are most closely bound to you by place, time, or opportunity, as if by chance."[5]

In the philosophy of Henri Bergson, whose influence has waxed and waned throughout the twentieth century, one finds a very different approach to the love of humanity. Bergson distinguishes between "closed morality" and "open morality" in the hope that human beings will someday attain a universal society in which the latter supplants the former. As he defines the relevant terms, closed morality arises from instinctual bonds that impose a sense of obligation upon each individual, while open morality consists in sympathetic identification with the creative vitality in all people.

In the open society, which Bergson recognizes to be utopian, we love all members of our species with a love that is God himself. We do the right thing not because the voice of conscience tells us to, but rather through a spiritual impulse to bring the world closer to an absolute goodness. According to Bergson, that is what motivates the saints and heroes who thereby transcend the limits of their own origins in a particular family, tribe, or country. Nature has provided us with instincts that enforce our allegiance to closed societies such as these. But the saints and heroes experience a love of humanity that Bergson deems superior. It represents a force in nature more ultimate than mechanisms of group survival or solidarity. Through this type of love, as Bergson describes it, the closed society is wholly displaced by the open society that truly shows forth our ultimate being.[6]

Leaving aside difficulties that I encounter in Bergson's conception of sympathetic identification, it seems to me that he is mistaken when he gives the love of humankind principal importance in questions of either ontology or morality. Not only can one doubt the notion that God is in the world as the creative energy that explains our biological or vital development, but also one may refuse to identify ideal morality with an attitude that subordinates every other social love to a love of humanity. What happens in friendship, in sexual and married love, or in the other relationships that we have studied can be equally valuable. Nature would be greatly distorted if the values they entail were swallowed up by an indiscriminate love of mankind. As with every other form of social love, and indeed love in general, devotion to creatures who are merely fellow humans must justify itself afresh on each occasion. Though we may eventually reach ideas about a supreme harmonization among the different types of love, we should not assume a priori that any one of them must always take precedence over all the rest.

At the same time, we can agree that open morality based on the undiscriminating love of human beings is more than just the "extension of an instinct." But what does this imply? Bergson thought that the love of humanity is fundamentally different from the love of one's family or even one's country. Hume had made a partly similar assertion. He called attention to the fact that the feelings we have for people who are remote from us are much weaker than our sympathy for intimates. He nevertheless thought that humanitarian love is strong in many persons and that it bestows upon strangers or unknown individuals a sympathetic concern that resembles what we experience toward those who are closely related to us. Since sympathy itself is limited in its scope, Hume concluded that we render our sentiments more general through an act of rationality. Our judgment tells us that all humans are alike and so we *treat* them in a similar fashion, even though the sympathy we actually feel is addressed only toward people we encounter. At this point Bergson disagrees. To explain how the love of humanity differs from other social loves, he invokes a separate mode of feeling, an intuitional faculty that goes far beyond the intellect.

In the degree that Hume's analysis considers the love of humanity to be the love of family or clan reconstructed through an act of reason, I think Bergson's critique is justified. To love another *as* a human being, though he or she may differ greatly from oneself, requires more than just the recognition that we belong to the same species. For one thing it involves what Shelley, in his essay on benevolence, describes as a unique employment of interpersonal imagination. We thereby put ourselves in the other's position, and thus vicariously undergo what he or she experiences. We resonate with emotions—fear, longing, whatever—that result from our identification with this other person, whom we may never meet or even see.

This complex of imaginative responses makes up a pattern of feeling as well as rationality. It includes more than calm reflections about the similarity in our states of being, and more than just a simulation of the sympathy we feel for persons in our acquaintance. Hume's description may explain the behavior of most people when they contribute to causes that benefit mankind. The philanthropist writing out a check for his favorite charity need not feel much at all. But the love of humanity expresses itself in other ways as well. Though we may not wish to accept the mystical implications of Bergsonian intuitionism, we can agree that people do have sentiments of love that enable them to identify with distant and unrelated individuals. This development out of, but also beyond, family love is suggested by phrases such as "the brotherhood of man." Its imaginative and emotional charge was embodied in the concept of *fraternité* that meant so much to millions in the Romantic period, and has remained as an ideal of modern humanism.

Fraternité is primarily a matter of feeling, rather than extrapolation through the intellect. But it is a feeling that presupposes our sense of life in the family. It is not a separate faculty, as Bergson claims. To the extent that we can have an open society we do not discard but merely redeploy the energies that bring the closed society into being. Family love expands beyond its own domain and this transforms the nature of affective experience. That is why there must be more at stake than just the extension of an instinct. But it is *through*, and not despite, their prior feelings that people acquire whatever humanitarian sentiments they may have. Reason is insufficient for this task, and nature affords us no other means of accomplishing it.

The love of humanity is an ethical ideal. The utilitarian standard puts it to practical use. Yet it is often associated with attitudes that exceed morality. Insofar as it overlaps with compassion for all who suffer or love for enemies and those who oppress us, it is more than merely social love. It is then part of religious love as well. This also happens when we love not only human beings but life itself, and possibly reality as a whole. At this point, love becomes a form of spiritual response. As such, it demands a new set of coordinates for its explanation.

5
RELIGIOUS LOVE

A discussion of religious love ideally requires an understanding of what is called the spiritual life. By and large, the former is a component within the latter that various traditions have cultivated as the embodiment of their particular faith. To analyze the life of spirit properly would take us beyond the scope of the present work. I hope to return to it in another book. Here I need only fit religious love into the general outline that I have been sketching.

At each point my schematic remarks have been based on differences among types of imagination. In religious love, the affective imagination operates on the largest ontological scale. As Santayana said that religion is poetry that "supervenes upon life," so too can religious love be seen as the imagination reaching beyond the limitations of self, friendship, family, nation, or humankind in a supreme attempt to embrace and accept all reality.

Even atheists must be impressed by this aspiration for the absolute. They themselves generally experience the allure of its questing attitude. Why else would they feel so intense a need to deny the existence of a deity? Even if they believe we have no knowledge in this domain, would it not be more convenient, and certainly more comfortable, merely to ignore the affirmations of religious people? Why go to the trouble of refuting them? Atheists often have a cosmic consciousness as highly refined as in the devout believers whose arguments they scorn. To that extent they too may be said to have a "religious attitude," as John Dewey also held. The love of nature or of universal spirit that is frequently substituted for a love of God is itself a form of religious love.

Almost any love approximates religious love when it becomes sufficiently dominant and all-inclusive. As we know from centuries of poetry, the young man or woman in love treats the beloved like a sun or fixed star about which the entire universe must revolve. Despite the astronomic wisdom that tells us the cosmos is not constructed along these lines, the lover is metaphorically expressing truths coherent with his or her own feelings. The divinity worshiped in such love has the same unutterable importance as the God that Jews or Christians or Moslems specify as the object of their devotion.

We might argue that the recipient of sexual love is just a meager droplet within the bottomless ocean of reality. But even if this is a difficulty for those who love only humans, the love of nature can take on the amplitude of total dedication and be as spiritual as any theistic faith. In pantheistic religions, or in the thinking of philosophers like Spinoza, who believed that God and Nature are really the same, naturalist fervor can even claim to be the *only* authentic religious love.

Even when espoused by guileless Christian mystics, pantheistic love has usually seemed outrageous to those who prefer more orthodox expressions of religious feeling. Whatever its faults, however, pantheism provides a theoretical resolution that is benign in at least one respect. It undoes a conceptual knot that theology has fumbled with for two thousand years. Christianity has always wanted to defend two conflicting dogmas. One of these holds that only God shall be the object of our love and that all other love—for instance, sexual love, the love of humanity, or the love of nature as a whole—must be sinful if it treats its object as inherently worthy of being loved. The second view, which has often permeated Christian life, maintains that since God created everything with a loving intent, even what is wholly material can be loved in and for itself. All types of human love are therefore potentially innocent attempts to love oneself or others or even nature not only as spiritual entities but also in the full materiality that God has given them.

Pantheism erases the distance between these two doctrines by taking as literally true the idea that God is in the world. His love and the love of him are then considered essentially the same, an underlying love that shows itself in every other type of love. However possessive maternal love may seem, and however passionate or libidinal sexual love may be, these are just embodiments of God's love carrying out its sanctified mission through natural means. This idea has been accepted and cherished by many people who belong to established religions but do not recognize, or would not agree, that the pantheistic vision is heretical.

I have no need to adjudicate the matter. Such questions are nevertheless worth studying because they illustrate how greatly the religious imagination pervades the life of meaning. Religious love creates meaning in life by affirming an overwhelming, even total, value that love attains once it is felt to emanate from ultimate levels of reality. In its comprehensive searching, the religious imagination functions in the manner of a spy-glass. It extends itself for objects at a variable distance and imposes a cosmic perspective upon them that may eventually guide each moment of one's life.

As I have mentioned, sympathy and compassion are dispositions that can be religious as well as social. This kind of love derives its religious import from the fact that someone cares enough about others to treat them as joint manifestations of life while also recognizing that they are different realities. Every love of persons does something similar, but only in sympathy or compassion does one focus on the fellowship of living together in a largely hostile world and suffering in the way that animate creatures do. Schopenhauer may have been too extreme when he claimed that suffering results from merely being alive, wanting what we need but do not have and never feeling completely satisfied with what we get. Still he was right in thinking that sympathy and compassion can be directed toward whatever suffering does occur, and that these responses unite us most effectively with all the rest of life.

According to Schopenhauer, as I interpret him, no loving response could be more religious or more truly metaphysical than this. Though he insists that such love is generally thwarted by more petty interests, particularly the ones he himself does not have, Schopenhauer scarcely tells us how we may attain the sympathy and compassion he so greatly admires. Possibly it is only an artist like Dante or Shelley or Beethoven in *Fidelio* who can portray the religious dimensions in our sympathetic or compassionate attitude toward persons we know to be different and yet respect as fellow participants in life's tragic comedy—persons we treat as being ontologically equal to us in that regard.

Though they overlap, sympathy and compassion are not identical. Nor is either the same as empathy. Each of the three employs the imagination in a different way. Empathy is a kind of mimicry. Through it we share other people's feelings in the sense that it causes us to undergo something comparable. If they are depressed, we feel heavy-hearted. If they are buoyant, we feel energized or encouraged. As a developmental phenomenon, this may be a preliminary for the eventual occurrence of sympathy or compassion. But affective contagion, as empathy is, need never be a form of *caring*. Empathy bespeaks a fascination with the joy or sorrow of someone who matters to us. For there to be sympathy or compassion, however, we must also care about the welfare of the other person. That emotional investment does not happen automatically, and our empathetic response may never issue into it.

Through sympathy we care about someone primarily as a creature whose feelings we recognize as not unlike our own. Sympathy is more than just a bland acknowledgment or purely cognitive observation: it is also an expression of felt kinship. Without duplicating the other person's distress, we feel it as an unwelcome intrusion whose existence we regret as we would if it happened to us. We sense our likeness as fellow mortals who are liable to the same kind of suffering. We commiserate with the other's sorrow, and rejoice when it is lessened, as a declaration of interpersonal solidarity. In part at least, this is what the Romantics meant by "sympathetic identification" that puts us in another's position. We identify *with* this person inasmuch as we experience the world in a similar way and care about similar things. But in itself sympathy is largely passive. It entails no subsequent or related action. It only *feels* for an individual and possibly contents itself with letting him know its feelings. Frequently it leads on to nothing further.

The other person may not want anything else. We have expressed our sense of likeness with him and shown that what he is undergoing concerns us too. That is something, and often quite sufficient. Yet this sympathetic attitude can also be shallow, both morally and emotionally. It scarcely specifies the nature of our bond, and it does not indicate that we will ever do anything to help the other person. We feel that the world is alike for us, but otherwise our sympathetic response may be wholly vague and indeterminate. It can easily turn into sentimentality. The kind of love that compassion fosters makes our identification more consecutive in our behavior. The imagination then presents the other not only as a human being who resembles us (if it is a human being) but also as one whose suffering we are prepared to alleviate or take upon ourselves even if we could avoid it.

Among the world religions, this employment of the imagination is best understood by Buddhism. While stories of gods and goddesses fill the peripheries of its message, like a beguiling filigree to entertain the mythic consciousness, Buddhism seeks to awaken compassion that causes us to immerse ourselves in the misery of everything else that lives and suffers. The Buddha may be revered as a divinity, but he originates as the all-too-human Gautama who progressively earns the reward of Nirvana but then refuses to accept it. His perfection consists in attaining infinite compassion. That is why he refuses to enter into paradise unless all the rest of suffering life is also admitted.

This gesture of universal love constitutes the supreme holiness of the Buddha, but it is also available to other men and women. No Christ is needed to purify them of their sinfulness. They themselves must learn how to work out their salvation through the diligence of a comparable love. Nor is there any reason to think that their compassionate feats will eliminate the pain of living. While striving to help others, they believe that misery is inevitable in life. When they identify with all the suffering in the world, they duplicate it in themselves as a way of attesting to its evil. They know their loving gesture will not eradicate it. But they have done what they can, and that is what matters most. This love may be purer than the kind that Western religions are usually able to imagine.

Seeking to be compassionate, we need not espouse traditional religions of either East or West. In my book on meaning in life I offered some ideas about an attitude I call "the love of life." I was playing upon the colloquial phrase we commonly use to denote a sense of well-being, a feeling that our own life is rich and refreshing and therefore something we love in itself. People who talk this way mean that they, at least, are glad to be alive. Love of life in this sense expresses and reveals self-love. To love one's life one must love oneself, which I was advocating. At the same time, however, I was referring to a love that we might also have for life as it occurs in all other living things. I knew that what I said might seem to be merely mystical, and I freely admitted my own considerable deficiencies as a lover of this sort. I realized, too, that many moralists would consider my ideas fruitless. That is unavoidable, since the love of life does not imply a single or unitary course of action.

The love of life includes both sympathy and compassion, each involving imaginative responses distinctive to such love. The love of life implies sympathy insofar as it asserts a concern about all instances of life regardless of the differences among them. A sense of community is thereby created, a quasi-social love that enables us to delight in the life that quickens everything that is not dead or inanimate. I am not the same as my dog or cat, but we belong equally to the class of living entities and I respond to them as such. It is as if they are peers within a society that I also inhabit, though possibly as just a surrogate leader or big brother.

To an even greater degree, the love of life involves compassion. My dog and cat are not merely animals I perceive as parts of a life that flows through me as well. I also see them struggling, as I am, to stay alive despite the hardships that are inescapable in fragile beings such as we. Each of us wants to retain our individual mode of existence, and to improve it, whatever fatalities may await us.

The cat and dog seem to have a love of self that is at least as great as mine. If I had an adequate love of life, above all as it appears in them, I would feel a compassionate oneness with their condition. They are pitiable despite the goodness of being alive, of having health and strength and access to many pleasurable possibilities. Their experience in life is worthy of pity and compassion, as mine is too, because it arises from material forces that constantly threaten our destruction even while sustaining us for the time being.

A truly compassionate life is one in which caring *about* shows itself in a willingness to take care *of*. Without intruding upon the autonomy of the other person, our sympathy transforms itself into action. Feeling and behavior then make a total unity that manifests an ever-increasing capacity to love life wherever it occurs, and in itself. This goal may be unrealizable, as I myself believe, but it is worth striving for.

Once we distinguish between sympathy and compassion, and appreciate their authentic function in a love of life, we see how different is the Christian notion that God descends to wash away the sins of humanity. This idea is offered as a proof of God's identification with man, and indeed Christ appears in the form of a human being, just as human beings are said to be created in the likeness of God. Through the incarnation a new society is born. Believers become members of Christ, as they are also members of their local tribe or nation. A grand bestowal of this sort would seem to be supremely compassionate, since Christ enables all people to surmount the sufferings that issue from sinfulness. But the doctrine is chaotic. For the God who sends his only begotten son, a person within his own divinity, is also the source of everything in the world that causes suffering. How then can he truly identify, in either sympathy or compassion, with his hapless victims?

Comparable difficulties attend the dogmas of the other Western religions. But if we supplant them by a more plausible materialism or atheistic naturalism, we encounter problems that are equally troublesome. These secular philosophies may help to justify the love of life, but they can also prevent us from experiencing it as *religious* love. Not only will we have discarded the love of God, to which I will presently return, but also the love of nature and the cosmos will need to be renounced or totally reinterpreted. People create religions because they recognize that life occurs within an immediate environment that is not itself alive. By loving an ever-present and ever-living God, or the gods in general, they assure themselves that all existence has meaning and may even be infused with love. Neither materialism nor naturalism, in most of their varieties, can offer that assurance.

In the Romantic era, philosophers and theologians often sought to resolve the issue by erasing the usual distinctions between the animate and the nonanimate. The love of nature that resulted was often just a love of scenery, a bestowal upon vistas or aesthetic objects that were said to emanate from nature but really manifested our poetic experience of it. Beautiful sunsets and starry nights were invested with extraordinary implications. That kind of love had been developing for many centuries in the West. One of its earliest stages occurs when Petrarch describes Mont Ventoux in 1336 not as a physical object or as a symbol of hierarchical being in the universe, but as something he himself ascends. His mere experience as an ardent mountain-climber signified to him the religious meaning that all of nature manifests. This humanization of the material environment may be soothing to those who think that life as it occurs in us is the goal of life itself, wherever and however it exists. To the extent that one considers such humanism overly anthropomorphic, however, the religious imagination will find neither comfort nor reassurance in it.

Pascal understood the problem as well as anyone. He speaks of the paralyzing fright he feels as a petty human being contemplating the enormity, and "the silence," of interstellar space. Even if there is life in other regions of the firmament, we may quake as he did at the awareness that the universe would mainly seem to be a set of tremendous furnaces. Pascal overcame his fear by believing that everything material was ontologically derivative from the infinite goodness of a God who creates all matter and can be loved as a person.

Without this leap of faith, the love of reality as a whole may not make any sense. Nature's laws, however science portrays them to us, are not inherently lovable. We can possibly understand Margaret Fuller's claim that she accepts the universe, but we also see the rightness in Carlyle's remark: "Egad, she'd better." The universe is *there*; we cannot escape it. If it is not alive in its totality, or produced by a living and benign progenitor, what reason have we to love it—assuming that we are even capable of such love?

One might say that we can love the cosmos as we also love our automobile or hometown. These are not alive, and yet they sustain us in our being. Can we not feel gratitude to even a purely material universe that does the same and more extensively? That would be reasonable if we had an adequate idea of what this universe is like in its entirety as a single entity. But though we may have considerable experience of an automobile or the town we live in, what we call "the universe" is mainly an abstraction to us. People can love parts of it that are present to their consciousness and amenable to their interests, but most of it defies comprehension—by human beings, at least—and we may wonder whether anyone can truly accept or love it as a whole.

Since cosmic love is so dubious, it is understandable that doctrinal faiths have generally tried to subsume it within the love of God. The crucial word is capitalized in order to distinguish him (her?) from the gods of more primitive religions. These had names of their own, as people do, and like human beings no one of them could combine within his or her personality all that we consider important in the universe. In the monotheistic religions God's being is taken to be the ground for Being as such. He provides an explanation for the occurrence of anything that exists, and his love enables us to love whatever might exist. God creates it all either in one act—as a single bestowal of love—or progressively through benign intervention, or even (as Leibniz thought) by getting things going and then letting them develop as they will, like a hand that puts the needle on a phonograph. Being a supernatural person, God could be loved as one also loves persons in the world. To love the world itself, one had to see it as the manifestation of God's loving creativity. Even in the parts or elements that we can know and appreciate directly, the world would not be lovable except as an offshoot of the deity whose personality we revered. God was identified with the very essence of love, as in Christianity, and only he was ultimately worthy of being loved.

This conception of God as both love and the uniquely suitable object of love has been attacked in many ways that theologians must take seriously but that we may well bypass in this place. What primarily concerns me is the idea that since no one but God can truly love and be loved all human love is merely derivative. The love that men and women experience is treated like a borrowed light reflecting back whatever luminosity it can garner from its supernatural source.

As I mentioned earlier, Christians—for instance, Luther—sometimes argue that by his nature man is unable to love; others, such as Aquinas, insist that God bestowed the capacity for love on human nature as an act of grace. In either event Christianity, which calls itself the religion of love, must face the anomaly of believing that its own practitioners, however devout, cannot love anything except in a secondary manner. Even when directed toward God, love would have to be a kind of wish fulfillment, something that we idealize above everything else but can never hope to attain without divine intervention.

The enormous pessimism in these views about our ability to love anything, including God, should encourage us to seek a more naturalistic analysis. If we look impartially at our condition, we find a mixture of nobility and depravity, portrayed in exhaustive detail by all the great poets and artists. To the innocent eye it seems obvious that people are capable of loving, though they may not do so wisely on many occasions. Love belongs to human nature itself. It is part of what we are as a species that has evolved on this particular planet. In that sense, it is one among other primary constituents of our being. Through bestowal and appraisal man creates value and therefore loves, sometimes with insight and great tenderness, much as the Judaeo-Christian tradition thought that only God does. The idea of God embodies our aspirations toward this ideal: it symbolizes a goal that human perfectionism seeks.

The love of God cannot be duplicated by other types of love. It would be a mistake to assume that it is comparable, even on a higher plane, to any of the previous categories I have discussed in this book. It transcends each of them individually while including them all. In the process, however, they imbue it with their own particular meaning. Not only is God referred to as a loving parent one should love in return, but also, in modern religions, he receives the same devotion as earlier faiths bestowed upon distant ancestors. Other types of love are involved as well. In seeking oneness with the deity, whether in merging or the wedding of spirits, the saints have often described their union in the language of romantic and even libidinal love. Christ is often portrayed as the bridegroom who unites with man's soul in a spiritualized equivalent of married love. Loving God as he does, the believer may feel certain he is responding to a divine presence that fills this world with a holiness that originates outside of nature. Since none of this is verifiable, however, the cash value of such intuitions resides in the earthly experiences with which the love of God is associated and to which it lends an aura of sanctification.

In the traditional view, nothing would be worthy of love unless there existed a God who freely bestows goodness upon the world. But if we believe that love is a natural response to which we have access as human beings, we avoid this bleak conclusion. On the other hand, we can see how even the love for a nonexistent God may be defensible when it strengthens our inclinations toward love itself. For the idea of God has a special function, and the love of God belongs in a class by itself. God, as religious people usually think of him, is more than just a perfect and eternal source of love. He is more than just an ideal creator of value. He is all-powerful and all-knowing as well as all-good.

Santayana found a contradiction in these ascriptions, since

knowledge and a concern for goodness pertain to a realm of spirit that he considered incapable of exercising power over a world that is ultimately material. To this extent, the love of God would seem to be internally confused. That may be the case. But the fact remains that all people desire power, knowledge, and goodness. It is not surprising that they should direct their love toward a perfect being who is not only a person but also one who manifests the values and ideals embodied in our longing for power, knowledge, and goodness. Religious faith that has developed in the West makes this kind of love an urgent reality, and even necessity, for men and women who might not have led meaningful lives without it. The fundamental incoherence of the established dogmas does not prevent them from transmitting viable systems of behavior. The religious imagination may even claim that this alone justifies its flight into the unknown. Using its resources in an attempt to love God, it makes its own realm of meaning, its own heaven on earth. Is any other defense needed?

❄

I myself have never experienced much religious love. I was reared in a religion that presented to my unformed intelligence a conception of a monotheistic and distinctly paternal creator whom I could always trust. I cannot say that I felt real love for this nebulous being. Although I greatly loved my father, I did not aspire toward a love of God. When I was very young, I had a sense of awe and frightened respect for this deity, but the relevant sentiments dissipated when I could no longer think of him as an ever-present person. That idea was, and is, too remote from my actual experience to have had much effect on me.

At the same time, I realize that I may not be representative in this regard. Love for a personal God who is omnipotent, omniscient, and omnibenevolent has united millions who might otherwise feel they have nothing in common. It is often the only kind of love that they can experience. I admire their ontological and affective audacity. I am grateful for the ritual and artistic productions through which their kind of mentality has frequently expressed itself. I appreciate the aesthetic value in religious works of art without sharing the faith that brings them into being. What I cherish is life disporting itself imaginatively at levels that only a religious attitude can reach. I feel no need to accept either the ideational formulas of religion or the repellent fanaticism to which they often lead.

To a naturalist in philosophy traditional ideas about religious love can be important for learning about human nature. What could be more natural than to love that which rules the universe, whether or not it is a person? It symbolizes and embodies the total mastery for which our own self-love hungers; its cooperation is essential if desire for any object is to succeed; it shows itself in the underlying sustenance the cosmos provides merely in allowing us to live and pursue our purposive goals. Reverence, even adulation, toward the source of power is possibly the most primitive love in human beings. Religious doctrines transmute such feelings into an idealized craving, satisfiable only by a supreme being who wields the greatest possible power. In our evanescent lives, shipwrecked on the strand of finitude and soon to be washed away, this desperate need for oneness with that than which nothing could be greater must surely resonate to some degree in everyone.

At the same time we learn sooner or later that the world defeats our attempts to understand its reality, even when we acquire useful information about it. We tend to identify ourselves with our consciousness—a fundamental mistake that engenders a multitude of errors. Like Socrates, though without his clarity or honesty, we gradually recognize how much we do not know. We perceive that memory is inaccurate, and predictions of the future uncertain. Our sense organs are often unreliable. Even vision, that symbol and conveyor of knowledge about the external world, is subject to myopia, distortion, and blindness. How wonderful it would be to grasp the truth about everything, to understand all manner of things instantaneously and to apprehend the universe in an intuitive glance more effortless than any faculty of ours can ever yield! It is understandable that our frantic imagination, spinning wildly in this religious fantasy and pushing aside all qualms about verifiability, should posit the existence of a being that is capable of such superlative cognition.

But in feeling love for the omniscient person we call God, can we understand what is meant by that *everything* he presumably knows? We use panoramic words like "ultimate reality" as if their meaning were apparent to us. But is it? As we are delighted with ourselves when we decipher something, we love the idealized person who knows all things spontaneously, from eternity, without limits, and to perfection. As if through a glass darkly, we seem to detect an absolute mind worthy of inspiring total devotion in creatures who are intellectually as frail as we are. Our quest for certainty is so obsessive that we scarcely realize that the glass may only be a mirror that reflects our own inadequacies, instead of giving us a means to overcome them through love.

What strikes most forcibly upon our heart of hearts, however, is God's capacity for omnibenevolence. We could accept our alienation from perfect knowledge or power if only we felt sure that the world is governed by the good. That is what sustains Piccarda in her abode on the outskirts of heaven, as Dante describes her in his *Paradiso*. She puzzles him by saying that she, like all the blessed spirits, finds peace in submitting to God's will even if this means being distant from his luminous presence. Dante has trouble with the idea that one can love God and yet tolerate remoteness from him.

What Piccarda has learned, and Dante eventually will, is that human beings can cheerfully forfeit their hopes for infinite power and submit to any cosmic necessity provided that the ruling order is a good one. Similarly, they can live with the recognition of basic ignorance about a world that systematically frustrates their search for total knowledge, if only they are assured that all is for the best. A God in whom we can truly trust must be one whose omnipotence and omniscience implement his unbounded goodness. In this sense the love of God finally depends on his being and remaining an omnibenevolent creator.

In effect, that was the staggering idea that Plato imparted to all succeeding generations. But Plato did not believe that love is itself the greatest of all goods. He thought it was merely that which propelled us toward the greatest good. In the Judaeo-Christian tradition, particularly as it developed in the concept of agapē, love is identified with infinite goodness. This notion constitutes an unparalleled development of the religious imagination. In saying that God *is* love, sheer bestowal of value expressing his essential being, Christianity invites its believers to seek a love for love itself and to realize that nothing can be better than the good that love entails. By asserting that the goodness of love is endlessly bestowed by the supernatural person who ordains that all things shall be as they are, Christian doctrine reassures us that our own love is grounded in reality.

This is what we all long for. The desire for an all-embracing love that is real and possibly reciprocal underlies our various attempts to love other persons. That is why religious love for a living deity more worthy of love than any alternative can be so compelling. It provides a framework within which all other loves may be accommodated in one fashion or another. It is a beautiful tapestry that the idealizing imagination weaves as either the background or the foreground of affective life. One would have to be aesthetically insensitive and spiritually dead not to recognize the grandeur of its design.

This is not to say that religious love has exclusive value or must be a major part of everyone's life. Pluralism is as relevant to religious love as to the other types. Unlike the essentialists in philosophy—Plato, Freud, and most Christian thinkers—I see no merit in defining love in terms of one or another of its varieties. Though we tend to associate love with the love of persons, even this may be of lesser importance to many people on many occasions. Similarly, we can assert that religious love (or sexual love or maternal love) is defensible or "primary" only after we have specified our personal interest and point of view.

If we are talking about individual development, mother's love may be taken as the source of all future possibilities. But it need not be wholly determinant beyond the temporal stages in which it occurs. At least, not for everyone. In its own dimension, sexual love—particularly when it involves libidinal instinct—may often take precedence. When I was a teenager in the army and in combat, I was struck by the extent to which the sex drive seemed to fill every moment of our lives despite our constant fear of death, or possibly because of it. In other circumstances, other social attitudes predominate. Religious love may certainly do so for those who have the faith, but that does not make it definitive of love in general.

Does this mean that religious thinkers are wrong to promote and extol the love of God? Not necessarily. It receives unique importance from its ability to incorporate every other type of love. It thereby reveals imagination functioning at its most sublime and also most precarious. The peril in religious love arises from its tendency, latent though not always actualized, to assume that all other loves have subordinate value. The true believer will scarcely admit that sexual love, parental love, or any of the others, can be simply what they are in nature and neither a showing forth of God's love nor a circuitous means of loving him. To the extent that it denies the independent validity of predilections that are merely natural, religious love violates the integrity of any love that is different from itself.

Despite this drawback, the love of God vividly illustrates two of the corollaries that must always accompany a satisfactory pluralism. The first of these is the principle of harmonization. Once we move beyond the essentialistic hope to find a one and only mode of behavior or choice of object that uniquely defines what love is, we realize that its diverse manifestations can be harmonized in different ways. To think that any one harmonization is preferential would be to reinstate essentialism at a higher level, and theories about the love of God are often guilty of that. But their attempt to effect *some* kind of harmonization that matters to human beings is surely praiseworthy. Having restored the naturalistic elements that were expunged or neglected by traditional dogmas, and having repudiated claims to literal truth, religious faith can then espouse whatever modes of harmonization it prefers. Such harmonizations need not conform to beliefs about the love of God that have prevailed thus far. Legitimate and wholesome religious love can be nontheistic or even atheistic as well as theocentric.

The second corollary turns upon the notion of dialectic interaction. For if we allow a plurality of loves, each potentially as authentic as the next and all of them requiring harmonization of some sort, we must expect them to vary in their response to one another. In life as we know it, everything is subject to change despite its conservative impulse to remain the same; and the changes that do occur often result from dynamic confrontation with external forces. The same applies to love in general, and specifically religious love as a human attitude that must coexist with all the different kinds of love that people have in their relations to each other.

Parental love as it interacts with the child's love may serve as a model of how human beings acquire the ability to experience love in any of its varieties. At every moment, each participant succeeds and fails in terms of expectations arising from the situation itself. Attempts to love develop responsively through intricate permutations from moment to moment. Love is formed by reciprocal adjustments that differ greatly in endurance and longevity. This affective process may be studied like any other fact of nature. It operates through causal vectors that establish what does or does not come into being. Whether good or bad, desirable or undesirable under the circumstances, each surviving harmonization establishes the emotional character of a person or a culture. It both fashions and reveals the meaning of love in that local setting. If we treat religious love as a phenomenon of this sort, as one among other ways of loving that contribute to consummatory experience, it may have a vital place in the good life. A priori, at least, it need not be excluded.

6
CIVILIZATION & AUTONOMY

Throughout Western philosophy we constantly encounter a distinction between two faculties of human nature, one of which goes by the name of "reason" and the other designated as "passion." Love was usually assigned to the second of these categories. But in Plato there had already occurred an attempt to harmonize love and reason. Though he describes Eros as a kind of emotional yearning, Plato's entire analysis tries to prove that love consists in a striving for metaphysical goodness that only rationality can discern. True love was thus a blending of the two faculties—emotion acceptable to reason, or even reason that has become emotional itself. The Platonic ladder of love shows struggling humanity how to transcend merely passional love by substituting an enthusiastic quest for values that our intellect discloses. This higher disposition was supremely rational, and yet it too was love—a love of abstract forms culminating in the Good.

When Plato's Christian followers eventually articulated similar ideas about the *ordo salutis* (ladder of salvation) that could bring us closer to God, they emphasized the extent to which the emotional element remains intact throughout. As in the words of the Bible, God was to be loved with all one's heart, soul, mind, and strength. Like Plato, the Christians insisted that spiritual love can prove itself wholly justifiable to any rational scrutiny. Properly understood, passion and reason could not be antithetical: in one who knows and appreciates ultimate reality, both faculties coalesce.

From the very outset, however, this belief in harmonization was repudiated by another way of thinking. Partly in Aristotle's teachings and surely by the time of the Stoics, there appears a conviction that passion and reason can never be reconciled with one another. Humanity had to choose between the values of emotion and cognition. The Stoics in particular, and even the Epicureans, who differed greatly from them in other issues, thought we must give up the experience of love if we hope to attain the good life. They extolled respect for rationality that runs counter to emotional exuberance. Since love pertained to strong and often passionate feelings, it necessarily undermined self-control imposed by reason. Spiritual liberation required a choice between the two. The harmonizing of love and reason might be a beautiful ideal, but it was thought to be unattainable even by enlightened or healthy-minded men and women.

In more recent centuries, traditional moralists have often rehearsed what by now has become a platitudinous contrast between love and reason. This was a common theme in the seventeenth and eighteenth centuries. The Romantic movement of the nineteenth century stood in opposition to all such distinctions. It found in emotion a kind of wisdom that the rationalists in philosophy had generally neglected, and it treated reason as inevitably subservient to more passional aspects of human nature. The Romantic outlook is beginning to recede from our immediate consciousness at the end of the twentieth century, but it must be kept in mind if we wish to understand one of the seminal works of the last hundred years. In *Civilization and Its Discontents* Freud attacks the optimistic belief that reason and passion can be harmonized with one another, or amalgamated in any of the ways that idealists such as the Platonists or the Christians or the Romantics recommended.

If Freud is right, civilization cannot be cured of the most basic of its discontents. Humanity is forever doomed to a split between its rational and emotional faculties that lingers ineradicably within its nature. Any theory of culture or psychology or politics that ignores this ultimate division must therefore end up with a wholly distorted perspective. If Freud is right, the potential consequences are enormous for psychiatric theory and the philosophy of love, and also for speculation of any sort about the human condition.

In the dualistic manner that is characteristic of him, Freud presented similar ideas at various times in his career. Distinguishing between the pleasure principle and the reality principle, he implied that the latter gives us reasonable advice while the former leads us to act on feeling or impulse. Throughout his mature thinking, he emphasized the conflict between cultural and instinctive elements of human psychology. In *Civilization and Its Discontents* this approach finally issues into his pessimistic belief that civilization and sexual love must always be engaged in war with one another. That in turn implied an ultimate and unavoidable limitation upon human freedom: since existence in society involves repression and the frustrating of innate drives, we can never achieve the freedom that would come from satisfying our nature as we would like. For this misfortune in our condition, Freud concluded, there is no possible remedy.

Despite the pessimism in these dualistic ideas, Freud recognizes that civilization itself develops by means of a love that is essential for its existence. This is love that binds the members of a group who have common interests. It consists of sublimations that have turned into religious or humanitarian love—the love of God as well as attempts to love one's neighbor and even one's enemy. Freud considers such love to be aim-inhibited since he believes that all love, however remote from apparent sexuality, reduces to the drive for libidinal satisfaction.

Though he is convinced that religious and humanitarian types of love are generally unrealistic, and therefore morally suspect, Freud explains their occurrence in terms of civilization's justifiable need to use them as instruments for the control of human aggression. In the process, aim-uninhibited love (i.e., sexual or genital love) is also throttled to some extent. Since it contains components of aggressiveness that civilization finds threatening, sexual love must be curtailed in its expression and even impaired within itself.

Though people want love as well as civilization, thinking they are both agencies for the attainment of greater happiness, Freud emphasizes the unavoidable struggle between them that often causes pervasive misery.

I do not wish to deny the value of Freud's pessimism. Compared to the utopian speculation of either his Marxist critics or his wilder revisionist adherents, he speaks with a sense of horrified realism that one must respect. Like the prophets of the Old Testament he has seen so much suffering, and so little joyfulness, among humans that he despairs of virtually all proposals about improving our lot on earth. Without determining how much happiness *Homo sapiens* may or may not be able to attain, we may nevertheless feel that Freud's analysis is unduly negativistic. The distinctions upon which it is predicated are inadequate for the devastating inferences he draws. In fact, his arguments are often circular: the premises he formulates already presuppose his dire but unsustained conclusions. Defining love, civilization, and the striving for freedom or happiness as he does, Freud misleads us about the harmonizations to which they may possibly contribute.

In the introduction to this book I suggested that Freud's conception of human experience was mistaken in two respects: first, in thinking that since everything past is preserved, the "found" is really a refound; second, in assuming that civilized responses are inherently noninstinctual and therefore that sexual interests must derive from the libido independently of civilization. The chapters that preceded this one have chipped away at these beliefs. We are now in position to attack them frontally.

At the most fundamental level, Freud's principal error consists in relying on a mechanistic model for his analysis. In his attempt to fashion a psychology that approximates sciences like physics or chemistry, he describes experience in terms of "energy" being employed for one or another purpose. He detects conflict between civilization and sexuality whenever the former takes this energy from the latter and puts it to its own uses. But though we can talk this way, as we do in remarking that a man neglects his wife's sexual needs because all his energy has gone into pursuing his career, such language requires amplification in a direction Freud does not take.

The man who directs his basic stamina toward business or a profession, rather than sexual fulfillment, does so as an expression of what matters most to him. Possibly he finds no other way to support his family and he may even tell us that "ultimately" he cares for them more than anything else. Whatever the details of the particular situation, each pattern of experience or behavior requires an explanation in terms of meaning and the making of individual choices. This implies an analysis that investigates, as no mechanistic model can, the ways in which human life manifests a search for values and a continuous reconstitution through the imagination of the world we recognize as our own.

Once we think of the relationship between civilization and sex or love in this manner, we see how indefensible Freud's dualistic vision can actually be. By "civilization" he means the instrumentalities of law, social opinion, custom, and regional belief that descend upon biological reality as an external imposition. Compared to the libido, which is oriented toward pleasure in the individual and reproduction of the species, civilization must always appear secondary or inessential. Libido shows what nature has ordained, Freud assumes; civilization must therefore be relatively artificial.

At the same time Freud recognizes that civilization also serves Eros, which is to say the life-force. He thereby acknowledges that civilization can be more than just a superficial restraint. What he does not see, or fully appreciate, is the extent to which civilization plays a creative role in the experience of both love and sexuality. Far from being artificial, it is an integral part of the quest for meaning that is distinctive of human nature as it appears in these affective areas.

In one place Freud relates the level of civilization to the "beauty, cleanliness and order" that has been achieved in advanced societies. He says that these three "obviously occupy a special position among the requirements of civilization."[1] He also identifies civilization with the "esteem and encouragement of man's higher mental activities—his intellectual, scientific, and artistic achievements."[2] Among these attainments he lists religion, philosophy, and a dedication to humanitarian ideals as foremost examples of civilized pursuits.

In contrasting civilization with sex or love, and in claiming that warfare between them can never be eliminated, Freud emphasizes the sacrifices that must be made if we wish to devote ourselves to one or another of these contending forces. He sees the life of the mind as an austere searching for truth that requires a virtual suppression of libidinal or hedonic possibilities. He approximates Goethe's Mephistopheles, who says: "All theory is gray, but life's golden tree is green." Freud perceives that a cultivated existence greatly differs from one that is animalistic. And he is right in thinking we may sometimes have to choose between these two forms of life. But he fails to recognize that they are paths within a single landscape: divergent as they may become, they also conjoin or crisscross throughout our experience.

Much of our sexual behavior, and much of what we feel as sexual impulse, is itself a product of civilization. Society provides us with our conception of what is beautiful in sexual objects, and it accentuates or diminishes our sensitivity to their charms in accordance with its own developed predilections. In human beings we rarely find an expression of wholly unadulterated lust. Appetite generally occurs through the mediation of acquired tastes or preferential selections that manifest standards of value in our cultural upbringing.

Nor is this civilized element essentially nay-saying. When he describes Western romantic love as "lust plus the ordeal of civility," Freud sounds as if the civilities of social life play only a negative or tactical role in lovemaking. But this is blatantly cynical, and surely mistaken. Though civilization may indeed demand renunciation, it also arouses affective interest. It often invites us to grasp and enjoy the delectable objects it embellishes, luring our sensory experience into imaginative possibilities that might not otherwise have presented themselves.

In general, civilization is bivalent just as sexuality is. Sex can be an aggressive acquisition of selfish pleasures, or else a humane sharing of mutual satisfactions. So too can civilization enforce harsh mandates that throttle pleasurability; or else it can speak in sweet and seductive tones that awaken our fondest dreams of amatory delight. It is because the latter function has been so highly esteemed in modern society that television commercials are able to succeed as well as they do. They represent what is meaningful and valued in our civilization. They show what matters to us as civilized people who live in the present.

In the Viennese society he knew best Freud was struck by the great amount of sexual repression that was prevalent. Had he wished to do so, he could have focused upon the sexual freedom that many people enjoyed in the same city and at the same time. Like most European capitals toward the end of the nineteenth century, Vienna encompassed libertine as well as puristic lifestyles. Freud explained the repressiveness that came to his attention as the price one had to pay for the amenities of modern life. He ignored the sexual opportunities and refinements that also belong to it.[3]

Over and above his ideas about civilization's effect on sexuality, Freud suspected that the sexual instinct itself may have been impaired far back in human evolution. In these musings about organic repression, as I mentioned earlier, he suggests that man may have lost his ability to satisfy the libido fully when he attained the bipedal position. The olfactory sense would then have diminished in acuity, and the genitals (of the males, at least) would have become more greatly exposed to attack. Freud considers this development crucial in the evolution of our species, and he wonders whether it may even have sparked the beginnings of civilization.

But if, and to the degree that, human sexuality was affected by organic repression of this sort, civilization cannot be charged with restraining it. We may also question Freud's overall assumption that human sexuality is more repressed than the sexuality of most other animals, quadrupedal mammals for instance. He seems to be thinking of ruthless appetitive beasts in the jungle springing with untrammeled potency upon their sexual prey, or else of infinitely receptive females eager to accept the discharge of a suitable mate.

This Romantic figment is quite remote from the facts about sexuality among nonhumans. Their libidinal responses are usually limited to highly circumscribed stimuli—and for the female, brief periods of estrus. Even some of our fellow primates are more repressed than *Homo sapiens*.

Drawing upon the vast and fertile imagination available to them in all areas of life, human beings have a sexuality that engenders and pervades many other activities throughout their individual development. This gives our experience an erotic and romantic tinge that is unique to humankind. But it does not follow that we therefore suffer a greater level of frustration. Though we are deprived of pleasures that our dogs can have when they encounter one another, we compensate by indulging in many other types of sexual gratification. To say that humans are inherently repressed, whether for reasons that are organic or socially induced, is highly inaccurate. One might even agree with behavioral biologists who claim that man is, if anything, "oversexed."

Over- or undersexed in which regard, and in relation to what standard? These are not matters that need to be resolved here. I am principally concerned to note that our theory goes awry if we assume that there is in human nature a wholly instinctive sexuality that can be separated from the alien influence of civilization. That essentialistic view is erroneous not only in treating these two elements as if they were independent but also in neglecting the fact that each of them benefits from their intermingling. Modifying his own conception through the idea of organic repression of sexuality, Freud might have recognized that civilization too suffers from an impairment within itself. It cannot procure the pleasures or amenities to which it is devoted without assistance from the imagination, and that is often imbued with sexual and biologic overtones beyond anyone's control. The puritan in a puritan society who accepts the comfort of a luxuriant mattress may find himself taking an unexpected interest in his wife's adjacent body. Civilization, as well as sexuality, is often strengthened by this kind of phenomenon.

I emphasize imagination as that which unites sex and civilization because it is so pervasive in our ability to create meaning. By sexualizing civilization while also civilizing sexuality, imagination renders both of them into meaningful possibilities for experience. In a way that is distinctive to itself, love goes beyond both sexuality and civilization. Sexual love, the combination of sex and love, is a means by which love uses sexuality for the creative ends of bestowing and appraising value. Civilization is easily directed to this purpose, and it operates in different ways. Though some kinds of civilized love are tamely rational, others are quite raw and demanding in their passionate urgency. Even the most civic or humane types of love can include libidinal as well as nonlibidinal impulses.

Freud thought that civilized society must restrain sexual love even when it is not explicitly libidinal. Since he believed that love is in any event reducible to sex, he had doctrinal reasons for concluding that civilization would ultimately be hostile to both. But apart from the difficulties in Freud's general reductivism, we may insist that even at its most superficial level civilization has often fostered love in virtually all its varieties.

It is not just a question of unifying people so that they may cooperate for reasons of survival. Civilization does use Eros in that way, as Freud points out. But also it identifies itself with other ideals that are prominent in one or another kind of love. Though Freud cites religion as one of the provinces of civilization, he fails to see that many religious sects, notably those in the West, cultivate what they take to be an indispensable love of God whether or not it has survival value. Moreover, in the last two or three hundred years our civilization has oriented itself toward the ends of romantic and even Romantic love. Far from seeking to thwart such attitudes, modern society has largely supported the view that happiness and fulfillment require their active satisfaction.

At many times and in many societies, civilization has promoted the love of family or the nation, and eventually it may find a way of instituting an effective love of humanity, even of life itself. Among these manifestations of love there has generally been much conflict. Each love tends to repress one or more of the others, and different civilizations variously serve opposing aspirations. A patriarchal state may thwart romantic love, such as Romeo and Juliet's, on the grounds that it encourages young people to avoid their appointed duties in that society. Civilization is not thereby attacking love, but only a variant that it wishes to throttle in favor of some other type—in the case of Shakespeare's play, family or clannish love—that takes precedence over individual attachments.

Freud is rightly alarmed by the emotional discontents of civilization. But he does not realize how much we suffer because civilization itself is inwardly divided. It has no monolithic structure any more than instinct might. Each of these consigns different aspects of ourselves to behavior and experience that become value-laden dispositions struggling against one another. The affective patterns that result pursue their own ideals and promote their own forms of meaning. The imagination, with godlike largesse, fuels all of them equally.

Though some purpose may underly this cacophony of values, it is frequently experienced by us the participants as sheer chaos and unhappiness. Nature is never benignly complacent in its operation. But in creatures like ourselves it often conduces to harmonious adjustments that register as moments of gratification and even joy. Having misconstrued the origins of our discontent, Freud's pessimism blinds him to a range of consummatory values that nature can also afford. Through love, combined with civilization as its ally and progenitor, human beings attain a freedom of expression that Freud denied or discounted as very improbable. Through love we savor the goodness of freedom itself. But what exactly does that mean? And what is the nature of the freedom that love entails?

From the very beginning of my work on the nature of love, I characterized it as an acceptance of another as he is in himself. I sometimes varied the language by speaking of the other as he or she "happens to be." I did so in order to emphasize, as against theorists like Freud (or Plato), that love does not necessarily require a particular type of object. By its mere definition, it is a bestowing of value upon anyone or anything that matters to the lover. In talking about acceptance, I meant that this bestowal does not seek to alter another in ways that are alien to his or her inclinations and desires. Whatever they are, whatever they involve, they constitute the other as that person happens to exist at any moment. We accept them as an indication of our loving fidelity to the one who has them. Our ability to love is limited because our capacity for acceptance is.

Acceptance of this sort must not be confused with liking. Though love is a way of delighting in another, this does not mean that we derive pleasure from all the many attributes that belong to this individual. Most we accept in an act of courtesy. Some may be too hard to change. Even if they are repellent in themselves, we tolerate them because they are properties of the person we love. Lovers may even treasure these unlikable traits, much as they might prize a letter from their sweetheart that has become besmirched in the mail. Usually, however, we cherish what does seem likable and desirable in the beloved. For those qualities make it easier for us to accept her as she is.

While having this variable relation to pleasure or likability, our acceptance is an interest in the other as one who is unique in her totality. Uniqueness does not mean that she is not similar to anyone else. It refers to the fact that a person's life is molded and largely created by her own preference and choice of meaning. These are uniquely hers in the sense that she is the one who determines what they are. To accept another is to show allegiance to her autonomy in this respect.

Personal autonomy can be violated in many ways. One can impose one's own desires, and even seek to crush what matters to the other. Malice entails a more or less conscious attempt to destroy someone's autonomous nature. More often, people are oblivious to the fact that others have an autonomy of their own. Human beings often disregard each other's separate being, or else aggress against it in the act of expressing their own autonomy. Love does not augment autonomy in the beloved. Love merely perceives and respects it. It bestows value on it by according great importance to its existence. The lover gives meaning to his or her life by affirming and attending to the sheer autonomy of the one he or she loves.

In saying this, I principally have in mind the love of persons.

Though in a trivial sense things and ideals may be uniquely what they are, they cannot be autonomous like people. They do not make choices, and they have no feelings to which we might respond. At the same time, the love of persons is frequently central to love in general. We often love things and ideals by treating them *as if* they were persons, or at least resembled them. This is a by-product of our need to bestow value. Through the imagination, our ideas about autonomy are easily extended to inanimate objects. Just as we consider it an infringement of a man's autonomy if he is forced to be a slave or an accomplice in his own destruction, so too do we feel that the autonomous being of a Victorian mahogany bureau is violated when someone thoughtlessly paints over it. For reasons of love alone, we may also care that trees in a forest remain as they are, authentically what they "want" to be, which is to say, alive and not cut down.

Characterizing love in terms of autonomy, we should beware of metaphysical quandaries. Some philosophers have thought that love penetrates to the secret essence of another person and respects the beloved's free will in some ultimate realm of being. That is not what I mean by autonomy. Accepting another as just the entity that he or she happens to be implies no philosophical belief about freedom of the will. As far as love is concerned, the autonomous other may exist in a deterministic universe, all of it subject to ineluctable causation. Such questions lie beyond the province and the expertise of love. It addresses itself only to what appears before it in the empirical world, what is presented to it and what it *makes* present by means of its attentive attitude. If the object is a person, he or she will manifest needs and desires, feelings and emotions, choices and inclinations that constitute a personality. Except for moments of physical constraint and social or psychological subjugation, persons have the capacity to direct their lives on their own. Therein lies their autonomy, which may or may not result from causal factors beyond immediate inspection.

Love is more than just respect for, or even concern about, the autonomy of its object. It is also a means by which the lover carves out his own autonomous destiny in relation to the object's autonomy. This is an act of freedom whether or not it increases other kinds of freedom that lovers have but sometimes sacrifice. The notion that love is by definition self-abnegation, a radical submission to another person, confuses it with masochistic imitations of the real thing. Love is not inherently sacrificial, even if—for reasons of love—one gives up some freedoms that might have been retained under other circumstances.

These freedoms, and the opportunities for happiness they could have made accessible, are often lost permanently through love. Yet the autonomy of lover or beloved is not thereby altered. It is not jeopardized by the fact that they have made sacrifices for each other. Choosing to be faithful, as they may, even promising to remain so forevermore, they are doing what they want. They have not been coerced into this mode of interpersonal response. The grandeur and instinctual goodness in their bestowal of value is not a sacrifice of *themselves*. What they give up are present and future possibilities that they now freely exclude. By refusing to cheat on their relationship, for example, they may renounce the freedom to behave with others as they do with each other; nor will they be able to abandon one another casually; or in general treat the beloved as just a thing to be used and thrown away. But they themselves accept these conditions, and therefore the residual autonomy of each remains inviolate.

Love is not a device for either finding new freedoms in life or preserving the ones we had before. People who avoid love because they wish to do exactly as they please, even if this means emotional isolation, correctly understand the risks that love involves. As a *feeling*, love can be joyous and exhilarating. But the life that includes this sentiment also consists of responsibilities, commitments, and obligations through which our loving attitude reveals itself. A parent's love appears not only in moments of delight or well-earned pride but also in steadfast endurance and unremitting effort. Far from weakening love, such loss of freedom strengthens it. Nor is the autonomy of the one who loves endangered, as it would be if he were compelled to live a life he has not chosen. Love is a relationship in which each participant acts autonomously despite the forfeiture of freedoms that inevitably results.

In making this distinction between autonomy and freedom, I recognize that it is often difficult to separate them. Think of a man who loves his wife, or would like to do so, but who finds himself revolted by her addiction to cigarettes. As frequently happens, she, too, is disgusted with herself. The husband believes that, at some level of her being, she does want to break the habit. Is he violating her autonomy when he takes cigarettes out of her purse, or interferes when she is about to light up? He may feel that he is motivated by love, and that anything less intrusive would border on coldness or unconcern. He may claim that since she wants to stop smoking, having insisted as much on many occasions, his actions reveal attunement to her autonomous being. In limiting her momentary freedom, he may believe that he is faithful to her deeper self.

On the other hand, the wife may feel that unless she has actually asked her husband to help in this fashion, his behavior is not an expression of love. She may say that if he really loved her he would be less revolted by her addiction than he seems to be and less prone to take such extreme measures. But what if the husband's patience and sympathetic affection are simply unavailing? What if the wife herself has lost all hope of controlling her need to smoke? We might conclude that it is destroying the possibility of love between these two people by preventing them from accepting what the other is autonomously. Or else we might say that they continue to love each other since they confront their problem jointly: their love, as in the words of Shakespeare's sonnet, "bears it out even to the edge of doom."

I see no ready solution to this ambiguity about love in relation to freedom and autonomy. One would have to know how much the would-be lovers cause suffering in each other, and how much their responses mask underlying hostility or resentment. If every possible solution has been tried and has failed, the couple may finally give up in the matter of cigarette smoking but love each other nevertheless. If they experience a feeling of helplessness, however, or anger in being yoked with this other person under these circumstances, their capacity to love each other may no longer exist. In that event, neither will be able to accept the other's autonomy, regardless of what they would like. Love is not vouchsafed to human beings in every situation. That universal aptitude is not a freedom anyone can have on all occasions.

To say that love is an acceptance of another person's autonomy is not to say that it is basically "unconditional." That term has been used to denote two different attitudes, neither of which I consider essential for love. One of these is an acceptance of the beloved in perpetuity. Regardless of changes that may occur in that person, and throughout the future alterations in his own feelings or emotions, the lover—or should we say, the *true* lover?—is thought to accept the beloved till death do them part. This is probably what Shakespeare meant in the sonnet I just cited.

A love of that sort is possibly heroic. It may sometimes be beautiful. But it can also be distasteful or unpleasant, and it is often harmful when it causes unwarranted sacrifices and prolongs avoidable weaknesses. The fortitude in such attachments need not be doubted; in some cases it may be quite admirable. This kind of unconditionality is not, however, definitive of every love that people have had for one another. Though it is an ideal that many have believed in and that the marriage service often enunciates, it is not a prerequisite for the love of persons. Even if human beings are capable of maintaining such devotion, it does not reveal the nature of love.

The second type of unconditionality that is sometimes invoked entails an acceptance of the other that is predicated on no appraisal whatsoever (at least, no positive appraisal). Acceptance of this sort involves a pure bestowal of value. As we saw, it is present in the agapē that Christians have generally identified with God's love. Having criticized that notion in various places, I need only remark how foreign it is to whatever love we mortals can have. All bestowal of love, including our own as human beings, exceeds appraisive considerations inasmuch as it means that value is being created over and beyond the goods that we discern through individual or objective appraisal. But this does not imply that for us bestowal can exist *without* appraisal. Though bestowal occurs spontaneously and in ways that may be unpredictable, it is always generated and accompanied by appraisive conditions within our affective nature.

We are animals, not gods or angels, however godlike our creative powers can sometimes be and however angelic some well-tempered persons may appear. We gravitate within each other's reach as appetitive and appropriative beings who seek to benefit from one another. To satisfy imperatives that are physiological and biological, we need each other and we need to be needed. As our bodies are nourished by elements of the physical world on which they feed, so too is our psyche replenished and fulfilled by the contacts with people that we are able to appreciate and enjoy. These realities provide the causal conditions to which appraisal is attuned and without which bestowal could not develop or even originate.

Consider a typical situation in which two strangers, a man and a woman, approach each other on the street. At a distance each knows very little about the other. To some extent, however, they have stored expectations of a fairly general sort. They can see that the other person is a human being of the opposite sex, and this alone induces relevant appraisive acuities. We do not experience inanimate objects as we do living things, and among the latter we experience fellow humans in a very special way. They can provide us with goods that other entities cannot, and we appraise them accordingly. When the man and woman in our example come closer to each other, they pick up further information that matters to them. The woman has a figure this man finds exciting; the man has a way of walking that attracts this woman. And so on through the innumerable clues about desired gratifications that each of them can possibly garner from the other.

Whether these two people take action related to the data they have accumulated in their brief encounter, or merely walk on without acknowledging the other's presence, they have participated in the complex processes of appraisal. These fill our ordinary existence throughout life. Appraisiveness partly determines our awareness of each other. It enables us to respond to one another. Without it, we could feel neither lust nor sexual attraction in any other form, and neither could we have the ability to love. Since love involves bestowal that goes beyond appraisal, it cannot be reduced to it. Yet bestowal would not occur in human beings without appraisal. Each is needed for us to experience love, or even sexuality, as we normally do.

The notion that love is definable as unconditionality neglects and misrepresents the importance of appraisal. It interprets love as gratuitous in the sense of involving no need or desire other than the need to love. If this were true, our usual appraisive standards would not apply and love would be a pure bestowal with no concern about benefits to oneself. Far from being evaluative or judgmental, love would merely affirm the being of the other person. But any such account falsifies the love that human beings do and can have in actuality. Love as we know it is always a mixture of creative bestowals and appraisals that variably develop as a relationship progresses.

Appraisal contributes to love directly, and not merely as a causal factor. We do not show our love by suspending judgment: that would be inhuman or a sign of indifference, both of which defeat the possibility of love. It must always include within itself a concern about what is good or bad *for* the other person and *in* the other person. Since it is also an acceptance of the autonomy of that person, bestowal does not impose its own criteria of good or bad. It creates value merely in attending to the desires and ideals of the beloved, which become valuable to the lover for their own sake. But this could not happen, and would have no reality, unless he also accepted the equal legitimacy of his own desires and ideals. Attracted to someone because of appraisive needs in himself, the lover is then able to bestow value on what this other person wants independently and from her own appraisive point of view.

Though human love does not exist without appraisal, it certainly excludes invidious types of appraisal. One who evaluates another in terms of an abstract moral standard, or acts from motives that are purely selfish, is not thereby manifesting love. Appraisal belongs to love when it is conjoined with, and awakens, bestowals of value that transcend appraisiveness alone. Each occurrence of appraisal provides a causal and constituent influence upon love's total experience. Far from being unconditional, love is an intricate network of conditions that we use to fabricate new ways of profiting from one another.

Love is freedom in the midst of conditionality. It freely creates meaning and value as an expression of each lover's autonomous nature. But in accepting the other's autonomy, both persons also accept whatever conditions that involves. Extensively in love, and possibly to some degree in life itself, bestowal and appraisal operate reciprocally.

Is there something paradoxical in this situation? If the experience of love includes appraisive attitudes, does that not make it essentially impossible to accept the beloved as-is? Appraisal estimates what the other person is worth, either to ourselves or to society at large; it reflects our desire to benefit from association with other people; it usually involves efforts to change them in accordance with our own needs and values. Purposiveness of this sort is inescapable in human relations. How then is it compatible with bestowing value on someone? If the lover accepts the beloved as she is, how can he make demands or impose standards she may fail to satisfy at any time? Acceptance of one's own appraisive autonomy would seem to make love as bestowal an impossibility.

If human beings cannot surmount this difficulty, we must conclude either that my analysis is faulty or else that people are just incapable of experiencing love as I have described it. We avoid both of these alternatives if we recognize that appraisal and bestowal are entirely coherent as elements in love. It is *because* we are always appraising one another, and must do so in order to get what is needed for survival as our own kind of person, that we make the compensatory gestures involved in bestowing value. Since we do and must appraise the beloved, we try to use or change her in accordance with what matters to us; but by placing these appraisals in a context that nevertheless accepts her as she is, in herself, we bestow value upon her as a separate and autonomous being whose reality is not definable by our own particular need or evaluation. The experience of love requires both responses.

The two components may nevertheless conflict. They then repudiate each other instead of interacting harmoniously. In that event love will not occur or long endure. It exists and flourishes, in human beings at least, only when neither element is absent or submerged and each depends reactively on the other. In love the relationship between appraisal and bestowal is dialectical, and therefore not contradictory. If either becomes totally dominant, love disappears. Otherwise it lives on, happily or unhappily, in that state of emotional ambiguity that characterizes so much of our existence.

❄

Though it must show itself in benevolent action, love is not always beneficial to those who experience it—any more than life is. As a combination of appraisal and bestowal, conditionality and freedom, reason and feeling, love can wreak its own kind of havoc in a society that is closed or hostile to it. But in the open society it can have a very positive function. Far from being a principal cause of civilization's discontents, it often serves as a remedy for them. It is not just a goal that only special communities, saintly or puristic, can pursue. It is a model of what constitutes the good life for all human beings, both as individuals and as social entities. Does this mean that it alone provides the key to a life worth living? And does it really help us solve our daily problems? Or does it merely complicate them? These are the questions we must finally consider.

7
LOVE, & DO AS YOU WILL

This book has studied the pursuit of love through a variety of categories and concepts. Like pieces of a jigsaw puzzle, they must be fitted together. We must ask ourselves how our disparate speculations interact with one another, and how they emanate from a single point of view. In this chapter I hope to answer those questions, while also suggesting how my present thinking needs to be carried further.

There are three dimensions to be explored. First, how do the ideas that I have been sketching provide a unified perspective upon problems about love and meaning that have troubled philosophers as well as nonprofessionals? I am not interested in formulating an abstract schematization consisting of necessary and sufficient conditions. I find that type of approach barren and unprofitable, however precise it may seem. Life can be understood only in its concreteness and complexity. Even the purest or logically most rigorous abstractions cannot reveal the elusive, though ever-present, reality of life. If, however, one's scattered thoughts attain no adequate consistency among themselves, we may wonder about their ultimate persuasiveness.

Apart from this need for a clarified general theory, it is also important to specify in greater detail how love can actually exist among human beings undergoing the pressures and emotions that constitute our normal existence. For most of us there is no exit from moment-by-moment relations with other people. We like them sometimes, but also feel variable amounts of fear, distrust, or even hatred toward them. Relying on them, we often become possessive, demanding, and intolerant of their usual desire to sustain interests different from our own. To some extent our affective interactions with one another are marketplaces in which we offer parts of ourselves as products that others may value and therefore accept in exchange for what there is in them that we find attractive.

How does love enter into this thronging busyness that is the social or interpersonal life that human beings live and often consider meaningful? I have occasionally watched, with no real understanding, birds that congregate by the hundreds on the bare branches of a tree. They screech in a manner I cannot fathom, and the purpose in their gathering puzzles me. Is there a subtle integument of love, or the search for it, that draws them to each other? And in our species is there a similar pursuit that causes us to flock together in the social worlds that we inhabit? If so, it will remain incomprehensible unless we can decipher its relation to many other kinds of feelings and dispositions that people generally experience.

A third kind of problem must also be examined more fully. In earlier contexts I mentioned the sentiment of many people nowadays that love should be avoided for the sake of personal equilibrium and freedom from psychological, even moral distress. What this entails is still unclear. Would the sexes be more likely to overcome their warlike inclinations toward one another if they curbed their appetite for love? And what can we say about conditions in which various authorities have insisted that love is undesirable or even wrong: for instance, sexual love when the lovers belong to the same gender, or are married to other persons, or are not yet married and may never intend to be?

This kind of issue has preoccupied virtually all societies, and most have contrived to punish those who do not respect whatever code is deemed correct. But is there a right or wrong in these matters? And how can any particular society determine the best attitude for it to adopt in relation to them? Or is it all a question of idiosyncratic taste?

❄

In trying to present a unified perspective, I begin by returning to remarks I made about animal love. The idea that animals have this capacity has often been attacked by theorists who consider love to be exclusively human. We are given to a sentimental fallacy, they say, when we believe the cat that presses against us or the dog that licks our hand is acting out of love. These organisms are thought to be motivated by preprogrammed instincts that must not be confused with the love that is available only to our species. On this view, human beings may possibly bestow love upon the animals they care about, but they are deluded if they think that their adored pets are able to reciprocate in kind. It is as if we believed that the automobile we mollycoddle with frequent tune-ups and oil changes responds with love when it runs efficiently.

In these deliberations, thinkers usually focus upon relationships that exist between humans and the animals they live with. Those who believe in a mutuality of love are sensitive to the values people receive from animals, as well as those they give to them. A purring cat makes one feel wanted, and a woman may act as if she were a surrogate mother toward the kitten that seems to like cuddling with her as much as she likes cuddling it. A devoted dog inspires trust, and a man whose canine friend accompanies him on long walks may feel they are companions in a joint enterprise that really matters. To determine the extent and character of animal love, however, we need to reflect about the way that animals live among themselves. Life in their own societies is very different from what it becomes when they enter ours. No other species has social structures identical with our own; none has linguistic or cognitive talents that are comparable; and few are capable of inventing ever-changing meanings as we do.

Even so, animal behavior often contains patterns of response that resemble human love. Maternal love is certainly not limited to *Homo sapiens*. Throughout the mammalian species it would seem to be fairly uniform, though subject to significant variations, as one would expect. If we think of lion prides or wolfpacks or monkey troops as similar to the tribes and clans we create, nonmaternal ties that resemble love can also be shown to exist among many species other than our own. Devotion to the group within an ant or termite colony may actually be a more compelling bond than any that primates such as us experience. Nor is there much point in ascribing these aspects of animal existence to instinct alone. We often have no way of knowing whether, or how much, life in creatures greatly different from ourselves includes learning processes on their part that we cannot understand. And, of course, our own responsiveness is also innate to some degree.

In general, it is very hard to appreciate the quality of experience in other creatures. Think of those ground moles that spend all their time digging for tuberous roots, scurrying with them through narrow corridors, and finally depositing the food where the queen and her consorts can eat it. This wholly repetitive behavior, and the entire life of these animals, has been considered meaningless by more than one philosopher. But possibly the worker moles, as well as all the others, are motivated by something like a sense of overriding mission in preserving their particular colony. For all we know, their actions may be caused by an equivalent of social feeling. Jostling one another in their corridors, they may even have affective relations—the rudiments of gregarious good will or competitive animosity, personal likes and dislikes—directed toward some other mole but such that we will never be able to detect or fully comprehend them.

In their relations with human beings, animals who are "domesticated," as we say, have learned how to expand their capacity for love. They do this for reasons of their own, as we do too in acquiring the ability to love them. In our case the loving relationship tends to be premeditated and carefully nurtured, sometimes because we have contrived to use these beings to make up deficiencies in our love for other humans. Having only meager powers of conceptualization, animals do not think in that manner. They have never inherited an ideology that leads them to believe that love is a supreme value worth cultivating under virtually all circumstances. If they cross the boundary between their species and ours, they do so with apparent spontaneity that we may experience as a gratuitous bestowal. Though we know it is to their advantage to have us feed and shelter them, we also feel that they enrich us by accepting our proffered intimacy.

As I mentioned in an earlier chapter, animal love differs from human love in being based on a diminished level of imagination as well as intellect. But since I have all along defined love as an act of acceptance that involves imaginative bestowal of value, should I not conclude that animal love must always be highly circumscribed? I do not think so. For though imagination is an important ingredient in both love and the creation of meaning, it is not the only one. The idea of acceptance includes the suggestion of both allegiance and constancy in one's attitude. In this respect animals experience love that is often greater than the kind we have. The fidelity we find so difficult to muster in our attempts to love one another comes more easily in some other animals. They, too, employ imagination, but it is weaker and less extensive than ours. They compensate for their poor (though adequate) imaginative powers by augmenting their capacity for devotion. They are less prone to fanciful distractions that might seduce more volatile and quick-witted creatures like ourselves.

These variations between animal and human love need not surprise us. Despite our tendency to anthropomorphize everything animate that we find lovable, the differences between species should not be minimized. In fact, one of the reasons we do love animals is because we intuit their generosity in freely admitting us into their varied lifestyles while also tolerating our desire that they share ours. Animals that take this attitude manifest an implicit courtesy toward us. Even among themselves, within their own species, they seem to have an extraordinary willingness to be serviceable, as when dogs enable each other to gather information (e.g., about the local food supply) by allowing themselves to be sniffed.

Living with animals, taking care of them, showing affection as well as receiving it, we make a place in our own system of values for what is meaningful to them. In response to their acceptance of us, we give them access to our privacy. We let them see what we would not allow fellow humans to observe. We open ourselves to them even if it can be injurious for us to do so. That is a characteristic of love in general. At its most extreme it is typified by the martyrdom of St. Sebastian, as portrayed by painters in the Renaissance. They depict the saint tied to a stump or pillar, his eyes rolling upward toward heaven, while archers shoot arrows into his body. Both the saint and those who execute him seem to be at ease in this situation. It is as if they are participating in an orchestrated act that shows forth the receptivity in St. Sebastian's ability to love.

I used to think that the scene symbolizes the condition of all artists (or philosophers) whose attempts to benefit humanity elicit nothing but the barbs of hostile critics. I now see St. Sebastian as one who accepts, for reasons of love, even his own destruction. What the legend describes as his martyrdom is really part of his saintliness. His attitude is saintly because he willingly subjects himself to whatever uses God has chosen for him, even if this means becoming an object of target practice. He stands at his post, totally exposed, like a constant lover in an intimate communion with people who do not wish him well and are actually engaged in putting him to death.

In our relations with animals that we cherish, and in our happier moments of love for other human beings, there is no question of martyrdom. Nor is saintliness the only goal that love pursues. St. Sebastian is paradigmatic only in portraying the receptivity of love. It usually asserts itself in behavior that is more clearly active. It creates mutual and healthy relationships. It overcomes hatred or disdain between those who feel isolated from one another. While relinquishing total rights to one's own person, it seeks benefits for oneself as well as others.

In the Western world the submissiveness in love has often been identified with the self-sacrificial behavior of Christ. That was what many theologians considered the basis of authentic love. Since God is perfect in himself, he does not benefit by descending as a savior and being crucified. As St. Paul said, this bestowal could only be a stumbling block for the Jews and an absurdity for the Romans. They did not believe that by its nature love was a renunciation of self. For Christians, however, that notion revealed not only the essence of divinity but also the path that each person must follow in trying to attain ideal goodness. One had to sacrifice oneself for others in a loving emulation of Christ.

At the same time, and running athwart this part of Christian dogma, there developed the idea—which is now quite orthodox—that Christianity is a joyful religion. Far from being self-sacrificial, it frequently exhorts its believers to enjoy the beauty of God's creation. The divine bestowal, either in making the world or in redeeming it from sinfulness, is then seen as a model of fulfillment and self-realization. Human beings who delight in their condition, and in the universe, are thought to approximate the love that is truly definitive of God. This outlook was already present in the Old Testament, for example in the Psalms. Christianity amalgamated it with heathen and naturalistic conceptions that were not too different. Nowadays many Christians assume that this is the correct approach, sometimes without recognizing how pagan it sounded to co-religionists of theirs in previous years.

Throughout the nineteenth century, romanticism sought to accommodate both aspects of Christian dogma. Idealists such as the youthful Ludwig Feuerbach argued that even death could be explained as a supreme act of self-sacrificial love. Feuerbach interpreted the death that each person undergoes as a surrendering of one's selfhood so that others may exist. He saw this not only as proof of a person's ability to love, but also as an indication of what love inherently entails. Other Romantics, developing the latent pantheism in Hegel's philosophy, insisted that God was in the world as the longing for consummatory goodness that propels nature forward. To realize the love that is divine, one had only to enjoy one's immersion in this process.

I mention these two currents in religious attitudes toward love as views that differ from my own. Human beings can sacrifice themselves for reasons of love, as a starving mother does in giving food to her child rather than eating it herself, or as soldiers have done in falling on a grenade and thereby protecting their comrades from its blast. But love is not inherently or necessarily a sacrifice of self. In being a bestowal of value, it creates rather than destroys. In accepting the autonomous being of another, it delights in it to that extent and thereby enriches the lover as well.

If one wishes, one can say that since love is a fulfillment of this sort it manifests God's presence in us. That is a nonverifiable article of faith about which I have no doctrinal beliefs. While I recognize it as metaphysical or theological poetry that some people have found significant, I feel no need to affirm or deny it. What matters most to me is the awareness that when we make ourselves available to others, admitting them into our personal being and allowing them to use it, our vulnerability creates the possibility of love but does not necessarily lead to self-sacrifice. It may often be the means by which one initiates openness in the other person and thereby induces a reciprocating love that benefits both without causing either to lose the good things of life.

This openness that makes one accessible to another without diminishing oneself enables love to be a form of self-realization. The creative bestowing of value augments the lover as well as the beloved. In the routine of ordinary life, we feel ourselves imprisoned by the same old habits, the same old relationships, the same old daily finitude. Anything that induces a new and satisfying experience will seem wondrous to us. Falling in love, particularly if it has happened rarely in our lives, gives us the feeling that we have transcended mundane existence. We sense the goodness in being alive, in having met just the right man or woman, in having the exhilarating feelings that now engulf us. Such love may well appear magical to us, and this magic may seem to issue from a merging with the person to whom we are now willing to give ourselves.

What seems like merging is, however, one or another type of sharing. Falling in love differs from "being in love" and "staying in love." In these relationships the sharing of selves becomes more permanent and more pervasive (though usually less emotionally charged) than in the love one has fallen into. But even the giving of oneself that occurs in that cataclysmic experience is really an incipient mode of sharing.[1] That is why the belief in love as merging, under these and all other circumstances, can only be illusory.

On the other hand, the sense of wonder is real enough. Love has the ability to strip away layers of accumulated dross that hide the potential beauty in everything. It makes life meaningful by revealing the newness in each moment of experience and the possibility that much of it can satisfy our desires. To the lover the beloved is not just another creature in the factual world but a marvel to behold. If the two feel that they have merged with one another, it is because they cannot believe that ordinary life is capable of yielding so ecstatic a relation as the one they are now experiencing.

Yet love, in all its variations, is a common occurrence in life. It exists as a supreme, and not infrequent, attainment in our natural condition. It is transcendent or miraculous only in contrast to the many examples of routine behavior and affective failure that life also includes.

Those who think love is merging are guilty of an error that sometimes occurs in reflections about musical aesthetics. The blending of notes in a chord, or voices that sing in harmony, may serve to illustrate actual merging. There is an exquisite oneness in that kind of fusion: it is not surprising that we feel uplifted by its frequent grandeur. We would delude ourselves, however, if we thought that the tenor and soprano whose overtones merge so beautifully in their duet are themselves merging (or even the personae they portray). Though the singers are at-one with each other and with the music, they must still remain separate human beings.

All arts are similar to love inasmuch as they issue from the imagination. But art and love differ in many ways. Art is inevitably abstract, even in voices that sing expressively. Love adheres to the concrete being of a person, thing, or ideal while also adding to it through creative bestowals. Art uses imagination to probe and represent reality, or else to enclose it within a formal structure, but love responds directly to realities and accepts them in themselves even when it alters them. Mergings that are possible in art generally tell us little about the nature of love.

Aesthetic productions can often heighten our appreciation of "the given"—life as it is lived from moment to moment. This happens when art increases our awareness of elements in experience that we might otherwise neglect or take for granted. In love such creativity in meaning occurs pervasively. By its very being love attends to whatever it bestows itself upon, and that may be almost anything that consciousness affords. Art and love are therefore correlative. It is not by chance that art, above all when it deals with the human search for meaning, so often finds a suitable subject matter in love of every sort.

Nevertheless, Plato was possibly wiser than most of the critics who condemn him for having banished the poets from his ideal republic. Accepting the given through a work of art is not the same as accepting it in real life. We can always ask ourselves whether a particular artist strengthens our capacity to love. The works he or she creates may often perform that service—but not necessarily, and certainly not invariably. Plato's utopian state was conceived as a haven for the love that he thought most desirable. There is no guarantee that even great art fosters that or any other kind of love—except, of course, the love of art itself. Proust's confusion about this vitiates his defense of art as well as his critique of (interpersonal) love.

❄

For some readers it will have seemed odd that these general comments originated with a discussion of animal love. I took this opportunity to counter the speciesism to which human arrogance has always been liable. The idea that animals are incapable of love results from an assumption that all values in the universe are generated either by God (whom we represent in our own image) or by members of our species. This is on a par with saying, as some philosophers have, that only we are truly rational, purposive, and capable of having meaningful lives. Descartes even insisted that animals are really just mechanical constructs, machinery artfully wound up and activated by the laws of nature. That conception runs completely against my grain. To me its wrongness is self-evident.

But also I began with remarks about animal behavior because I believe that human nature cannot be understood in any other context. This need not blind us to the splendid uniqueness of human love. During the discussion that followed a public lecture I delivered at a large university, I was surprised by a question from someone in the audience. "Do you love your wife," a student asked, "as much as you love your dog?" I was taken aback since I had mentioned neither in my lecture. The two kinds of love are different, and not really commensurate. Instead of saying that, however, I replied: "Well, my dog doesn't criticize me . . ." There was an outburst of laughter, and I turned to the next question. Though I may not have shown it, my answer troubled me. Was I being sufficiently honest, either then or in my lecture? In my attempt to share my thinking, had I concealed the reality of my condition as a human being? Or was I revealing too much about my own limited and imperfect capacity for experiencing love of any sort?

I will not burden the reader with these private issues, but it might well be unfortunate if someone did love animals more than he or she loves men and women. Having been born to members of our species, we are faced throughout our lives with the need to solve most of our intimate problems in relation to them. Love for pets or even wild animals can augment our ability to love, and to some degree we may use them as substitutes for humans we would like to love but do not. But even so, the principal relationships that emanate from our natural condition must always be those that we maintain with other people.

What exactly are these relationships? In large part they depend on developments in the history of ideas about love, as I argued earlier. Trying to map out a possible taxonomy of concepts and attitudes that men and women have established in their affective bonding with one another, I once outlined a fivefold cycle. Limiting myself to the Western world, I described a historical and recurrent progression along the following lines: first, ideas that approach love from the point of view of male supremacy, subsequently countered by the dominance of the female, then by conceptions that extol an equality between the sexes, followed by beliefs about a spiritual transcendence in love that takes both male and female into a higher realm, only to be succeeded by a deflationary attitude that reduces love to a physical and largely sexual congress between men and women who delude themselves if they think they are capable of spiritual oneness. I gave examples from different periods of history, and I speculated about the possibility of a dialectic that internally binds each of the five stages to those that follow or precede.[2]

Without summarizing the details of that discussion, I now wish to suggest that the fifth stage can be thought of as a cumulative achievement rather than just a reaction to the elevated approach it considers unnatural. In my examples from the Middle Ages, I mentioned *The Romance of the Rose* as a realist rebuttal of the idea that human beings can have for one another the spiritual love that Dante depicts as his relationship with Beatrice. But though *The Romance of the Rose* makes this critique, one can also find in that work (and in many others during the same period) elements of a more positive approach to human possibilities. Men and women are shown to be capable of healthy, moral, and wholly commendable love within the confines of their natural condition. A tincture of the idealistic aura of Dante's vision was thus perpetuated. Despite its interest in pure spirit, it could be retained to some extent by all enlightened realists.

If this emendation is accepted, we may also emphasize how greatly some of the other stages incorporate the best of what comes earlier in time. The love between Dante and Beatrice was itself presented as a synthesis between religious love and the humanism of courtly love. The latter had reached its highest level in the legend of Tristan and Iseult. I interpret that legend, and the myth it represents, as an attempt to show how sexual love unites male and female in an equalized relationship that defeats prior conceptions of either women submitting to the domination of men or of men making themselves subservient to women. This equalization enunciates within a secular and naturalistic framework the ideal of a well-formed marriage based on reciprocal love that Christian doctrine had often advocated but that church and state both conspired to defeat throughout the Middle Ages. Far from being a glorification of adultery, as most critics have thought, the myth of Tristan and Iseult—for instance in the writings of Chrétien de Troyes—reveals the dimensions of perfect matrimony.

This particular perfection is shown to occur when godlike creatures such as Tristan and Iseult live together in a total oneness that they forge for themselves even though society condemns it and finally brings about their death. Their sexual union is not only a moral consummation but also one that reveals the sanctity of love as it exists between those who are made for one another. Though its physical implications are portrayed in a realistic manner that even *The Romance of the Rose* would approve, the nobleness of life appears in the sacred bond that unites these lovers permanently.

For our purposes in this book the myth of Tristan and Iseult has particular relevance. Its many versions and aesthetic transformations exist within the history of romance literature, which flourished in the Hellenistic period, reached a high point in courtly writings of the thirteenth and fourteenth centuries, and played a major role in the romanticism of the last two hundred years. As an efflorescence of the imagination, romance contributes to what I have called the romantic aspect of sexual love. The relationship between romance and the romantic needs further investigation.

When I discussed the romantic in a previous chapter, I emphasized the fact that it involves a search for permanent oneness with another person. Romance literature presupposes this interest on the part of the reader but often narrates the story of a couple who experience love only as a result of extraordinary events they could never have foreseen. The young man and woman find themselves enmeshed in circumstances that wrench them out of their routine expectations. Being cynical or worldly wise or simply unenlightened about their emotional capabilities, they have initially no conscious desire for either oneness or a permanent relation. These come upon them as a consequence of the adventures they experience together in escaping the problems of their former life. Having succeeded in their separation from the rest of society, having overcome fabulous perils with and because of their fellow escapee, they finally attain a passion for one another that they denote as love. They realize not only that they too feel a craving for romantic oneness but also that their mutual escapade, the romance we have been reading or watching on the screen, proves that they cannot live without each other. They see themselves as permanently united.

That having been accomplished, conventional marriage can occur as a happy ending that reconciles the lovers with the world they formerly tried to leave behind. But their life in that society, which is to say the marriage as it actually exists now that romantic possibilities have been fulfilled, is not a part of their romance. The details of matrimony belong to another reality, after the yarn is finished, after the storybook is closed, after the curtain comes down, or after the film announces that it has reached "The End."

From the Hellenistic period (and earlier) through the latest Hollywood love story, the genre of romance frequently treats nature as the locus of escape that liberates the eventual lovers from their social origins. In some versions the hero who is out hunting encounters the Fairy Queen, herself the embodiment of nature. She makes him her special darling. Occasionally he stays with her and never does return to ordinary life. But in the more usual scenario, the hardships and delights of living in nature teach two heroic mortals, a man and woman, that they love each other. Once they have learned this, they can beneficially assume their normal obligations in society.

The Wood of Morois or the Forest of Arden or the untamed

countryside of Connecticut or Pennsylvania, as in *Bringing Up Baby* and *It Happened One Night*, are settings for both escape and return. They enable the lovers to act with abandon—abandoning the roles that society had imposed upon them and abandoning themselves to natural desires and emotions. But they also reintroduce the lovers, now united, to a world they have changed if only in changing themselves. Having undergone their emotional transfiguration, they are able to enact love not only with one another but also (in different ways) with other human beings.

These elements of evasion and return via nature might be seen as further illustrating the struggle between sex and civilization. That is how Freud would interpret them. But the fables usually move in other directions. Many, and possibly most, weave their tales of adventure and abandon in ways that show the interpenetration between sexual and civilized aspects of our being. In *It Happened One Night*, for instance, the young heiress played by Claudette Colbert leaps off a yacht to escape a father who wants to control her choice of a husband. She shares a series of adventures with an aggressive journalist, played by Clark Gable, who constantly ridicules the phoniness of her pampered existence. Throughout their tribulations Gable instructs Colbert in the facts of life. He teaches her not only how to avoid discovery by her father's detectives, but also how to sleep on straw out of doors, how to survive on raw carrots, and even how to dunk a donut in coffee.

In having her romanesque adventure, the Colbert character realizes for the first time what it is to spend all night on a bus, to stand on line for a shower at an autocamp, to be subjected to the many hazards and indignities that the poor encountered during the Depression. By the end she understands the social reality from which her father's wealth had always shielded her. But also she observes and participates in a freedom and spontaneity that she has never experienced before, as when her fellow travelers on the bus begin to sing about the man on the flying trapeze who—unlike anything she has ever known—flies through the air with the greatest of ease.

It seems inevitable that this young woman should fall in love with the Gable character who maneuvers her through these vibrant and liberating events while also participating in them. In providing her course of enlightenment, he makes a woman of her—as all Pygmalions do. The happenings by day and night reveal to her, as he knew they would, what ordinary people experience within the social conditions that mold their feelings and emotions. The heiress and the journalist are themselves more than ordinary. They are stars in the romantic firmament, the equivalents of gods and goddesses despite their sheer humanity.

It Happened One Night is a comedy with a happy ending: the well-matched pair finally get married, and their abandonment to natural impulse becomes harmonized with the life-enhancing possibilities of civilization. The walls of Jericho, the repressive blanket that prohibited lovemaking, come down when the lovers have not only resolved their interpersonal problems but also sanctified their sexual union through socially approved matrimony. *Romeo and Juliet* is a tragedy because there civilization has crumbled. The harmonization of human values has been defeated. The failings of society prevent the lovers from surviving as a married couple. Shakespeare's play is also an archetypical romance, however, for it shows how the lovers achieve complete romantic oneness by jointly evading social impediments even though they die as a result.

These ideas about romance in relation to the romantic are worth pursuing because they pose a major problem about sexual love, and possibly all love between human beings. Is it rational to hope that a permanent, or even lasting relationship will retain the excitement and fulfillment that romance dramatizes? In its aesthetic independence, romance literature could be thought to be merely escapist. One might say that it is *because* life in the real world—whether in medieval Europe or in America during the Depression—is heartless and embittering that the imagination feeds on fantastical tales of enchanting unity between idealized men and women.

On the other hand, we can also see the lovers' oneness as a touchstone of what is possible for all human beings under optimal circumstances. The legends about their incredible exploits then appear as myths that penetrate to a core of our reality. They show what inheres as a potential in each of us, and they challenge all particular societies to allow the fullest expression of the love that these fictional characters experience.

To say this, however, is not yet to answer the fundamental question that romance introduces. Even in the most permissive and advanced society, the one that is most humanely civilized, how can the daily grind of routine marital chores, of inevitable struggle with the environment, of continual fluctuations in emotional attitudes, of misunderstandings and disagreements that intimacy creates when it is not actually breeding contempt—how can all this be surmounted by romance or the romantic, or for that matter by any other element of interpersonal love?

In the glow of libidinal completion, the explosive ecstasy of orgasm may give us a feeling that all obstructions to harmonious love have been washed away. In the playfulness of erotic titillation we may sense an organic attachment that makes life with another person both rewarding and meaningful. But these libidinal and erotic satisfactions are generally short-lived. After having sex we still must get dressed and deal with everyday necessities. Despite the other person's sensuous allure we still perceive him or her as one among other humans, some of whom are also attractive to us. What seemed like permanent oneness can always degenerate into a mutual nightmare, as Shelley says about married people who "With one chained friend, perhaps a jealous foe, / The dreariest and the longest journey go."

Some have thought that only an enchantment, a literal magic, could overcome the difficulties of sexual and marital love. Because that suspicion lingers in us all, we may readily treat romance as always wish fulfillment, make-believe, charming and delightful deception that lures the unwary into bonds that are ultimately injurious. If we are to avoid this baleful conclusion, we must give adequate reasons for thinking the love that romance glorifies can have an irreplaceable value within the good life. In his attempt to defend romantic love, Bertrand Russell argued that not to experience it means missing out on one of the joys of life. But Russell did not believe that this special sense of oneness with another person would endure, and he maintained that once marriage and the formation of a family have occurred romantic love becomes anachronistic. Did he underestimate its durability, its lasting importance?

If we assume that romantic love is just a refinding of childhood feelings people outgrow in becoming adults, we may well consider it a transitional phenomenon that stable and prolonged marriage will ultimately eliminate. It would seem to have no place within the complex of mature responsibilities, duties, sorrows, and even joys inherent in matrimonial relations. But the married state can also include a kind of friendliness that well-adapted spouses may have with one another. And within this particular friendship there can be a feeling that just in staying together, standing by each other despite everything that impinges on them, the couple are jointly validating their romance and still experiencing the vestiges of it.

There are those who say that romantic love depends on obstacles and that romance depicts the overcoming of these obstacles prior to marriage. Once the lovers have married each other, it is argued, there can no longer be the circumstances that generate either romance or the romantic. But it is not only premarital love that never did run smooth, as the character in Shakespeare suggests: the same is true in even the happiest of marriages. Life never has or ever will run smooth. Living with another person is itself a condition fraught with obstacles to the perfect and harmonious adjustment that married people desire but achieve only on occasion. At moments of crisis, when they and those they care about are seriously ill or threatened by outside forces, the oneness between them may be accentuated by the realization that their fragile bond must constantly be defended and renewed. They need not tell themselves that they are living a romance, and their emotional state will have altered greatly since the distant days of courtship, but if they are able to face their major problems together—as friends united by a perilous situation—that alone will preserve the romantic for them.

If we consider friendship a mutual assertion of equality, as I suggested earlier, we may find that it is crucial to married as well as sexual love. Separated at the wedding ceremony until appropriate words are uttered, the bride and groom leave the church hand in hand like friends who accept a mission that only they can carry out. Acceptance of this sort defines their friendship and draws them further into each other's life, enabling them to elude the rest of society to that extent. This alone provides an element of romance as they venture into the unknown wilderness of exploration and discovery between themselves.

It does not matter that something similar has happened to millions of others and that society condones its happening to these two. Within their own microcosm they are Adam and Eve confronting a virgin land outside of Eden. Though they are not being punished and need not feel that they have transgressed in any way, they too must create a new world for themselves. At the beginning, at least, the wonderment and excitement of their personal romance is capable of extending their sexual love into the altered circumstances of matrimony.

But how long can it last? As long, perhaps, as their friendship does. In Renaissance literature, as in several others, the word "friend" is often used to mean "lover." The conflict between friendship in that sense and official marriage is the dominating theme throughout Shakespeare's *Antony and Cleopatra*. At the end, Cleopatra dies with the happy thought that now she can join Antony in a better realm where he will be to her both friend and husband. This higher love was not available to them during their lifetime, and many will assert that marriage in the world as we know it is always inimical to the desired coalescence.

A great deal depends on the individuals involved in each marital bond, the social mandates that surround them, and in general the reigning ideology as it exists at any moment. Still there may be some advantage in determining how marriage or sexual union can actually render itself compatible with friendship. Those who identify interpersonal love with merging often do so because they are struck by the fact that the lovers' passion seems to have melted all barriers between them. But friendship requires barriers, or at least boundaries and lines of demarcation that recognize individual autonomy. To have a friend one must feel a sameness or similarity with a person who responds equally but nevertheless remains different. This could not happen if we merged or fused into something else.

On the other hand, the condition I have called a "wedding" of separate personalities may also be incapable of creating romantic friendship. What is merely joined at the superficies can easily be put asunder. A friendship that stirs the emotions and promises permanent oneness usually requires more than that.

In the 1960s and 70s, "open marriage" was sometimes advocated as a kind of matrimonial friendship that would be compatible with sexual freedom, even promiscuity, as opposed to any search for merging. Since the attempt to merge can lead to unrealistic expectations that undermine marital harmony and whatever romantic love may have preceded it, open marriage not only acknowledges that husband and wife are separate persons but also that they may have interests vastly different from one another's. Having agreed that each is free to follow independent goals, to have love affairs and experience unshareable relations with other people, the married couple can presumably establish between themselves a love that is based on friendship they might not have attained through traditional matrimony.

One may nevertheless wonder whether the friendliness and the love afforded by an open marriage provide everything that men and women have generally wanted in either a romantic or a marital situation. Even if jealousy and smoldering resentment have been lessened by the recognition that each is free to do as he or she desires, other components of sexual love may also have been eliminated. One cannot have a sense of adventure or intensity in a marriage unless that marriage exists as an integral and somewhat binding unit. Insofar as open marriage loosens the emotional rivets between the spouses, does it not forfeit its ability to retain the romantic elements of sexual love? The advocates of open marriage would have to show that nothing worthwhile has been lost through this arrangement.

One thing of value that might be lost is "marital passion," as I called it in my trilogy. I distinguished it from ordinary romantic passion as a way of suggesting that lasting intimacies might still include some though not all of the passionate sexuality that may have existed before marriage. What now seems to me equally important is the fact that even when sexual drive has declined, as it does in everyone eventually, spouses may continue to have strong emotions and a longing for one another at various moments in their marriage. These feelings reinforce their sense of the romance they live together throughout their persistent effort to maintain romantic oneness.

❄

Since the interpersonal love in marriage is social as well as sexual, the sense of romance between the parents may also affect the family that results. Duties within the society they have created may still be onerous to the spouses, and they will always have to deal with them as persons liable to individual anger and hatred as well as love. But they may also pride themselves on a commonality that contributes its own consummatory goodness. Though feelings of unity within the group become most evident when its members are threatened by death or injury, they also appear in celebrations that presuppose a residual love among those who have endured each other's company.

In the course of this marital journey, as distinct from the one that Shelley mentions, the spousal friends will have participated in an enormous gamut of joint experiences and mutual interests. The yoke of marriage that so often limits one's freedom will be easy because it generates a meaningfulness that can exist in no other context and that reverberates throughout the years. Looking back on what they have been through, the couple will not only share a fund of memories but they may also feel that their life together—difficult and even tormented as it was at times—has attained an interwoven meaning that each of them can cherish.

These comments may help to clarify what I referred to as being in love and staying in love. They can also illuminate the concept of interdependence. People who avoid marriage or even sexual love usually do so in order to protect themselves against the evils of mere dependency. They do not want to be saddled with someone who demands too much of their attention, who cannot cope without them, who may even seem to have no life other than the one that issues from the intimacy itself. Most men and women also realize how dangerous it is to be themselves dependent on another human being in the massive way that love readily induces. It is as if one has then become addicted to the foreign substance which is that other person. Hegel described a similar state in his analysis of the master-slave relation that causes each participant to destroy the other's freedom and to acquire the other's weakness. The bond between master and slave drags them both down. But interdependence is something else.

When people are interdependent, they too depend on each other for many of the benefits that human beings can get from one another. As in ordinary dependence, there need not be an exchange of similar goods. That sometimes happens, for example, in kissing on the lips, when the pleasure that one person bestows elicits responses that yield the same kind of pleasure in the other. More often, however, interdependence employs a division of labor within a system of mutual bestowals. Each person satisfies the other by intentionally providing goods *because* the other wants them. The result is more than just an exchange of what is valued. For that might involve nothing but a willingness to make payment for what one selfishly desires. The relationship would then depend on little more than appraisals that underlie purposive behavior as a whole. For our affective attitude to become interdependent love, it must also include an interest in the welfare of the other as an autonomous being.

This acceptance and reciprocal benevolence make the couple interdependent. They each depend on the other not only as a source of what they want but also as a person on whom they can bestow value. Bestowal of this sort is inherently enjoyable. Frequently, though not on all occasions, human beings *like* to help other creatures, to take care of them, to sustain the independent goodness of their living as they choose. Most of us derive pleasure just from seeing life burst forth in anything animate and healthy. Moreover, we all need, and want, to feel that we are both needed and wanted by others. Being needed is not enough; nor is being wanted, if we are not needed. Interdependent love arises when we are both needed and wanted by someone whose sheer vitality makes us need and want this other person. The bestowal we then make, assuming we are capable of it, is beneficial to us as well as to the other.

Because the bestowing of value means so much to human beings, people sometimes become obsessively dependent on it. The pursuit of love is then pathological. But when lovers are interdependent, they combine appraisal and bestowal in a way that enables them to accept their oneness as an ideal condition worth cultivating. Theirs is nothing like the bondage of master-slave. Though they need one another, they are not subservient to each other. They do not relinquish their sense of autonomy or their faith in the importance of being what they are as individuals. They may regret the loss of former freedoms, but they have no reason to doubt the love they acquire as a result. Satisfying each other as well as themselves, they may indeed feel that they have reached what is deepest and most meaningful in human nature.

At this point it will be useful to consider an example that Sartre employs in *Being and Nothingness*. Illustrating his notion of "bad faith," Sartre describes the phenomenology of a waiter who presents himself as nothing but a waiter. In relation to his customers he would seem to be enacting a role with which he has totally identified himself. He stands at attention awaiting orders, he holds his folded napkin on his arm with almost geometric precision, he uses the formal terminology of servile politeness. Sartre finds the waiter guilty of bad faith because in pretending that he is *just* a waiter the man denies his own existence as a human being. Like any other person, he is free at every moment and can always transcend the conventionalities related to his vocation. Even in accepting them as requisite for appearing as a waiter should, he is already manifesting a freedom that his attitude negates. This kind of inner contradiction, Sartre maintains, constitutes bad faith.

As against Sartre's analysis, we might argue that putting oneself in a particular role and trying to perform it to perfection, as actors on a stage also do, need not involve bad faith. If we are perturbed by the spectacle of the waiter engaging in rigid acts that he prescribes in order to define himself *as* a waiter, it is because we feel that his imagination has alienated him from the interpersonal situation that gives meaning to his profession. To be a waiter is to provide people with food or drink at their request, to serve them in a manner that makes the occasion enjoyable for them, and to receive the emoluments that such service warrants. If one makes the activity into an abstract role played out apart from its human context, in proud isolation as it were, one denies all possibility of interdependence. Waiter and client will remain dependent on each other—one taking orders, the other giving them—but they cannot become interdependent. They can only approximate the master-slave relation.

In his robotic preoccupation with technique, the waiter is revealing that he does not really care about the people he is serving. Neither does he expect them to care about him. His patrons are not persons whose autonomy matters to him. For him they may even be objects to be used and turned into ready cash. This has its advantages since it armors him against the hazards that are present in all personal contact. Still his manner is disquieting. It precludes the possibility of our responding to one another as fellow humans. It is as if we were indeed robots, we as well as the waiter, and therefore incapable of experiencing an authentic love of persons.

At the same time as we are shocked by the waiter's performance, we know that our capacity for creating and maintaining interdependent love must always be limited. Nor would we want to take upon ourselves, in relation to every waiter we encounter, the responsibility and concern that such intimacy demands. Even sexual response (to say nothing of sexual love) cannot be extended to so wide a compass. The barnyard gallantry of Don Juan makes sense as an expression of the libidinal and the erotic; but when he repeats the same romantic protestations to all the women he meets, his playacting becomes dishonest and somewhat ludicrous. The same applies to love that is not sexual. We would find ourselves constantly defeated if we tried to establish interdependence with all casual acquaintances who happen to cross our path.

Jean-Jacques Rousseau had a vision of a perfect society in which everyone would feel love of one sort or another for everyone else. In the world of actual humanity, however, nothing like that is available to us. We might want Sartre's hypothetical waiter to recognize that we are both persons, and we might hope that his devotion to the ideal of being a perfect waiter would be affected by this realization. But unless he becomes a friend of ours, we also prefer that he keep his distance and respect our privacy. With him we do not crave the interdependent love that we may desire with someone else. While acknowledging the autonomy of the waiter, and expecting him to show that he is aware of ours, we may well avoid a relationship in which each fully cares about the extensive welfare of the other. That kind of loving attitude we usually reserve for very few people. If we try to experience it with many, we are likely to find that it survives only in a highly attenuated form. This may be sufficient for a love of humanity, but sexual and marital love (or even close friendship) require emotions that are more intense and more binding one-to-one.

Having read this far, some readers will feel disappointed. Where are the graphic case histories, they will say, the stories of star-crossed lovers, of people drawn as by magnetism to one another, of heroic devotion or molten passion that we usually associate with love? Where is the practical advice to the lovelorn, to the dysfunctional paramours, to the loners who never find Mr. or Ms. Right despite their earnest search for "a meaningful relationship"? In countless books journalists, psychiatrists, even scientific researchers have accustomed us to the intimate secrets of Mrs. A, who desperately needs help in restraining her philandering husband, or Mr. B, who seems to expect his wife to love him as his mother did, and so on.

As a working philosopher, I am not equipped to purvey such

engrossing revelations, though I, too, am interested in them. Life is inherently fascinating for those who observe it with aesthetic appreciation, particularly if they can do so at a comfortable distance. In trying to determine what it all means, however, and what it amounts to, we need insights and theories that elucidate the nature of human relations. We need a cartography of concepts that maps out the affective terrain and enables us to find whatever path we individually wish to follow.

Even in matters of love, however, philosophical theorizing should help people deal with practical problems. When Freud wrote articles such as "'Civilized' Sexual Morality and Modern Nervous Illness," he spoke with the voice of a moralist drawing upon his experience as a psychologist. That article in particular is relevant to the concrete issues I mentioned at the beginning of this chapter. Freud describes how society as he knew it stringently controls sexual and marital conduct. Sounding almost like a libertarian, he deplores the extensive harm that social mandates unwittingly cause in prohibiting premarital sexuality and in condemning adultery. He recommends greater awareness of each person's need to solve such problems as he or she decides and without interference from public opinion or communal authority.

To a large degree, though not uniformly, Freud's influence has prevailed in these areas of morality. Sexual intercourse prior to marriage is tolerated nowadays throughout the Western world much more than when he first wrote. A hundred years ago unmarried men were permitted to have carnal relations with prostitutes, but respectable young women had to remain chaste. And since church and state both considered marriage an inviolable bond, divorce as well as most forms of extramarital sexuality were thought to be scandalous and even sinful. Nowadays we are generally horrified by these enforced limitations upon the freedom of males and females alike. We feel that human nature is distorted and abused by society's refusal to respect personal choice.

Despite his pleas for tolerance, Freud himself was divided as a thinker in these matters. For in his own theories he retains essentialistic views about sex and love that have always been used to justify the manipulating of other people's conduct. This essentialism assumes that there is in principle a single and unitary way for all human beings to realize their sexual drive and inclination to love. Through a proper use of reason as well as observation, it was thought, one could discover the lineaments of this preferential orientation. It alone revealed the structure in human nature that indicates what sexuality and love must be for our particular species. With that superior knowledge at hand, could we not discover how men and women *ought* to live in order to attain objectively desirable responses? And should they not be encouraged—forced, if necessary—to behave accordingly? This mode of reasoning was employed for centuries by secular and ecclesiastic authorities who sought to prevent moral turpitude in those who might be swayed by wayward impulses.

Freud adopts, and fosters, this attitude inasmuch as he reduces human sexuality to a universal and basically innate pattern that belongs to our biology. His theory of the libido is predicated upon the assumption that we, like other animals, are all programmed to engage in coital behavior that serves as the norm for sexuality. Though Freud recognizes that this imperious drive can lead to what he calls "the tyranny of the genital," he maintains that it exists as an ultimate force that defines our nature as affective beings. The conflict between sex and civilization perturbs him as much as it does because he thinks that civilization regularly disrupts the preappointed functioning of sexuality. When he delineates the differences between male and female sexual interest, more sharply than most recent sexologists would, he posits subsidiary uniformities—one for each gender—within the overall pattern imposed by libido as a whole.

Freud's essentialism is present in everything he writes about sex or love, and it raises doubts about his pleas for greater tolerance toward those who deviate from standards others impose upon them. In asserting that there is a single preferential means by which men and women can satisfy their sexual drive, is he not prescribing norms himself? Freud and his followers have always rejected this inference. They claim to be scientific investigators reporting facts about human nature and whatever is needed to fulfill it. Since they identify natural fulfillment with happiness and the achievement of organic health, they deny that their approach mandates constraints upon sexual behavior. But essentialism is itself a constraint. It gives normative importance to particular goals of sexuality as opposed to others. It assumes that some practices are sick or undesirable merely because they run counter to the ends of reproductive coitus. The concept of "perversion" operates in Freudian theory much as it does in the ideologies whose repressiveness Freud lamented.

I have fully discussed Freud's essentialism elsewhere, and there is no need to repeat my criticism in this place.[3] But his essentialistic ideas about sexual perversion have special relevance here. Though Freud believed that human sexuality always includes homosexual components, he thought that health or normality requires their sublimation. From this it would follow that fully consummated sexual love between people of the same gender can only be unfortunate and more or less diseased. Such deviations from the innate biological program would have to be deleterious. Homosexuality as a life-style must therefore be incompatible with either psychological or social well-being.

In opposing this approach, gay liberationists have frequently maintained that, far from being a legitimate norm, heterosexuality is just an affective taste that certain people have. In this view it does not matter that the great majority of human beings have the heterosexual taste: that is just a statistical datum from which one cannot derive normative conclusions. Moreover, it is often argued, all sexual orientations are largely composed of responses that were acquired or somehow learned in childhood. Some gay theorists even claim that under conditions of total liberation everyone would find homosexuality just as gratifying and conducive to health as anything people nowadays hope to attain through heterosexuality. Sexual instinct is gender free, according to these theorists—it may be used for reproductive purposes, and of course that currently requires heterosexual relations, but in itself it can be satisfied equally well by physical behavior between persons of the same sex.

What interests me most in this controversy is the fact that

neither side puts an adequate emphasis upon the differences between sexual love and sexuality apart from love. Even if the human organism is programmed toward reproduction, as the Freudians think, this alone would not prove that sexual love of a benign or desirable sort must always be heterosexual. On the other hand, one need not defend the possibility of homosexual love by asserting that the alternative lifestyle is just an acquired and wholly variable taste. The homosexuality or bisexuality that may be appropriate in some people may not be beneficial in those (at present, the great majority of human beings) who are exclusively heterosexual for reasons that are hormonal and temperamental as well as social.

These differences in sexual disposition become less significant once we focus on their relative ability to be enacted with love. It is conceivable that sexual love between people of the same gender is not the same as sexual love when both genders are involved. But there is no reason to think that either relation provides love that is inherently better or worse than the love the other yields in a society that is amenable to it.

For this pluralistic reason alone, the concept of perversion as it has often been employed is both obnoxious and unnecessary. It has generally served as a mode of denigration designed to limit sexual freedom. To envisage a sexual relationship that is or can be an expression of love, one need not ordain which combination of genders must be included. The participants can determine that for themselves, following their destinies as they wish and without a sense of guilt whatever they happen to choose. Their choice may be unfortunate or unwise, but a priori no alternative is preferable and each can be expected to involve losses as well as gains. In an open society all the varieties of sexual love, however they occur, will have the right to be considered with absolute equality. We need ban only those that prove hurtful to others.

Similar conclusions apply to questions about adultery and premarital sexuality. Traditional moralists have opposed such modes of self-expression on the grounds that they undermine the integrity of marriage, and are therefore pernicious. In taking this approach, these authorities have generally assumed that monogamous marriage favored in the West conduces to the only goal of oneness that society should condone. Ideally, at least, marital love would emanate from sexual love between the spouses and result in social love throughout the family. For the most part, however, this conception paid too little attention to the fact that love is often defeated in married life. By condemning extramarital sexuality, society did not improve the likelihood that love would occur between husband and wife. People struggling to find a relationship that was right for them were merely hampered by the realization that their friends or parents might look askance at even their successful experiments.

One tends to forget how recently the so-called sexual revolution occurred. Nowadays the majority of unmarried men and women in the Western world feel little need to control their sexual behavior or search for love in accordance with the prohibitions that were so prevalent before. I remember reading an article thirty years ago by the anthropologist Margaret Mead in which she advocated a major departure from the sexual mores that were then common in this country. She suggested that instead of remaining virginal or repressed before they get married, young people should feel free to engage in any intimacies they desire. Mead thought emotional and educational benefits would accrue from allowing the young to be promiscuous, to live together in trial marriages, to find for themselves whatever love was or was not meaningful to them.

Ideas such as these were novel at the time. They seemed quite radical, even though Mead predicted that after a period of exploration the young would settle down in marriages of a conventional sort. Divorce and extramarital dalliance might even occur less frequently, she thought, since the previous period of trial and error could help people find a mate who is right for them. Having played the field, husband and wife would be better informed about their interpersonal capacities and more likely to establish an enduring love within their marriage.

These suggestions may seem obvious to us. In the three or four decades since they were enunciated, they have been accepted to an extent that neither Mead nor anyone else anticipated. Are today's young men and women closer to attaining the ideals of sexual or marital love that underlay her thinking? The world has changed in so many other ways that it is hard to give a definite answer. The greater freedom in sexual behavior of any sort has convinced some people that the game is not worth the candle. Previously it was, for large segments of the population, virtually the only game in town. Sexuality fed the imagination of many who had no other talents to develop. All that has changed considerably.

The constraints that society used to impose, including the idea of marriage as a prerequisite for sex, provided quasi-formal coordinates within which the art of sexual love could occur. When sex is indiscriminate or too easily satisfied, it loses much of its aesthetic appeal. Marriage is a means by which sex becomes more discriminating, if only because it then involves a person whose intimate being one experiences directly, and contributes to, over a period of time. Sex remains accessible but more fully encased in the many other interests that a couple can also have in common. These make possible a sense of beauty that transmutes pleasure into consummatory appreciation. In our new enlightenment are we neglecting this kind of value?

In a course I once taught on concepts of sexual love, a student succinctly posed a problem about marriage that his generation faces: "Why marry the cow if you can get the milk for nothing?" If the student had been a woman, she might have wondered why one should marry the bull. Is this cynicism a sign of moral decadence? Or is it rather honesty about one's feelings at an age when nothing is certain other than hormonal urges?

In trying to answer such questions, or give advice in general, one should not assume there must be a solution that is right for everyone. Human beings are free to create whatever life is meaningful to them. We are a mixture of quasi-instinctual drives and acquired responses that variably enable us to survive in the environment we inhabit at any moment of history. To succeed in love, or anything else, we must have the courage to follow our intelligence as well as our strongest inclinations. The outcome will not be the same for all persons. Nor should it be.

I return finally to the heading of this concluding chapter. It was originally St. Augustine who told us to love and do as we will (*Dilige, et quod vis fac*). He meant that those who love God properly are incapable of doing anything that is wrong. When Rabelais affixed the words "Do As Thou Wilt" above the portal of his fictional Abbey of Thélème, he had in mind a very different concept. Rabelais thought that if one followed natural impulses one would thereby experience a type of love that is truly desirable for human beings. In the Romantic period the two perspectives were synthesized in the idea that wherever it occurs love is itself God. The person who undergoes it in the course of realizing his or her natural condition, whatever that might be, would perforce be living the good and holy life. For love was an epiphany showing forth not only the nature of God but also his sacred presence in us and in the world.

I recognize the allure of this Romantic faith. It is a by-product of the philosophical idealism that enriched the life of millions in the nineteenth century. It seems hardly defensible today. Nevertheless we can make suggestions in opposition to those who claim that love should be avoided. We may remind them that the creation of meaning belongs to life itself, and that human beings attain meaningful lives through love of any sort. Love is not to be avoided, but only the harm that may possibly come from it. Under specifiable conditions some forms of love are clearly preferable to others, and every love can become suspect. None is sacrosanct or immune from ethical evaluation. But though there are objects and occasions of love that should be rejected, the acceptance, even love of love can make life vibrant and infinitely rewarding.

If we think of love as in itself the answer to all the problems human beings face, we will constantly be disappointed by it. If we search for perfection in a mate and refuse to be satisfied by anything less than that, we will never really experience sexual or marital love. If we are unwilling to undergo the interpersonal negotiations, the bickering, the inevitable annoyance, animosity, or anger that is part of living with another person, we will never be able to give our love to anyone. Since love does not simply happen, as I have been suggesting, it must emerge as the saving remnant of our endless yearning for happy and meaningful lives.

Nor is there any guarantee that love will yield both happiness and meaning. The pursuit of love provides meaning in life, but the experience of it varies greatly in the quantity and quality of the happiness that results. Though love may often make life worth living, no one can promise that any life—including a life of love—will always be a rose-garden of delight. It rarely is. Even heroic or saintly individuals who devote themselves to the care and welfare of other persons may be denied the glorious recompense they have so greatly deserved.

To want to avoid love is unnecessarily extreme, and probably counter to our nature. It is equally wrong, however, to formulate rules about a love that must take precedence over all the rest regardless of the consequences. Each man or woman must determine afresh which love matters most and is most justifiable in a particular circumstance. Philosophers can sometimes help in this endeavor. They can reveal the logical and empirical implications within alternatives that are actually feasible. This is what I call mapping out the conceptual terrain. Though I have left much territory uncharted, that is all I have tried to do in this book.

Notes

INTRODUCTION: LOVE AND MEANING

1. Willard Gaylin, M.D., *Rediscovering Love* (New York: Viking, 1986), p. 43.

2. Martin Bergmann, *The Anatomy of Loving: The Story of Man's Quest to Know What Love Is* (New York: Columbia University Press, 1987), p. 159.

3. In his book, *The Interpersonal World of the Infant* (New York: Basic Books, 1985), Daniel N. Stern reaches a similar conclusion: "Since the traditional clinical-developmental issues such as orality, autonomy, and trust are no longer seen as occupying age-specific sensitive periods but as being issues for the life span, we can no longer predict the actual developmental point of origin of later-emerging clinical problems involving these issues, as psychoanalysis has always promised" (p. 12).

4. On transference as "both a new creation and a repetition," see Arnold H. Modell, *Other Times, Other Realities: Toward a Theory of Psychoanalytic Treatment* (Cambridge: Harvard University Press, 1990), pp. 20, 60–86.

CHAPTER 1: TWO MYTHS ABOUT LOVE

1. See Robert C. Solomon, *About Love: Reinventing Romance for Our Times* (New York: Simon and Schuster, 1988), p. 24. See also his *Love: Emotion, Myth and Metaphor* (Buffalo: Prometheus Books, 1990), and my discussion of Solomon's ideas in *The Nature of Love: The Modern World* (Chicago: University of Chicago Press, 1987), pp. 341–42, 409–11.

2. William James, *The Principles of Psychology* (Cambridge: Harvard University Press, 1981), 1:279.

3. On this, see Ilham Dilman, *Love and Human Separateness* (Oxford: Basil Blackwell, 1987), pp. 93–108. For a somewhat different view about merging, see Robert Nozick, "Love's Bond," in *The Philosophy of (Erotic) Love*, ed. Robert C. Solomon and Kathleen M. Higgins (Lawrence: University Press of Kansas, 1991), pp. 417–32. For a vastly different view, see Mark Fisher, *Personal Love* (London: Duckworth, 1990), pp. 26–32. See also the rejection of psychoanalytic theories of merging in Stern, *The Interpersonal World of the Infant*, pp. 104–7. On uniqueness and identification, to which I return in later chapters, see Alan Soble, *The Structure of Love* (New Haven: Yale University Press, 1990), pp. 48–67, 270–73.

4. Gaylin, *Rediscovering Love*, p. 103.

5. David Hume, *A Treatise of Human Nature* (Oxford: Clarendon Press, 1888), p. 365.

6. Ibid., p. 576.

CHAPTER 2: PERSONS, THINGS, IDEALS

1. On idealization, see my extensive discussions in *Meaning in Life: The Creation of Value* (New York: The Free Press, 1992) and *The Nature of Love: The Modern World*. See also *The Nature of Love: Plato to Luther*, 2d ed. (Chicago: University of Chicago Press, 1984), pp. 39–42.

CHAPTER 3: SEXUAL LOVE

1. In *The Goals of Human Sexuality* (New York: W. W. Norton, 1973), pp. 17–22 and passim.

2. See ibid., pp. 41–65.

CHAPTER 4: LOVE IN SOCIETY

1. Erich Fromm, *The Art of Loving* (New York: Bantam Books, 1956), p. 49.

2. On friendship as having something in common, over and above liking one another, see Elizabeth Telfer, "Friendship," in *Other Selves: Philosophers on Friendship*, ed. Michael Pakaluk (Indianapolis: Hackett, 1991), pp. 250–67.

3. George Santayana, *Reason in Society* (New York: Dover, 1980), p. 35.

4. *The Poetry of Robert Frost*, ed. Edward Connery Lathem (New York: Holt, 1979), p. 38.

5. Saint Augustine, *On Christian Doctrine*, trans. D. W. Robertson, Jr. (Indianapolis: Bobbs-Merrill, 1958), pp. 23–24.

6. On these ideas, see Henri Bergson, *The Two Sources of Morality and Religion* (Notre Dame: University of Notre Dame Press, 1977).

CHAPTER 6: CIVILIZATION AND AUTONOMY

1. Sigmund Freud, *Civilization and Its Discontents*, trans. James Strachey (New York: W. W. Norton, 1961), p. 40.

2. Ibid., p. 41.

3. For a contemporary view of sexuality significantly different from Freud's, one need only look at the work of the artist Gustav Klimt. See Carl E. Schorske, "Gustav Klimt: Painting and the Crisis of the Liberal Ego," in his *Fin-de-Siècle Vienna: Politics and Culture* (New York: Knopf, 1979), pp. 208–78.

CHAPTER 7: LOVE, AND DO AS YOU WILL

1. These ideas are discussed at greater length in *The Nature of Love: The Modern World*, particularly pp. 383–90, 406–17, 438–40.

2. See ibid., pp. 35–37.

3. See *The Goals of Human Sexuality*, particularly pp. 15–25, 155–57.

Index

Library of Congress Cataloging-in-Publication Data

Singer, Irving.
The pursuit of love / Irving Singer.
p. cm.
Includes bibliographical references and index.
ISBN 0-8018-4792-3 (alk. paper)
1. Love. 2. Love—History. I. Title.
BD436.S523 1994
128′.4—dc20 93-34176